BONES OF THE INNOCENT

A MASON COLLINS CRIME THRILLER

JOHN A. CONNELL

NAILHEAD PUBLISHING

GET A FREE MASON COLLINS NOVELLA

The relationship between writer and reader is a special one for me. If you are interested in going beyond what you read here and wish to receive occasional newsletters from me with details on new releases, special offers, and other news relating to the Mason Collins series, you can sign up to my mailing list, and I'll send you a free Mason Collins introductory novella.

See the back of the book for an offer for a free Mason Collins novella that is not available anywhere else!

COPYRIGHT

CONTENTS

S omehow they always knew when she awoke, and they would come. And those footsteps, like pounding drums in the cave-like passageway, always meant anguish and terror. The trouble was, she couldn't remember why.

Cynthia stiffened, clamped her eyes shut, and continued the steady rhythm of her breathing as if still asleep. At some point during her nightmares, she had wound up in a fetal position on the floor. The stone felt cold on her face, and the coarse sand, like ground glass, etched her cheek. The odor of dank earth and the contents of the bucket assaulted her nostrils. Her head, her throat, her heart, her entire insides, seemed like one throbbing bruise. Despite this, she kept very still.

She tried to recall the events leading to her abduction, but the only thing she could remember was being with her mother in the medina. She had just turned eighteen, and her mother offered to take her on a shopping spree to celebrate. But the actual abduction and these last few—days, weeks?—of captivity seemed like one continuous nightmare, asleep or awake. Time stood still in this coffin of rock.

Just below the thumping of her heartbeat, she could hear the moans from other prisoners in the midst of their own nightmare. Someone coughed, the sound echoing off the rough-hewn rock walls. Sometimes it was soft crying, and sometimes a desperate prayer in a language she didn't understand. Always the voices of the young, and some seemed to be children.

Oh, God, let it be a nightmare so vivid it only seems *real. Let me go home. Let me go home!*

A voice startled her. She clamped her hand to her mouth, realizing that she had spoken the last phrase out loud. That prompted a few other prisoners to sob in their cells. They weren't supposed to talk. Even crying might bring the stout woman with the cruel eyes. From another cell, a boy shushed the others with panic in his voice.

An odd staccato clacking came again, the one that had woken her from sleep. It was closer now. As much as she tried to keep her eyes closed, she felt an overpowering need to see the source of the noise. Slowly she opened them. The cell had no illumination, though a harsh light from a single bare bulb in the hallway found its way through the ill-fitting slats of wood that made up her cell door. It produced razor-thin slashes of light, and one cut across the small room, directly at her head, only to veer off at the last moment. The backlit grains of sand made it seem like she gazed upon an alien landscape. That illusion captured her thoughts a moment, insistent, mesmerizing. It drew her in and refused to let go.

Her captors must be giving her some kind of drug. That was the only explanation. But for what purpose? Who had taken her prisoner, and why were they keeping her in a drug-induced stupor? Cynthia had never taken drugs before, but she was sure that was what it must feel like. When the drug's influence was at its worst, she often saw relatives she knew from England, like her long-dead grandmother, who seemed to be standing right next to her. Spirits and voices whispered to her.

A moment later the clacking began again and a cockroach crossed the beam of light. It stopped next to her face. Its antennae wiggled in the air, as if analyzing her breath. Despite her urge to recoil, she remained still. The hard light hit it from behind, making it translucent amber. The cockroach reminded her of *Alice's Adventures in Wonderland* and the strange creatures Alice had encountered. Like the caterpillar on the mushroom, this cockroach seemed to be communicating with her. She knew that was silly, but the creature gave her a sense that she wasn't so alone. A calm came over her—or was that the drug still having its way with her?

Her mind suddenly cleared, and with it, alarm gripped her heart. Like clockwork, they would come soon. They knew. Somehow they always knew. That thought forced her to rise up on her elbows, and the cockroach scurried away. She had to find a way out or she might go crazy.

Crazy like the one young woman—girl really—who had been dragged away—yesterday or the day before?

The young woman had screamed in her cell, a scream that froze Cynthia's lungs. And the big woman and man came for her. They always wore Venetian carnival masks of white, with grinning mouths and evil eyes, making them even more terrifying. The young woman cried and struggled against the strong chains that held her as they dragged her away. Cynthia caught a glimpse of the girl's body through the cracks of her cell door, as she was forced toward some unknown fate. She wore a gown like Cynthia, and she growled and snapped and wailed. It had made the others cry out. The man yelled warnings at them in Italian. Several heavy doors slammed in succession behind them, bolts shoved into place, until the girl's primal screams had faded to weak echoes. They took her away, and she never returned.

That memory drove Cynthia to her feet. She panted with

panic. She knew she would end up like that girl. Soon they would take her away.

Why was she here? Why were any of them here? What was happening to them? Would she ever see daylight again? Her mother?

She pressed her hands against her temples as if her head might explode. Moaning from the pain, she staggered in tight circles. How long had she been here? When would it end? She spun faster and moaned louder. It was the only way to control the cold, invisible hands that threatened to crush her mind. She became aware of the others moaning along with her. Then other voices loudly begging her to stop.

"They'll come!" some girl said. "Then you'll be sorry."

Another pleaded, "You'll make us all suffer."

Cynthia threw herself against the door and pounded her fists. "Get me out of here! Please!"

Others were screaming now. Was she in an insane asylum? Was she losing her mind? She pounded the door and cried.

A boy yelled at her in a foreign tongue. There was terror in his voice. Begging.

Cynthia's violent efforts dissipated the effects of whatever drug they had given her. And more memories came. The shadow of a man hovering over her like a ghostly and evil spirit. She was helpless, as she lay... where? His hot breath. His hands.

Cynthia pulled at the iron bars inserted in the small window of her cell door. She pulled so hard her shoulders ached. Then she heard herself growl like she had gone mad. She didn't care. "Get me out of here!"

Like the crack of a rifle shot, a heavy bolt was pulled back. The sound was so terrifying that she stopped. She held her breath and froze. A distant door's hinges creaked.

They were coming.

More doors and footsteps. Cynthia backed away. She held her

arms tight around her and backed up slowly until she hit the rock wall. Footsteps were loud now, and Cynthia clamped her hands to her ears.

Maybe if the sound disappears, they won't come. Maybe—

Cynthia's cell door opened with a clang. A tall, dark figure, silhouetted by the harsh light, stood in the doorway.

Cynthia screamed.

MARSEILLE, FRANCE
June 1946

M ason Collins sat at one of the sidewalk café tables among
a multitude of others taking advantage of the sun and
soft sea breezes in the plaza overlooking Marseille's Vieux Port
and the Mediterranean. The view of the bay, with the fishing boats
sailing out of port with the tide, and the sparkle of sun on the
whitecaps of the unsettled sea, wasn't the only thing Mason kept
his eye on. He was also watching the three men stationed at
strategic positions in the rectangular plaza. This was the first time
he'd seen up close the team of assassins pursuing him.

They looked American, though definitely not tourists. Maybe
ex-intelligence, maybe ex-cops. One examined a rack of post-
cards, one snapped photos like he'd never seen anything more
captivating than this plaza of crowded café tables and modest,
turn-of-the-century buildings, and the third eyed the same page of
a newspaper long enough to memorize the article word for word.
But their eyes were unfixed as if they were concentrating on
everything except what supposedly held their attention. Ever so

slightly, they tilted their heads, their eyes and ears collecting and assessing data while they pretended to be part of the passing crowd.

Whoever had hired these assassins wasn't taking any chances this time, sending at least three men to surround him in broad daylight. Mason had put another two-man team out of action in Freiburg, Germany, and then evaded the same team somewhere south of Paris, then Lyon, but after reaching Marseille, he'd dropped his guard and stayed too long.

He should have known better.

"*Putain pigeons*," Claudette said as she shooed away another pigeon that had landed on the table, hoping to steal the remainder of Mason's almond croissant.

Claudette sat across from him, small but fierce, and more intelligent than she let on. She'd been in the French Resistance during the war, and worked with the Special Operations Executive, Britain's clandestine military organization. Being from an Irish mother and a French-Algerian father, she spoke English with a French-Irish accent, which delighted Mason. Sometimes he felt content simply to sit and listen to her talk. They'd met outside Lyon a little over three weeks ago. Lust at first sight.

She had been rambling on about her family again: her brother still missing since Dunkirk; her mother killed during the bombings at Caen; and that rundown always leading to her father's current situation.

"*Chéri*, let's go someplace quieter. And without all these disgusting pigeons."

Mason closed his eyes and tilted his head toward the sun, which was about to drop behind the buildings. "I just want to enjoy the last rays. After two arctic winters in Germany, I feel like I'm still thawing out."

A moment of silence passed between them.

"There's something I need to tell you," Claudette said.

"My guess is it has something to do with those three goons with guns moving in for the kill."

Mason kept his eyes closed, but he could hear her suck in her breath and forget to exhale.

"It's about your father, isn't it?" Mason said. He imagined Claudette scrunching her face in indignation, with her heavily plucked eyebrows forming a high arc over almond eyes, which added to her fierce but seductive air. "You were telling me, once again, that your father was arrested by American intelligence in Berlin for passing classified diplomatic communiqués to the Russians."

He heard Claudette pour another glass of white wine for herself. Without opening his eyes, he covered his glass with his hand before Claudette could fill it. "I've got to stay sharp," Mason said.

He noted that Claudette didn't ask why.

"Is that why you sold me out?" Mason asked, then opened his eyes and looked at her. "To save your father?"

Claudette dropped her hands into her lap.

"If you're going for that popgun of yours, I wouldn't advise it."

Claudette stared at Mason with tears forming in her eyes. "They offered me a deal. They would help my father if I set you up. You must have angered some very influential people."

"So that *was* you, in Lyon? That's how they found me."

"Yes. But then we left before they could set the trap."

"I bet they offered you a bunch of money on top of saving Daddy."

"I'm sorry, *chéri*."

Mason nodded. "Yes, I believe you are."

"What are they going to do with you?"

"If I have my way about it, nothing. Someone sent them to kill me, so it might go that way."

8

"Why do they want you dead?"

"I busted up a crime ring operated by some powerful people. Some people hold a grudge for way too long."

She pointed her chin at one of the men. "The pigs are probably lying about helping my father."

Mason glanced at the three men. They had moved in a few yards, tightening the circle. "It's time for you to go, Claudette."

Claudette gathered her cigarettes and lighter and put them in her purse, probably nestling them against the Browning 1905 mouse gun she had started carrying a few days ago. She hesitated, her eyes moist as she stared at Mason.

"Go *now*, Claudette."

She shot up from the table and hurried away. She passed one of the hit men without incident and disappeared out of sight. As Mason watched her go, he felt the bitter sting of betrayal, but he had bigger things to think about at the moment. He shifted in his chair to face the table, purposefully turning his back on two of the men. They might try something here, but with scores of witnesses to worry about, they would probably wait for him to step into one of the side streets. That's why Claudette had wanted them to leave the plaza—part of the setup.

Mason put an unlit cigarette in his mouth, then searched through his pockets, ostensibly for his lighter. His right hand dug into his brown sport coat pocket and adjusted the position of his Colt 1908 Pocket Hammerless pistol for a quick draw. The same pocket contained his lighter, but before he could remove it, someone reached across from the neighboring table and held a flame from a gold, engraved cigarette lighter in front of Mason's nose. Mason's entire body tensed. He gripped the pistol as he turned to the man.

"I thought I recognized you," the man said with a British accent.

9

Mason kept his hand on his pistol while he sized up the man. He leaned forward, putting the cigarette to the flame.

"Carson Trusdale," the man said as if that would surely ring a bell.

Mason figured Carson to be in his midthirties. He wore a white linen suit and a dark blue button-down shirt, a red handkerchief in the breast pocket, and brown leather shoes with ivory linen insets—shoes Mason had seen on the Boulevard Saint-Germain at a price worth four months of his former army investigator's salary.

"British liaison?" Carson said. "McGraw Kaserne, Munich military-government offices?" When Mason still offered no response, Carson added, "I was present at the U.S. Army general staff meeting about your investigation into the crime ring. Specifically about what to do with the British officers exposed in your investigation."

Mason checked the three men in his peripheral vision. They had stopped, hovering fifty feet from his table. Was this part of the plan? Or something unexpected?

"And you just happened to be in Marseille, sitting at the next table."

"Why, yes," Carson said, acting somewhat perplexed. "Business brought me here, and this happens to be one of my favorite cafés."

The explanation seemed legitimate, but Mason didn't believe in coincidences. "I'm curious, what kind of Munich MG business would bring you to Marseille?"

Carson chuckled nervously. "Once a detective, always a detective, heh?" His crooked smile faded when he saw Mason's stony face. "I'm not in the service anymore. I work for the diplomatic corps in the International Zone of Tangier. Morocco."

If this guy happened to be the leader of this particular group of cutthroats, he was an odd one. It didn't add up. But Mason had no time for chitchat either. "Good for you," he said, and started to rise from the table.

Carson put his hand on Mason's arm, while his eyes locked on one of the assassins. That made Mason curious enough to hesitate.

"I overheard your conversation with the young lady," Carson said.

Mason leaned in and lowered his voice. "If those three clowns get the idea that you know what's going on, you're not going to leave Marseille alive. Take your hand off my arm and forget anything you overheard."

Carson pulled his hand away. "Please sit down and hear what I have to say. What I propose could be beneficial to both of us. If you don't like it, then you can walk away and take your chances."

Maybe this guy did work for the men who wanted him dead, and he was there to extend a deal on their behalf. Mason sat, his table now in shadow. "You'd better talk fast. Those guys aren't going to wait much longer now that the sun's going down. And the more you talk, the more they're going to think you're involved."

Carson took a cigarette out of his gold, engraved cigarette case and lit one as if he had all the time in the world. "I have to be honest. I didn't just happen to sit down. I saw you as I was passing by." He paused and smiled demurely, as if embarrassed by the confession. "Of course, I recognized you immediately. And I've had direct experience with your methods and reputation as a detective. It was fortuitous, really—"

"Get to the point."

"I may have a job for you."

"I'm not looking for one."

"A case. A detective case."

"Even more reason to say no."

Carson started to say something, then furrowed his brow. "I don't understand."

11

"You don't need to."

"Granted, but it could be a rather healthy sum of money."

"They don't have detectives in Tangier?"

"Incompetent or crooked. Or both. Let me tell you about the case—"

"I'm not interested."

"Considering your current situation, I thought you would be."

"Money won't solve my current problem."

Carson's face went crooked and his eyelids fluttered as if a particular thought caused him pain.

"You have something else to confess," Mason said.

"I'm afraid, I …" Carson paused as if looking for the right words. "I exaggerated the truth regarding when I first saw you. It was earlier in the week. You were with that woman Claudette. I made some inquiries. I know you left the army and Germany under less-than-ideal circumstances, and I wanted to find out if you'd joined one of the nefarious gangs that are so prevalent here—"

"Carson, get to the damned point."

Carson twitched in his chair at Mason's bark; then his words came tumbling out: "I know you haven't any money. You're— were—living with the woman on her meager funds. Even if you manage to elude your present stalkers, how long can you last without money? I offer you an ideal opportunity for escape *and* to make a small fortune." Carson stopped for a breath, and his eyes flicked wide in alarm when he saw how close the assassins had come. He leaned in and lowered his voice. "From what I gather, this isn't the first time you've been pursued since leaving Germany."

"Unless you intend to get in the line of fire, you'd better get on with it."

"I have a private boat at my disposal. My employer's boat. Very fast. We shove off at midnight. Pier three, berth seventeen.

View it as an opportunity to slip away. Erase your trail for good. That is, if you manage to extract yourself from this predicament."

The sun had set below the horizon, leaving the plaza in a gray twilight. The lamps were still unlit, and everything took on a muted, indistinct quality. A perfect time for the killers to make a move. And, sure enough, as if some unseen puppeteer had pulled their strings, the three men readied their guns still concealed in their suit coat pockets and moved forward.

A waiter with the ubiquitous white apron and black bow tie came up to Carson's table, causing Carson to turn away from Mason for a moment ...

Mason sprinted from the table and raced full speed toward the entrance of the café. He glanced back to see a stunned Carson still seated, and his three pursuers running through the maze of tables after him. They'd obviously expected him to make a dash for the busy port, not flee into the café and risk being cornered. Mason had counted on that, and he'd picked this café for a reason: he knew from scoping it out on his first visit that it was a straight shot through the café and out the back exit.

Inside, the place was nearly empty. Mason dodged a waiter, turning over empty tables as he passed. Just as he got to the back door, he heard a shout from the pursuer at his rear, and a crash of tables being tossed aside.

Mason exploded out the back exit and into a narrow alley. One pursuer in the café. That meant the other two planned to cut him off at either end of the alley. He had to act fast. He pushed his back against the outside café wall and waited next to the hinged side of the door, with his pistol at the ready. The door burst open, and just as the pursuer was halfway out, Mason shoved the door into the man with all his strength. But the pursuer had anticipated this and jumped back, then countered Mason's move by shoving the door back into Mason. Mason recoiled from the blow. The pursuer slipped out and swung his pistol around to aim.

Mason grabbed the SIG Sauer's slider with his left hand and pushed it away. The gun fired. The bullet ripped through Mason's suit coat. The man pulled the trigger again, but Mason grabbing the barrel had jammed the gun.

Mason yanked on the pursuer's gun arm and struck the man's vulnerable wrist with his right hand, while he used his body to push the heavy door to trap the pursuer. But his assailant anticipated that move as well and seized Mason's hand to diminish the blow. The man managed to squeeze through the door, spinning while trying to pull Mason off-balance.

Thrusts with feet, elbows, and knees were answered with counterthrusts. The two had received the same level of hand-to-hand combat training, both throwing blows only to be blocked by the other. Mason knew the other two assassins would be charging down either end of the alley, closing fast with guns drawn.

In a final desperate move, Mason tried to stomp on the top of the man's foot. The man avoided the blow, but the move distracted him for an instant. Just what Mason was hoping for: Mason threw his forehead with everything he had and connected with the bridge of the man's nose. He felt the crack of nasal bone resonate through his skull.

Still grappling for the gun, the man collapsed backward into the open door, pulling Mason in with him. At the same instant, gunfire rang out in the alley, and bullets splintered the wooden door just above Mason's head.

The stunned man fell onto the floor, with Mason coming down on top of him. Mason then delivered several blows, knocking the man senseless. Mason grabbed the gun, jumped to his feet, and kicked the back door closed.

One of the killers hit the door, but Mason blocked it with his body. He dodged behind the adjacent wall just as several bullets pierced the door. He cleared the jamb, then jumped away with arms extended, ready to fire at whoever burst through the door. But no one came.

Behind him came several shouts at once: "*Police! Les mains en l'air!*"

Mason knew that phrase well enough. He ignored them at first, still waiting for one of the killers to try, but when he heard the click of a revolver's hammer cocking, he dropped his gun and raised his hands.

3

M ason exited the thick wooden doors of Les Baumettes prison, flanked by two guards. They prodded him out into the pouring rain. By the time the guards closed the doors behind him, Mason was soaked through his haggard street clothes. He didn't mind. The cool rain felt wonderful after the stifling air and stench of the overcrowded prison cell.

It was after eleven p.m., almost twenty hours after his arrest. Spotlights swept past the paved entrance, illuminating the sheets of rain and the stone facade of the prison walls. He remained a few feet from the doors and tried to peer through the darkness. The assassins could be waiting for him in strategic positions beyond the small pool of light.

In front of him and fifty feet into the shadows, a car's head-lights came on. A man in silhouette emerged from the car and leaned against the front fender. Mason stood still for a moment, reviewing his options. He wasn't about to beg the guards to let him back into that hellhole of a prison. He might as well take his chances and face what awaited him.

He moved forward, clearing the pool of illumination and step-ping into the dark night. He paused to let his eyes adjust, balling his fists and tensing for fight or flight—or the crack of gunfire and the impact of a bullet.

The silhouetted man's arm rose, and to Mason's dread, the man held something long and thin in his hand. But instead of leveling the rifle-shaped object to aim it at Mason, the man's arm continued upward until the object pointed to the sky. Then, pop. An umbrella unfolded and snapped open. At the same moment, a spotlight swept past, causing the umbrella to glow, temporarily bathing Carson Trusdale in a grayish light. He smiled, clearly enjoying himself.

Mason stepped forward. "Something tells me you were the kid everyone beat up on the playground."

"Now, is that any way to talk to the man who got you out of prison? And for your information, I went to Eton, Mr. Collins. There was no playground. Besides, being the third son of the Earl of Bedford, the only boys who beat on me were those of higher peerage than my own."

Mason stopped in front of Carson. "What are you doing here?"

Carson kept the umbrella to himself. "I thought that was evident."

"How did a low-level English diplomat get the French to let me go?"

"You're soaking wet, Mr. Collins. Why don't you get in the car?"

"Just because you got me out of prison doesn't mean I'm obliged to go with you."

"I'd rather thought you would do so for your survival. The French released you under my care. Do, please, get in the car. We wouldn't want you dying of pneumonia."

Mason walked around the front of the car and got in the passenger's seat. Carson slipped in behind the wheel. He reached around to the backseat and brought a towel forward, dropping it in Mason's lap.

Carson started the engine, but before he put it in gear, he said, "I'm afraid it's too dangerous to go to your ex-girlfriend's to get your things."

"Don't worry about it. I've got what I need."

"Oh, that reminds me." Carson reached in his coat pocket and pulled out Mason's .380 Pocket Hammerless and held it up by two fingers. "You dropped it in the scuffle. I had to bribe the café owner to give it up."

Mason took it as he wiped the rain off his face. "Thanks."

Carson put the car in gear and pulled out of the small parking lot. "I took the liberty of purchasing a number of items for you. Some clothes, a nice suit, hat and shoes." He gave Mason a sweeping glance from knees to shoulders. "I sized you up in the plaza."

"If you cook and do laundry, we're all set."

Carson pressed his lips in a frown. "I bought them because the boat trip to Tangier will be cold at night."

"I hate boats. But what I hate more is feeling like I'm being shanghaied for a shady job nobody else wants. In *Africa*, no less."

"Mr. Collins. I told you I work for the British consulate in Tangier—"

Mason put his hand on the door latch. "Forget it. Stop and let me out."

"Really, Mr. Collins, it's quite legitimate, I assure you."

"Now, why should I believe some oddball Brit who fabricated a tale about why he's sitting next to me in the plaza just to offer me passage to some hellhole in Africa? Give me a good reason why in hell I would step foot on a boat and go on a fool's errand."

"I believe escaping those assassins qualifies."

"I can head for Spain or Italy."

"Without a shilling to your name?"

18

"I'll get by. Stop the car."

"Be reasonable. This is your best chance to elude your pursuers. You try to escape on foot with no money, and they'll surely catch up to you. And do you know what lengths I had to go through with the bloody French to get you out of that prison? I offer you sanctuary and a pocketful of money—"

Carson's mouth clamped shut when he saw Mason had his pistol pointed at him. His eyes were wide with fear, and he struggled to keep his eyes on the road.

"On the other hand," Mason said, "what's to stop me from taking your money, your clothes, and the car?"

Carson stole glances at the gun and Mason as he negotiated a sharp curve.

"Stop the car, or I take it and leave you by the side of the road."

With a dramatic sigh, Carson slowed the car, and it rolled to a stop. Mason opened the door.

"Three girls have gone missing," Carson said quickly. "Abducted most likely. And there may be more. They're in their teens, but still children."

That stopped Mason. He settled back into his seat and waited for the rest.

"The three we know of are fifteen, sixteen, and eighteen years old. The first one, right about a month ago. A Dutch girl named Sabine de Graaf. The second, Valerie Meunier, three weeks ago. And the last, Cynthia Brisbane, twelve days ago."

"What about the local police?"

"They're doing what they can, but haven't any results to show for it."

"And no ransom demands?"

Carson shook his head. "No notes, no witnesses. Absolutely nothing." Carson paused to study Mason's reaction, but Mason continued to stare out the windshield. "The parents are desperate.

There aren't any local private investigators who can handle a case like this. I've seen the results of your investigative skills in Garmisch and Munich. I also know of your reputation as an unstoppable and passionate investigator. If anyone can help us, it's you. I'm sure of it. I've already contacted the British consulate and one girl's parents, and they're delighted. They'll pay handsomely."

"I don't care how much smoke you blew up their asses, Mr. Trusdale. I don't work miracles. In the majority of cases, if the abductee isn't found within the first couple of days, then they're either gone or dead."

Carson fished around in his jacket pocket and pulled out a small photograph. He held it out for Mason to see. It was a portrait of a pretty girl with blond hair done up in a traditional braid. She had light freckles and a big, toothy smile. "This is Sabine de Graaf. Fifteen. She played the clarinet and sang in the school choir. She loved Greek mythology, and was a whiz in mathematics."

Carson began to fish for another photograph when Mason slammed the car door shut. "You don't need to show me any more."

Carson smiled and started the car engine. "You won't regret this."

"Oh, yes, I will. Beginning with the goddamned boat ride."

Page 20

4

S till a mile and a half distant, Tangier blistered under the North African noonday sun. Mason stood with his back against the boat's wheelhouse with his hands firmly gripping the rail. The rush of cool, salty air helped control the remnants of his seasickness. He hated small boats only a little less than he hated open water. After spending close to twenty hours in his cabin— and steps away from the head—he'd planted himself in this position on the deck.

Twice on the voyage from Marseille, they had rendezvoused with other boats in the middle of the sea. Then a few hours before dawn, they had docked at Almería, Spain, to take on a mysterious cargo. That short time on land and, luckily, the calm seas crossing the Strait of Gibraltar, had helped alleviate the worst of his gut-wrenching nausea.

The boat was a decommissioned Royal Navy motor launch, and from the empty cannon and machine gun emplacements, it had obviously been a submarine chaser. But the crew's quarters had been converted into luxury cabins and cargo holds, and the two engines had been beefed up to propel the boat at close to thirty knots. More than a few times during the trip, Mason had wondered why the British consulate would require such a fast boat. And why it had left port in Marseille at midnight. And not for the first time in the thirty-six-hour voyage, he wondered what exactly he'd gotten himself into.

Carson sauntered up to him, wearing a white linen suit more fitted for the tropics. He held his white, straw fedora secured to his head with one hand, and a tall gin and tonic in the other, a drink he consumed at regular intervals, day and night.

Carson waved his glass of mostly gin, making the liquid slosh near the rim. "Well, look who's finally emerged from their cabin."

Mason ignored the remark and continued to stare at Tangier, as if doing so would impel the boat to close the gap with lightning speed.

Carson walked up to the rail and spread his arms wide as if to take a long-lost lover into his embrace. "I'm back, my darling." He looked back at Mason and pointed to Tangier. "Look at her. Shangri-la on a drunk. Like a trollop who's given so much to so many and is showing all her wrinkles because of it."

It wasn't Tangier's wrinkles that concerned Mason.

Tangier's whitewashed, square buildings with equally square windows clung to the crescent-shaped slopes rising from the edge of the Mediterranean. To the left and center, modern buildings of concrete and glass spread out along two intersecting ridges. To the right, a chaos of streets encircled by the crenulated ramparts, the crumbling walls and peeling paint of the old part of the city. Instead of palm trees and rolling dunes spreading out toward the Saharan horizon, eucalyptus and oak trees dominated a tortured coastline. A long beach lay along the city's left flank, and directly in front of them was the crowded port, where a U.S. Navy cruiser, yachts, speedboats, and motor cruisers outnumbered the fishing vessels. It looked more like the bastard child from a one-night stand between San Diego and Tijuana.

"I can see the disappointment in your face," Carson said. "But let me assure you, there's never been any place quite like Tangier, ever."

"Some people might take that as a blessing."

Carson joined Mason at the wheelhouse. "I have a feeling Tangier is going to be just your kind of town."

"At the moment, I couldn't call any place 'my kind of town.'"

"Oh, this one is special. Some call it the wickedest city in the world. Talk about a den of iniquity, this city takes the crown." He leaned in as though sharing a secret. "Fertile ground for a detective."

"From where I'm standing, I don't see what would attract anyone to the left armpit of the Mediterranean."

"Tangier is in the International Zone belonging to nine different Western countries. Can you imagine getting nine countries to agree on anything? Tangier's politics are neutral—almost anyone can enter, no questions asked. Prosecution of Westerners is rare—with the exception of rape and murder. Mix that all together and you have a blessed haven for international spies, ex-Nazi war criminals, unlicensed doctors, and defrocked priests. One can make a fortune with the nonexistent banking laws and the permissive import/export policies, all of which attracts smugglers, pirates, gunrunners, and gangsters—how's that for starters?"

Mason remarked that Carson took great delight in the prospect of returning to his den of iniquity. "Who do you really work for, Mr. Trusdale?"

Carson acted as if he'd been slapped. "Your tone implies my employment is somewhat sinister."

"A fast boat with expanded cargo holds. The midnight rendezvous with other boats, then the mysterious cargo we picked up in Almería, now under lock and key. Trips to Marseille, a favorite port of entry for every kind of contraband."

"Mr. Collins, I am a vice-consul under Sir Wilfred Brisbane, the British consul general for Tangier. This boat was ceded to the consulate for diplomatic purposes. The cargo is fresh fruit, olive oil, Spanish wine, and port. You may conduct a search, if you like."

"I don't really care if what you're doing is legal or not. I like to know who I'm dealing with, and you're as slippery as they come."

Carson feigned hurt feelings but said nothing. They both watched in silence as the boat glided up to the dock. The engine shuddered when the screws reversed direction, and the boat rested against the dock. The crew moored the boat, then stood aside to let Carson and Mason disembark.

Mason stepped onto the dock with the suitcase Carson had purchased for him in Marseille. He looked up to a raised pier that accommodated the ferries bringing passengers from Gibraltar and Spain. A large ferry was docked there now, disgorging its passengers. The Moroccans were made to wait while the Westerners descended the gangway. Most of the Moroccan men wore hooded robes and struggled with huge bundles on their backs. The women herded packs of children while balancing an infant on one hip and a cumbersome sack on the other.

Carson stopped next to Mason and nodded toward the Moroccans. "They work in Spain for weeks or months, then come home whenever the job is done or they're forced out. Franco doesn't take kindly to illegal immigration. For five hundred years the Moors kicked the Europeans around—then the last five hundred the Europeans have been returning the favor."

"I read the Moroccans are pushing for independence."

"Yes, France and Spain are refusing to let go, but I'm afraid they can't hold out much longer." Carson leaned in and lowered his voice. "It's a shame really. Losing Tangier would be the end of an era. I'm not sure what will happen to our queen of decadence if she is taken over by the Moors. One by one, the colonial powers are losing their colonies. What will dear old England or France do when there are no more dark-skinned people to kick around?"

Mason wondered whether Carson was dreaming of a better future or a better past.

The mostly white, well-dressed ferry passengers had to navigate a mob of Moroccan men in hooded djellabas or long white robes and turbans that formed a gauntlet. The merchants called out to the passengers while they held up baskets, brass teapots, or beaded jewelry. Another man in a blue robe and a blue round hat held the reins of a donkey burdened with so many rolled carpets tied to its back that only the legs and head were visible. Most of the passengers did their best to ignore the cacophony of voices, while a few brave souls stopped to haggle over prices.

"Shall we?" Carson asked.

Mason walked next to Carson along the dock. A Spanish man with sunbaked skin trundled along behind them, pushing a hand-cart containing Carson's prodigious steamer trunk. The hot sun brought up odors from the brackish water of fuel, algae, and sewage.

"What kind of minefield am I going to be stepping into with the local police?" Mason asked. "They're not going to take kindly to a private dick tromping all over their turf."

"You're probably right. But the British consulate will pave the way as much as possible. This wave of abductions is unusual. Very few homicides are reported, and serious crime is low for a city of this size. Though I wager the city officials encourage the police to look the other way except for serious offenses committed in broad daylight. The city administrators and businessmen are very anxious to create an image of Tangier as a crime-free city to encourage investment and upper-class immigration. Just recently, Barbara Hutton, the heiress to the Woolworth fortune, set up a residence here. Real estate is booming and lining everyone's pockets. They want to keep it that way. Something like this abduction business has them all in a tizzy. You solve this, and you'll be given the key to the city, not to mention coffers of gold and all the gems of Araby."

"I didn't agree to take this case for the money."

"Which is why I showed you the photograph of the girl, instead of opening my checkbook."

Mason cut in front of Carson and got in his face. "The missing girls are the only reason I didn't leave you by the side of the road in Marseille. So stop dangling money in front of me, and stop trying to play me for a chump. And if I find out you've been using those girls to set me up in some game of yours, then I'll break your scrawny neck."

Carson acted as though he still possessed the moral high ground, but his eyes watered from fear. "Really, Mr. Collins. This is a genuine cry for help."

"As long as we're clear. Let's get on with it."

Mason and Carson began walking again. It didn't take long for Carson to recover his composure, and he strode up to the police kiosk standing at the end of the network of private docks with open arms and a politician's smile.

"Sergeant DuBois," Carson said. "So good to see you."

"The same to you, Monsieur," the sergeant said.

The sergeant had two small electric fans mounted in opposite corners of his kiosk. They blew hard enough to make the whiskers of his handlebar mustache twitch in the breeze, but did nothing to control his perspiration under the heavy uniform. Still, he sported a smile, one that seemed to express hungry delight at seeing Mr. Trusdale.

Carson indicated Mason with a sweep of his hand. "Sergeant, may I introduce Mr. Mason Collins. He's traveling with me."

Carson handed over his passport. Mason realized just then that he had left his passport behind in Marseille with the rest of his worldly possessions. The sergeant eyed Mason but neglected to ask for his passport. Then Mason saw why: the sergeant leafed through Carson's passport just long enough to spot the wad of French francs tucked inside. He slipped the currency into his pocket with the deftness of a magician.

Carson said, "Mr. Collins is traveling under the protection of the British consulate."

"I understand," the sergeant said as he handed Carson his passport. His smile dropped to an officious frown when he addressed Mason. "Monsieur, the deputy chief of police, Capitaine Rousselot, requested that you see him as soon as you arrived."

Carson slipped in front of Mason and said to the sergeant, "Tell Capitaine Rousselot that Mr. Collins and I must see the consul general before anything else."

Mason stepped around Carson and said to the sergeant, "Tell Captain Rousselot that I'd be happy to see him right away." With that, he headed for the gated exit.

Carson caught up, with the poor crewman now far behind. "I have strict orders to take you to Sir Wilfred Brisbane as soon as we docked."

"If you and your boss want me to conduct an investigation, the first thing I need to do is get whatever information I can out of the deputy chief of police. Then I'll see your boss." Another thought came to Mason. "And how did the local police already know I would be involved with the case?"

Carson was about to respond, but the answer came in the form of a gaggle of reporters rushing up to them as Carson and Mason cleared the gate. They called out Mason's name and hurled questions at him at the same time. Camera flashbulbs burst in his face.

One particularly aggressive reporter got within inches of Mason's advance. "Mr. Collins, what makes you think you can find the missing girls?"

"Why did you *really* leave the army?"

"Isn't it true that you're only doing this to take the bereaved parents' hard-earned money?"

Mason plowed through them, clearing a path for Carson and his baggage handler. They were in a small parking lot that fed onto a roundabout. As they crossed the lot, the reporters jostled around Mason like hungry piranhas. Carson rushed ahead and guided them to a gray Jaguar SS coupe parked in a covered space reserved for wealthy boaters. Mason climbed in the passenger's seat, while Carson and the baggage handler wedged the enormous steamer trunk in the rear cargo hold. Carson squeezed in behind the steering wheel. He then honked the horn to get the reporters to clear. When the reporters finally relented, Carson pulled out onto the roundabout and into the slow-moving traffic of cars, trucks, donkeys pulling wagons, and two riders on camels.

Mason said, "How am I supposed to investigate a case with a herd of reporters nipping at my heels?"

"I assure you, this wasn't my doing."

"Then who? I can't do my job with the local police and the press scrutinizing every step I make."

"I telegraphed the consulate that I had employed you—I had to get their approval, after all. I then telegraphed the good news to the consul general that you had agreed and we were on our way. Someone at the consulate must have released the information to allay some of the fear that's gripping the populace."

"You mean it was a publicity stunt for Tangier's principal investors."

"The British consulate will do everything in its power to aid you in your investigation, but we can't control the press."

"I want one thing straight right now: I work alone. No more press releases. No daily reports. No supervision of any kind. If I need the consulate to smooth things over or grant access to normally private information, they give it to me. No questions asked."

"You can tell the consul general himself. That's where we're headed after seeing the deputy police chief."

"I want to talk to the parents of the missing girls before I see His Holiness."

Looking contrite, Carson said, "I'm afraid you don't understand. The consul general *is* one of the parents."

5

C arson navigated the car through a roundabout and climbed up Rue de Portugal, which ran alongside the medina ramparts. Up close, Tangier began to show another side: palm trees lined the streets, flowers graced balconies, and sunbathers or cocktail-sipping partyers enjoyed views from the medina's flat-roofed buildings. It seemed half the city's population was out on the town: men in their neutral-colored hooded robes and women in broad straw hats and multicolored garments.

When they turned left and away from the medina, suddenly everything took on a Western appearance: large department stores, sidewalk cafés, jewelry stores, and restaurants. Most of the pedestrians were dressed in suits and ties or dresses. If it weren't for building signs in French, Spanish, or a smattering of Arabic, Mason would have thought they were driving through a small city in Florida.

They stopped at a six-pointed intersection, where a dark-skinned cop gesticulated wildly and blew his whistle as trucks zoomed by, or Moroccans with donkey-powered carts and robed men on camels risked life and limb as they moved serenely into the chaotic tangle of streets.

Finally, Carson managed to take the second left through the controlled chaos and onto the Boulevard Pasteur. Modern buildings lined both sides of the wide boulevard, with street-level jewelry and designer shops, and rows of banks from a dozen countries. A few more turns brought them to Rue Michel Ange, and finally Carson pulled into a small parking lot serving Tangier's police headquarters. The building was a throwback to an older colonial era, probably late eighteen hundreds, with neoclassical columns way too massive for the diminutive temple to law enforcement. Two police sedans of 1930s vintage, an army-surplus jeep, and two horses were stationed in front.

Mason and Carson exited the Jaguar and headed for the entrance.

"The chief of police is a Belgian chap, Commandant Lambert," Carson said. "Captain Rousselot is second-in-command. And contrary to what you might expect, the Belgian commandant is the pompous ass—trying to out-French the French. The captain is the one who should be in charge. He's quite intelligent and speaks five languages, including a remarkable command of English. He can be a rather ill-tempered fellow, but very professional and sometimes helpful."

"Competing egos *and* different nationalities," Mason said. "And the lower ranks end up stepping all over each other just trying to stay out of the line of fire."

"You don't know the half of it. The next six senior officers are either French or Belgian—then the force is a hodgepodge of maybe two hundred men: Moors, Spanish, French, and about ten percent is a mélange of individuals from all over the world. I would swear they recruited half of them by roaming the streets and picking up anyone dim-witted enough to take the oath."

As Carson led Mason up the shallow steps, they passed four policemen wearing either French blue or Spanish green, and having a heated argument in two different languages.

"How does anything get done around here?" Mason said.

"It doesn't. Now you see why I was so desperate to have you on the case."

They entered the expansive lobby, and the first thing that hit Mason was the seeming lack of oxygen. Ceiling fans swirled overhead but did nothing for the stifling heat. It looked like the place had been a bank or an administrative office building before the police had taken it over. There was a long wooden counter with windows that had probably been for bank tellers or clerks, then an open area behind for desks. A balcony ran along three sides of the second floor, providing access to the offices. A glimmer of nostalgia for his time as a Chicago detective hit Mason, and despite the building's unconventional layout, it still looked like any modest-sized police station in the States: scuffed black-and-white tiled floors, chairs lining the street-side lobby wall with drunks, vagrants, and waiting civilians.

Mason and Carson approached the desk sergeant. Carson made the introductions in French. The desk sergeant barked at a Moroccan uniformed clerk, who jumped to his feet and rushed to open the swinging gate as if his life depended on it. The clerk ushered them up two flights of stairs.

The deputy chief of police, Captain Jean-Marie Rousselot, occupied the second-to-last office off the short hallway. It sported walls of mahogany and a tiled floor, with arched stone windows looking out over the bay and the marina. The office had been designed for some former bank executive, but Captain Rousselot had turned it into a cop's work space, as it looked like someone had tossed a hand grenade into his file cabinet. Something Mason appreciated.

Captain Rousselot rose from his desk. He sported a cordial grin, and with quick, short strides came out from behind the desk and shook Mason's hand. He stood at five feet five and was lean but muscular, exuding a bigger persona than his short stature would indicate. He seemed less interested in Carson and gave him only a curt bow before returning to his position behind the desk.

"I am pleased to meet you," Captain Rousselot said in excellent English. "Monsieur Brisbane has told me much about you. Please, sit."

Mason and Carson settled into two wooden chairs that creaked under their weight.

"So, Mr. Collins," Captain Rousselot said, "I understand you are going to grace us with your uncanny skills and find these girls."

"I haven't promised anything."

Rousselot rocked back in his swivel chair and gave Mason a wry smile like a professor with an errant student: "But you have agreed to take the case even after my entire police force has discovered nothing. You, without resources, will succeed where we have failed."

Mason wanted to say that from what he'd seen so far, he hadn't been very impressed with the police force, but he knew it would be best to avoid a pissing contest; he needed the captain's cooperation.

Carson took advantage of the brief staring contest to say, "Capitaine, I'm sure you welcome any help in finding these girls. That is more important than professional pride."

Rousselot glanced at Carson, then returned his gaze to Mason. "What Mr. Collins is aware of that you are not is that outside interference by individuals can disrupt an investigation. Witnesses harassed. Evidence tampered with."

"Captain," Mason said, "if you've interviewed every witness, collected any evidence, and searched the crime scenes, then I don't see what I could do to screw things up."

The heat in the room seemed to rise another ten degrees after he said it. Mason disliked this new role of private detective. He'd always been in a position of authority, backed by and sanctioned by either a city police force or the U.S. Army. He'd never met a private detective he liked, and many achieved only one result: extricating hard-earned money from desperate clients.

Carson leaned forward in his chair. "Capitaine Rousselot, Mr. Collins has been contracted by the British consul general, and he will conduct a parallel investigation, with or without your cooperation."

Mason looked at Carson. "That's not what I'm going to do. Without Captain Rousselot's help, I'll be going in circles and following dead leads, wasting everybody's time." Mason turned back to Rousselot. "Sir, you know time is critical in abductions. I'll stay out of your way, and anything I turn up I will report to you. Let me help either find the girls or bring the perpetrator to justice."

The captain still hesitated. He held his head back and stared at Mason down the bridge of his nose.

Mason reached into his pocket and slapped down the three photos of the missing girls that Carson had given him. "These girls are all that should matter."

Rousselot launched forward in his chair. "Do not talk to me like a suspect in an interrogation room."

Mason could tell the captain struggled to avoid looking at the pictures, but only a moment passed before he lost the battle and looked. His gaze finally rose up to Mason, and his stern expression had turned to concern. "I have a daughter about their same age."

Rousselot thought a moment, then stood abruptly. "Come with me." He grabbed his cap and briefcase.

Mason and Carson stood and began to follow Rousselot out of his office, but the captain held out his hand to stop Carson. "You are not going."

"But I represent—"

"No civilians."

"But he's a civilian," Carson said, pointing at Mason.

"He is different," Rousselot said, and walked out of the room.

"Rather mysterious of him," Carson said.

Mason shrugged. "If this takes a while, then I'll meet you at the British consulate."

Carson shook his head. "I have strict orders to take you to see Sir Wilfred. I'll wait for you in the lobby."

Mason nodded and joined Captain Rousselot in the hallway.

The captain waited until they were descending the stairs to say, "We believe one of the missing girls' bodies has been found. About an hour ago."

"Do you know which one?"

Captain Rousselot looked at Mason with a grim expression. "Unfortunately, it will be difficult to tell."

6

C aptain Rousselot led Mason to a police sedan. A Moroccan police driver snapped to attention and opened the door for the captain. Once Mason and the captain had taken their seats in the back, the driver got in and pulled out onto the busy street.

Rousselot set his briefcase on his lap, pulled out a series of files, and opened the top file folder. "The first girl to disappear, Sabine de Graaf, is fifteen. Dutch. Her father is a banker. Thirty-one days ago, she was on the beach with her mother. The beach was crowded with sunbathers. Sabine asked her mother permission to buy an Italian ice from a Spanish fellow who was selling them from a cart nearby. The vendor was no more than fifty meters from their spot. But according to the vendor, he never saw the girl. In fact, no one noticed her or witnessed anyone abducting her. She just disappeared."

"And the mother saw nothing?"

"The mother claims she looked away for what she swears was only a moment. That was at three in the afternoon. She says that when she turned back to look for her daughter, the sun had dropped to the horizon, and there were fewer people on the beach. She was shocked to realize that four hours had somehow passed."

"She wasn't drinking alcohol? No medical problems?"

"No. It could have been sunstroke, or she went into shock when she realized her daughter had gone. It is hard to tell. And it will be pointless for you to talk with her. She is hysterical and in the hospital under heavy sedation. We barely got that information out of her before she went into an uncontrollable fit."

"Did Sabine have any behavior problems? Rebelliousness? Could she have run away?"

"Not according to her father. She was a quiet girl, with few friends, despite her beauty. We retraced her day as best we could: shopping with her mother, lunch at a café on Place de France, then the beach. She never reported any enemies or anyone following her."

While Rousselot closed that file and opened the next, Mason noticed the Moroccan driver studying him in the rearview mirror. He had intense dark brown eyes, but there was nothing malicious in the look. More curious about the American talking to the deputy chief of police like an equal.

"Valerie Meunier," Rousselot said, as he turned another page in the file. "Sixteen. French. She disappeared exactly three weeks ago. She, too, was with her mother, shopping in the Grand Socco."

"Did the mother have the same four-hour blackout?" Mason said.

"She had a brief episode of confusion, but not as extreme as Madame de Graaf. Though she felt more ill—a severe headache and nausea."

"And no one saw Valerie or her abductor?"

"That is not particularly surprising in this case. It was market day, and the Grand Socco, the main open-air marketplace, is always extremely crowded at that hour."

Mason thought for a minute as he stared out the window. It had taken less than twenty minutes to leave the city behind. The road of cracked concrete followed a valley floor between high mountains to the east and a lower cluster of hills to the west. He turned back to Rousselot. "It could be the mothers were drugged somehow. But chloral hydrate would have knocked them out. Barbiturates and Sodium Amytal, the same thing. What about opiates? Were the mothers tested for drugs?"

The captain cleared his throat and shifted in his seat. "The detective in charge only thought to check the two mothers after it was too late."

"Any reason to suspect the abductors were Moroccan? Maybe revolutionaries seeking revenge or the release of political prisoners?"

Mason noticed the Moroccan driver looking at him again.

"There are some radical elements, yes," the captain said. "We've had a few small demonstrations, some incidents of violence, but nothing compared to French Morocco. In Rabat and Casablanca, for example. Tangier has been relatively calm."

Captain Rousselot filled Mason in on the third missing young woman while they bumped along the country highway. Cynthia Brisbane had disappeared twelve days ago. And like the others, she had been with her mother, though the mother had been drinking heavily. After visiting the Grand Socco, they had ventured deep into the medina before the mother noticed that Cynthia was gone.

Captain Rousselot leaned forward to speak to the driver. "*Le plan de Tanger, s'il te plaît.*"

The driver rifled through the glove box and passed back a folded map. Rousselot flattened it out, revealing the city of Tangier—to Mason's mind, shaped like a fat-barreled derringer, with the top of the barrel running along the coast and pointing west. With a tap of his finger, Rousselot indicated an area in the upper right-hand corner of the city. "This is the medina, the old, walled part of the city."

The medina was shaped like a primitive axe, with the "blade" side facing north and the sea. Whoever had built the medina didn't believe in straight lines, or in the concept that streets should lead somewhere, anywhere. The layout reminded Mason of a tangle of barbed wire, the streets twisting in on themselves or simply ending into nothing.

The captain pointed to the only spot within the medina walls that came close to a recognizable shape, and a very small one at that. "This rectangular area here is called the Petit Socco, or little market. The mother and daughter were just west of this spot. They proceeded up Calle Cristianos, then turned left on Calle Seba. About fifty meters farther on, Cynthia Brisbane disappeared."

He then pointed out the long, crescent-shaped beach that began near the marina and followed the shore of Tangier Bay. About halfway down the beach, Sabine de Graaf had vanished. And finally, the captain indicated the Grand Socco, a rough oval plaza sitting just outside the main gate to the medina. "Valerie Meunier and her mother dined at a café, then shopped at several vendors' stalls in the Grand Socco. According to her mother, Valerie never left her side, but within ten minutes she was gone."

Mason studied the map for a few moments, realizing that the abductor could easily slip through that maze of medina streets and disappear without a trace.

The driver turned off the concrete highway onto a dirt road. It was four p.m. The sun still sat high in the sky and baked the barren landscape. An occasional holm oak or gnarled olive tree dotted fields of dry grass and provided shade for small herds of goats and sheep. They met very few cars or trucks. Most of the traffic was the walking kind, local men in hooded djellabas, with the women in billowing red or striped garments following behind.

Finally, about thirty minutes from Tangier, the driver pulled to the side of the dirt road, where a police jeep, a black sedan, and a station wagon converted into an ambulance were parked. Mason and Rousselot exited their car. The captain said something to the driver in French; then he and Mason moved toward a group of four men standing among the scrub brush thirty yards off the road. A few vultures and a lone hawk hovered overhead. The desiccated shrubs and spiny plants cracked under their feet. The sun pressed down on Mason's head, and the dry wind immediately sucked the moisture from his mouth and lungs. He'd developed thick blood after three years in northern Europe during the war, making the heat even more oppressive.

The two uniformed policemen came to attention and saluted the captain. The two other men wore white short-sleeved shirts and striped ties. They nodded to the captain and took a few steps to join them. The captain introduced them as Inspecteur Réne Verger and Subinspecteur Armando Rincon. Verger, a man in his early thirties, had sandy-blond hair, while his younger partner, Rincon, had dark, curly hair and olive skin.

Inspecteur Verger eyed Mason warily, then talked with the captain in French. Mason turned to look at who Mason assumed was the medical examiner. He squatted near two tall bushes a few feet away, with his back to the group, blocking Mason's view of the body. Mason stepped around the medical examiner and stopped midstride.

Any initial impression Mason had that this landscape was barren and lifeless vanished when he looked at the poor girl's corpse. Only patches of blackened skin on her face and legs below the knees remained. What flesh the vultures and hyenas hadn't consumed, the maggots and beetles were finishing off. Her matted hair was obviously blond, but all three of the missing girls had similarly colored hair.

The medical examiner appeared impassive as he examined the victim's throat with a magnifying glass. He looked up at Mason, then over his shoulder at the captain and detectives. "You must be that American detective we've heard so much about." He was British by the accent.

Mason nodded. "Broken hyoid bone?"

"Yes. And what's left of her esophagus appears to be perforated, though that could be an animal bite. It will be impossible to tell for certain if strangulation is the cause of death, but it seems the most likely."

Captain Rousselot came up to stand at Mason's side. Inspector Verger remained where he was and barked orders in French to his junior partner.

"How long do you think?" Mason asked the medical examiner.

"In this heat, putrefaction happens very quickly. And by the accumulation and type of insects, I'd guess four to six days at the most."

The Spanish subinspector began to take photographs. He breathed rapidly through his mouth, his skin ghostly gray. The medical examiner stood and lit a cigarette with his soiled gloves still on his hands. "Definitely female," he said to Mason and the captain. "Probably mid to late teens. We should be able to get good dental imprints, but forget fingerprints."

"All three came from wealthy families," Captain Rousselot said. "They should have dental records."

"You measure her height yet?" Mason asked.

"I estimate she was one hundred sixty-five to a hundred and sixty-eight centimeters."

Mason looked at Captain Rousselot, who said, "Two of the girls are in that range. If I remember correctly, Cynthia Brisbane is closer to one hundred and seventy-five centimeters."

"That's assuming this victim is one of the three girls," Mason said. He walked over to the corpse and knelt beside it. He had never become used to the sight and smell of a decaying corpse, despite all the bodies he'd seen during his time on the Chicago police force and the war. He could even imagine these bones fleshed out into a lovely and vibrant teenager, full of hope and life. She had surely suffered and lived in terror her last days on earth, before her life had been snuffed out and her body discarded in such a hostile and lonely place. And there were two other girls —if not more—who might suffer the same fate. Children, probably violated, then murdered and discarded. Mason had promised the captain to tread carefully in the investigation, but now there was no way that was going to happen.

Mason noticed faint geometric patterns on the soles of the girl's feet. He pointed out the area to the medical examiner. "Tattoos of some kind?"

"More than likely henna tattoos. Moroccan. Different designs mean different things. Good fortune or warding off evil spirits. It's fashionable with the Western girls to get these types of tattoos."

"Where do they have them done?"

"By Moroccan women in the markets or impromptu stands in the streets."

Inspector Verger stomped over to the captain and launched into a one-sided yelling match. Though Mason didn't understand French, he got the idea well enough, as the inspector kept jabbing his finger his way. He sauntered toward Verger with a passive expression but steely eyes. Verger's tirade continued, but he took short steps away from Mason's advance, blurting out only a few words, then stealing uneasy glances at Mason. His mouth clamped shut for good when Mason came within inches of his face.

"Mr. Collins," Captain Rousselot said with a tone of resignation. "We should allow my detectives to work without interference."

Mason gave the French detective one final glare before turning and walking back to the car. He joined the Moroccan driver, who leaned against the car. The driver offered him a cigarette by shaking the pack in Mason's direction. Mason took one and nodded his thanks. The driver lit it for him, and Mason took a puff. He nearly gagged and tossed it away.

The driver laughed. "They're Egyptian. You do not like them?" To Mason's surprise, the man spoke English with only a slight accent.

"Tastes like they were soaked in formaldehyde."

The Moroccan held out his hand. "Tazim Daoud."

"Mason Collins."

Tazim shook Mason's hand vigorously, then saluted. "I am *gendarme adjoint brigadier chef*, first class."

"You don't need to salute me, Tazim. I'm not in the army anymore."

"Yes, I know, but you were a chief warrant officer four. A criminal investigator." Tazim smiled at Mason's look of surprise. "Oh, I heard about you. And you were an army intelligence agent during the war, yes?"

Mason nodded, not sure where this was going.

"I worked for U.S. Army intelligence, too. Counterintelligence agents hired me before the American army invaded Morocco. I was very proud to help kick the Vichy French and Nazis out of my country." He tapped his head with his index finger. "I know things." He then nodded toward Verger. "Like I know that man could not find his testicles if they were not attached to his penis. He makes wind to hide his incompetence."

Mason chuckled. "It's called being a blowhard, not making wind."

"Capitaine Rousselot is a good man, even though his countrymen still colonize us. He promoted that Spaniard, Rincon, to detective only a month ago. I tried to convince him to promote me, but Moroccans are kept to the lower ranks."

"You think you're ready to be a detective?"

"*Bien sûr.* Of course."

"Okay. Do you know how the victim's body was taken to that spot?"

Tazim pointed to a mark on the dirt road where the detectives' sedan was now parked. "You can see old tire tracks where the stupid detectives parked right on top of them. The wind in this valley blows very hard. There has been no rain for one month here; therefore, the tire tracks are maybe four days old."

Mason nodded. "That's right. Broad tire tracks with deep treads. Probably a jeep or desert vehicle. And did you see their foot tracks?"

"Did you?" Tazim said skeptically.

"Yes." Mason gestured for Tazim to lead the way.

Tazim launched himself off the car and walked over to the traces of the tire tracks. He scanned the area just off the road. "Here."

Mason walked over. Tazim crouched at the edge of the road and pointed at the ground. "The police wear shoes, but there is an outline of a boot, a heavy person." He then pointed to where a spindly ground plant was broken at the stem. "A tall man, perhaps." Then he pointed to a much fainter print. "It's harder to identify this one."

"Sandals, maybe," Mason said.

"Yes, of course. A lighter, thinner man." He looked up at Mason. "Moroccan?" he asked as if hoping for another answer.

Mason shrugged. "Maybe a European who likes sandals."

"Or someone wanting us to think he is a Moroccan."

Mason nodded. "That's possible."

Tazim looked where the body had been dumped and pondered a moment. "Or perhaps they are amateurs or incompetent."

"Or believe they're above suspicion or so self-important not to care."

"That would mean Nazarenes." At Mason's confused look:

"That's what we call Westerners. Christians. The local Moroccans are called Tanjawis."

"And you're not a Tanjawi?"

"I am from Casablanca. I was brought to Tangier by your army to help expose Moroccans working as Nazi informants. And they exposed some Nazarenes. You might be surprised that there are still a number of Nazarenes in Tangier who were Nazi sympathizers."

"Not after where I've been the last two years."

Tazim stood and faced Mason. He glanced over at Captain Rousselot, who was making his way back to the car. "Let me be your assistant," Tazim said.

"You've got a job. Stay with it. Get experience. And when Morocco gets its independence, you'll be ready to take over."

"France and Spain will never let Morocco go." A thought then came to Tazim. "I could be your eyes and ears in the force. I help you, and you teach me."

"And then if the captain, or someone else in the department, finds out you're spying for me, we'll both be sent packing."

Captain Rousselot yelled out to Tazim in French as he stepped onto the road. Tazim's brow wrinkled in disappointment. He rushed over to the car and opened the door for the captain. Mason scanned the horizon and wondered if there were other girls left out here. Maybe ones whose remains had already been claimed by the desert. Nothing but bones and memories for the grieving parents.

"Are you coming, Mr. Collins?" the captain called out from the car.

For now, Mason thought, *though I have a feeling I'll be back here soon.*

7

Tazim pulled the sedan into the police headquarters parking
lot. Carson stood in the shade of the building's portico and
fanned himself with his white straw fedora. It had been a silent
ride back to the city, though Captain Rousselot did say that
because Inspector Verger had complained so vociferously, Mason
would have little cooperation from the police. When they exited
the car, the captain leaned so no one would overhear. "I will give
you what little help I can, Mr. Collins. I'm sorry, but my hands are
tied." He gave Mason a curt good-bye and headed for the
entrance.

Tazim faced Mason, came to attention, and saluted him.
Mason made a halfhearted swipe at his saluting arm. Tazim
winked, spun on his heels, and then jogged to catch up to the
captain.

Carson seemed reluctant to come out into the sun, but Mason
remained where he was. Carson let out a theatrical sigh, jerked
the lapels of his suit coat, donned his hat, and left the sanctuary of
the shade. As he walked, he said, "Where have you been?"

"My dear Mr. Trusdale. We're arguing already, and we
haven't even made it to the honeymoon."

Carson looked chided. "It was a simple question."

"I said you could wait for me at the British consulate."

"I was afraid you'd wander off and forget that we have to talk to Sir Wilfred. He's the one responsible for bringing you here." When all Carson received from Mason was an amused smile, Carson marched over to the Jaguar and opened the door. "I don't appreciate being treated like an errand boy. I've been assigned to facilitate your investigation. I bailed you out of prison, perhaps saving your ungrateful life. And without my continued endorsement, you could find yourself out on the street without a penny to your name." With that, he got in the car and slammed his door.

Mason debated whether to get in the car or walk away. In the end, he got in the passenger's seat, and Carson pulled out of the police headquarters parking lot.

"They found a girl's corpse out in the desert."

Carson jerked his head in Mason's direction, his eyes wide with dread. "Is it Cynthia Brisbane?"

"The remains are too far gone to know. She was about five five or six, with blond hair."

Carson's shoulders relaxed. "Thank God. Cynthia's taller." He looked back at the road to avoid Mason's stare. "It's tragic, of course. For the young lady."

"Of course."

"I didn't mean to sound callous. I'm just happy for Sir Wilfred and Mrs. Brisbane."

"The girl was strangled so hard it broke her hyoid bone. She was stripped, and her body dumped out in the desert."

"Lest you think me a self-serving bastard, I'm simply relieved that a man I respect hasn't lost his only daughter."

"What you should be thinking is that if the victim is one of the abducted girls, then when he's done with them, he kills them and dumps them in the desert to rot."

Carson's momentary elation turned sour. "Perhaps we shouldn't tell Sir Wilfred what the police found."

"He's going to find out, if he hasn't already. You've got to tell him."

Carson looked at Mason with alarm. "Not me. I might deny being a self-serving bastard, but I'll readily admit to being a coward. At least when it comes to Sir Wilfred."

"Cowards are almost always self-serving bastards."

"Insult me all you like, but I'm not going to be the one to tell him."

"Why are you afraid of him? You think he's going to beat you?"

Carson set his jaw and gripped the steering wheel as if a furious debate raged in his mind. "Let's put it this way: he has a volatile temper. He's a brilliant diplomat, except when it comes to the people who work for him."

Mason shook his head. "Oh, this just gets better and better."

Carson turned onto a street that circled a large oval plaza. The interior was full of vegetable and flower stands and booths with carpets or baskets or brassware, all shaded by a cluster of tall oaks. Restaurants and bars, offices, and shops ringed the plaza. Throngs of Westerners and Moroccans circulated through the space or sat at the sidewalk café tables.

"Is this the Grand Socco, where Valerie Meunier disappeared?" Mason asked.

"Yes, and Cynthia Brisbane and her mother had just entered the medina from here, before Cynthia disappeared. *Socco* is a Spanish translation for *souk*, the Arab word for market. The locals come for the produce or the flowers, and the tourists come for souvenirs. It's the heart of the city, and it's always crowded like this."

"I want to come here after we see your boss."

Carson only grunted a response. At the opposite end of the

plaza, he turned on a street that skirted along the walls of the medina and climbed up a steep grade. It eventually leveled off above the city and followed the twists and turns of the ridgeline. Through the pine and eucalyptus trees, Mason caught glimpses of the sea and, far in the distance, the hazy brown coastline of Spain. Mansions lined both sides of the road, each house a different architectural style, each trying to outdo the others in sprawl and opulence. Carson informed him that they were on what the locals called "the mountain," though it hardly qualified for such a lofty title. The road was aptly named the New Mountain Road, which was just an updated version of the old mountain road. The only signs of life on that hot afternoon were the Moroccan nannies, gardeners, chauffeurs polishing cars, and the occasional security team.

Carson pulled into a driveway and stopped in front of tall, wrought iron gates. Beyond was a large estate overlooking the high cliffs and the sea. The British consul general's mansion was of Spanish-style architecture, a two-story gargantuan with a red tile roof, arched windows, and beige stucco walls. A British-uniformed gatekeeper exited a kiosk and instructed them to pull into the small graveled parking area by the side of the house.

A man with ginger-colored hair and mustache met them at the car. He held his head at a slight tilt as he gave them a fraction of a bow, all the while keeping his hands clasped and close to his chest. Carson greeted the man and introduced him as Norwood, Brisbane's butler and personal secretary. He reminded Mason more of an undertaker. Norwood led the way along a paving-stone walkway, up the colonnaded portico, and to an arched front door. They entered a large foyer of marble and mahogany. Great care had been taken to replicate an old English manor, from the architectural details to the antique furnishings and paintings depicting sailing ships or dead relatives.

Norwood stopped them and leaned in, speaking in a hushed

tone. "Sir Wilfred has not arrived yet. You can wait in the study, if you like."

"Mrs. Brisbane is here, or you wouldn't be whispering like that," Mason said.

Norwood and Carson exchanged a look, before Norwood said, "I believe Sir Wilfred would prefer that he alone gives you all the facts."

"Mrs. Brisbane might remember details that Sir Wilfred wouldn't. I need to speak to her."

Carson leaned in like Norwood and whispered, "Mr. Collins—"

At full volume, Mason said, "You want me to investigate this case, then let me talk to Mrs. Brisbane. Their daughter has been missing for almost two weeks. The only hope we have for preventing her body from ending up in the desert is to start asking everybody difficult questions."

Carson and Norwood exchanged another look; then Norwood led them down a long hallway. He moved as if entering a sacred tomb. They turned into a spacious library, like the foyer, all marble and mahogany. Floor-to-ceiling bookshelves lined the walls, with a rolling ladder affixed to a metal railing, allowing the browser access to the books on the higher shelves. There was a large mahogany table, high-back, carved chairs, and a plush red carpet.

Norwood stopped at a door almost hidden between the bookshelves. "This is Mrs. Brisbane's personal study." He moved to knock on the door, but Mason put his hand on Norwood's arm to stop him.

"I'd rather you two wait out here."

"The consul general would never hear of it."

"Norwood," Carson said gently, "Mrs. Brisbane might feel more comfortable talking to Mr. Collins without us present."

"Talk to a complete stranger? Without an introduction?" Norwood said this as if they were both completely mad.

Mason began to realize that dealing with English aristocrats might be more difficult than an army general. "Make a quick introduction, then leave. She'll talk to me if it means a chance at finding her daughter."

Norwood hesitated, then said, "I feel it necessary to warn you that Mrs. Brisbane is very upset. News of what the police found in the desert has already reached us."

Mason shot a glare of frustration at Carson. Gossip in a small town couldn't move any faster.

Norwood continued, "Please take that into consideration, and not assume that her behavior is in any way usual. And I ask that whatever occurs during your interview will remain confidential."

A husky woman's voice came from the other side of the door. "For heaven's sake, Norwood, I can hear everything you've said. Let the man come in, and remain where you are, as he requested."

Norwood opened the door and stepped aside. Mason crossed the threshold and had to push away a mass of palm fronds and hanging ivy. Mrs. Brisbane's study had been built as a greenhouse, and ferns, palms, and orchids filled the space. Heavy curtains of deep reds and gold were drawn across the windowed walls. Swags of multicolored silk hung from the ceiling, giving the impression of being inside an exotic Persian palace. Thick odors clung to the beads of moisture in the air, and each seemed to deposit its distinct fragrance in his nose: wet earth and vegetation, sandalwood incense, and Mrs. Brisbane's sickly lilac perfume. But dominating the others was a scent like burning weeds. Mason knew that smell from his time as a detective for the Chicago PD—marijuana.

Mrs. Brisbane wore a silk caftan and gold turban, and lounged among a mass of pillows. Mason would have found that screwy enough, but a towering black man dressed in a flowing white robe stood over her, stirring the damp air with a large fan of peacock feathers.

Mrs. Brisbane said nothing, as her mouth was busy drawing in smoke from the tapered end of a tall hookah pipe. She looked at him with bloodshot eyes underlined by dark, puffy circles. She motioned for Mason to come forward. She appeared to be in her late forties, and despite her unusual appearance, she exuded elegance and had a youthful softness to her angular features, giving her an air of a timeless beauty.

"Mrs. Brisbane, I'm Mason—"

"Yes, I'm aware of who you are," Mrs. Brisbane said, her words slurred and her head listing to port. "My husband has extolled your virtues." She narrowed her eyes as she peered at Mason. "Do you believe you will find my daughter?"

"I can only promise that I'll try, ma'am."

"Beatrice, please, Mr. Collins." She held up the hookah. "Do you imbibe? It's a mixture of tobacco and hashish. Particularly effective in calming my nerves."

"I'll stick with alcohol, ma'am."

"Beatrice," Mrs. Brisbane said again in a faraway voice, and she took another hit off the hookah.

"If you'd rather I come back another time …"

Mrs. Brisbane exhaled slowly and patted a neighboring pillow. "Sit. I'm going to get a cramp in my neck if I have to keep looking up at you."

Mason struggled to sit on the soft pillow. The bizarreness of it made him think of those Westerns in which the cowboy hero had to sit and smoke a peace pipe with the belligerent Indian chief.

Despite the drug's relaxing effects on her facial muscles, Mrs. Brisbane's eyes expressed deep anxiety and sorrow. "I heard about the poor girl the police found in the wilderness."

Mason gave her a nod. "They haven't identified her, yet. She may not even be one of the other missing girls."

"Don't patronize me, Mr. Collins. I'm stronger than I appear at present."

"You last saw your daughter twelve days ago, correct?"

Mrs. Brisbane looked off to some distant place, and said with some effort, "What is today?"

"It's Saturday, the twenty-ninth."

"Then, yes, twelve days ago."

"Did she say that anyone was harassing or following her?"

"She's a beautiful girl. There was always some lad in heat following her."

"Being clever isn't going to help me."

Mrs. Brisbane smiled. "Forgive me. Old habits. One must be clever if one is to be the wife of a British diplomat." She paused. A look of bitterness passed across her face. "No, dear boy, Cynthia reported nothing out of the ordinary. No enemies or ardent suitors that I am aware of."

"And she disappeared in the medina?"

Mrs. Brisbane nodded. "At around three in the afternoon. We had done some shopping in the new town and the Grand Socco …" Her voice trailed off, and her expression turned grim. "We'd gone into the medina for a stroll, when I lost track of her. In fact, I lost track of myself." She tried laughing it off, but it fell flat. "When I became aware of my surroundings again, I noticed she was gone. I thought maybe she went 'looking for kicks,' as she would say. As if that phrase might minimize her constant acts of defiance. But in fact she had disappeared." Mrs. Brisbane took a long draw off her hookah with a shaking hand.

"Had she done this before? Maybe to meet up with a secret boyfriend, and they decided to run off together?"

"Do you have young daughters, Mr. Collins?"

"No, ma'am, I don't."

"They are as silly as can be." She paused as tears came to her eyes, and she unconsciously wiped at one lingering on her cheek. "But she wouldn't do such a thing, despite how she might have expressed her disdain for parental authority. She just vanished, and it's all my fault."

She leaned into Mason as if revealing a secret, her lilac perfume now rancid from being mixed with the smoke. "I believe we were under some kind of spell," she said matter-of-factly.

"Sorry, ma'am, but I don't follow."

Mrs. Brisbane took a long drag on the hookah, as if the pause would give her time to consider her response. She took in so much that it caused her eyes to partially roll up in her head.

"Mrs. Brisbane?"

She exhaled a prodigious cloud of smoke. "Morocco is a strange and magical place. The West has forgotten the lore of spirits, sorcery, and potions, but Morocco has not. The majority of Moroccans *do* believe. Which, in my opinion, makes it manifest. It may not be real to you ..." Her voice trailed off as her eyes focused on something unseen.

"Mrs. Brisbane?"

Her eyes shifted to Mason, though her head remained where it was.

"So," Mason said, "you suspect a Moroccan may have used magic or some kind of potion to hypnotize you both and lure Cynthia away?"

"I don't suspect—I know it."

"And why is that?"

"They're all very crafty. Always wanting handouts or to trick you out of your money and possessions. They're like ignorant schoolchildren, but with a streak of larceny and greed."

Mason looked up to the statuesque African, but the man remained expressionless, even bored. He'd probably heard these words countless times. Mason asked her, "If the Moroccans are greedy, why do you think there hasn't been a ransom demand?"

"Such individuals don't behave rationally, even in crime."

With Mrs. Brisbane's last word, her face drooped as if every facial muscle had given in to gravity. She had fallen under the influence of the hashish—the one potion Mason could believe in. He wondered how much the drug spoke for her, how much of what she said was reliable.

Mrs. Brisbane looked at him, as if she knew what he was thinking. "Don't assume that because of my present state of mind, I don't know what I'm saying. Or that I do not love my daughter very deeply. I lost two other children in childbirth, so Cynthia is very precious to me. She is vexing and irresponsible, but I cannot bear the thought of life without her. Please, find my daughter, Mr. Collins, before it's too late."

It seemed the effort to bring her fears to the surface and articulate a coherent thought had taken her last ounce of willpower. Her eyelids drooped, and she began to stare at the tiled floor.

Mason hoisted himself off the pillow. He arched his eyebrows at the black man to share in the bizarreness of the situation. The man only glanced at him with the same stone-faced expression before returning his gaze to the middle of the room.

Mason gently laid his hand on Mrs. Brisbane's shoulder, then fought his way through the tangle of plants as he headed for the door. Just as he reached for the doorknob, someone jerked the door open from the other side.

A tall, thin man with hair dyed black and a pencil-thin mustache hesitated just long enough to give Mason an icy glare before blowing past him. Sir Wilfred Alastair Brisbane had arrived.

Mason followed him just far enough into the room to clear the palm fronds. The consul general stood in front of his wife in silence as he flexed his fists. A moment passed; then he knelt in front of her. His back remained stiff as he leaned forward to examine her eyes. Sir Wilfred was at least five years her junior, but he gave her the scolding look of a strict parent. Mrs. Brisbane looked past him, though Mason doubted she was unaware of his presence. There was no exchange of tenderness, no shared distress.

Brisbane stood, turned on his heels, and marched up to Mason. "In my office, if you please." He then continued his march out of the room.

A few minutes later, Norwood ushered Mason into a second-floor room. Unlike the rest of the house, it was modestly decorated with an oak desk and two rigid chairs. Another set of austere chairs and a padded bench faced a stone fireplace. Behind the desk, a bay window offered a view of the treetops and the sea beyond. There were a few file folders and law books on the desk and single shelf, leaving Mason with the impression that the man spent little time in the room, unless his tastes were as Spartan as the look on his face.

Brisbane stood at the bay window. He angled himself in such a way as to have a view of both the room and the sea, a position that expressed an indifference to both. "Have a seat, Mr. Collins."

Mason shook his head. "You stand, I stand."

Brisbane's lip trembled at the impertinence. "I expressed my disappointment to Norwood for failing to shield my wife from your inquisition. Not to mention the potential for embarrassment."

"For you, or your wife?"

Brisbane turned. "How dare you—"

"You want me to help find your daughter?"

"The local authorities seem incapable."

"That's not what I asked."

Brisbane turned back to face the window. "That's why I had you brought here. To help."

"In order to do that, I had to talk to Mrs. Brisbane. I'm not here to judge her method of coping with your daughter's disappearance. It's not any different than turning to the bottle to drown your sorrows."

"This habit of hers has been going on for some time. Morocco got to her long before Cynthia was abducted." Brisbane faced Mason and arched one eyebrow. "Did she claim that her lapse of judgment and Cynthia's disappearance was due to black magic?"

"I figured that was the hashish talking."

Brisbane shook his head. "Among other absurdities, she swears that one of the maids keeps leaving little bags around the house. Bags containing a myriad of ridiculous ingredients to make her ill, so the maid can take over the household."

"She says Cynthia vanished into thin air."

"Cynthia has slipped out of this house easily enough, past these high walls and twenty-four-hour guards. She would have had no problem with her mother in the medina."

"Any reason why you think she would slip away? A boyfriend, say?"

"She's eighteen, Mr. Collins. We had arguments, and I had to take disciplinary actions. But none of those actions would warrant her running away. As far as a boyfriend is concerned, there are many things she refused to share with us. However, I have forbidden her fraternization with boys until she shows she can act like an adult."

"How about Cynthia's friends? Do you know any of them?"

"I'm too busy to concern myself with their names."

"Mrs. Brisbane seems to think that a Moroccan may have taken her."

"I wouldn't rule it out."

"Is it common for Moroccans to abduct Western girls?"

"Heavens, no. But Tangier has more than its share of white and colored criminals. Then there's the slave trade—" Brisbane stopped, and just for a brief second, he let his worry peek through.

Mason allowed himself to assume that the worry was for his daughter.

"I'll ask the local police to give me a list of suspected criminals, but I need you to write down any of Cynthia's routines you're familiar with, extracurricular activities, clubs."

Brisbane regained his composure, his expression returning to that of a dignified sneer. "That will be a short list. Those kinds of trivial things are more my wife's concern." He moved to his desk and sat. After retrieving a sheet of stationery and a fountain pen, he began to write. Without looking up from the paper, he said, "I've tried to rein in my daughter's rebellious side. I've tried to convince her that her loose morals would get any young woman into trouble, let alone a beautiful one like my daughter. It's a constant battle, and one I'm afraid I've lost." Brisbane stopped writing for a moment. His eyes remained fixed on the paper as the fingers of his left hand stroked his hair.

"I have to ask you, sir: With the British consulate at your disposal and your position as consul general, why didn't you try to enlist the help of someone from British intelligence? Or a retired officer, for that matter?"

"My frustration with the police investigation only came to a head recently, and you came highly recommended. Plus, I wanted to steer clear of any hint that I'm taking advantage of my position in using government resources."

"In other words, you want to keep this private."

"Use any words you like. The fact is, you are here and I'm asking you to help. That should be enough."

"Do you know whether your daughter had any connection to the other two missing girls?"

It took Brisbane a second to answer. "Passing acquaintances, perhaps, but the Dutch and French girls went to different schools." Brisbane looked up at Mason. "I suppose you'll be investigating the other two disappearances because of the possible connection. However, I insist that you put your energy into finding Cynthia."

"Sir Wilfred, if the disappearances are related, then if I find one, I find all three."

"I brought you here to find *my* daughter."

"I thought I was asked to come to help find all three."

"I'm willing to pay handsomely, but if I discover that you are making deals with the other parents, or neglecting any leads having to do with Cynthia in favor of those other girls, I will have to reconsider my offer."

"If you're going to dictate the terms of my investigation, then you can find another stooge."

"I was led to believe that you would be more amenable."

"You mean Carson led you to believe I was spineless."

"I'm offering you twenty thousand pounds, Mr. Collins. That's almost thirteen thousand U.S. dollars."

That gave Mason pause. Thirteen thousand dollars was about three years' worth of salary for a Chicago police detective, and four years' pay as an army investigator. He could do a lot with thirteen grand, and the possibilities were already rolling around in his head.

"One thing we have to get straight: I won't ignore the other disappearances. I have to follow leads as they come up. I concentrate on Cynthia, but I *will* be checking out the other two."

"Then let me be clear: the twenty-thousand-pound reward is for finding her alive. Do you hear me? Alive. I'm paying for your lodgings and giving you a small stipend for your time and living expenses. Ten pounds a day. You will come by every day to report your progress and collect your day's allotment."

"Keep me on a leash, more like it."

Brisbane smiled at Mason's stern expression. "If you stay away from the prostitutes and the underground gambling houses, you can get by in Tangier very cheaply."

The small amount of money didn't bother Mason. He'd gotten by on far less. It was Brisbane's attempts at controlling him by waving a wad of money in front of his nose. He wasn't about to make it a one-sided investigation. And Mason wondered how long he would be able to put up with this before giving his-royal-pain-in-the-ass a right cross to the chin.

8

"Here we are," Carson said as he parked the car in front of a building declaring itself the Hôtel Maison Rose.

Mason and Carson climbed out of the convertible, and Mason retrieved his suitcase out of the backseat.

Carson noticed him inspecting the hotel's cracked stucco and peeling paint. "She has faded in her glory but retains her charm. It's rumored that Matisse stayed here. Although I think that story was started by the Frenchman who owns the place—a rather proud fellow from Montmartre."

"No luxury too extravagant for the British consulate."

Carson attempted a sympathetic smile. "This is where I leave you," he said, trying to sound cheerful.

"I thought you were going to show me the spots where the girls disappeared."

"Sorry, but I'm done for the evening." He pointed to the end of the street. "That way is the Grand Socco. On the other side of the Socco is the main entrance to the medina. I wouldn't go too far, though. You can get turned around in there if you don't know where you're going."

Carson dived into the driver's seat before Mason could protest further. He waved and shouted "Cheerio" before driving off.

Mason watched the Jaguar race up the road as he considered Carson's quick getaway. All of a sudden he was in a hurry to leave, when the rest of the time he'd hovered close like a persistent fly.

Mason entered the hotel's lobby, which hadn't changed—or been renovated—since the teens. The French belle époque decorations had a patina of dust and age, which included the gold statuary of draped women holding candelabras, chandeliers exploding with crystals, and green wallpaper with filigreed gold patterns, now turning brown with age and tobacco smoke. After checking in, he took an open-caged elevator that clanked and groaned up to the fifth floor. The floorboards in the hallway creaked underfoot. Gold-leafed candelabras hung at neglected angles with dim bulbs that only gave off a simulation of light, while lace curtains on the hallway window fluttered in the breeze, throwing patterned shadows on the dark green walls.

Ever since he'd stepped onto Tangier's dock, everything had seemed surreal. A few days ago, he was sipping wine in Marseille, and just a few months ago, he was fighting for his life in a small town in Germany. If he didn't know better, he would have thought it a dream brought on by inhaling too much of Mrs. Brisbane's clouds of hashish.

Mason found number 527 and unlocked the door. The room shared the same musty odors as the lobby. The floral wallpaper had separated at the seams, and a long brown water stain extended from the ceiling and disappeared behind the brass bed. He'd been in plenty of dives before, but this was Brisbane sending him a message: he'd been bought and paid for, like the rest of the chattel in his sumptuous mansion.

Mason walked to the window and peered out along the rooftops. A minaret poked up above the chaotic streets of the medina. A sea breeze helped cool the heat of the late-afternoon sun. The breeze also brought in the miasma of traffic and urban decay, but under the coarser scents mingled the perfume of the sea, of spices, cooking oils, and baking bread.

Experiencing Tangier wouldn't be half-bad if it weren't for the gnawing at his gut that nothing appeared as it seemed. That no one he'd met so far had told him anything near the truth. On top of all that, he hated the idea of being a detective for hire. But for the moment, he was stuck; he had willingly backed himself into a corner. After seeing the girl's corpse, he knew he would pursue the case, money or no. He thought about Laura, the love of his life, somewhere in the damaged heart of Europe, and what she had said about him. That because he came from a broken home and had suffered bitter betrayal while with the Chicago PD, he compensated by trying to fix everything broken in the world. Single-handedly bring criminals to their knees, and save the world from pain and suffering. A lone crusader. A hero with a chip on his shoulder. She was right, of course.

So be it ... Plus, a wad of cash didn't hurt.

It seemed to start as a distant melancholic voice. A second later, another voice much closer called out, both echoing among the buildings. Then the city became quieter. Mason knew it was the Muslim call to prayer, but he'd never heard it before. The words meant nothing, but the voice had a timeless sound.

The exotic scents and sounds, the tangled city simmering in the heat, the twisted people, and the melancholy sound of the call to prayer—he could appreciate how someone might see ghosts and shadows where there were none, believe in spells and black magic.

Surreal, indeed.

~

MASON SAT AT THE LONG MAHOGANY BAR OF THE HOTEL'S lounge and restaurant. A bartender wearing a white uniform and a red fez hat came up to him. He was a tall man with soft brown skin and large eyes. Mason ordered a thick steak, French fries, and sautéed onions. He hadn't eaten since leaving France, so his stomach leapt at the prospect of solid food, and lots of it. The bartender brought him a draft beer, which Mason planned to nurse while he waited.

Mirrors on the back wall extended along the entire length of the bar, and they afforded Mason a view of the room behind him. The lounge/restaurant had the same faded green-and-gold motif as the lobby. Tables and wood-paneled booths lined two walls. Tall palms sat among the lounge chairs arranged in the middle of a red Oriental rug that had a patina of brown from decades of foot traffic. The blue light of dusk filtered through four paneled art nouveau windows and highlighted the cigarette smoke.

A bony, middle-aged man sporting a thin mustache settled onto the barstool next to Mason. He was dressed in a turquoise suit and matching tie, and the man's noxious cologne threatened to ruin Mason's appetite. Mason rose to move down a few stools, but then a tall man and a muscular blond in his early twenties sat on Mason's other side.

Mason felt a gun barrel poke him in the ribs. The turquoise man leaned in.

"We prefer that you stay where you are," the man said. He spoke with a British accent, though Mason thought it sounded like he had marbles in his mouth.

"What do you want?" Mason asked, as he put his hand in his pocket and felt for his pistol.

"We want to talk."

"We? Does it take all three of you to form a sentence?"

The turquoise man poked Mason deeper into his ribs with the pistol. "You gonna take your hand off that gun, chum? You might get one good shot off, but then you'd be dead. What's the advantage in that?"

The guy had a point. Mason had already asked the important question, so he just sat there in silence.

The man in turquoise, obviously the leader, made a show of reaching in his inner coat pocket with only his thumb and index finger. He pulled out an envelope, bulging slightly from whatever was inside. He put it on the bar and slid it over to Mason.

Mason crossed his arms, refusing to take the envelope. "I'm guessing that's get-out-of-town money."

The leader gave one quick nod toward the envelope. "Five hundred quid and a one-way ticket for a plane to London."

"Who's it from?"

"Do you think if he wanted you to know, he'd have sent us?"

"Good point. And the reason your buddies came with you is in case I refuse?"

"That's right," the leader said with a smile.

"If your employer wants me out of town, and he's willing to have me killed if I refuse, then why not just kill me and be done with it? That saves him the five hundred, plus the expense of the ticket. Seems to me he didn't think this whole thing through."

The leader dipped his eyebrows as he tried to process this.

"Now I'm really getting curious," Mason said. "You guys are hired guns for this one job, and your boss is an amateur. A rich one, probably, and desperate enough to hire three overdressed gunsels to deliver his bribe. My guess is he's probably paying you guys about three times the amount in the envelope so you don't just take his money and run.

"And here's a tip for you: The guy you're working for has something to do with three abducted girls. One of them was just found dead, probably raped and tortured before she was strangled to death. Do you really want to be in business with a guy like that?"

The leader said nothing. A bead of perspiration had formed on his brow, more than likely from the effort to analyze everything Mason had said.

Mason continued. "The guy probably has a lot more money where this came from. You could shake him down for a big pile of cash. He's an amateur. He'll break in about ten minutes flat. And because he's involved in the biggest crime this town has seen in a while, he won't go to the police."

The turquoise man grinned as if he prided himself on having inside information. "I know for a fact that he's got some powerful friends. You don't mess with those kinds of people."

"Ah, now we're getting somewhere. It's a man, he's rich, and he has powerful friends. Anything else you'd like to tell me about him?"

"Are you going to take the money, or are we going to have to stuff it up your ass?"

"Then think about this for a moment—"

"I don't want to do any more thinking," the leader said, and nodded for his two companions. They stood, and one of them poked Mason in the back with his pistol barrel.

Mason ignored them and said, "The abducted girls' parents, they all have more money than they know what to do with. You turn this guy over to me, and I'll see that you all get a nice chunk of change as a reward. No one has to know that you're the ones who pointed the finger."

"Not a chance. Now shut up, take the envelope, and we'll escort you to the airport."

Mason ignored him. "Say I take the envelope … Then what? You going to escort me all the way with your rods in your pockets, like we're one big happy family, past the hotel lobby full of people, and out onto a busy street?"

"That's right. You don't give us any trouble, and we don't kill you."

"And I'm supposed to believe that you won't just shoot me anyway and take the money? Seems like I've got nothing to lose. But you guys do if you gun me down in front of a bunch of witnesses. Is that worth what your employer is paying you? That's just bad business."

The turquoise man yanked open Mason's jacket and jammed the envelope into his inside breast pocket. "Get up and move."

Mason complied while he ran through his options. He knew that once they got him in the waiting car, the men were just as likely to kill him and keep the money as to take him to the airport.

The leader prodded Mason forward with the pistol jammed in his back. "Nothing stupid, okay, sport? I can put a bullet in your back and get out the door before anyone knows what's happened."

Mason moved for the bar exit with the leader using his gun barrel to nudge Mason along. His two companions took up the rear. The turquoise man had made his first mistake—aside from pissing Mason off—by having both of his guys bring up the rear. One of them should have gone in front to limit Mason's options.

Unfortunately, none of Mason's escape options guaranteed he wouldn't get a bullet in his back.

9

The turquoise man shoved Mason out into the hotel lobby. They walked at a slow pace. The check-in counter was on their right and, to the left, a wide space with faded-green upholstered benches and twenty people.

A short, stout, white-bearded man of about seventy stood by the front exit. He locked eyes on Mason, and a broad smile spread across his face. Using a cane with a black shaft and silver handle, he propelled himself with surprising speed across the room. He headed straight for Mason.

"Mr. Collins, I presume," he said with a British accent.

The stout man stopped right in front of Mason, blocking the procession. Mason had no idea who the man was—he figured another journalist—but he welcomed the distraction.

"Get out of the way, you old codger," the leader said. "We got business."

The old man ignored the remark. "I wasn't sure this was your hotel, but knowing Brisbane, I surmised he would put you up in an establishment of"—he took in the surroundings—"lower standards, shall we say. I wonder if we might have a few words."

One of the gunmen began to move around the group to shove the old man aside.

It was now or never.

Mason spun on his heels, grabbing the leader's gun and shoving it away. In the same fluid motion, he jabbed the man's throat just below the hyoid bone with his stiff fingers. The man went rigid as he gagged, loosening his grip on the gun. In the time it took for the tall gunman to draw his pistol out of his pocket, Mason already had their leader in a choke hold and control of the leader's pistol. He aimed it at the tall gunman. That still left the blond gunman to his right. But just as he was turning to cover the blond, he heard a swoosh, then a crack of bone. The blond cried out, followed by the sound of the gun hitting the carpet. Another whoosh and the blond gunman fell through Mason's peripheral vision and crumpled to the floor.

People in the lobby screamed or fled as Mason held the leader's neck tight enough to cut off the man's breathing. He kept the pistol trained on the tall man. "Place your gun on the ground. Nice and slow. And kick it toward me."

The tall gunman complied.

"Now collect your friend and get out of here."

The tall gunman hoisted his blond companion to his feet and helped him limp out the door. Mason twisted the leader around, grabbed him by his turquoise coat lapels, and shoved him into the checkout counter. The turquoise man still tried to regain control of his throat muscles as Mason jammed the pistol in his throat.

"Who hired you?"

"I don't know," the man finally got out. "Messenger. All done by messenger."

The man looked too frightened to lie. "Open your mouth," Mason said.

The leader's eyes popped wide, but he did what Mason asked.

Mason grabbed the envelope out of his pocket and stuffed it in the man's mouth.

"Make sure that gets back to your employer. If you see me on the street, I'd advise you to run the other way."

The leader gave a desperate nod. Mason half lifted him and pushed him toward the hotel entrance. The leader staggered the last few feet to the door and exited. Mason scanned to see if any bystanders had been hurt. The few people who hadn't fled the lobby seemed unsure of what to do next. Mason eyeballing them prompted a few more to hurry away, while others stood stock-still and stared at him.

The old man stood just off to Mason's right, with his feet spread and leaning on his cane with both hands. He still wore that same sly grin, and Mason wondered whether he had continued to grin while taking down the gunman with his cane. He was dressed in elegant summer whites and sported an equally white Vandyke beard. He reminded Mason of the Coca-Cola Santa Claus on summer vacation. His bushy eyebrows were arched high into his forehead, and his double chin rolled over his collar.

"Thanks for the help," Mason said. "You're pretty handy with that cane."

"You didn't do too badly yourself."

Mason stepped over and held out his hand. "Mason Collins. But you knew that."

The old man leaned heavily on his cane as he grabbed Mason's hand and pumped it in a grand handshake. "James Melville. It looked like you could use a little help."

"You knew what they were up to?"

Melville shrugged. "I have keen powers of observation."

"Lucky for me. How about I buy you a drink?" Mason said, pointing to the bar. "We're going to have to wait for the police anyhow."

Melville made a slight bow. "I would be delighted. They make ghastly drinks, but I find the atmosphere comforting. I can show you some of the best bars in town, if you like. You'll find that here they are the social heart of the community, therefore important if you want to make contacts with the European residents."

They entered the hotel bar, and Melville made a beeline for a booth near the bar.

As they settled in, the waiter hurried over with Mason's cooling steak. Mason dug in with relish.

After consuming several large mouthfuls, Mason said, "What did you want to talk to me about?"

"Hmm?" Melville said absentmindedly as he glanced at a copy of the London *Times* newspaper left on the table. He shook his head as he read. "Another bombing in Casablanca. Went off in a marketplace—three dead and fourteen wounded. Then the bloody reprisals by the police, army, and vigilante colonials. Terrible business." Melville pushed the newspaper aside. "Fortunately, Tangier has been spared the worst, but I wonder how long that will last."

Melville was about to say something else, but a passing waiter distracted him. He waved the waiter down as if his life depended on it and ordered a martini. Mason ordered a scotch on the rocks.

Melville leaned in when the waiter left and said, "Normally I would cringe at the idea of you ruining a scotch with ice cubes, but the scotch they serve here doubles as embalming fluid." He settled back. "Now, where were we? Ah, yes, why I wanted to talk with you. Anyone who reads the local papers knows who you are by now."

"Exactly what I was afraid of. Those punks, for example."

"Yes, I know what you mean. But notoriety can sometimes open doors that normally would be closed. People always like meeting a celebrity. Even a flash in the pan, like yourself."

"You haven't said what you want to talk about," Mason said after consuming more of his steak.

"The case, dear boy."

"You're not a reporter or an ex-cop. I can tell that much."

"True, but I wonder how you came to that conclusion," Melville said. He then winked and tapped his broad nose. "The nose tells all, eh?"

"That's one way of putting it."

The waiter came over with their drinks, and before he had time to set Mason's on the table, Melville took a gulp of his. He grimaced and said to the waiter, "I believe the bartender has confused a martini with a Molotov cocktail. Bring me a gin and tonic instead."

The waiter took away the martini with a promise of a quick return.

"Consider me the town snoop," Melville said. "I'm curious about everything and everyone. I should write a book one day on the outrageous and nefarious denizens who inhabit this singular city. You and this case interest me."

"You're wasting your time, Mr. Melville. I can't say anything about an ongoing investigation."

"I understand. However, as much as this case fascinates me, you fascinate me more. Retirement affords me leisure time, and one of my pursuits is studying human nature. What little the newspapers write about you only recounts your exploits, famous *and* infamous. I would very much like to get to know you." He held up a hand to interrupt Mason's response. "And before you think my purpose is to put you under a microscope, that is not the case. I would like to see if we could become friends. I have so few of them, but I believe we could get along famously."

"Thanks for the offer, but as soon as I'm done here, I'm gone."

"From what I've read, this place should be your cup of tea."

"You're the second Brit to say that. Maybe you guys think all

Americans want to be cowboys in the Wild West, looking to shoot it out in Tombstone."

Melville shrugged. "Tangier has its similarities to a frontier boomtown. But I think it's more you're an adventurer who doesn't know it yet."

"Or a lone crusader looking for the Holy Grail."

"Aptly put, Mr. Collins."

"Yeah, well, someone's said that about me, too."

Mason spotted two policemen—Spanish by the green uniforms—talking to the hotel manager near the check-in desk. He quickly finished his meal and pushed the plate aside. Melville looked in the direction of Mason's gaze and started to pull out his wallet.

"This is on me," Mason said. "I owe you that much." He downed his drink, then stood and headed for the lobby, knowing Melville would follow.

Melville did most of the talking to the policemen, as he spoke Spanish and the two policemen spoke nothing else. The two policemen threatened to bring both of them in for questioning—that much Mason could understand—but somehow Melville talked them out of it. He put his hand on Mason's back as if presenting him as a local celebrity. The policemen made note of Melville's account of the events, and after corroborating the story with several witnesses, they seemed relieved to get away from Melville's constant chatter.

Mason said, "I didn't understand a word, but I could tell that was some smooth talking."

The waiter brought out Melville's gin and tonic, and Melville downed it in one gulp. "I managed to make them more confused than when they arrived."

"In that case, I owe you a few more drinks. But we'll have to make it for another time. Right now, I want to see the spots where the three girls were abducted."

"It would be my pleasure to show you. I know the exact spots, and the one in the medina is not that easy to find. Perhaps afterwards, you can fulfill your promise of more drinks."

"Done."

Out on the street, Melville walked alongside Mason, tapping his cane as if strolling in Hyde Park. Mason wanted to hurry along, but the older man was taking his time, and Mason started to regret taking up Melville on his offer.

Pedestrians far outnumbered cars as entire families strolled in the cooling air or bought their evening's dinner from the butcher shop or grocer: a mix of Westerners and Moroccans; men in suits or long hooded robes, women in dresses or covered head to foot in burkas or robes of white and red.

They turned right and entered the Grand Socco. The bustle of the crowds, cars, buses, and donkeys pulling carts formed an endless flood that made it difficult to distinguish sidewalk from street. The crush of humanity seemed to increase the ambient temperature and further reduced the already low levels of oxygen choked off by the volumes of exhaust and dust. Hundreds of people mingled among the bright-colored tents and makeshift booths that crowded the central plaza.

Everywhere Mason looked, the city repeated the extreme contrast from the Moroccan to the Western: the ugly modern buildings of concrete built astride the ancient crenulated medina walls, the camels and the cars, the excesses of wealth and the worst forms of poverty. Beggars, adults and children, with black teeth and scars or deformities from skin diseases or malnutrition, moved among the middle-class and well-heeled crowds with their hands out, mumbling supplications.

Melville touched Mason's arm and pointed toward an ancient arched gate, a relic of the original walled city. "The Catherine Gate. That's approximately where Valerie Meunier disappeared. I say approximately, because it's the last place anyone remembers seeing her, including her mother. It's the main gate that leads into the medina. There are seven others that circle the walls. The Kasbah, the former palace, sits at the highest point of the medina, surrounded by its own wall."

Mason and Melville had to walk in single file through the crowds along the inner circle of the Grand Socco. There were women weaving baskets or selling herbs. Men hawked their brass pots or carpets or musical instruments. There were the food vendors, the vegetable, fruit, and flower stands. Then one turbaned man in the middle of it all, "charming" a lethargic cobra. Chaotic and crowded, and it wasn't even market day, when Valerie had disappeared. In this place, anyone could have slipped the mother and daughter something to confuse or stun them. The prick of a drug-tinged pin or a cup of tea, or a tinged apple for that matter.

They then crossed traffic again before stepping up to the medina gate. The gate was wide enough for two small cars to pass, and it led to a street that ran straight for a city block before curving to the right. Several small streets branched off from the main street, which was packed with shoppers and vendors. Mason wondered how there had been no witnesses in such a crowded place.

Mason and Melville's second stop was the crescent-shaped strip of beach that extended for a half mile from the docks and marina to a natural barrier of high cliffs. Mason walked the length of the beach, while Melville waited patiently by the docks. The beach was only fifty yards at its widest, and quickly became narrow as it extended outward. A scattering of ramshackle buildings, dive bars, and primitive bathhouses ran parallel to the beach. A couple of mansions and a hotel were under construction along a dried stream bed. Then after that, little except for a cluster of Moroccan fishing vessels pulled up on the edge of the beach for the night. Beyond the sand in the interior lay only scrub and grassland bisected by railroad tracks.

Now that the sun had set, a cool breeze came off the water, and the stars had begun to appear. A couple of freighters floated past in the distance, and beyond, the lights along the Spanish shoreline flickered like stars in the humid air. Off in the distant hills, a few bonfires had been lit and shadowy figures hovered around them. From one of the near houses, Mason could hear a lute playing a melancholy song, the exotic mixture of notes foreign to Mason's ears. And somewhere farther on, drums began to pound out a fast rhythm. The wind carried both and blended them, making it seem as if the sounds came from many places at once. It created a sense of otherworldliness, and Mason could see how, in this land, some would begin to believe in the presence of spirits and potions and dark forces.

Suddenly, out of the murky night, Mason saw the silhouette of a man walking toward him. He wore a djellaba, which hid his feet, making it seem that he floated on the sand. Mason felt for his pistol snugly cradled in his coat pocket.

"Mr. Collins," the man said loudly over the rush of wind and lapping waves.

Mason recognized him when he got closer. "Tazim, you should know better than to sneak up on a man."

Tazim displayed a broad smile. "I knew you would be investigating the scenes of the abductions."

"What are you doing out here?"

"I have come to help you."

"We've already been over this."

Instead of arguing, Tazim pointed to a spot fifty yards from where they stood in the center of the beach. "That's where the Spanish vendor was selling the Italian ices."

"And how do you know that?"

"I read the witness statements and the detective files. I am the captain's driver and secretary and manservant, therefore invisible. No one thinks it odd if they see me with the captain's files." Tazim said it without a tone of resentment.

Mason said nothing, as there was nothing to say to counter the obvious prejudice in colonial Morocco. He'd seen enough of that in the service.

Tazim held out a package wrapped in brown paper and tied with string.

Mason took it. "What's this?"

"Copies of the detectives' notes and photographs from the case, including the photographs of the girls and their parents."

"This could get you in serious trouble."

Tazim held up a small Minox Riga camera. "I made copies with this. A gift from the man I worked with in American intelligence."

"If they had caught you—"

"I am here, no?"

Mason held up the package. "Thank you. But don't do it again. They could boot you off the force and throw you in jail."

Mason looked toward the scrubland that bordered the interior edge of the beach. "I'm trying to figure out why the abductors chose this place. There's no real cover for one or two men to conceal themselves, or make an easy getaway with a panicked fifteen-year-old girl."

"And the beach was very crowded that day," Tazim said. "Mostly Nazarenes and tourists from the cruise ships."

"No Moroccans?"

"Some vendors who sell water or trinkets. Some children come to beg. Most Moroccans do not have the leisure time to relax on the beach. I understand why you ask. A Moroccan man would be noticed carrying away a white woman."

Mason nodded as they walked along the beach. "Hard enough for a white guy to do it." He surveyed the surrounding area. "And why take a girl in the middle of so many beachgoers?" He pointed inland. "It's got to be a good sixty yards to the brush. Why not snatch a girl closer to the bushes?"

"According to the detective files, all three girls are from wealthy parents."

"There haven't been any ransom demands, so money doesn't seem to be the reason. And if the abductors don't care about money, then they would have fewer problems with victims of poor parents. Rich ones have the influence to pressure politicians and police forces."

"Or the money to hire a private detective," Tazim said with a knowing smile.

That notion still stung Mason. He turned and headed for the marina and Melville, prompting Tazim to do the same.

After a few moments, Mason said, "The only thing the abducted girls have in common is that they come from wealthy parents. The parents don't know each other, and the daughters don't seem to run in the same circles. There has to be some reason why they abducted these girls. Something that links them. The first thing we should do is look into their parents."

Tazim smiled. "So, you will let me help you?"

"It looks like I'm not going to get rid of you. But don't breathe a word of this to anyone at the police department. If we're seen together, we're just acquaintances. That's it. No need to explain more."

Tazim chuckled. "A Nazarene and Tanjawi. Together."

"That doesn't happen in Tangier?"

"Many will assume that if we are acquaintances, it is for sex."

"Goddamn, Tazim. What kind of town is this if two men can't work together without the gossip?"

"It is Tangier, Mr. Collins."

10

"What do you know about Mr. Melville?" Mason asked Tazim as they walked along the beach.

"I have little respect for a man who spends his days drinking alcohol. But he is good to the Tanjawis. He has organized a charity to give food to the poor, but he is like many who use charity as a way to feel superior to those he gives, like a shepherd to his flock of sheep. He uses this to influence some to cook and clean for him. And he has some who constantly inform him of people's activities."

"So, the town snoop has a ring of spies."

As they approached Melville, Tazim's smile became forced and his pace slowed.

"I was about to send out a search party," Melville said to Mason, and nodded toward Tazim. "I see you've picked up a stray."

Mason introduced them and said, "Tazim and I met at the police station. He's agreed to be my guide. At least, when you're not around."

Melville regarded Tazim with a smile, though he eyed him in

an odd way that Mason couldn't quite make out. "Shall we convene to the medina? I believe you still owe me several drinks."

"Join us, Tazim," Mason said.

"I don't drink alcohol."

"It's against their religion," Melville said. "I swear half the tensions in the Muslim world could be solved if they were allowed alcohol."

"Alcohol did not stop Hitler or Mussolini," Tazim said.

Melville gave Tazim a slight bow. "Well said, my Moroccan friend. I stand corrected."

"I'll buy you a cup of tea, then," Mason said.

Tazim accepted and they entered the medina through a small gate almost hidden by a turn in the wall. Just inside the gate a doglegged, asphalted intersection constricted into three small streets of paving stones. Mason tried to keep track of the many narrow streets they traversed. The streets twisted and sloped uphill or down, while others ended abruptly. Often the buildings on either side leaned forward, almost touching, or the two opposing sides were connected by an enclosed bridge, blocking out the moonlight and the star-filled sky.

They finally came to a five-pointed intersection of no more than fifty square feet, with one broad street heading south, and three other streets—more alleys—splayed out in different directions. A perfect spot to nab someone and disappear.

Tazim pointed down the broad street. "Mrs. Brisbane and her daughter came up that street to this intersection." He then pointed to what seemed like a continuation of the broad street, though it took a sharp turn to the left. "Eyewitnesses stated that Mrs. Brisbane continued to walk up that street, but no one saw Cynthia Brisbane after passing through this square."

"And no one saw Cynthia being abducted, or heard cries for help?"

Tazim shook his head.

Melville leaned on his cane with both hands and grinned at Tazim. "Tazim, tell him what the locals think."

"How is that useful, Mr. Melville?"

Melville used his cane to point to a small rectangular fountain hewn into the stone wall opposite them. A short rusted metal pipe stuck out from the wall just above the brackish water collected in the trough.

"This used to be a public fountain for gathering water, but it hasn't been used in many years. Whatever system supplied the water doesn't exist anymore, but somehow water continues to collect in the trough. The locals avoid going near it." He turned to Tazim. "Would you care to tell Mr. Collins why?"

Tazim turned to Mason with a wry smile. He said in a pseudo-British accent, "You must forgive Mr. Melville's rudeness, talking to me like a schoolchild." He then continued in his own voice. "Most Brits speak to Moroccans that way. But to answer the question, many Tanjawis believe a djinn spirit lives in the fountain."

Melville asked Tazim, "Do you believe a djinn resides there?"

"Do you believe in angels or demons because the Bible says they exist?"

"What are djinn?" Mason asked Tazim.

"Like your Bible speaks of angels and demons, the Quran talks about djinn. They are another type of being, humans and angels being the other two. The Quran says Allah made them from smokeless fire—" He stopped. "You don't really need to know this. It is legend. Myth."

"But most Moroccans believe they exist," Melville said. "Djinn are invisible to us mortals, but they can see us. Our word *genie* comes from djinn."

"Like the genie in the bottle," Mason said.

"And you have elves and leprechauns," Tazim said.

Mason turned to Melville, and he wondered why Melville was

bringing this up. "So, you're saying that Cynthia was carried off by an invisible being, who lives in that fountain?"

"They exist because most Moroccans believe in them," Melville said. "There are things in this world that science cannot explain."

"That's what Cynthia's mother thinks. You two must be going to the same shaman."

"Three girls disappear without a trace in crowds of people. No one sees them. No one hears their cries for help. Poof. They're gone." Melville snapped his fingers. "I would simply advise not to discount the inexplicable in a land like Morocco." He turned and pointed in the direction of the broad street. "May we find further inspiration in a glass or two of alcoholic spirits?"

Mason and Tazim accepted, and they wound their way along the street until they came to a rectangular plaza still within the walls of the medina. The contrast between the dark and silent streets and this bright and lively spot was jarring. Bars, nightclubs, and restaurants ringed the entire plaza. Music blared and neon lights flashed. A Moroccan man led a cow by a rope and offered fresh milk to outside customers. A priest stood in the middle of all this, preaching against sin and to seek the salvation of God.

Melville chose an outside table at a Spanish restaurant. The three of them sat, ordered their drinks, and took in the spectacle. Somewhere inside, a guitarist strummed a flamenco tune, in harsh contrast to the big-band sounds of the neighboring restaurants and the Moroccan music accompanying a snake charmer. A fistfight broke out amid the outside tables. Drunks staggered among Westerners dressed to the nines and children deformed by disease and malnutrition who begged for money or candy. Two Moroccan teenagers dressed in skintight shorts and billowing tops eyed Mason for a few moments with puckered lips and come-hither expressions.

"Tell me someone accidentally left the gates to the loony bin open," Mason said.

Melville shrugged. "A typical reaction from a Tangier novice. Where else could you get such a parade of humanity in all its glory and degradation? And all for the price of a drink. I come here, as many locals do, for the sheer spectacle."

"I do not like it here," Tazim said. "It represents all that is wrong with Western colonialism."

"It appears we have a rebel in our midst," Melville said.

"You're talking to an American, Mr. Melville," Mason said. "We kicked out the British a while ago. Maybe it's Morocco's turn."

"Yes," Melville said, "it seems inevitable, but I, for one, intend to enjoy this orgy of eccentricities as long as possible."

Their drinks arrived: a beer for Mason, a whiskey for Melville, and a mint tea for Tazim.

"The Petit Socco is only the part you can see," Tazim said. "There is another hidden behind closed doors. There are secret sex clubs, where only those who have enough money can enter, and then only to those who can afford the high price and are invited by another member. To require that much secrecy has to mean unspeakable things go on in those places."

"Come now, Tazim," Melville said. "These secret clubs are only rumors. Nothing remains a secret in this town for long. Especially one so salacious as you're imagining."

Mason was ready to change the subject. "Tazim, one of the mothers of the abducted girls claims that she and her daughter were put under some kind of Moroccan magic spell."

"You cannot believe this."

"I was interested in what you think."

"Spells, magic potions, djinn spirits—Morocco has all of them. But it is mostly the poor and uneducated who truly believe."

"This mother is well educated and very rich."

Melville said, "Mysterious circumstances and tragedy have a way of convincing normally rational and intelligent people to turn to the occult for explanations. Religion, for example. Sir Arthur Conan Doyle delved into the occult after the death of his son. Closed-minded is the man who claims science explains everything."

Mason asked both of them, "Do you know of any Moroccan potions that could explain the mothers' stupor during the girls' disappearances?"

Melville and Tazim shook their heads.

Mason downed the rest of his drink. "I'm going to turn in. I haven't had a decent night's sleep in four days." He got up from the table. Both Melville and Tazim offered to accompany him back to the hotel, but Mason declined. He needed to think.

The streets were full of people, many of them Moroccan men in hooded djellabas topped with knitted, brimless caps or fez hats, and some had their hoods pulled over their heads. A perfect wardrobe choice for someone up to no good. Crowded streets and anonymity added up to a dangerous combination.

Back at the hotel, Mason secured the door and windows as best he could, and made sure his gun was within easy reach at all times. He then went through everything Tazim had included in the packet: case files, transcripts of interviews, and photographs of the abducted girls and their parents. He tried reviewing the transcripts, but he kept nodding off. Finally, he dropped into bed without washing. Despite the group of Moroccan musicians singing and pounding on drums just down the street, Mason fell asleep in seconds.

He dreamed he pursued a hooded man who dragged a girl along the twisting streets of the medina. The girl looked like Sabine de Graaf, and she kept calling out his name, but he couldn't catch up to them. He rounded another sharp turn and saw the girl looking back at him with pleading eyes. And just before the man pulled her around another corner, the girl looked at him —this time with disappointment.

11

A taxi dropped Mason off at the British hospital. It sat on the edge of the cliffs overlooking the Mediterranean and just west of the medina. The view was as spectacular as the hospital building was mundane. It featured unadorned white walls and a red tile roof, with a central building of three stories and several single-story auxiliary buildings to the left and right.

It was close to eleven a.m. Mason had slept later than he'd wanted, but his exhaustion had dictated otherwise. The ringing of his hotel room telephone had woken him. On the other end of the line, Rousselot told him that the corpse had been tentatively identified as Sabine de Graaf. The news enraged Mason and propelled him out of the room.

At the hospital's ground-floor reception desk, Mason was directed to go to the top floor, east wing. There, he stopped at the nurses' station and asked for Mrs. de Graaf's room.

The nurse looked at him over her reading glasses. "Family?"

"No, a friend."

The nurse shook her head as she glanced at her paperwork.

"Mr. de Graaf. Is he here?"

"He's with her most days, but he's not here now."

"Do you know when he'll be back?"

"This is not a hotel, sir. I don't keep track of the comings and goings of visitors."

"How about her doctor? It's important."

She let out an impatient sigh. "Dr. Amoretti should be done with his rounds in an hour or so. You can wait in the visitors' lounge."

Mason noticed that the nurse's eyes had unconsciously shifted to her right when she'd answered the question. She turned to address some paperwork on the desk behind her, signaling she would not waste any more of her time. He didn't need anything else; she had given him what he needed. He thanked her and stepped inside the lounge.

It took about five minutes for the nurse to forget his presence and become distracted by one of the other nurses. With quick strides, Mason slipped out of the lounge, turned left, and walked down the hallway. He asked a couple of nurses he encountered where he could find Dr. Amoretti, telling them that the doctor wanted to speak to him. One of the nurses pointed to a tall man discussing something with another nurse down the hallway.

Mason went up to him. "Dr. Amoretti?"

The doctor ignored him for a moment while giving the nurse last-minute instructions. He had the hunched posture that very tall people sometimes acquire. His oblong head was completely bald, except for a smattering of black hair along the back of his collar. His face was pale, soft, and unremarkable, like the shell of an egg, except for the massive tangle of eyebrows that seemed to be swallowing up the black frames of his glasses.

He finally turned to Mason. "What can I do for you?" he asked with an accent Mason surmised as Belgian. He'd heard that accent plenty during the war.

"Actually, I was hoping I could talk to Mrs. de Graaf."

"I'm afraid that's out of the question."

"Sir, it's vital. It has to do with the investigation into Sabine de Graaf's abduction. And to save time, no, I'm not with the police. I've been hired by the British consul general to investigate all three of the girls' abductions. Anything she can tell me about that day would be helpful."

"Follow me, please."

Mason followed the doctor to a room three doors down. They stepped inside, and the doctor pointed to a woman standing by the window, staring out between the narrow gap in the dark green curtains. Her eyes were blood-red; her hair, while clean, was tangled. She wore a silk full-length gown with a floral print—obviously something brought from home. She looked fragile and broken, her eyes fixed, as if staring at some unseen horror.

"This is Mrs. de Graaf," the doctor said.

"Ma'am?" Mason said to the woman. "Would it be all right if I ask you a few questions?"

The woman remained as still as a wax figure representing a character in a tragic tale.

"You see now that she is completely incapable of human inter-action," Dr. Amoretti said, and walked out of the room.

When Mason met him in the hallway, some distance from the room, the doctor said, "Madame de Graaf is severely traumatized and under sedation. Even if you could get through to her, you might induce another attack of hysteria."

"Then why is she here and not in a mental ward?"

"I am her personal physician. I wanted to keep her here under my care. I think I'm more qualified to determine where she should receive treatment."

"Fair enough. Has she said anything to you that might help me? Something about the day of Sabine's abduction?"

"Even if she were coherent—which she hasn't been since that day—I couldn't divulge anything."

"I'm not asking for confidential information. Something overheard, something she said to the nurses. The smallest detail might help."

The doctor thought a moment. "How can you assure me you're working for the British consul general?"

"Call his office, if you like. I can wait."

The doctor looked into Mason's eyes, then nodded. "I can tell you what I've already told Inspector Verger. She has no recollection of that afternoon. Nothing at all, until coming out of her stupor."

"Do you have any idea what caused her to lose an entire afternoon? Was she drugged?"

"Possibly, though I can't rule out some kind of psychotic attack. As far as I know, she was in good mental health before that afternoon. However, I've known patients who were seemingly healthy one day and mentally ill the next."

"One of the other mothers of an abducted girl had a similar blackout. She also experienced hallucinations, but they didn't last beyond a couple of hours after she regained her senses."

The doctor suddenly seemed annoyed, though Mason wondered if it was something else.

"Look, Doc, Sabine was held captive for over three weeks, possibly raped, definitely strangled, then thrown out like the trash. Give me something that's not going to compromise your Hippocratic oath, and help me find who did this."

Dr. Amoretti let out an impatient sigh. "Her initial symptoms were extreme hallucinations, which are still present, confusion, loss of memory, nausea, aversion to bright lights. Most are consistent with a severe psychotic episode."

"What kind of hallucinations?"

"She claims she has a foreign entity in her chest that won't let go. She sees people who aren't there. Dead relatives, ones who were killed during the war. She was in Rotterdam when the Nazis bombed it to rubble. Her daughter's abduction could have brought on latent guilt about surviving after so many had perished."

"You don't think these symptoms could have been brought on by a drug?"

"There's no reason to think she was drugged without her knowledge."

"How about someone slipping something in her food or drink?"

"That doesn't explain her continued exhibition of symptoms."

"I've seen guys with battle fatigue, and drugs just made them worse."

"So now you're the physician?"

"I'm saying that at least two mothers experienced similar blackouts. I'm saying that's too much of a coincidence."

The doctor thought for a moment. "It's possible the effects of whatever drug she was given could have triggered her hysteria. She may be one of those cases where a drug set off a psychosis deep in her id. However, I will indulge your amateur theory, so that I can get back to my patients. Aside from being administered orally or by injection, drugs can also be administered through inhalation or subcutaneously—through the skin. Obviously, she would have noticed something introduced by injection or inhalation."

"What kind of drug could be introduced through the skin?"

"Mr. Collins, I am not an expert in exotic hallucinogenic drugs. Now, I must go. Please."

"Just one more question. I understand Mr. de Graaf is here most days. Any idea where he is now?"

The doctor hesitated with a mournful expression. "The police telephoned him here this morning to say that they had identified his daughter's remains, probably by dental records. He is at the police station to make arrangements for his daughter's remains."

Mason nodded while he studied the doctor's face. This obviously made the man nervous, as he said, "If you will excuse me," and walked away.

Mason watched him for a minute. He tried to decide if Amoretti was hiding something, or afraid to say. Was the good doctor treating Mrs. de Graaf, or keeping her quiet?

12

Mason sat at an outside table of a café across from police headquarters. While he waited for de Graaf, he scanned a newspaper's scathing opinion piece about himself. The editor mentioned everything about Mason's past, from his expulsion from the Chicago Police Department, to those accusing him of being an agent provocateur in Germany. That his reckless behavior was the cause for his shortened career as an army investigator. Things a newspaper could acquire in such a short time only from the same man or men who wanted him gone. The piece went on to criticize the local police for incompetence, and declared it was a slap in their collective faces that a good citizen of Tangier had felt it necessary to hire such a disreputable detective.

Mason folded the paper and slammed it on the table. His third cup of espresso tipped over into its saucer, spilling the last of the coffee. He'd already told one reporter to get lost while sitting there. He debated whether to leave before another reporter showed up, or to suck it up and order another espresso. He held up his hand for the waiter when a sullen-looking man emerged from police headquarters.

Mason checked one of the photographs from the packet Tazim had given him. It was de Graaf.

De Graaf crossed the small parking lot and turned right on the sidewalk leading to the medina. He had his hands jammed in his pockets and stared at the pavement with haunted eyes. Mason left money on the table and dodged traffic as he hurried across the street.

Mason caught up to de Graaf at an intersection. "Mr. de Graaf?"

The man jerked his head around, startled by the sound. He looked at Mason with bloodshot eyes.

"My name is Mason Collins—"

"I don't want to talk to any more reporters," de Graaf said in perfect English. "Please leave me alone." He crossed the street when the light changed, and Mason kept up with him. Mason felt bad for the man. He'd just learned his daughter had been murdered. But Mason couldn't wait.

"Mr. de Graaf, I'm not a reporter. I'm working for the British consul general, investigating your daughter's abduction."

De Graaf stopped abruptly and spit his words in anger. "It's not an abduction any longer. It's murder. My Sabine is dead."

Mason had to urge him to the curb before the traffic light changed. It was then that he noticed the same man, in a dark gray suit, who had exited police headquarters right behind de Graaf. Initially, the man had turned in the opposite direction, but now he was just up the street, leaning against a building and watching them.

"Mr. de Graaf, I'm going to do everything I can to find those responsible. But in order to do that, I need your help."

"My help? Where were you when my daughter was abducted?"

"I only got here yesterday and started on this case. I need to do some catching up. And one of those things is getting information from you."

De Graaf removed his handkerchief and wiped the tears and sweat from his face. "I've told the police everything I can, and they've achieved nothing. They're all incompetent or corrupt." He turned and continued down the sidewalk.

"Look," Mason said, "I feel like a heel talking to you after what you've been through, but please, can you answer some questions?"

De Graaf answered with a feeble nod as he continued to stare at the pavement.

"I believe your wife and daughter were drugged that day. It was slipped into something they drank or ate. From what I understand, they did some shopping in the medina and Grand Socco before heading to the beach."

"That was their plan, yes. I wasn't with them, so I don't know. I told the police that."

"Was this something they did on a regular basis?"

"Yes. About twice a week."

"Did they have a routine? Always shopping at the same stores or eating at the same restaurant before going to the beach?"

"I don't know about the shops, but they usually stop at one of two restaurants in the Grand Socco, the Blue Eagle or Chez la Vie. Sometimes they have refreshments at La Coté Socco."

"Okay, that's good. Did Sabine say anyone was bothering her or following her?"

"The police asked me the same questions, and that's no." De Graaf stopped and looked at Mason. "You should know this if you've been talking to the police. Or are you not talking to them?"

Mason debated how to answer this. The way de Graaf thought about the police, Mason decided to go with the truth. "The French detective resents me working his turf."

De Graaf just grunted and continued walking.

Mason said, "Sabine had a henna design on the soles of her feet and on her ankles. I'm guessing from the day of her abduction. Was that something she did often?"

"A couple of times previously. Her school discourages girls from coming to class with the tattoos, so Sabine waited until the end of the school year."

"Do you know where she had it done?"

"The Grand Socco, I suppose. My wife had it done with Sabine this past May. She thought it would create more of a connection between them. They came home and laughed when they saw the shock on my face."

"Did your wife have it done this last time?"

De Graaf slowed his walk and looked at Mason. "Yes. Her hands had a paisley design." He smiled but with sad eyes. "Supposedly for good luck and fertility."

They had to stop at an intersection, and Mason used the opportunity to check his periphery. Sure enough, the man in the gray suit was still there, stopping when they stopped. Whether he was keeping his eye on de Graaf or him, he didn't know. "Mr. de Graaf, don't take this the wrong way, but do you have any enemies? Someone who might want to take revenge?"

"I'm a banking executive, Mr. Collins, so not everyone you do business with is going to be happy with you. But no one I can think of would ever consider murdering my—" He couldn't continue. He choked on his last words and fell back into a deep melancholy.

"The other thing I'm trying to make sense of is how the three girls—Sabine, Valerie Meunier, and Cynthia Brisbane—are connected. There must be some reason they were picked. I know they didn't go to the same schools, but what about outside activities or mutual friends?"

De Graaf turned to look at Mason. He was about to say something when he froze after noticing something or someone over Mason's shoulder. Mason knew the presence of the man in the gray suit frightened de Graaf.

"Who is that man?" Mason asked.

"I have no idea what you're talking about," de Graaf said. He turned and continued walking. "I am growing weary of your questions, Mr. Collins. I've told the police most of these things. I don't see the reason that I must repeat them. I am not very social. I have no business dealings with the other fathers. We don't go to parties or bridge nights."

"I'm asking about the girls, Mr. de Graaf. Your daughter was murdered. I'm sure you want the killers to be brought to justice."

De Graaf started to cross the street without waiting for the traffic, and Mason had to pull him back to the curb. He looked rattled and nervous, and Mason could tell he fought the temptation to look at the man behind them.

"Please, no more questions," de Graaf said. "I am so very tired."

"I understand. How about I come by your house at a later time?"

"Absolutely not," de Graaf said loudly—probably hoping it was loud enough for the man in the gray suit to overhear.

De Graaf started to cross the intersection, but he stopped and looked at Mason. Almost under his breath, he said, "Check out the equestrian center, south of town." He then walked away.

Mason turned on his heels, but the man in the gray suit was gone. The man had definitely frightened de Graaf, and the way de Graaf had revealed the equestrian center seemed to imply that this was something not to be uttered. The center looked like the best lead to pursue; then he'd check into the henna as a clever way to introduce a drug. Like a delayed-release capsule, the drug could soak into the skin and into the bloodstream, only to manifest minutes or hours later.

Mason looked up at the sun. After brutal winters in Germany, he'd dreamed of being under a blazing sun. But now it felt like his clothes would burst into flames at any moment. Without a car, he would have to hoof it to the equestrian center. At least he had some leads to pursue—if he didn't wind up just a pile of ashes on the roadside.

13

The frigid water stung like fire. It took Cynthia's breath away. It pummeled her like fists of ice and hot coals. Would it ever end? The force of the water shot from the fire hose knocked her feet from under her, but the manacles clamped around her wrists held her firm and upright, stretching muscle and tendon. Her screams of pain and pleadings for mercy went unheard as the big woman in the mask meted out the punishment.

Cynthia had violated the rules once again. Talking to the other captives—talking at all—was forbidden. And when they had discovered that she tried to learn their names and stories, and gave them encouragement, that had infuriated her captors even more.

The others refused to speak or hissed warnings that she might disappear, or that they, too, might be punished. They obviously believed that blind obedience might save them, despite the two others who had been dragged away by their captors and never seen again.

Finally, the water stopped. Cynthia's frozen leg muscles refused to support her any longer, and she hung from the manacles. She was too exhausted to hold up her head and watch her torturer walk wordlessly out of the room. The heavy door slammed shut, and the heavy bolt pulled closed with a clank. Then all was silent except for her heavy breathing and pounding heart.

Her soaked gown clung to her like icy fingers, and the burning sensation turned to numbing cold. Her entire body shook with violent convulsions as it tried to generate enough heat to keep her alive.

But alive for what purpose? What was happening to her?

There were days—or was it hours?—when they kept her drugged just enough to remain in a twilight daze. Then a day came when she was so heavily drugged that she lost all consciousness, only to wake up to the nightmare once again. And when the drug cleared and her awareness returned, she became conscious of the pain down there. Mercifully, she remembered nothing from her blackouts, but she knew she had been violated. The very thought sickened her. The revulsion made her retch.

How many times on each of those days ... or nights? And by whom?

As she hung helplessly, as she endured the pain, she fought back her tears, the terror of helplessness, the impulse to crumble into despair. She willed her rage to the forefront of her mind.

She vowed not to give up. Not to give in.

Cynthia commanded her legs to respond, to stand. And even as her body shook so hard that it seemed her bones rattled, she used her rage to summon her strength. Somehow she would fight back. Somehow she had to survive.

14

Dusty and his shirt drenched in sweat, Mason finally reached the equestrian center and polo field. It was south of the city, on the edges of the recent urban sprawl. The center consisted of a two-story clapboard house at the edge of a broad field divided into a polo field and a forty-meter dressage arena. A circular racetrack ran around the perimeter, with stadium seating situated on one side. A series of stables stood behind the house.

He crossed the gravel parking lot to a wide lawn—a great, green oasis in the surrounding brown. In contrast to this playground for the rich, and not more than a quarter mile past the park, lay a jumbled mass of lean-tos and tin shacks, like shantytowns Mason had seen as a teenager during the worst years of the Depression. The locals called them *bidonvilles*, because many of the huts, no bigger than a child's playhouse, were made from crushed army canteens, or *bidons*. He'd read in the newspaper about the severe drought and poverty that had brought Berbers from the Rif Mountains to Tangier, and most lived in squalor at the city's limits.

Mason approached a silver-haired man coaching a twenty-something woman upon a chestnut horse. He held what to

Mason looked like a buggy whip as he urged the woman to ride the graceful horse in tight circles. Mason introduced himself and asked if either of them knew Sabine de Graaf or Valerie Meunier. The woman ignored him, and the trainer simply pointed toward the house. The house would be Mason's last stop.

First he hit up the stable hands and groundskeepers, a mix of Westerners and Moroccans. It took about thirty minutes for Mason to ask just about every one of the employees on the grounds. If any of them did know the two girls, they weren't saying. It was as if they had been instructed to keep quiet. He finally made his way to a small paddock near the house, where a young woman in a riding outfit was saddling her horse. Mason walked up, introduced himself, and showed her Sabine's photograph. "Do you know Sabine de Graaf?"

The girl eyed him warily. "That's the girl who was murdered?" she asked in a British accent. "Why do you ask?"

Mason decided to act on a hunch. "I'm here because Sabine's father said that she, Valerie Meunier, and Cynthia Brisbane were in a riding club together."

"That's right, though I wouldn't call it a riding club. It's more a clan of wealthy parents who don't want their kids to be in the same classes as daughters of merchants and rich Jews. Heaven forbid they might get contaminated."

"Does that create some resentment from the other people coming to the center?"

"Not really. Everyone accepts those kinds of attitudes from those who live on Mount Olympus. I don't blame the girls. They're as sweet as can be—most of them, anyway. But the parents ..."

Mason was about to ask another question when the stable manager came stomping up to him. He was thin, though muscular, with a weather-beaten face. He tried intimidation by getting in

Mason's face and staring him down with eyes as gray as his combed-over hair.

The intimidation worked on the girl, as she made a quick retreat.

"Stop asking questions of the clients," the stable manager said with what sounded like an Italian accent. "And stop bothering my staff. This is private property. You will leave. Now."

A broad-shouldered, middle-aged woman appeared at the front door of the house. "Niccolo, what's going on?" she asked in American English.

"This man is a private investigator. He asks questions, and he is bothering the help."

"You," she said to Mason, pointing her finger. "I want you off this property. Now." She walked across the front porch with a muscular gait like she'd worked around stables all her life.

Mason walked up to the base of the front porch to meet her. "The first American I've met in this town," he said with all the charm he could muster. "My name's Mason Collins."

Her anger defused slightly. "Marjorie Ravenna. If I'm the first American you've met, then you haven't been here very long."

"Just got in yesterday."

"You're that ex-army detective I read about in the papers," she said almost as an accusation. "It's going to take more than a pretty face and American ingenuity to find those girls."

"What do you know about the case?"

"Nothing. But my late husband was a prosecuting attorney for thirty years, so I know that girls who've been gone this long don't stand a chance in Hades of being found. Now, I want you off this property. No more snooping around."

Mason looked up at the sun, then took his hat off and fanned himself. "It's a long way back to town on foot. Mind if I get out of this heat for a few minutes?"

She gave him an impatient glare but nodded. "You can have a glass of water. You've got five minutes."

Mason followed her into the house. The front room had a series of desks, a blackboard, and a small counter to one side. On the counter was a clipboard with sign-up sheets. Electric fans pushed hot air around the room. Marjorie stepped behind the counter. She pulled out a pitcher of water from the small icebox and poured two glasses.

Mason help up the glass. "Bottoms up."

Marjorie held up hers. "Finish your drink and get."

Mason took a long gulp, then exaggerated a satisfied sigh. "Thanks." He leaned on the counter. "You been in Tangier long?"

"Three years. My husband died last year, and I haven't had the heart to move on."

"My sympathies. You're too young to be a widow."

She gave him a world-weary look, but she seemed to appreciate the remark all the same. She couldn't help a smile, then caught herself. "Listen, Mr. Collins—"

"Mason."

"Look, I'd like to help, but I've got to keep matters private. Some of the members would have my hide if they knew I was giving out their information."

"I get that. Are there a lot of rich girls in the exclusive club? Must be tough keeping track of who's in, and who might contaminate the group."

She raised a hand. "I know what you're doing. You can stop right there."

Two women dressed in expensive riding outfits came into the office. They complained about the condition of their horses' stalls, and that their horses were not ready. They insisted that Marjorie come out to see for herself.

Marjorie came around the counter and pointed her finger at Mason. "Time for you to go."

Mason downed the rest of his water, thanked Marjorie. He took his time stepping out the door and descending the front porch steps. As he strolled across the front lawn, he observed the three women exit the house, then Marjorie locking the door behind her. She shot a glare Mason's way. Mason smiled and nodded, then continued his stroll. He heard the women's boots clomp across the porch and down the steps, and listened as their voices faded on their way to the stables. He made a sharp curve around the rear of the house. A gardener tended some flowers about fifty feet away, but was facing the other way.

Mason rushed up to the back door and turned the doorknob. The door was locked. He went on one knee and pulled out a tension wrench and paper clip he'd fashioned in his hotel room. A couple of seconds later, he opened the back door and slipped inside.

He went to the front counter first and leafed through the sign-up sheets. Nothing relevant. He rushed over to one of the desks and rifled through the things on the surface. Nothing. He checked the drawers, through the file folders. Again nothing. He tried the second desk, and after going through the center drawer, he found what he was looking for: a list of members that included de Graaf, Meunier, and Brisbane. As much as he'd expected to see Cynthia Brisbane on the list, it still gave him an uneasy feeling.

He heard Marjorie clomping up the front porch steps. He quickly folded up the list, stuffed it in his pocket, and then rushed to the back door. He opened it wide enough to check the surroundings. Luckily, the gardener had moved on. Just then, the front door opened behind him. Mason crept out the back door and closed it without a sound.

As he crossed the field to the parking lot, he wondered why Brisbane had left out this tidbit of information. Maybe this was all innocent. Maybe the Brisbanes knew nothing about the other girls being members. Possible, but he doubted it. Then why did the parents withhold the fact there was at least a minor connection between the three girls? De Graaf had steered him in this direction, but why was he too afraid to say more?

More questions than answers.

As he crossed through the parking lot, Mason saw Melville step out of a late 1930s Rover 12 sedan. "I thought you might like a lift," Melville said as he dabbed perspiration from his brow.

"Come to watch young ladies prance around on ponies?"

"Not my particular sport."

"What is your sport? Keeping tabs on my movements?"

"Far more interesting, I'd have to say."

"Was that your guy I spotted earlier, near Place de France?"

Melville seemed surprised to hear it. "Seems you have more than one enthusiast following you."

"Is that what you are, Mr. Melville? An enthusiast?"

"Would you like a lift back to town or not?"

"I won't say no."

Once they were settled in, Melville started up the reluctant engine and drove off.

"How did you know I'd be at the equestrian center?" Mason asked.

"A gossip hound, such as myself, has local sources of eyes and ears. I know following you seems a bit odd, but you must indulge a lonely man's appetite for a little adventure."

Mason studied him for a few moments. The older man looked to be enjoying himself, beaming as he used his lead foot to race down the busy highway. "I haven't figured you out, Mr. Melville."

"When you've done so, please inform me."

Melville veered around two men with donkeys pulling their carts with the skill of a race-car driver. Mason looked in the side-view mirror to make sure Melville didn't leave a dead body in the middle of the road. That's when he noticed another car keeping pace with them, despite Melville's daredevil speed.

Melville asked, "Did you find out anything during your visit to the equestrian center?"

"That there is a connection to the three abducted girls. They all belonged to an exclusive riding club at the center."

"That's not particularly unusual. And statistically plausible. The wealthy have nothing else to do but rake in the money and be members at exclusive clubs, or attend ladies auxiliaries, bridge clubs, Masonic lodges, gentlemen's clubs, charity organizations. With wealth comes leisure, and besides competing for the most outlandish parties, the clubs and societies keep them from getting bored."

"It still comes back to the question of why these three girls were chosen."

"Don't discount human eccentricities or randomness. The abductor would have his own reasons for choosing each of his victims, and quite possibly beyond our understanding."

"In my line of work, randomness may look like that, but once you dig deeper, you find the pattern."

"I fear you're making assumptions through your prejudices, and looking in the wrong place for connections."

"Sometimes the gut knows better. I'll stick to my prejudices."

"Suit yourself."

"Another theory I'm working on: Sabine de Graaf and her mother had henna tattoos hours before the mother lost consciousness and the daughter was abducted. Since you're so versed in Moroccan culture, do you know of any potion or drug in their culture administered that way?"

"Henna? Not that I know of."

"Mr. de Graaf said that his wife and daughter had more than once gone to the Grand Socco to get the henna tattoos."

Melville was compelled to stop by a traffic cop at a busy intersection. "Shall we head for the Grand Socco?"

Mason checked the side-view mirror. The same car was behind them. "Don't go anywhere." He got out of the car, rushed up to the driver's door, and leaned in the open window. "Who are you working for?"

The man calmly pulled out his police badge.

"If Captain Rousselot wants to know where I'm going, all he has to do is ask."

The man shrugged and said something in French. The only thing Mason could get out of it was "police" and "Capitaine Rousselot." He then pointed toward town and repeated "Capitaine Rousselot."

"Gah," Mason said with a wave of his hand.

Mason got back into Melville's car and said, "Seems I've got to pay a visit to Captain Rousselot. I don't know how long it will take, but if you're interested in tagging along in my investigation, meet me in the Grand Socco at six. We'll see what kind of henna-tattoo artists we can dig up."

15

Mason entered Captain Rousselot's office and dropped into a chair while the captain finished a phone call. He turned Rousselot's fan in his direction. He then pulled out his camera and took a few shots of Rousselot. Rousselot gave him an annoyed glance while he talked on the phone.

Rousselot finished his conversation and hung up. "So nice to see you again, Mr. Collins."

"I'm busy. What do you want?"

"The same thing as you: to find the abductors and save the other girls. But I also want you to stop interrogating the parents. Especially a grieving father."

"I can't hold off until de Graaf feels better. The clock is ticking, Captain. Sabine was killed a little over three weeks after her abduction. My guess is the abductor gets tired of them after that much time and kills them. That's just a guess, of course, but that means Valerie Meunier has four, maybe five, days from today. Cynthia Brisbane has no more than two weeks."

"Your aggressive nature may do more harm than good. Intimidating witnesses, for example. Harassing employees at the equestrian center. And I heard about the incident at your hotel. Not a very good beginning."

"In my book, being threatened is making progress. Someone is desperate enough to hire a gunman to run me out of town. Maybe he's afraid that someone like me, someone not hamstrung by bureaucracy and the people running this city, is going to see things as they are."

"And what have you discovered that is hidden from our eyes?"

"How about you tell me what you've learned in the past twenty-four hours, and I'll return the favor?"

The captain smiled. "We confirmed that the corpse was Sabine de Graaf, but you already know that. The medical examiner feels certain it was death by strangulation. The body was too decomposed to conclude anything else. And his original estimate of four to six days that her body was out in the elements still seems likely."

Mason waited for more, though he knew the captain had nothing else. "That's it? You're not holding anything back?"

"There are a few avenues of investigation my inspectors are pursuing, but not enough to share anything of value." He smiled and clasped his hands at his stomach. "And what do you have for me?"

Mason felt the folded list sitting in the breast pocket of his coat, but he decided not to share that tidbit just yet. "I'm pretty sure the mothers and daughters were drugged somehow. What kind of drug, I don't know, but something to make them docile and amnesiac without knocking them out completely. One method of delivering this drug would be in their food or drink."

"I agree with you," Rousselot said. "We checked out the employees and owners of the two restaurants and bars Mr. de Graaf said the mother and daughter usually frequented. But we found nothing suspicious."

"This is a long shot, but it could be the drug was given through the skin. Sabine and her mother may have had henna tattoos that day." Mason shrugged. "Like I said, it's a long shot."

"Interesting theory," Captain Rousselot said as he studied Mason. He took a cigarette out of his humidor on his desk. He offered Mason one, but Mason declined.

"Why didn't you tell me that the three girls were in the riding club at the equestrian center?"

Rousselot lit a match, but it never got to his cigarette. "I was not aware of this fact."

"Then either Verger didn't connect the dots, or the parents withheld that information."

Rousselot used the time to light another match and put it to his cigarette as he processed this. He looked toward the door as if checking to make sure no one was listening. Finally, he said, "Valerie Meunier's parents might be worth your time." He wrote something on a sheet of paper and slid it over to Mason. "That's their address."

"What can you tell me about them?"

"They are strict Catholics. Monsieur Meunier made his fortune as an industrialist, with enterprises all over Europe. He and his family moved here after the war, and he's now furthering his fortune in Tangier's real estate market. They've been cooperative with us, answering our questions. However, neither speaks English, so you will need an interpreter. I suggest you take Corporal Tazim Daoud. I know he has shared information with you and wants to be your assistant. I think this would be good experience for him."

Mason hid his surprise, as much at Rousselot's tolerance of Tazim as at his knowledge of Mason's activities. "And Tazim is to report back anything I get from the interview."

"We both benefit. I think it's inevitable that Morocco will gain its independence in the near future. I'd like to see Tazim be in an advantageous position when that happens."

"Why, Captain, an open-minded Frenchman."

Captain Rousselot didn't crack a smile, but neither did he deny it.

Mason said, "I'm happy to do it, but why do you want *me* to go back at the Meuniers?"

"It is—how do you say—a hunch. He's hiding something. Being a private detective does have its advantages."

"I think you've watched too many American gangster films."

"Monsieur Meunier has a way of bringing out a man's more primitive instincts. As far as I am concerned, allow those instincts to inspire you to use whatever means necessary to discover the truth."

Someone entered the office, prompting Rousselot to stand at attention. Mason turned to see a gray-haired man with a protruding belly, made more so by his odd stance. He leaned back as he stood there and peered down his nose as if that was the only way to bring his vision into focus. He wore a tunic that strained under the weight of massive epaulets and enough gold braid to rope a horse.

"*C'est qui, ça?*" the man asked in booming French.

Rousselot said in English, "Commandant Lambert, this is Mason Collins."

Lambert continued in French. He ignored Mason, looking only at Rousselot. They went on for some time, the commandant talking in an imperious tone, and the captain using a measured one. The commandant jabbed his finger at Mason, made a declaration, and left the room.

Rousselot shook his head, sighed, and turned to Mason.

"I get it," Mason said. "You don't have to say it. He wants me out of here."

Rousselot shrugged an apology. "Good luck with the Meuniers. You will need it."

MASON FIGURED CAPTAIN ROUSSELOT WAS GETTING DESPERATE for results, since he loaned out his car as well as Tazim for the interview with the Meuniers. He sat in the front passenger's seat, while Tazim drove up into the hills of the Marshan district. The mansions in the Marshan were older than the opulent upstarts on the New Mountain Road.

Tazim drove through the unattended gate of a six-foot-high brick wall. Before them sat a turn-of-the-century French Provençal affair. He stopped the car on a pebbled area off the driveway.

As they approached the house, Mason said to Tazim, "While you translate my questions, watch for their reactions. Their eyes or hands might say something different than what's coming out of their mouths. And I want you to translate everything they say. The things they say to each other. Even if it's insulting."

"To me, or to you?"

"Anything and everything."

A few moments after he knocked, an older man in a black suit answered the door. By his stiff appearance and dour demeanor, Mason figured he was the butler. The man arched his eyebrows when he saw Tazim in his policeman's uniform.

"We're here to see Mr. and Mrs. Meunier," Mason said. "We'd like to ask them a few questions pertaining to their daughter's abduction."

Tazim began to repeat this in French, but the butler said, "I speak English. Captain Rousselot called to tell us you are arriving."

The butler opened the door and stepped aside, but as Tazim

moved to enter, the butler held up his hand and said, "*Il peut entrer, mais pas toi.*"

Tazim said to Mason, "He—"

"Yeah, I don't need a translation to know what he said," Mason said, and turned to the butler. "Look, mac, this man's a trained policeman and here under Captain Rousselot's orders. If you have a problem with him, then you have a problem with me. And I'm betting you know all about how unpleasant American detectives can be." For effect, he got in the butler's face. "I advise you to let us both in."

The butler took a few steps back to get away from Mason. He waited at a safe distance to let them enter before shutting the door. He waved them into a small sitting room, then left for another part of the house. The sitting room was decorated with French antiques—Louis-something-or-other. The sofa, love seat, and chairs all looked painful to sit on, with every available space of wood carved in over-the-top ornamentation. There was a clock on the black marble mantel that outdid the rest: black-bronzed maidens swooned around its base, with birds and angels, filigreed flowers and vines, exploding from the urn-shaped clock. The clock hands were as unmoving as the stale, hot air.

There was a tiny drawer in the base of the clock. Mason's fingers started to itch, as they always did with the compulsion to open drawers and cabinets. Especially one in a nonfunctioning clock. He opened the drawer. Inside was a lapel pin fashioned in the shape of a double-bladed axe with the tricolor of France. Mason recognized the emblem, but he couldn't quite place its significance. His rumination was interrupted when he heard the butler plodding down the hallway. He closed the drawer just as the butler opened the double doors.

"Monsieur and Madame Meunier will see you now."

The butler led them down a long hallway and to a larger, sunnier room. Though the warm light did nothing to brighten the dark furniture and faded paintings. Monsieur and Madame Meunier sat in upholstered, high-back chairs, with a small table between them. They were both very still as if posing for a portrait painting. Monsieur Meunier wore a charcoal-gray suit and a heavily starched shirt under a maroon tie. Madame wore her braided hair up in a sensible bun, as sensible as her heavy, thick-heeled shoes. She held her clasped hands on her black, pleated, midshin skirt, which was topped off with a black suit coat and blouse with a silk bow across the neckline. The sun poked through the lace curtains and highlighted the dark circles under Madame Meunier's eyes and the unevenness of her makeup.

In unison, their eyes glanced at Mason before locking a disapproving glare on Tazim. Obviously, the butler had warned them about a brown man invading their sanctuary, since neither voiced any objections.

Mason sat and covered the usual litany of questions, with Tazim translating. After several questions, Mason found the translation process frustrating. He had no way to pace his questions, improvise, or read between the lines. So he used the gaps in conversation to study the couple. Mrs. Meunier remained silent, with her jaw clamped shut as if fighting the urge to speak. Her hands were pressed firmly into her lap like she was forcing herself to remain seated. Mr. Meunier sat rigid, almost statuesque, though his upper lip curled as if he smelled something foul in the room. His stiff posture, reluctance to answer questions, and short responses were all telltale signs that he was hiding something. Both of them were.

"I understand Valerie was in the same riding club as Sabine de Graaf," Mason said.

After Tazim's translation, Mrs. Meunier glanced at her husband, then nodded.

"Also, the third girl abducted, Cynthia Brisbane. As a matter of fact, quite a few wealthy individuals have sons or daughters in the riding club. Can you think of anyone in the club who you might suspect is behind the abductions?"

While Tazim translated, Mason noticed over Mrs. Meunier's left shoulder, on a small corner table, another lapel pin placed discreetly next to one of Valerie's dressage trophies. This one had the simple tricolor of France without the double-bladed axe. Then it came to him: the lapel pin he'd seen in the clock's drawer was the emblem of Pétain's Vichy government, which had collaborated with Hitler. Mason had seen that symbol on plaques and flags as the U.S. Army pushed the German army out of France.

Meunier had been a Nazi collaborator, probably making his fortune as an industrialist for the Nazi war machine. Perhaps Captain Rousselot knew Meunier's association, and that's why he had encouraged Mason to play rough.

Which was why Mason decided to hit them with a hammer.

Mason said in German, "Herr Meunier, Captain Rousselot and I estimate your daughter has no more than a week before she is killed."

That stopped Meunier cold. They both looked at him in shock. Tazim looked back and forth between the two parties.

Mason continued in German, "I see you understand. Good." He went on to explain that the time frame was based on the date of Sabine's abduction and the time of her death. "If you and Frau Meunier wish to have any chance of saving your daughter, you will answer my questions."

Mrs. Meunier obviously understood him, too, as she looked like she was about to break down into sobs.

"I think you both know why I asked about the riding club. There has to be a connection as to why these three girls were abducted. But there's more to it than just them taking dressage lessons at the same club, isn't there? The real connection is with the girls' parents."

"That is nonsense," Meunier said in German. "We believe Moroccan slave traders abducted them."

"Sex-slave traders do it for profit. Sabine de Graaf was violated, tortured, and killed. All right here in Tangier. These abductions have nothing to do with Moroccan slave traders."

Meunier shook his head in annoyance. "Then ordinary Moroccan criminals. Perhaps they are revolutionaries." He looked vexed, but there was no conviction in his voice.

"What is it you're hiding, Herr Meunier?"

Mason's shock tactics worked. Meunier fell silent. Mason would let them stew in juices of their own making.

Moments later, Mrs. Meunier used her eyes to urge her husband to speak. Mr. Meunier's stony expression softened to one of contrition.

Continuing in German, Mr. Meunier said, "I became acquainted with several of the fathers of the girls in the riding club. In our conversations, we discovered we shared many political and economic ideals." He hesitated and pointed at Tazim. "Does he understand German?"

Mason turned to Tazim and asked in English, "Do you?"

"Do I what?"

"I'll explain later," Mason said, and shook his head at Meunier.

Mr. Meunier continued, "We decided to form a club. A gentlemen's club."

Mason wanted to say, "A fascists' club," but he didn't.

Mr. Meunier said, "But this has nothing to do with Valerie's abduction. All you have proposed is a place where the three girls met. It could be one of the horse trainers or stableboys. It could be any number of people who come to watch the training or exhibitions."

"Everyone is a suspect until they aren't. How many members are in your club?"

"I don't know the exact number. Perhaps thirty."

"Are Mr. de Graaf and Mr. Brisbane members?"

"I don't see how that is useful."

"I need all the members' names."

"I will not violate the other members' trust, their right to privacy."

"Herr Meunier, your daughter's life is at stake. And time is running out."

"I refuse."

"Henri!" Mrs. Meunier said with horror. She proceeded to yell at him in French.

Tazim translated quietly, "Do you think your honor is more important than our daughter?"

Meunier looked at his wife for a long moment.

"I'll make it easy for you," Mason said. He pulled out the list of the exclusive riding club and held it out to Meunier. "Check off the names of those who are members in your club, and write down the names of members who aren't there."

Meunier hesitated, but his wife pivoted in her chair and glared at him. He took the paper and moved to a table to fill in the names.

While Mr. Meunier did that, Mason asked, "Frau Meunier, could you repeat the places you went in the Grand Socco the day Valerie was abducted?"

Mrs. Meunier named every stop before they went to the Grand Socco to eat lunch and shop for groceries. She named the same brasserie, Chez la Vie, that de Graaf had mentioned. "Then, after lunch, Valerie wanted so much to have a henna design. There are two young Moroccan women who are always at the Grand Socco, so we stopped there."

"Did you have one of the women do a design for you?"

"Yes, just on my hands. Normally I would never do such a thing, but Valerie insisted. We were having such a good time that

I couldn't say no. It made her so happy …" She trailed off into sad reflection.

"Can you describe the woman who did your tattoo?"

"She was young, perhaps late twenties. No veil and quite lovely for a Moroccan. She was with another henna artist in her midforties. The other woman had a small mark or scar over her left eyebrow. Why are you asking so many questions about that woman?" Her eyes narrowed. "It must be her. That Moroccan woman must have given us some kind of poison."

"I plan to question the henna artists, but there were many opportunities to slip a drug into your food or drink."

Mr. Meunier finished writing and gave the papers back to Mason. "I've done what you asked. Now it's time you leave. You have treated us like criminals for long enough."

Mason disagreed. He looked over the list. Other than the three fathers, he didn't see anyone else who stood out. He didn't think Meunier had provided all the names, and he might've even tried to add a few false leads, but it was more than when he came in.

He pocketed the amended list and said his thanks.

On their way out, the butler opened the door as if showing out unwanted animals.

Mason stopped in front of the butler. "What were you doing the day Valerie was abducted?"

The butler pulled his head back, as the door prevented him from retreating any farther.

Mason said, "Valerie was abducted by someone she trusted. That's why she didn't call for help. That makes you a suspect. I'm going to be watching you very carefully."

Mason walked away before the butler could protest. He knew it was childish, but the man had pissed him off. At the car, Mason turned on his heels and glared at the butler. The butler rushed to close the door.

As Mason settled into the passenger's seat, he said, "Next stop, the Brisbanes'."

Tazim started the car. "Not very professional of you, but thank you for scaring him."

"I suspect everyone. Who knows? This time the butler could have actually done it."

16

M ason filled Tazim in on what the Meuniers had said as they made their way to the Brisbanes'. Fifteen minutes later Tazim pulled the car up to the gate. The guard let them through without question or checking IDs. Mason figured the guard thought he was a big shot since he had a "Moroccan driver."

"I will leave you here," Tazim said. "My orders were to return after we interviewed the Meuniers."

Mason nodded. "We can't have you in the doghouse the first time Rousselot lets you out on your own."

"Doghouse? I don't understand this reference."

"Never mind. And you can tell Rousselot everything, except about me having this list of members. Okay? I haven't looked it over yet, so I don't know who's who."

"Do you suspect Capitaine Rousselot?" Tazim said, then caught himself. "Ah, you suspect everyone, until you don't."

"That's right."

Norwood, Brisbane's butler, met Mason at the front door and led him inside. He was in a hurry to get Mason up the stairs. "Mr. Brisbane has been waiting for you for some time now."

Norwood knocked on Brisbane's office door and opened it without waiting for a response. Brisbane whirled around, as if he'd rehearsed this dramatic gesture for Mason's tardy return.

"Where have you been? I expected you hours ago."

"I didn't come here to check in with you."

"I said my daughter is your top priority, and your daily reports are part of the stipulation of your employment."

"And I said that you let me do my job the way I want. It's the only way this is going to work."

Brisbane took a moment to calm down and rubbed his forehead—probably rehearsed as well. "You can't imagine the stress I'm under."

"Imagine the stress your daughter is under... So why don't you tell me everything to help get her back?"

"I have told you everything."

"Yeah? You told me the three girls have no connection. When you knew damn well they all belong to an exclusive riding club. And the fathers are members of a secret men's club."

Brisbane blanched, and his jaw went slack. "How did you find out about that?"

Mason crossed his arms. "I didn't. You just told me. What do you guys do in this club? Plot to take over the world?"

A flash of relief spread across Brisbane's face, though he masked it quickly. "It's simply a group of men with conservative principles in economics."

"Fascists?"

"Don't be ridiculous."

"Really? Meunier is ex-Vichy. De Graaf somehow financially thrived and survived the Nazi occupation. If I look into your past, will I discover the same thing? I still have a few friends left in intelligence."

While he was saying this, Mason had the feeling Brisbane thought he had been referring to another type of club. One that had struck fear into his heart. So much so that he didn't get upset at Mason's implications.

"That club has nothing to do with my daughter's disappearance. Do you think we planned among ourselves to kidnap each other's daughters?"

"A few moments ago you reacted as if I was talking about another club. What sort of club would that be?"

"That's absurd. You are grasping at straws, which makes me very concerned that you're at a loss in your investigation. Perhaps I've chosen the wrong man for the job."

"Is that why you only want me to investigate your daughter's abduction? So I won't sniff around and discover your dirty laundry?"

"How dare you? One more word about this ... this is a ridiculous line of questioning, and I'll cut you off without a shilling."

"You'd rather save your own hide than save your daughter? Sabine de Graaf was murdered and discarded after a little over three weeks. The abductor gets tired of his captives once he's used them up. That means Valerie Meunier has maybe five days, and Cynthia has less than two weeks. If you want to gamble with her life, or prolong her suffering, then send me away. That's on your head. But I will continue to search for her and Valerie and hunt down the abductors. With or without your help."

Mason turned to go, but Brisbane said, "Stop. Please."

Mason faced him.

"I swear there is no other club, sinister or otherwise. If there is a connection between the girls and the club, then by all means look into it."

Mason pulled out the list from the equestrian center that Meunier had amended. "We are going to go through this list of names. You are going to tell me about them, and if any of them are potential suspects."

"That would violate the trust of the group."

Mason wagged the list at Brisbane. Brisbane snatched it out of his hand and took it over to his desk. Mason looked over Brisbane's shoulder as the man wrote. The list of names came to twenty-six. There were judges, company CEOs, a dozen diplomats from a handful of countries, highly placed government officials, and, to round out the list, royalty from half of Europe.

"I'm certain that not one of these members could be considered a suspect," Brisbane said. "They are all gentlemen and honorable men."

"Then why do you all feel it has to be kept in secret?"

"That is not relevant. And I resent you treating me as a suspect. I am a victim."

"Your daughter's the victim. Not you."

Brisbane turned red with anger—or it was fear. "You know perfectly well what I mean. I will not discuss this any further."

Brisbane pulled out his wallet, counted out ten pounds sterling, and slapped it on the desk. Mason took it, as he no longer felt dirty about taking money from someone like Brisbane.

Mason started to leave, then stopped and turned back to Brisbane. "One more question."

Brisbane made a pained expression. At that moment, it was obvious that the man still had some dark secrets.

"Did Cynthia ever get a henna tattoo in the Grand Socco?"

"Yes, and strictly forbidden to ever do it again. Why do you ask?"

"Just something I'm working on. I'll be in touch," Mason said, and left.

17

M ason stood on the edge of the outer ring of the Grand Socco. It was six forty-five p.m., and the sun had settled just below the heights above the city. The neon lights of the night-clubs and restaurants had come on, and music drifted out into the streets. Customers filled the café sidewalk tables and took in the din and swarm of the place.

"Looking for me?"

Mason turned around and saw Melville standing behind him. "I'm not going to ask how you slipped up on me with that limp of yours."

"Shall we seek out some henna ladies?"

Mason and Melville wove through the locals buying that evening's dinner and tourists doing their last-minute shopping before heading back to the waiting cruise ship. Mason saw two henna women by an oak tree who fit Mrs. Meunier's description. They were busy applying henna designs on a couple of giggling tourists. Mason and Melville watched the younger woman doing the final touches of an intricate floral design on a middle-aged woman. She used a syringe to apply the henna paste. She would draw the dark green paste into the syringe from a bowl containing the mixture, then use the needle in quick motions to make small petals of the flowers. That heightened Mason's suspicions, but if the woman had punctured any of the victims' skin, they would have felt it and complained. The young woman worked fast, drawing the design from memory.

Melville said, "The more traditional way is to use a stick, but that requires too much time for impatient tourists."

The young henna artist finished. The tourist paid her and left. Mason and Melville approached her as she went about organizing her tools for the next customer.

"Do you speak English?" Mason asked.

The woman looked at him and shook her head.

"*Parlez-vous français?*" Melville asked.

Again, she shook her head.

"This is going well," Mason said.

"She's probably a Berber from the Rif Mountains," Melville said. He tried, "*¿Hablas español?*"

When she finally nodded, Melville said to Mason, "Shall I give it a go in Spanish?"

Mason nodded. "Ask her how long she's been working here. Does she work here every day, and does she make her own paste?"

While Melville and the young woman conversed, Mason looked at the older henna artist. She still worked on a tourist in her midtwenties. The older woman kept glancing at Melville out of the corner of her eye. She looked agitated or frightened. Mason couldn't tell which.

Melville turned to Mason. "She's been here in the Grand Socco doing this kind of work for three years. Yes, she works here every day, except the holy days. And yes, she and her companion make their own paste, which consists of henna powder, lemon juice, brewed tea, and the pièce de résistance, donkey urine, an ingredient that makes their tattoos darker and last longer."

"I'm guessing they don't tell the tourists that. Tell her three girls who got henna tattoos from them became sick, as if drugged. Ask her if she knows anything about that."

The older henna woman said in English, "That was not because of the henna." She said it with anger, and her eyes flicked between Mason and Melville.

"What is your name, ma'am?" Mason asked.

"My name is Jamila, and she is Fatima. We do not make people sick."

Fatima burst into rapid Arabic and was near tears as she spoke. Jamila responded in a gentle tone, then said to Mason, "Fatima say, one of the Nazarene women who came was not sick. She was possessed. Possessed by a djinn." She peered into Mason's eyes as if waiting for him to scoff at her. But he motioned for her to continue.

Jamila said, "There is evil at work on those girls."

"Come now, madam," Melville said. "This sort of talk does not help us."

Mason held up his hand to quiet Melville.

Jamila would not look at Melville. "This evil came with the Nazarenes. They brought it here, and now they are paying the price."

Mason squatted in front of Jamila. "What sort of evil?"

"There are Nazarene men possessed by evil spirits, and that evil will come to you if you stay among these men."

"Which men?" Mason asked.

Jamila barked something to Fatima in Arabic. They began packing up their things.

Mason said, "Jamila, which men are you talking about?"

"I will say no more," Jamila said, as they grabbed up their things.

"I'm not the police. I'm not here to arrest you, but I need to know why all three women became drugged after having henna tattoos done by you two."

The women were almost frantic to tuck their burdens under their arms and hurry away.

"What has you so frightened?" Mason called out after them.

Melville said, "A perfect example of the local folklore and superstitions. Or perhaps there *are* djinn spirits targeting Nazarenes."

Mason watched the two women scurry away. He had no proof and he couldn't force them to talk. Plus, the exchange had attracted too many angry stares from the other Moroccan merchants. He did feel Jamila was not far off the mark that there were some evil Nazarenes lurking in Tangier. He would talk to the women again, and next time with Tazim's help. They might speak more freely to another Moroccan.

"Speaking of spirits," Melville said, "shall we convene in the Petit Socco and drink our share of them?"

As they walked toward the Catherine Gate and the medina, Mason asked, "Do you know Carson Trusdale?"

"Everyone knows of Mr. Trusdale. By reputation, at least. A gentleman smuggler, they say, though he's never been exposed as such. He's a vice-consul for the British legation, you know. It is an open secret that most personnel of the diplomatic corps in Tangier take advantage of their immunity by smuggling to one degree or another. The joke in Tangier is that while the 'CD' on a diplomat's automobile license plates stands for *corps diplomatique*, or 'diplomatic corps,' it really stands for *contrabandier distingué*. 'Distinguished smuggler.'"

"I figured as much. He and I are overdue for a heart-to-heart talk."

Melville stopped. "Well, then, if you need to talk to him, he can be found most evenings at Dean's Bar. We can kill two birds with one stone."

They walked up Rue du Statut and turned left on Rue Amerique du Sud, and there, in an unassuming building, was an equally unimpressive bar. Cramped and smoky, the bar was packed to the walls. Melville had informed him that the bar was legendary, mostly because of its owner, Joseph Dean. Celebrities and criminals rubbed elbows while listening to Dean's endless stories of the outlandish and notorious residents of the city.

Mason spotted Carson sitting at a table in a corner. "I'd like to speak with him alone," he said to Melville.

"Of course. I'll be at the bar."

Carson was with a beautiful dark-skinned woman with high cheekbones and enough mascara to make her eyes look black. He was dressed in a tuxedo, and the woman wore a matching tuxedo and bow tie, but with nothing underneath the jacket. They were so busy yammering that Carson didn't notice Mason. Carson had an unlit cigarette to his lips and was searching his pockets for his lighter.

Mason stuck out his lighter in front of Carson's face. "Let me light that for you."

Carson tried to jump up from the table, but Mason put a hand on his shoulder and forced him to sit. Mason took a seat between them. The woman seemed unfazed, as if she'd seen this happen to Carson before. She plucked the cigarette from Carson's mouth and put it to hers. She then took Mason's hand and guided the lighter to her lips. She didn't smile. She said nothing. Her clothes and hairstyle might have been masculine, but her touch, her smells, her charms barely hidden by the tuxedo jacket, were all feminine.

Carson tried to use the distraction to rise again. Without looking, Mason forced Carson down again. He pivoted in his chair to face him. "Who paid you to set me up?"

"I have no idea what you're talking about."

Mason helped himself to one of Carson's cigarettes and lit it.

"It struck me as odd, you zipping away from the hotel yesterday afternoon, like you couldn't get away fast enough."

"I dropped you off and saw no reason to linger."

"Then, lo and behold, three morons with guns show up at my hotel. And I wondered, how did these birdbrains know exactly where I was staying and when I'd be there?"

"You think I had something to do with that?"

"Usually guys with something to hide answer cops with questions. I just moved you out of the suspicious column into the guilty one. You were a go-between for those thugs and whoever wanted me out of the picture."

"Do you realize how absurd that sounds?"

"There you go again."

"I'm not a part of any sinister conspiracy. I'm the one who found you, bailed you out of jail, and hired you."

"You did all that because you thought I was so desperate that I'd knuckle under to any of Brisbane's demands. And you misrepresented me to Brisbane, telling him that I was a patsy and a stooge, so you could get a lucrative contract."

"Has Carson been a naughty boy again?" the woman said. She spoke British English with a slight Arabic accent.

Carson pointed to the woman with his open hand. "Mason, this is Sara. A completely demented artist from Beirut."

"And you are a swindler who finds people only to con them," Sara said.

"That's not true," Carson said to Sara. He looked at Mason contritely. "Well, not always true. It wasn't for a lucrative contract. I already have lucrative contracts with Brisbane and a number of wealthy clients. It was in exchange for a promotion to consul. I needed the diplomatic immunity. A venture went bust, and I ended up owing some of those clients a great deal of money."

Mason dropped his hand on Carson's shoulder and squeezed.

"You'd better spill it, Carson. Who hired you? I don't have much patience with people who set me up. I might just drag you into an alley and skin you alive."

Carson closed his eyes and took in deep breaths, as if summoning the strength to resist—or confess. There was a break in the tension when a waiter came up to the table with an ice bucket containing a bottle of champagne. He laid out three glasses and said, "I assumed the gentleman will be joining you."

Before Mason could say no, Sara said, "Yes."

The waiter opened the bottle with great ceremony and poured champagne in the three glasses. It seemed to take an eternity, and all the while, Mason continued to squeeze Carson's shoulder.

When the waiter left, Carson let out a big groan. "All right! I told those three where to find you."

"I'm more interested in who hired you."

Mason used his thumb to press into the nerve above Carson's collarbone. Carson grimaced; sweat broke out on his forehead.

"I don't know who. It could be any one of them."

"Any one of who?"

"My wealthy clients," Carson said as he squirmed to get away from the increasing pressure of Mason's grip.

"Carson, that's not helping. Give me some names."

"I can do better than that. I'll take you to them."

Mason released his grip. Carson sucked in air as he slumped in his chair and rubbed his shoulder. "Look, I'm sorry. I had no idea there was to be any foul play. One of my clients threatened to ruin me if I didn't do what he said. I don't know who, but I could narrow it down to four or five. And they'll all be at this party this evening."

"That's why you're all dressed up?"

"Yes, a filthy rich American named Anthony Jennings is hosting this gala event for charity. Some 'sisters-of-whomever' mission hospital for the poor."

Sara said, "These bourgeois pigs have parties every week, each trying to outdo the other. If this Jennings would just give all the money he spends on his parties, they would not need a charity ball."

"I accept your invitation, Mr. Trusdale." Mason downed the glass of champagne. "I'd be delighted to go to the party with you and Sara."

M ason found himself on the New Mountain Road again. Carson drove his Jaguar, with Mason folded into the front and Sara in back. On the way, Carson had insisted they pick up a tuxedo for Mason, and somehow convinced a British tailor to open his shop, using his clout as a consul and mumbling something about national security. The tux coat was a little snug around the shoulders and chest, but fit otherwise. He looked at it as wearing another disguise, though he wished Laura could see him. He felt pretty dapper.

Carson slid down in his seat as they passed Brisbane's mansion. Just five houses up from there, they came to a high wall that extended for two hundred feet. Palm trees and hedges of flowers lined the pink stucco walls. Conversation and music emanated from the other side. Carson parked on the street, next to a line of Rolls-Royces, Cadillacs, and Mercedes-Benzes.

Mason pulled out the gentlemen's club member list that Meunier and Brisbane had emended. He handed it to Carson. "I want you to point out anyone we see inside who is on that list."

"We're either going to have a very busy evening or get thrown out on our bums."

A few minutes later, Mason, Carson, and Sara walked through the large, arched gate. Before them stood a sprawling Mediterranean-style villa with white stucco walls, tiled roof, and Moroccan details of arched and latticed windows and an onion-domed front door. A circular driveway led up to the front door, where Moroccan valets dressed in gold djellabas and turbans with peacock feathers opened car doors. The passengers were decked out in tuxedos or beaded gowns and furs.

"Kind of like *The Wizard of Oz*," Mason said.

"You're the tin man without a heart," Carson said.

"And you're the cowardly lion," Sara said to Carson.

"Oh, ha ha," Carson said.

The front door was at least twelve feet wide and nine feet high with huge double doors of wood and iron. Around the onion-shaped top and along each side was an intricate gold, green, and blue geometric pattern. A tall black man in the same gold and peacock outfit checked Carson's and Sara's invitations, then eyed Mason.

"My cousin from Ireland," Carson said, and glanced back at Mason with a glower. "The Earl of Blarney."

The man eyed them skeptically but let them pass. Mason led the way inside, but he didn't get more than two steps before he stopped. That was the only way he could take in what he saw. The foyer alone would have dwarfed his grandmother's house in Ohio. And instead of beholding marble columns or crystal chandeliers, he stared at a desert scene. The floor had been covered in sand. From the walls and ceiling hung painted backdrops simulating a desert landscape under a starry sky, accentuated by theatrical lights that created a silvery cast of imaginary moonlight. The sweeping staircase at the far end of the foyer was covered in tent material creating a nomadic encampment in an oasis of palm trees and ferns, which threw patterned shadows on the walls from the forest of torches. Most exotic of all, three men in indigo robes stood with their camels near the tent-covered staircase.

"Jesus," Mason said.

"Christ had very little to do with this pagan bacchanal," Carson said. "If I know Jennings, this is just the prelude to what's waiting inside."

Sara harrumphed. "The pigs occupy a land, then make symbols of their colonial occupation."

"You didn't have to come, you know," Carson told her. "Please behave yourself in there."

Two muscle-bound Moroccans parted the tent flaps, and they passed through the opening. Carson was right; the foyer was simply a prelude. The immense ballroom carried the same theme: swaths of red, green, and white canvas hung in swags from the ceiling and draped down the walls, creating the illusion of a giant tent. The entire room was covered in scores of Oriental rugs. At the far end, a ten-piece Moroccan band of handheld drums, large brass castanets, lutes, and other stringed instruments pounded out exotic rhythms. Like a three-ring circus, Moroccan dancers hopped around the front of the band while belly dancers wove through the crowd, and a fire-eater juggled torches, then spit flames. In the opposite corner, acrobats performed balancing acts, and a sword swallower engorged long blades. A large cage sat on a platform to the side of the band with two leopards pacing nervously.

"Like Rome having one last orgy before it falls," Mason said.

Sara said, "It reminds me of the decadent party in the novel *Steppenwolf*. You and I are the wolves forced to live among humans."

Mason had read the book, and he could see the same conflicts within him, being both a lone wolf and human. Though he couldn't identify with the main character's obsession with inevitable suicide—unless he counted the times he'd run headlong into dangerous situations, like this one.

Mason and Carson stepped into the reception line, but Sara would have none of it. "I will not bow to these people. I will find a rich man to seduce, then ruin." With that, she sauntered off, on the prowl.

"I haven't figured out why, but I like her," Mason said.

"A fire-breathing dragon with an amazing figure."

"I would've never pictured the two of you together."

"Good heavens, she and I are not lovers. She's a brilliant artist, and she's always great for a good laugh. We're like quarreling siblings who feel a great affection for one another."

Mason and Carson made their way near the front of the reception line. Mason stepped out of the line to get a better look at Jennings: a tall, lanky man in his early sixties. He had a formal, courtly manner about him, with his gray-streaked black hair that was slicked back, emphasizing his high forehead, long nose, and sharp jawline, which ended in a chin flat enough to be used as a blunt instrument. His dark eyes and smile advertised his notion that he had the world at his fingertips. He had the habit of making big, quick hand gestures as he talked, taking up the room and intimidating anyone who dared to stand too close.

Next to him stood a woman of no more than forty, glamorous and elegant. She held his arm with one hand and shook guests' hands with the other. Tall herself, she appeared to be an ex-model, as she could produce a smile when called upon, and her elegant poise had that practiced air of a professional. She wore a white silk gown that wrapped around her long torso, then flared in a swirl and draped on the floor.

Jennings didn't skip a beat when Mason stepped up. He thrust out his hand and flashed a Hollywood smile. "Mr. Collins. I don't recall sending you an invitation, but I'm delighted to see you, nonetheless."

"I thought it only right to come to your party. Especially after meeting three of your hired hands. I hope I didn't disappoint you, turning down the offer."

"I'm afraid I don't know who or what you're referring to."

Jennings continued to smile, but his dark eyes, so glossy they reflected the chandelier lights high above, probed Mason, as if measuring him up for the level of trouble he would have to go through to get rid of him—or the size of the plaque required to mount Mason's head on his trophy wall.

Jennings's eyes flicked to the corner over Mason's shoulder. Mason had already scoped out the room and noticed a tuxedoed bodyguard in the very same corner. Jennings's gaze returned to Mason for an instant before landing on Carson. "Mr. Trusdale, I never know where your tastes lie. The last time I saw you, you had a lovely woman on your arm."

"Yes, of course. I believe that's when you had another lovely lady on yours."

Mrs. Jennings flashed an evil look at Carson, and then her husband. She left Mason for last. "You're holding up the line, Mr. Collins. We should give other guests our attention."

"I hope not the kind of attention your husband has given me."

"If you're not here to enjoy our hospitality, then I would invite you to leave."

"I'm already enjoying myself, Mrs. Jennings. And I'm looking forward to meeting your other guests."

Mrs. Jennings ignored Carson and turned her attention to the next guest in the line. Mason and Carson walked deeper into the ballroom. Carson pointed out a couple in their forties, both standing regally together, drinks in hand, dressed in the full regalia of ribbons, medals, and, for the woman, a diamond tiara.

"The Baron and Baroness von Litchten," Carson said. "The baron is on your list. I believe the royal title cost them a king's ransom, but Tangier's high society doesn't care if it's inherited or paid for. A phony-sounding name if I've heard one, but for the right price, anyone can become royalty here."

Mason pulled out an Ansco Memo camera he'd bought cheap at a store near his hotel. Tiny in his hands, he held it up and photographed the couple.

"Would you please stop that? We're going to get thrown out."

Mason pocketed the camera. "Let's go talk to His Highness."

Carson groaned but followed Mason. They sauntered up to the couple. Carson introduced them, telling them Mason's name, but nothing else. Their English was halting but passable.

Once the pleasantries were out of the way, Mason said, "Terrible about the abductions of the young women."

The baroness shook her head at the tragedy of it. The baron said, "Yes, terrible." There was nothing sincere in his voice. Either he didn't find it terrible enough to be bothered, or he knew more than he wanted to reveal. Almost as an afterthought, he said, "I hope they find the scoundrels."

"In fact, Sir Wilfred Brisbane asked for my assistance in the search."

At this, the baron seemed surprised. "You, sir? Have you made progress?"

"Some. But would you believe that someone hired armed thugs to intimidate me? Even threatening violence?"

The baron and baroness acted aghast at the idea.

Mason added, "And I understand that person is a member of very high standing in Tangier society. I have to say, whoever it is, they sure appear guilty by doing such a thing."

"Do you have a name, sir? This should be brought to the attention of the police."

Again, there was no sincerity in it. The "baron" had mastered detached, polite conversation, but Mason bet he lacked the skills to hide the telltale signs of guilt. In his gut, Mason felt the baron was evasive for some reason, but not for hiring the three stooges.

Mason had Carson lead him to other candidates on the list. Mason took photographs of each man, and then Carson would take him over and introduce him: two judges, a Spanish consul on the Committee of Control, two bankers, and one who Carson had no idea how he'd made his millions. In one fashion or another, Mason probed each of them. Some appeared sincere and had nothing to hide. Others fell into the baron's category of vaguely guilty of something, but not of hiring the thugs.

Carson said, "Can we take a break? I'd like to enjoy the party before I become persona non grata on everyone's guest list."

"How about some fresh air? There might be more members we haven't talked to outside."

Carson reluctantly agreed, and they made their way through the ballroom to the French doors leading out to the patio. The world suddenly changed from surreal Morocco to *The Great Gatsby*. Spread out on the immense lawn, a twenty-piece orchestra played a Cole Porter song for the people that packed the dance floor installed for the party. Everything was decorated in black and gold, from the gold dance floor to the stage draped in black. Gold lanterns hung from a grid of wires and, above, a mirrored ball spun, throwing flecks of light upon the dancers.

"I'm getting a drink," Carson said, and headed for one of the three bars, also draped in gold.

Someone came up behind Mason and took his arm. It was Sara.

"You're going to ask me to dance."

Mason offered her his arm and led her onto the dance floor.

Sara said, "You had some success?"

"Not much. And what about you?"

Sara shrugged. "I am too aggressive, I think." After a pause, she said, "So, now what? What's your big plan?"

"I'm sure the word is spreading by now. Whoever it is, I'm betting they'll make a play this evening."

"Why don't I like the sound of that?" She looked up at Mason with seductive eyes. "I'm trying to imagine how many women's hearts you've broken."

"It's more like the other way around. I've been accused of lacking charm."

"I'll reserve judgment until I get to know you a little better."

"I'm not looking for romance. I'm here on business."

"But you won't stop me from enjoying myself."

"Knock yourself out."

"Just so you know, this isn't romance for me either. Just sex."

"What can you tell me about Carson? Is he mixed up with Jennings? Other than his smuggling business."

"I doubt it. Carson has no loyalties, except to himself and His Royal Highness the British pound note."

"What about you? Are you mixed up with Jennings somehow?"

Sara stared at Mason for a moment, as if calculating her answer. "I fucked him once."

"So much for hating bourgeois pigs."

"I did it for the sport. And why are you asking about Jennings?"

"Jennings interests me. What do you think about him?"

"Fucking him once doesn't make me his psychiatrist." She glanced at something over Mason's shoulder. "Better yet, why don't you ask him? Two of his bodyguards are headed this way."

19

Like sharks in tuxedos, Jennings's two bodyguards cut through the dance floor with their eyes fixed on Mason. They weren't muscle-bound hulks, but sure-footed, like track-and-field athletes—or ex-soldiers. They stopped in unison, each taking flanking positions next to Mason.

The bodyguard sporting a full mustache said with an American accent, "Mr. Jennings would like to have a word with you."

"He didn't have to send the two of you. I was hoping he and I could have a chat."

The bodyguard with the mustache motioned for the patio door. "If you will follow us, please."

Mason said to Sara, "You should go home now."

"You can't get off my hook that easily. Besides, I want to see what condition you're in after your little chat."

Mason followed the two bodyguards across the patio. He caught Carson watching him with wide eyes from one of the bars. And as they crossed the ballroom floor, Mason spied Brisbane and Lambert talking with a group of guests. Brisbane froze in midspeech when he saw Mason and his escorts. A heartbeat of alarm spread across Brisbane's face, though Lambert used the opportunity to glare at Mason.

The two bodyguards led Mason across the simulated desert to the back of the foyer. One of the men opened tent flaps and motioned for Mason to enter. He found himself at the base of the stairs that led up to the second floor. One man stayed below while the mustached bodyguard escorted him upstairs. Outside the influences of the party, the real world returned. Real in a sense, because the opulent surroundings were far from Mason's experience except for museums he'd visited in the past. They crossed to large double doors with gold handles.

The man held out his hand. "Your pistol, please."

"What are you? Ex-army or law enforcement?"

"Out of respect, I'm not going to frisk you. Just hand it over."

Mason fished the .380 out of his pocket and handed it to him. The bodyguard knocked on the door, then opened it for Mason. He said, "I'll be waiting out here. No funny business."

When Mason entered, Jennings was standing behind a large mahogany desk. Two high-backed leather chairs faced the desk, while on the other side of the room, a plush leather sofa faced a Buick-sized fireplace.

"Come in, Mr. Collins. Can I offer you a drink? I have some thirty-year-old bourbon."

"I can't remember the last time I had a good bourbon."

Mason waited while Jennings turned to a table behind his desk and poured the drinks. Jennings offered Mason a cut-crystal highball glass filled with the amber liquid.

Jennings motioned to one of the chairs. "Have a seat."

"I prefer to stand."

"As you like." Jennings raised his glass to Mason, then took a sip.

Mason said, "You must be pretty desperate to send three armed goons to get me out of the picture."

"Right down to business. Who said I sent these men?"

"You did, by summoning me to your office just now."

Jennings took time to settle into his plush desk chair behind the desk. "Showing up here like you did made me curious. That's all this is."

"I don't buy it."

Jennings took a few moments to study Mason. "Buying it or not isn't my concern. But say I sent those men. Why would I do such a thing?" He paused and smiled, exuding an air of superiority, as if talking to a child. He leaned on his elbows. "It's because you're bad for this community. You're bad for business."

Mason didn't see that coming, so he said nothing and waited for Jennings to continue.

"So far, we've been able to keep the news of these abductions local. A terrible thing, but a local affair. Hardly newsworthy in a postwar world with so much deprivation and death. I checked out your background the moment I heard Brisbane had hired you. A disgraced Chicago police detective who has a reputation for busting heads and no regard for authority. Suddenly, there's a story that makes reporters sit up and take notice; a vigilante detective defies police authority and stirs up trouble."

"So you're the one who fed that info to the press."

Jennings shook his head. "That would be contrary to our goals. That makes headlines we don't need. Suddenly, newspapers in Europe and the States start writing sensational reports about the abductions, the incompetence of our police, and the dangers of our fair city. A bad reputation discourages new investment in business and real estate. Wealthy individuals would think twice about setting up residence here. There is even serious talk about bringing the new United Nations organization to Tangier. Can you now see what's financially at stake? Tangier investors could potentially reap vast benefits from a thriving environment, but a bad reputation could ruin it all. So, perhaps a group of investors decided to take the initiative and see if you could be persuaded to leave."

Jennings sat back and rolled the highball glass in his hands. "If this group offered you five thousand dollars, would you reconsider?"

"At least three girls have been abducted, one of them murdered, and you and your buddies are worried about the city's reputation and increased profits. And I don't think it stops there. I think sending three goons to get me out of town tells me that someone in your group of investors—either you or some of your rich cronies—is responsible for the abductions and murder. That makes me very angry. I'm going to do everything in my power to see that person or persons go down hard."

"How about twenty thousand?"

"You think this is some kind of auction? You and your cronies figure twenty thousand is enough to compensate for three girls' lives? Fuck you."

Jennings finished his drink. He got up and went for another. "You know, having money does help uncover all sorts of information. I learned something very interesting about you. From ... associates, you might say. I don't like them, but they have been useful in arranging certain business transactions without all the red tape. In fact, I've heard they have a price on your head. Let's be honest with one another. You didn't come here to save three girls. You came here to escape an assassin's bullet. I haven't called these associates yet, because I usually like to get something of value in return. So, here's what I propose: You take the twenty thousand and go away, to wherever you want. With that amount of money, you could go far indeed. And in addition, I won't make that call."

"You'd go through all that trouble and expense to persuade me to leave town? If I had any doubts, I don't have them anymore. And here's my thinking: You have no guarantees that once I fly out of here, I wouldn't come back or keep my mouth shut. Being a successful businessman, you would never take such a shaky deal. Especially with an unpredictable guy like me. Unless you had an insurance plan. What I figure is, you'll have a team waiting for me at whatever destination you have planned for me. Or maybe arrange something before I get on a boat or a plane out of here. You have no intention of holding up your end of the bargain. No dice, Mr. Jennings."

"Then I fail to see why you came here if it wasn't to make a deal."

"Someone rich and desperate hired those goons. I needed to know who. You were happy to accommodate me."

"I have nothing to do with either of your accusations, Mr. Collins. But I am prepared to go to any length to preserve my financial interests."

"Enjoy the rest of your party, Mr. Jennings. If I have anything to do with it, it'll be your last."

Jennings stood there with a look of rage in his eyes. Mason knew he wouldn't risk creating a scene at his own party, or have Mason disappear after so many people saw him being escorted upstairs. But all bets were off once he stepped out of the man's compound. He raised his glass and downed the last of his bourbon. "Thanks for the drink."

He turned and walked out the door. The bodyguard returned Mason's pistol.

Mason said, "You're working for a real asshole, you know that?"

The man said nothing.

"I'll see you out there on the shooting range," Mason said, and walked away.

Mason found Sara and Carson in the foyer talking to a tall blond beauty in a beaded gown. Carson cast furtive glances at the crowd of guests, and the blonde looked more interested in her surroundings than in Sara's banter.

Mason came up to them and said "Excuse me" to the blonde while leading Carson and Sara away to a quiet corner. "We have to leave before Jennings rallies his troops," Mason said, and looked back at the bodyguard still standing by the stairway.

"I couldn't agree more," Carson said.

"It's that bad, huh?" Sara said.

As Mason ushered them toward the front door, he said, "I need a place to stay. And not at either one of your places. Those are the second and third places they'll look."

"I knew this wouldn't go well," Carson said.

"I'm surprised you made it out of there in one piece," Sara said.

Carson said to Mason, "I want to thank you for getting me in the middle of this. I'll drive you wherever you want, but then I'm taking the boat and making a shipment to Spain."

"You're running away?" Sara said.

"I'm not running away. I'm simply staying out of sight for a few days. And this may be my last profitable run before they see to it that I'm thrown in jail."

"Coward," Sara said. She turned to Mason. "I know of a place. It's an apartment in the medina. It belongs to a girlfriend of mine. Veronique is in Lyon for a month. She won't mind if you stay there for a while."

Carson dropped Mason and Sara off at Mason's hotel.

Sara made an obscene gesture at Carson's Jaguar as it disappeared. Mason scanned the area. No one appeared to be following them, but he wasn't taking any chances. Five minutes was all it took for him to jam his things in the suitcase and collect the files and photographs that Tazim had given him and the ones he'd collected on his own. They then walked at a brisk pace to the Place de France, where they caught a taxi. Sara spoke French to the taxi driver, who took off down Boulevard Pasteur.

"The medina is that way," Mason said, pointing in the opposite direction.

"We're going to stop off at my apartment first. I need to get the key to my friend's place."

The taxi dropped them off at Sara's apartment, which was situated near a small park on Rue de Belgique. Mason waited in the lobby. He concealed himself behind a return wall and watched the entrance. Fifteen minutes elapsed before Sara came down with a suitcase and large leather bag.

"That's a pretty big key."

"I'm going to stay with you for a few days."

"That could get you into a lot of trouble."

Sara just winked at him and headed for the door.

Mason took her arm. "Wait here."

He exited first and scanned the street. A couple walked arm in arm away from the apartment building. Two Moroccan men in djellabas sat on a bench by the park and talked among themselves. Mason waved for Sara to follow him; then they walked to a corner near the British consulate and hailed another taxi.

They stopped the taxi at the Marine Gate of the medina. Inside this part of the medina, the streets were dark and quiet. Their footsteps echoed off the walls as they made several turns before Sara stopped at a green door and unlocked it. They entered a dark room. Mason used his lighter to find the switch for a floor lamp. They were in a small living room, modestly furnished, with an open kitchen at one end. The lamps were draped with beads, and the walls were covered with charcoal sketches of people and desert landscapes.

Sara dropped her suitcase and crossed her arms. "Exactly what did you say to Jennings that could put us both in danger?"

"I refused his offer of a payoff and to get out of town."

"I don't get it. Why don't you just take the money and go?"

"Because, dammit, three innocent girls were abducted. One was tortured and murdered, and the other two aren't far away from the same fate."

Sara responded with a mocking laugh. "You really are something."

Mason stared back at her, waiting for her to explain.

"I am half-English, but I am also half-Lebanese. I'm offended that all of your concern, all of your inquiries, are only for the three white girls. Nothing for the missing brown girls and boys."

"What are you talking about?"

"No one has mentioned the missing Moroccan children?" At Mason's look of bewilderment, she said, "I'm not surprised."

"How are these kids connected to the three girls?"

"They're all in their teens, and they disappeared. What other connection do you need?"

"Did they disappear around the same time? Did they just vanish, like the others? I need to know if they're connected to the girls' abductions."

"What difference does it make? They're all missing."

"How many, and when?"

"I don't have all the information. Only that within the last five months, there has been a rash of disappearances of Moroccan children. The parents went to the police, and the police said they would look into it, but nothing. It's not until white, rich children go missing that everyone goes into a tizzy. The police, the press. And the rich and powerful bring in an ex-army detective and offer to pay him lots of money to rescue their white daughters. Why don't you use some of your experience and balls to help the brown people?"

Mason smiled. "That's the reason for the seductress routine. You were hoping to convince me to help the Moroccan kids."

Sara said nothing and only continued to glare at him.

"Why didn't you just ask me?" Mason said.

Sara shrugged. "You're doing this for the money, aren't you? The poor Moroccan parents can't pay. I haven't seen a white man yet who would lift a finger to help brown and poor people."

"I didn't come here for the money. I didn't come for the parents. I came here because of the kids. Goddamn, lady, don't think you know me because I'm white and have a dick."

Sara still had her arms tightly crossed, but some of her anger seemed to dissipate.

"Can you take me to some of the parents tomorrow? I'd like to question them. Find out what I can."

"Where they live, white people would rather avoid. They don't live in mansions with servants or have anything to offer."

"What did I just say about a dick and a white face?"

A smile softened her scowl. "You would really do this, wouldn't you?"

Mason answered her with a glare of his own. Sara loosened her bow tie and let the ends fall. She unbuttoned her tuxedo jacket and slipped it off. "It's such a beautiful face."

With the ends of her bow tie draped over her ample breasts, she began a slow walk toward him. Mason met her halfway and embraced her, pressing her to him and kissing her soft, full lips. His need to have her outweighed any misgivings. Was she an ally or an opportunist? Would she sleep with him tonight, then turn him over to Jennings in the morning? Right then, he didn't care. She was like embracing fire, giving him unbelievable warmth, but she might just burn him in the end. But he knew that was what inflamed his passion—the danger of it.

Her full breasts and hips, her taste, the way she skillfully touched him, brought out a wild passion. He stripped her, lifted her by the buttocks, and entered her immediately.

He felt nothing ... and everything.

20

M ason felt a surge of excitement when he realized Sara
was taking him to the same *bidonville* he had seen near
the equestrian center. He looked over at Sara but said nothing.
They hadn't talked about last night, and Sara had a serious
expression. She was all business now, and that was fine
with him.

Mason had awakened that morning to discover Sara had
already been out to buy him a djellaba and sunglasses. She had
purchased a wide-brimmed straw hat and sunglasses for herself,
and fit right in with her dark skin. But after three years in northern
Europe, Mason was as white as the stripes on his djellaba. They
sneaked out of the medina just after sunrise and found
Veronique's rusted Renault in the marina parking lot.

Mason stripped off the djellaba as they drove up the dirt road
toward the encampment. "How do you know these parents?"

"I do charity work, mostly food distribution, for the Tangier
Benevolent Society."

Mason looked at her with a smile.

"What?" Sara said.

"Surprised. That's all."

"Just because I'm bonkers doesn't mean I can't help those in need."

Sara parked the car near the dry riverbed. There, before them, the sprawling *bidonville*. It seemed much bigger now that Mason was up close. Walls of garbage defined the outer borders. Children and emaciated dogs wandered through the rotting piles. A dirt path led them over a wooden footbridge that spanned a shallow ravine, where water must gush in the winter rains but now held only a dribble of greenish-brown sludge.

The shacks of corrugated tin and cardboard started twenty yards ahead, jam-packed on this lower level, then spreading out and up along the contours of the hills. Men in djellabas and women in colorful capes and straw hats stared at them with suspicion. Camels and donkeys stood among the shacks. Rivulets of fluid waste trickled toward the ravine.

A group of children in dirty clothes, none older than eight, ran up to them. Some yelled in Arabic, while some of the younger ones climbed on the car. Mason and Sara got out of the car in an area of hardened earth. A couple of the children froze in place when they saw Mason.

Sara said something in Arabic to one of the older boys. The boy ran off into the depths of the camp, while other men and women watched from a safe distance. A few minutes later, two men dressed in djellabas came out to greet them.

The two men headed for Mason, but Sara intercepted them. They talked for a few moments, while Mason waited. Some of the children held out their hands to Mason, obviously asking for food or money. All he had was a half pack of cigarettes and a lighter. He wasn't about to give them either, but the scene stirred up memories of the German orphans he'd encountered daily in Munich.

Sara motioned for Mason to come. The wind had gained in strength and tore at the patchwork walls; the loose pieces banged and rattled. Dust and loose garbage flew up around them as they entered the encampment. Men, women, and children came out of their hovels to watch as the two men led Mason and Sara up the dirt path. They turned left, then right, up a parallel path, and finally came to a large shack made of corrugated tin.

Mason had to duck down to enter the single room. It had a dirt floor covered with tattered rugs. Two lanterns threw a weak light in the space. It was furnished with battered wooden chairs and a table, with some mattresses on the floor. One of the men, Rachid, said something to Sara and gestured toward the two chairs.

"They're going to bring some of the parents of the missing children. This is how many Moroccans live in the paradise that is Tangier. They're mostly Berbers from the Rif Mountains seeking work and food. Summer is the hardest. But they're not beggars or thieves. They're farmers and artisans. They're servants and janitors, and are paid pennies."

Mason had seen similar misery as a kid during the Depression, and in Germany after the war, and he didn't like being preached to by anyone. "And if the king of Morocco and his rich cronies take over, will these people live better lives? Things aren't going to change once another group of rich and powerful take over, so don't look to me to be a revolutionary."

Sara remained calm. She didn't yell slogans or chastise his pessimism. "You came here, and no one paid you to do so. You agreed to listen to these people, when no one else will."

The two men returned with eight others: five women and three men. Rachid seemed to be the leader of the group, and he explained that some of the other parents were working or searching for work, but he and these eight represented the missing children. They greeted Mason and Sara with "*As-salaam alaikum.*" Some sat on a legless sofa, and some on the ground. Mason and Sara sat on the ground facing them.

Mason said to Sara, "I'll need descriptions of the children, where they were last seen, their usual routines, where they went, anything they reported to their parents, like suspicious people or rumors of suspicious activity. Then instruct them to ask others about suspicious persons or activities, and be on the lookout for any. If these people work together, they'll have thousands of eyes and ears."

Mason handed Sara his notepad and pen. "It's better if you write it all down. That way you won't have to stop the interviews to translate."

Mason looked over Sara's shoulder as she wrote down the parents' responses.

One by one, the adults told their stories. A few spoke broken English, but Mason had Sara translate everything to make sure all the details were clear. They told him that nine children had disappeared from this encampment alone. That there were stories of at least a dozen more children who'd vanished from the other slums and shantytowns over the past year. The youngest was eleven, and, surprisingly, a boy. In fact three of the nine were boys. The oldest was a girl of eighteen.

Mason asked how they were sure that they weren't abducted by slave traders. A father, whose name was Youssef, said that the slave traders had no need to abduct children from stable homes. There were enough poor parents with too many mouths to feed who sold them for a few hundred pesetas, thinking they were being taken in as servants. Then those unscrupulous people turned around and sold them to the traders. There were also the runaways or those turned away by their parents—easy pickings for slave traders. None of those circumstances pertained to their missing children.

"When were the first and last abductions from this shanty-town?" Mason prompted Sara to ask.

Sara asked the group, and as she wrote down the response, she said, "The first was at the beginning of January. A seventeen-year-old girl named Karima. Rachid, the man who helped us in the *bidonville*, is her father. She was on her way to a place near the Marshan Gate of the medina. Three times a week, food is handed out to the poor there."

"That was about six months ago. And the last?"

Sara asked and translated the response. "The last they know of was about five weeks ago."

"Ask if they know about any of the abductions aside from this place."

Sara complied, and said, "They've heard stories of maybe six other abductions starting around this time last year."

Two of the mothers and a father started yelling and gesticulating. Sara got into a shouting argument with them, and they eventually quieted down. "They, and many others, are angry nothing has been done by the authorities. The Nazarenes don't care about them. There are threats of mass protests. I told them you, a Nazarene, are here to help. Not all Nazarenes are bad." She paused as if reluctant to go on. "I promised them you would do everything in your power to find the children and bring them home."

Mason kept a neutral expression, though he wanted to give Sara an earful for making half-baked promises. They nodded and smiled at him. Some kept saying "*Shukran.*"

Mason said to Sara, "Tell them I promise to try, but there are no guarantees."

"They understand."

A woman started speaking rapidly to Sara, and Sara began writing it down in Arabic. "It's too fast to write in English," she said to Mason. "I'll tell you later."

The exchanges went on another forty-five minutes. Mason had hoped for some kind of pattern to emerge, but other than the parents claiming their teenagers were all beautiful or handsome, there was little to go on.

Finally, Mason and Sara exited the shack after many thanks from the parents. Two of the women spoke to Sara in rapid Arabic. While Mason waited, he lit a cigarette and looked around the encampment. Children held infants. Dogs sniffed through the dirt in search of food. Emaciated cats sunned themselves or skittered about between the shacks. And all Mason had to do was turn his head to the right to see the equestrian center and, beyond, the gleaming city, like Oz at the end of the rainbow.

Three men in their twenties came up to Mason. The trio's self-appointed leader and bigmouth got in Mason's face. He said things in Arabic in a taunting tone. Punks were the same everywhere, and these three were looking for trouble. Mason fought the temptation to smack him, but popping the punk on the chin was not a wise move in a hostile crowd.

Then, not a moment later, another four men, a little older this time, came up and chimed in. Each one encouraged the other, and their voices rose in volume and hostility.

Sara tried to talk to them, but they ignored her. The two Moroccan escorts, Rachid and his companion, tried to calm the growing crowd. The young men turned their anger on Rachid, though not with the same intensity.

Sara touched Mason's arm and noticed how tense his muscles were. "Keep calm," she said, and urged him forward. "We should leave."

As they descended the hill, people flocked to the disturbance, some glaring at Sara and Mason. The two had to navigate around groups who stood in their path. The whole way, Mason's hands were clenched into tight fists, his body tensing, ready to fight his way out of there.

Finally, they made it out to the clearing, and only curious children followed them to their car.

"I'll drive," Sara said. "You'll probably snap the steering wheel in two."

As they drove away, Mason said, "That little display doesn't make me feel much sympathy."

"They're dirt-poor, uneducated people, who are angry at all the injustice."

"That place feels like a powder keg ready to go off. What are those people going to do if all I find are corpses?" Mason looked at Sara, who said nothing. "The chances are remote of finding those kids alive. You shouldn't make promises in my name I can't keep."

"So, you don't intend to try?"

"That's not what I said." After a pause, he asked, "What was it you had to write down in Arabic when that lady was talking so fast?"

"That they're suspicious that someone, a Nazarene, is paying some Tanjawis a lot of money to do some evil things. That's how they put it, anyway. These men are also being paid to keep quiet about it."

"Do they have any idea what this evil thing is?"

"Uneducated people search for explanations in superstition and the occult, so I wouldn't take what they say literally." She paused, either because she had to enter the main road into town, or she was trying to frame her thoughts. "According to the rumor, the captives are taken belowground. I didn't get exactly what they were alluding to—a cave or cellar, I'm not sure. But there, evil men—Nazarenes—perform evil rituals. Sacrifices. Satanic rituals."

Mason watched the equestrian center pass by out Sara's window. "I don't buy the satanic rituals, but stories like this usually have half-truths. Maybe they are in a cave or large basement. They couldn't name the Moroccan men being paid for these evil deeds?"

"I'm afraid not."

Mason thought of something, then looked over Sara's notes.

After flipping through a few pages, he found what he was looking for. "Turn the car around."

"Where are we going?"

"The last Moroccan girl was abducted just before Sabine disappeared."

Sara glanced at Mason. "The girl found dead in the desert?"

Mason nodded. "I want to check out the place where Sabine was found."

"What do you think you'll find?"

"I hope nothing, but Sabine's probably not the first victim to be dumped out there."

"Oh, my God."

Sara turned the car around and headed south.

21

M ason recognized a gnarled cork oak tree near a pile of boulders. "Pull over, just there," he said, and pointed to a spot fifty feet ahead.

They both climbed out of the car and walked slowly toward an area that had been disturbed by several vehicles.

"Is this where Sabine was found?" Sara asked in a quiet voice.

Mason nodded and pointed toward a thick clump of bushes and high, brown grass in the distance.

"What are we looking for?"

"Old tire tracks or footprints."

They came to the spot where Tazim had parked Rousselot's car two days earlier. There was a confused jumble of tire tracks: Rousselot's police sedan, Verger's car, the ME's, and the ambulance. Then, underneath, Mason could still see traces of the tire tracks left by the men who had dumped Sabine's body.

The scrubland winds had blown sand and dirt into the impressions. Two days had passed, and the impressions were already becoming obscure. Older tracks would probably be gone by now, and Mason began to wonder what he was thinking by coming back out here. The abductors' dumping ground might be in this

158

area, but it could extend for miles in every direction. It would take teams of men days to scour a space that large, and that was assuming the abductors used the same locale for the rest of their gruesome work.

Mason continued past the disturbed ground, taking careful steps. Sara followed him in the middle of the road, her arms crossed tightly across her chest. She kept scanning the bushes on either side, as if expecting—and dreading—to see a corpse of a murdered child.

"You can wait by the car," Mason said.

"I'm not going to stand there, all alone. This place makes my flesh creep."

The sun pressed down on Mason's shoulders, and the back of his neck was already burned. The winds blew hot air and biting particles of sand. He tried to ignore it as he continued for a half mile from the two-day-old tracks. He was about to call it quits when he spotted a set of tire tracks barely visible in the center of the road. They indicated a heavy vehicle with deep-treaded tires had pulled off to the side, crushing the dry shrubs in the process. Though faint, the tires had etched their pattern deep into the soft shoulder of the road.

Mason squatted to examine the pattern. He used his pencil to flick away some of the particles of dirt and sand that had been blown into the grooves. He made a sketch of the pattern in his notepad. He then followed the entire line of the tracks, looking for unique markings or flaws of both the front and rear tires. And there it was, a chip out of the rear tire tread.

"The tire tracks match the ones near where Sabine was found," Mason said.

"How do you know those tire tracks are the killers'?"

"I don't," Mason said, and stood, looking out to the expanse of scrubland. "Stay here."

Mason moved into the brush. He scanned the low shrubs and

dry grasses, but he was no Indian scout. The traces of broken branches and disturbed ground he encountered could have been made by wild animals, or the Berbers who passed through here on the way to the city. He took his time, working a straight line out from the road, going thirty feet, then shifting to his right, coming back, then shifting again. On the third pass in the zigzag pattern, he came across a barren area where the dirt had been heavily disturbed. The trail of disturbance led straight ahead, to a thick row of bushes that showed something or someone had passed through.

Mason followed the traces, some fifty feet farther, when he spotted an odd shape along the ground a few yards to his right. He worked his way through the shrubs, knowing what he would find.

His chest contracted at the tragedy of it. A corpse lay on its back. Nothing but blackened skin and bones, the poor girl's black hair swept out behind her head. He squatted near the remains. What the hyenas and scavenger birds had neglected was almost mummified from the dry, alkaline soil and baking sun. She had been there at least a few weeks. He felt around her neck, where little skin had remained, and like Sabine's, her hyoid bone was broken, snapped in two by the extreme force as she was strangled.

Mason put his hand on her head for a moment. "I'm sorry."

He didn't know what else to say. He stood and scanned the area. There were no distinct footprints or other evidence. The wind and animals had taken care of that. It was hard to tell if she was Moroccan, though it seemed likely, since Sabine was the first reported Western girl. Regardless, her murder was connected to Sabine's. The tire tracks and being dumped in the same area confirmed that.

Why had the abductors neglected to bury Sabine and this girl? Were they that confident or just reckless? Maybe whoever was tasked with getting rid of the bodies had started by burying earlier victims and become careless over time. There could be others, somewhere out there, waiting to be discovered.

This seemed to prove that the killer or killers had started out by abducting Moroccan children, then switched to Western girls. Had the abductor become tired of Moroccan victims or simply decided to change the ethnicity of his quarry? Or was it something more sinister and audacious: for the sport of preying on rich, wealthy victims?

Was it just one man paying laborers to do the dirty work, or a group of men united by the same perverted cause? He had no direct evidence, but the Western girls and the Moroccan children were also linked by locale: the equestrian center. Sabine, Valerie, and Cynthia were all members of the riding club, and the Moroccan children came from the shantytown less than a mile away.

Mason heard Sara suck in her breath and blurt out a sharp cry. He turned to see her standing there with horror in her eyes. She backed away and ran toward the road.

"WE HAVE TO GO TO THE POLICE!" SARA SAID AS SHE DROVE back to town.

"We wait. It's too late for the girl. A few more hours won't matter."

"You're using that poor girl as a pawn?"

"I want to deliver the news, face-to-face, and watch their reactions."

"That's callous and cruel."

"This business is callous. These crimes are cruel. And the three fathers are putting up a stone wall of silence, even after one of the daughters has been murdered and the next one's not far behind."

"You don't know that. You really think the fathers would withhold information if there were the slightest chance of getting their daughters back? Just because you're callous doesn't mean everyone else is."

"I've seen what fathers can do to their wives, their sons and daughters."

"I'll have no part of it. I'm scared, but I'm more disgusted at how you're using a dead girl to get information. I'm going to the police."

"No, you're not. You wanted me to help those parents, so let me do it my way. The police investigation has gone nowhere. There's no evidence, no witnesses, and all three fathers are hiding something. You should be disgusted with them, not me."

Sara was about to pull into the marina parking, but Mason said, "Not here. Stop by the gate. I need to borrow the car."

"Why? Where are you going?"

"To deliver the news personally to the first on my list."

"One of the fathers?"

"Yes, and the weakest link in this chain of silence."

THE DOOR OPENED, FLOODING THE CELL WITH LIGHT, STINGING Cynthia's eyes. Someone slid a metal tray through the gap in the door; then the door slammed shut and the padlock clacked in place. Cynthia's stomach cramped with the need for nourishment, and her mouth secreted saliva. Food. Finally something to eat.

Despite her nearly unbearable craving, Cynthia waited. She waited for her eyes to become accustomed to the dim light. It was important to see what they had brought her. A moment later, she crawled across the floor and looked into the bowl. Her stomach rejoiced, though her mind filled with dread.

Her only way to mark passing time was by the meals brought

in at long intervals—if they brought food at all. And most meals consisted of cabbage and potatoes or a tasteless gruel, and just enough to keep them from starving. After consuming those meals, she would feel a numbing stupor, but she was still vaguely aware of things. She was sure the drugs were concealed in the food or the rancid tea, and those meager meals contained only enough of the drugs to keep her and the other captives sedated.

But she knew that when a big meal came—like the meat stew and bread in front of her—and she devoured it in a desperate act to assuage her hunger, the drugs would be so potent that she would lose all awareness. She would remember nothing but indistinct images and a dreadful fear. Fear like a nightmare where some unseen beast hunts her, and no matter how far she runs, no matter where she hides, the beast keeps coming.

This time, though, she had a plan.

She had held off defecating for the most part of two days, even as her bowels protested. She fought off the burning urge to gobble down the food, as she held the plate over the bucket and dumped half the stew into it. She then hovered over the bucket and relieved herself. Using the spoon provided for the stew, she stirred the contents, holding her nose and grimacing at the disgusting task. She used some of the tea to rinse off the spoon, and then with both hands on the bowl, she downed the remaining stew.

She would be drugged, but perhaps not enough to make her into a zombie. She might see a means of escape, or witness her violations. As horrible as the prospect was, she needed to see who was doing this to her. She needed to know who would pay for their deeds, who would rot in prison, then rot in hell.

2 2

De Graaf had a stately mansion in the Marshan, just one street over from Meunier's. He had the requisite butler, team of servants, gardener, and chauffeur, but the house felt like a tomb when Mason entered. De Graaf had made his money in banking, and according to Carson, he had some vague familial connections to Dutch royalty. Whether his move to Tangier was to increase his wealth or to escape retribution for Nazi collaboration, Mason didn't know, but the latter would fit the men's club's fascist leanings.

The butler ushered him into a small sitting room, where de Graaf waited in a black suit with a black armband. This time, de Graaf tried to exude a regal air. He stood straight, shoulders back, though he used the fingertips of his right hand on the back of a chair for stability.

"I don't know why you've come, Mr. Collins," de Graaf said with an impatient air. "I've told you everything."

"That's not exactly true, is it, Mr. de Graaf?" Mason said, and paused to let that sink in. "I wanted to ask you about your membership in a conservative men's club. I know that Mr. Meunier and Sir Wilfred Brisbane are also members."

BONES OF THE INNOCENT

It took de Graaf a moment to process this. "Those ... those connections have nothing to do with Sabine's murder."

"I think they do. Why didn't you tell me about the men's club? And why did you say you had no connections to Meunier and Brisbane?"

"For the same reason: those facts are not relevant." De Graaf shook and sought greater support from the chair.

"You see, leaving out things like that just makes a guy like me suspicious. It makes me wonder, what else is the guy hiding? Like the abductions, for instance."

"I don't have to stand here and take your insults. You will leave at once."

"If that's what you want. It just makes me more convinced you're hiding something. Don't get me wrong. I'm not saying you're involved with the actual abductions, but there's definitely some connection between the fathers. One that's so damning that all of you are holding back information that might help bring the murderer or murderers to justice. Maybe save Valerie's and Cynthia's lives."

"If you don't get out of my house now, I *will* call the police." De Graaf made a move for the telephone.

"I found another corpse a few hours ago not far from where Sabine's body was abandoned."

That stopped de Graaf.

"A girl about her same age. She'd been there about three weeks before Sabine. The heat and sun mummified the remains. Still, I could tell she'd been a pretty Moroccan girl. Long black hair, delicate features. Strangled just like Sabine."

De Graaf covered his face and dropped into a chair. Mason suspected this behavior was as much from profound guilt as it was grief.

Mason said, "I think you wanted me to find this connection

when you sent me to the equestrian center. Out of guilt, I imagine."

"You're making me regret that decision. I was distraught and—"

"What are you hiding, Mr. de Graaf?" Mason asked, interrupting. "What is the connection between the fathers?"

De Graaf kept his head buried as if Mason—or something in his past—might go away.

"Mr. de Graaf! Tell me."

De Graaf needed a final push. Mason charged, grabbed de Graaf's chair, and leaned into him. "The men's club was for more than just political meetings, wasn't it? You didn't sit around someone's living room, smoking cigars and talking economics. You all were going to town on boys and girls, raping and sodomizing—"

"No! It couldn't be. It just couldn't."

Mason stood and waited. It took a few minutes of weeping before de Graaf was able to calm down. He finally lifted his head from shaking hands and stared at the fireplace.

"I'm only telling you this because my poor Sabine was murdered. The secret brotherhood I belonged to—belong to, I guess, because it's forbidden to leave—is an order adhering to the principles of Aryan identity and destiny. It's the Brotherhood of the Temple of Hercules—"

"A fascist cult."

De Graaf sneered through his tears. "Call it what you like. I will not bother trying to make you understand our beliefs." His anger dissipated and his melancholy returned. "One of the brotherhood tenets is our belief in sexual magic. Intercourse under the appropriate ceremonial procedures can imbue the seed-giver with the power to transcend."

"With children."

"It's not what you think. Virgins are preferable, but that just wasn't practical. We used prostitutes of a young age in our cere-monies to be as close as possible to virgins."

While he listened, Mason's thoughts bounced all over the place, from wondering if de Graaf had lost his reason, to the excitement of finally getting somewhere with the case. He'd heard stories of organizations like this, but he still found it hard to believe educated men actually did this sort of thing.

"You talk about this like it's in the past."

"It is. We stopped after ..." De Graaf paused, his eyes drifting to some unseen place.

"After what?"

"After one young Moroccan girl died." De Graaf looked away and wiped the perspiration from his upper lip with a shaking hand. He recovered a second later and turned back to Mason. "We did not kill her. She died of natural causes."

"You're not a doctor. How do you know it was from natural causes?"

"That's the only explanation. We had completed our ceremony—"

"How many men raped her?"

"It was not rape."

"How many?"

"Eight were involved in the sacred ritual. Afterward, she went into the room we had set aside for the participants to wash and dress. When she didn't come out, we went in there and found her dead. She had to have died of natural causes ..."

"Did you call the police?"

De Graaf shook his head. "You've got to believe me. We did nothing to harm this girl."

"Was she drugged?"

De Graaf nodded. "A mixture of morphine and scopolamine. But what does that have to do with it? She was a prostitute.

Maybe we gave her too much, or she was in bad health and the drug was too much of a shock to her system."

"And you disposed of the body?"

De Graaf squirmed in his chair as if a more comfortable position would ease the guilt. "Yes. In the same area where Sabine was found. But this was five months ago, and we put her in a deep grave. The girl you found wasn't her."

"Who were the eight members present for the ceremony?"

"There are only eight members in the brotherhood, but I took a blood oath never to reveal names. I am sworn to secrecy."

"Someone from your group killed Sabine. Someone killed that Moroccan girl the day of your ceremony and hasn't stopped. Give me the names so I can discover who killed Sabine and abducted the other girls."

"I assure you that none of them had anything to do with that girl's death."

"Was Meunier there? Brisbane? Who?"

"Your badgering is pointless. Sabine is dead!"

"How about Jennings?"

De Graaf looked at Mason. His eyes widened with realization and rage. "Do you suspect he is behind the murders? Did he kill my Sabine?"

"Right now, I have a city full of suspects, Mr. de Graaf."

"But you asked about him for a reason."

"I asked about Meunier and Brisbane, too. Now that I know Jennings is a member—"

"I never said he was."

"You didn't have to. You suspect him, so that means he was there and knows what happened. I'll be definitely looking at Jennings, but I don't have any proof or witness testimony."

"It must be him. He has a reputation as a philanderer. Some of the members of the political club despise him, and I suspect that's because he's seduced some of their wives and daughters. He's ruthless and cruel. No morals. I'm telling you, it's got to be Jennings."

"Let's get back to you—"

"You must see that I'm right."

"Mr. de Graaf, I'm trying to figure out why the abductor chose Sabine, Valerie Meunier, and Cynthia Brisbane. Why those girls? Why not any of the other pretty young girls with well-to-do parents? There are plenty to choose from. How many of the eight had teenaged daughters?"

"I wouldn't know for sure. Our mission is to preserve the old order, not gossip about our families."

"Did you threaten to reveal the brotherhood's secrets? Maybe out of guilt over the death of the girl?"

"Revealing its secrets would implicate me. I was not about to do that."

Mason wanted to give de Graaf a good backhanded blow across his jaw. The man was more concerned about exposing the brotherhood and his reputation than finding his daughter's killer. *And he's only revealing this now after his daughter is murdered and his wife lost her mind.*

"Where did the brotherhood meet?"

"We moved it to a different location each time: a house, a theater—one time we rented a hammam."

"Where was the last one?"

"A half-finished hotel on the east end of the beach. The Hotel Alcazar. But that was almost a month ago. Our meetings stopped when Sabine was abducted. Why are you wasting your time on this? You should be going after Jennings. He's guilty of Sabine's murder. I'm sure of it."

"Until I or the police have solid evidence, we can't go after him or anyone else."

De Graaf shot to his feet. "The police are incompetent, and you're harassing me on the remote chance that some unidentified member is the culprit."

Mason lost his patience with this self-serving fascist. "I'll harass any of you I want to get at the truth!"

"Get out of my house!"

"Give me the names, Mr. de Graaf."

"This is pointless. I don't care about your investigation. I've already lost my daughter, and I could very well lose my wife. Now get out!"

De Graaf picked up the phone and asked the operator to connect him with the police. Mason grabbed his hat and blew past the shocked butler. He didn't leave because of de Graaf's threat to call the police. He was afraid of what he might do to de Graaf if he stayed any longer. He got in his car and growled, jerking on the steering wheel until he *did* almost break it in two.

Mason took his time driving away from de Graaf's mansion. Meunier was next, but he wanted to plot out the best strategy to break Meunier. The man hid behind his religion and his staunch belief in his superior status and breeding.

Mason braked at a stop sign, but just as he was about to accelerate, a black Mercedes raced past, blowing through the intersection. Mason got only a glimpse of the driver, but it was long enough: de Graaf. This looked bad.

23

The Renault was no match against de Graaf's Mercedes, and Mason fell behind. He lost sight of the Mercedes, but there were only two ways to go at that point on the road: east toward the medina, or west to the New Mountain Road. Mason turned west.

Mason pushed the Renault to the limit. After several sharp curves, the road straightened out, and far ahead he caught a glimpse of de Graaf's Mercedes before it took another curve. He cursed de Graaf's stupidity. He knew where the man was going, and blamed himself for pushing him too hard.

After negotiating the final curve, with the Renault's tires screeching, Mason saw de Graaf's Mercedes a quarter mile ahead. It turned into the iron gates of Jennings's estate. The gate exploded inward, and de Graaf's car took a slice out of the security kiosk.

As Mason covered the quarter mile, de Graaf's Mercedes raced across the front lawn. It skidded to a halt at the base of the steps of the front portico.

Mason sped past the damaged gate. The security guard in the

kiosk had recovered enough to get off one shot. The bullet rico-cheted off the driver's door and shattered the side-view mirror.

De Graaf jumped out of his car and ran up the steps. Jennings's butler opened the door, and de Graaf fired two shots from his 9mm at the man. The bullets pierced the door next to the butler's head. He ducked, then fled for safety. De Graaf charged inside.

Mason locked his brakes, and the tires dug into the lawn, coming to a halt. He jumped out of the car and ran toward the front door. "De Graaf! Stop!"

Two security guards were running from opposite sides of the house. One fired a warning shot, but Mason ignored it and ran inside. He heard de Graaf screaming for Jennings. It came from the ballroom at the end of the hall.

Mason made it to the ballroom. De Graaf stood in the middle of the room aiming his pistol at Jennings, who ran for his life. De Graaf's hand shook when he fired. The shot missed, and Jennings dived behind a grand piano.

"De Graaf!" Mason said. "Put the gun down!"

De Graaf swung the pistol around and aimed it at Mason. "You try to stop me, and I'll kill you too."

Jennings started to make a move for the back door, but de Graaf fired, hitting the piano. Jennings threw himself onto the floor behind the piano bench.

De Graaf advanced. "This bastard killed my little girl," he said as he fired a bullet with each step. Just as he was close enough to have a clear shot at Jennings, he pulled the trigger once more. The gun clicked. Empty.

Two security guards burst through the patio doors and aimed their pistols at de Graaf. Mason yelled that the gun was empty, but the explosions of the security guards' guns drowned out his voice. The guards put five bullets in de Graaf before he fell to the floor.

Mason was about to charge forward, when he felt the barrel of a gun touch the back of his skull. The gunman said, "Don't move." Another guard patted him down and took his pistol.

Jennings walked up to Mason. He was smiling, but Mason could see he was rattled, and not a little embarrassed. "Did you put him up to this?" he asked.

"I tried to stop him. His gun was empty. Your guards gunned him down in cold blood."

"Lucky for me he's a lousy shot."

"I'd say that's a shame. I don't like fascists. De Graaf told me you're a member of a fascist cult that violated children with some twisted idea that raping them gave you power." Mason glanced at both his guards. "Did you hear that, boys? Your boss is a Nazi."

"That's absolute nonsense—" Jennings stopped when he heard his wife walking down the hallway.

Mrs. Jennings strolled in as if nothing out of the ordinary had happened. She did freeze when she saw de Graaf's body lying in a pool of blood. She averted her eyes and walked up to Jennings. "Another jealous husband of one of the wives you've seduced?"

"I'm fine, darling."

"You didn't answer my question."

"Just a case of mistaken identity. A delusional man."

Mason said, "He's one of the fathers of the abducted girls. The one found in the desert. He seemed to think your husband is somehow involved. Maybe even connected to the death of a young Moroccan girl during one of his fascist ceremonies."

"My husband is a philanderer, but hardly a murderer or a fascist. He's too much of a coward. So cowardly, he can't face his wife and admit the truth. And before you accuse my husband of such wicked things, you'd better have proof. Do you, Mr. Collins?"

"I haven't accused him of anything. Yet. But to answer your question, no."

"Then please leave my house."

"He was just leaving, my dear," Jennings said. "Why don't you go make arrangements with the maids to clean up the mess, once the ambulance takes the body away."

"It's your mess. You make the arrangements." With that, Mrs. Jennings turned and walked out of the room as nonchalantly as she'd entered.

Once his wife was out of earshot, Jennings said, "Our friend performed one good service. He brought you to me on a silver platter. No need to hunt you down." He said to one of the security guards, "You know what to do with him."

The security guards started to take Mason away at gunpoint, but the wail of police sirens stopped them.

"Whoops," Mason said. "It's going to look awkward dragging me out now."

Jennings walked up to Mason. "It doesn't matter. You're dead already. I made that phone call I was telling you about. The man was very appreciative. He assured me he would send enough shooters to make sure you don't get away this time. That is, if one of my men doesn't get you first."

"You're not the first person who said that to me and ended up talking out of the other side of his mouth."

"We'll see," Jennings said. He nodded to the security guards and walked out of the room. The guards released Mason, and the leader gave him his gun, minus the bullets.

Mason joined Jennings on the front porch. The police had just arrived in three squad cars—probably the required number for a disturbance at one of Tangier's wealthy residences. Mason was more troubled than surprised to see Captain Rousselot exit one of the vehicles. A captain rarely showed up at a shooting unless it was so high profile he was compelled to go. Mason wondered if Captain Rousselot was in Jennings's back pocket. He hated to see a good cop become corrupted, but unfortunately it wouldn't be the first time.

Rousselot did a double take when he saw Mason. He gave Mason a disapproving frown as he walked up to the porch. Verger ran up and called out orders to his junior partner, Rincon, and the uniformed officers.

Rousselot said to Jennings, "I assume there is no longer any danger."

"No, thank you, Captain. My security guards stopped the man before he could shoot me."

"More like the guards shot a man with an empty gun," Mason said.

Rousselot spun to Mason. "I'll take your statement after I talk to Monsieur Jennings. Please wait here." With that, he and Jennings walked inside.

Mason went through several cigarettes while he waited. He was anxious to get started again. Time was not on his side. De Graaf's revelations went a long way to explain why the fathers were so reluctant to reveal their connection. Then there was Jennings. He had nothing to pin on the man—aside from being an asshole and a fascist—but de Graaf's accusations definitely moved Jennings up the list. Regardless of the man's guilt, Jennings had made Mason a target, and Mason intended to return the favor. Somehow.

At the moment, he faced a more pressing problem: how much to tell Rousselot about de Graaf and the other brotherhood members' extracurricular activities. The captain seemed like a good cop, but Mason had been wrong before. The police investigation into the abductions had yielded little information and fewer results. Some of that could be because Verger was so green, but Mason felt sure someone on high was hampering the investigation. Someone on high, like the captain.

Rousselot finally emerged from the house and signaled Mason to follow him to a place under a tree and away from the squad of police. "I warned you about harassing that family. And now this."

"You want my side of the story, or have you and Jennings already cooked up a tidy one?"

"If you think I am taking bribes from Monsieur Jennings, you are seriously mistaken. I ought to arrest you for interfering with a police investigation, trespassing, and harassing a potential witness —a father so stricken with grief that he felt compelled to commit murder."

"But you need me out here, doing what your detectives seem unable to do."

"Your boasting does not suit you."

"I'm angry, Captain. I'm angry at a father so twisted that he would rather let his daughter suffer than reveal his dirty secrets. Secrets I believe Meunier and Brisbane share."

"What are you talking about?"

Mason told Rousselot about the daughters' connection through the riding club, and the fathers being members in an ultraconservative men's club. Mason handed him a copy of the list of members. That's as far as Mason was willing to take it.

"They kept this a secret from the police for a reason. Why, I don't know. Oh, and you'll notice Jennings is on that list."

"I suppose de Graaf didn't give you any other concrete evidence?"

"I don't think he had much more to give," Mason said, lying.

"And de Graaf, completely on his own, came to the conclusion that Monsieur Jennings is responsible?"

"I asked him about a bunch of names, including Jennings." Mason paused. "I also might have mentioned that Jennings is on my long list of suspects."

"Then you made a grave error divulging this notion to a man desperate for answers."

"I didn't give him the gun and the keys to his car. And how come your detectives never made this connection? Why didn't they ever look into the disappearances of close to two dozen

Moroccan children over the last year? I've got to wonder why the police brass decided to stifle that investigation. Is it because they don't care about Moroccans?"

"Your efforts to anger me or confound me will not work. We did look into the disappearances. But because there are so many missing Moroccan children or they're sold by their parents, the detectives dismissed them as too doubtful to pursue."

"The parents claim the Moroccan kids are being used for evil purposes and kept captive in a basement somewhere."

"And where is your proof?"

"All you have to do is talk to some of the Moroccan parents. Did anyone in the department do that?"

Rousselot softened his expression, as if he was pained by something. "The suppression of that investigation came from Commandant Lambert. He was probably told to do this by people of higher authority."

"Then you better look real hard at Lambert. If you don't, then I will."

Rousselot folded the list with such force that he crumpled it. "I would be happy to do more if you could provide proof." His face turned red with frustration as he jammed the paper in his front pocket.

Rousselot turned on his heels to go.

Despite his misgivings, Mason blurted out, "I have one piece of evidence. A Moroccan girl. You'll find her corpse not far from where Sabine de Graaf was discovered. Naked, strangled, and dumped, just like Sabine."

Rousselot spun around, his face twisted in anger. "When did you find this corpse?"

"A couple of hours ago."

"And you waited until now to tell me? *Putain!*" He whirled around and barked orders. A few of the police milling around jumped at his commands and got into one of the squad cars. He looked back at Mason as he marched over to the car. "You're coming with me."

Mason got in back with Rousselot. As the car reversed out of the driveway, Mason saw Jennings watching them from the porch. Jennings formed his hand into the shape of a pistol and aimed it at Mason.

24

Mason stood outside the command tent. Inside, Captain Rousselot consulted with his squad leader, the medical examiner, and a man mapping out the area of their search. In the distance, a phalanx of police with two search dogs had fanned out across the parched land and advanced in a single line.

Mason had already pointed out the corpse of the girl he had found, and within the first half hour the search party had found another corpse in a clump of bushes—this time a boy of no more than twelve. He'd been strangled, naked, and mummified like the latest girl.

Tazim was out on the search line, and he looked shaken by the recent discoveries. Earlier, when Mason had Tazim alone for a moment, he'd asked Tazim why he hadn't said anything about the reports of missing Moroccan children. He had felt the same as the rest of the department. That, sadly, many parents were too poor to feed all their children and sold them as servants, who then became no more than slaves. Countless impoverished Moroccan children disappeared without a trace. He felt ashamed for making that assumption, and now he was out on the line, searching for more victims' remains.

Rousselot must have pulled out everyone with a uniform, leaving headquarters almost empty. At least the massive effort assured Mason that the captain was willing to put his money where his mouth was. Maybe he could trust him after all. At least a little.

Rousselot stepped out of the open-sided tent and stood next to Mason. "I still haven't decided whether to arrest you for withholding evidence."

"You can add me not telling you more of what de Graaf said to me. He and seven others formed a pagan fascist organization, the Brotherhood of the Temple of Hercules. They held ceremonies using Moroccan child prostitutes. The kids were drugged, then raped, supposedly to give the men transcendent powers. About five months ago, a Moroccan girl died right after their ceremony, and they dumped her body out here."

"*Mon Dieu,*" Rousselot said.

"And before you ask me: no, de Graaf wouldn't give me any names. The way he reacted to my questions, though, leads me to believe that Meunier, Brisbane, *and* Jennings are part of this brotherhood. No, I don't have a speck of proof. And, yes, de Graaf could have been out of his mind."

"Perhaps one of the members decided to take the ceremonies further."

"That's what it looks like to me. De Graaf was convinced Jennings is our man, but he didn't offer a reason except that Jennings is a relentless skirt-chaser."

"Then there's still the question of why Sabine, Valerie, and Cynthia."

"I haven't figured that out yet. Not for sure, anyway."

"It could still be Moroccans seeking vengeance or scaring the Nazarenes into leaving Tangier. Or Moroccan pedophiles."

Mason opened his mouth to say something when he noticed Rousselot staring at the line of police. The line had stopped about six hundred yards from where they stood, because one of the dogs had become excited about something. That had happened a couple of times with no results. This time, however, the sergeant motioned for the men with shovels and pickaxes. That prompted Mason, Rousselot, and the medical examiner to begin the long walk. They took their time. None of them were in a hurry to see another corpse.

Only a few minutes passed before the sergeant waved his arms as a signal they had found something. Mason, Rousselot, and the medical examiner quickened their pace.

Everyone was silent while the excavation team went about the gruesome task. As they removed earth from the shallow hole, torsos, arms, or legs revealed more bodies. The work progressed quickly, as the hole had been dug up and covered over several times. When they were done, four corpses of children lay side by side. They were desiccated, but spared from the hot sun.

The medical examiner said, "The fools used quicklime on the bodies. They must have thought that it would make them decay faster. All it did was prevent insects and predators from getting to them."

The four bodies were intact enough to see that they were all young. One boy and three girls. The boy was white, and the girls looked to be Moroccan. Mason exchanged looks with Tazim, who had tears in his eyes.

Silent and grim, the team of police fanned out again and continued their macabre search.

DONNA NIVENS WAS HAVING A GOOD DAY. DESPITE THE STIFLING heat and buffeting crowds at the market, she smiled. She had convinced her fifteen-year-old son, Eric, to come out shopping with her. Normally, it was impossible to pry him away from his favorite radio shows, or a book from under his nose, but he'd finally conceded after she told him he needed fashionable clothes to impress his new girlfriend. He even seemed to be enjoying himself, as he'd agreed to accompany her to the Grand Socco to get some fruit and a bouquet of flowers. Donna had bought her son a beer at the *cervecería*, and she'd had a cup of tea. She'd only taken a sip of the wretched stuff. She should have known not to order tea at a Spanish pub.

This was their last stop before heading home. She picked out just a few flowers, as she felt a headache coming on, along with a queasy stomach. *Never order tea at that place again,* she told herself. She paid the man, tucked the bouquet under her arm, along with the shopping bags full of clothes, and turned to look for Eric.

Eric was gone. She had left him two booths down, at a leather craftsman's booth selling belts, bags, and hats. He had grown quiet and unresponsive, but what teenage boy didn't have wild mood swings? "I'll be a minute," she had said, and asked him to stay put. Otherwise finding him in this crowd would be impossible. But now, of course, he had wandered off.

Donna negotiated the crowd of shoppers and returned to the leather craftsman's booth. She asked the craftsman if he had seen which direction Eric had gone, but the leather craftsman just shrugged. Her insisting he could do better just elicited a scowl from the man.

With an exasperated sigh, she pushed her way through the shoppers. Frustration, then a growing sense of uneasiness, gnawed at her stomach. Eric could be stubborn and sullen, but he had a protective streak when it came to his mother and would never just walk off in a place with so many foreigners and unsavory characters. She called out his name, while trying to catch a glimpse of his red hair through shoulders. Her gentle pushing turned to shoving. She felt short of breath, and suddenly the heat of the afternoon threatened to cause her to faint. She found it hard to concentrate, making her panic grow.

She yelled his name this time. Heads turned; people stared at her. She broke through the crowd to the street circling the plaza. People asked if she was all right, but she didn't hear them. She surveyed the area in ever-growing panic. She cursed the endless stream of cars, trucks, and donkey carts.

Then, through a gap in the traffic, she saw him. His back was to her, but she could tell immediately it was her son. Panic turned to hysteria when she saw two Moroccan men in hooded djellabas on either side of Eric, holding his arms. Eric looked docile, almost like he was sleepwalking, as the men pulled him toward the Catherine Gate and the twisted streets of the medina.

Donna screamed his name and tried to run across the busy street. A speeding taxi honked its horn and flew past. A slow-moving bus blocked her path. She slapped at the bus and scurried around it. Cars screeched to a halt. Horns blared at her.

She made it to the other side and ran through the gate. "Somebody, help me, please! They have my son. Help!"

A crowd gathered. A few people rushed to her aid, but Donna ran on. She ran, but Eric and the men were gone. She stopped, gasping for air between tears, only to scream out again. People gathered around her, asking her questions. Their mouths moved, but Donna heard no voices. Words had no meaning.

She burst into a run again, calling his name. But she knew it was hopeless. Evil men had taken her son. There was nothing to do but run.

Run, until she collapsed or her heart burst.

25

Mason and Rousselot rode in silence on the way back to town. Mason imagined that the captain wrestled with his thoughts; that he had done nothing to counter the commandant's dismissal of the Moroccan claims, and he had just witnessed the grim results of his inaction. They had remained at the site another hour, but the intensive search had yielded no other graves.

Rousselot pulled out the copy of the list Mason had given him of the fascist organization and looked it over.

"Pretty sickening, isn't it?" Mason said. "To think so many died to defeat fascism, and here are a bunch of guys embracing the same cause."

"You did not think that defeating the Nazis ended fascism, did you? Unfortunately, there are many such groups in France, England, and Italy. A number of the more radical groups include mysticism and the occult in their belief systems. When I was a detective in Paris, I encountered one such group. They worshipped the Norse gods and believed the Aryan race came from the lost city of Atlantis."

Rousselot folded up the paper and pocketed it. "We'll bring in these members for questioning."

"I'd like to be there when you do."

"Only as an observer."

The small caravan of police cars pulled into the headquarters parking lot, and they got out of the car. Mason wanted to press Rousselot about being in on the interviews, but the desk sergeant called out to the captain, running across the parking lot. Rousselot looked tired. He waited for the desk sergeant while he brushed dirt from his uniform. The desk sergeant rattled off something in French.

Rousselot looked at Mason with alarm. "There's been another abduction in the Grand Socco. A white male, this time. An Eric Nivens. Fifteen."

They all hurried for the entrance. A small group of reporters fired questions at them about the bodies and the Nivens boy's abduction. Rousselot ordered several policemen to keep them at bay.

"Was the mother with him?" Mason asked.

The desk sergeant said in English, "Yes. She saw two Moroccan men take him into the medina."

Mason and Rousselot exchanged looks of surprise. "Was she able to get a look at the two men?" the captain asked in English for Mason's benefit.

"No, sir. She only saw her son for a brief moment before they disappeared into the medina. She ran after them, but they had vanished."

"Does Mrs. Nivens show any signs of being drugged?" Mason asked.

"She is complaining of a headache and nausea, but that could be from the shock." The desk sergeant continued as they entered the building, "There are many witnesses. They all said the men looked Moroccan, but they were wearing djellabas with hoods. Some were able to see portions of their faces. One tall. Both thin with dark skin. One had a mustache, and one was clean-shaven.

One had a pointed chin. That's all the description we have. There are four two-man teams still out there searching. It was all we could spare."

"Do you have any idea where the abductors went in the medina?" Mason asked.

"They turned off Rue des Siaghins, heading northwest. From the witnesses, we were able to track their movements until they seemed to vanish near the Marine Gate."

At the bottom of the stairs, the desk sergeant said, "Inspecteur Verger has Madame Nivens in the second-floor interview room."

Rousselot thanked the sergeant and told him to get every arriving policeman out on the search. He then turned to Mason. "You know you can't go up there with me."

Mason nodded. "Just make sure Verger finds out where they ate or drank, and if he or she got a henna tattoo."

"Verger will be thorough in his questioning."

"You realize this doesn't fit the pattern. The mother doesn't seem to be drugged, but the son is. A bunch of witnesses, when no one saw a thing during the other abductions."

"Perhaps they are getting ... how do you say ... sloppy?"

Mason shook his head. "There's something not right about this one."

"Are you, perhaps, disappointed that it may turn out to be Moroccans after all?"

"Do me a favor, Captain, and don't let everyone jump to conclusions just because they want this case solved."

"And don't try to dictate police matters to me."

"Just one cop to another, I've seen it before: the pressure is so strong that everyone looks for easy answers."

"Ex-cop in your case, Mr. Collins." Rousselot's expression softened, as if he regretted what he'd just said. He pulled out a notepad and wrote something in it. He tore off the paper and handed it to Mason. "My home telephone. If you do discover anything relevant to the case, please call me on this number. Regardless, I ask you to remain in Tangier. I may still feel obliged to put you in jail."

~

THE BUSTLE IN THE GRAND SOCCO HAD SCARCELY SKIPPED A beat. There were fewer Nazarenes now that the word was out about two dangerous Moroccans kidnapping white teens. A two-man police patrol passed among the vendors, asking questions. Mason figured the police had already gotten as much information from the vendors as the latter were willing to give. Mason's plan was to question the waitstaff at the *cervecería* where Mrs. Nevins and the boy had ordered drinks. That was until he noticed the empty spot where the henna artists, Jamila and Fatima, usually offered their tattoos.

Mason approached a potter who had been there the day Melville and he had talked to the henna artists. "Have you seen the henna ladies who are usually here?"

The potter shook his head that he didn't understand. Mason then stepped over to a woman weaving baskets and asked the same question.

The woman said, "No, sir. They are no here today. The family no see them. They are very worried."

"I'd like to talk to the family."

The woman shook her head. "The family live in the medina. I do not know where."

"Do you know anyone who might know where they live?"

The woman gave a quick shake of her head and went back to her weaving.

Mason thanked her and asked several other vendors, who offered the same response. A few of them eyed him with suspicion and refused to answer, except to imply that after Melville and he had interviewed the two women, they had disappeared. He wasn't going to get anywhere like this. He decided to try the bars and restaurants on the outer ring of the plaza. As he crossed the plaza, he noticed Melville sitting at one of the outside tables. Melville gave him a hearty smile and raised his cane in a salute.

Mason walked over to him. "Don't you ever go home?"

"If there was someone to greet me, I would. Perhaps."

"Sorry, I'm spoken for," Mason said, and sat.

"Ah, yes, the young Lebanese woman you met at Dean's Bar."

Mason was surprised that Melville would know this, since he and Sara had been together for less than twenty-four hours. "You should think about joining British intelligence."

"Then I'd have to put in an honest day's work."

"I don't think that particular young lady is in the picture anymore."

"That's a pity. She's quite attractive."

"No one in your life?"

Melville kept his smile, though the rest of his face said something else. "I don't want to bore you with the details. However, I'm a widower. For some time now. My wife died of tuberculosis in 1922, and my daughter left home when she was fifteen. With a man, I suppose. I haven't seen her since."

"I'm very sorry, James."

"Don't be," Melville said, and lifted his glass. "Life goes on." He took a long swig of his whiskey.

Mason thought it best to change the subject. "You heard about the boy's abduction this afternoon?"

"I was here, though too far from the action to see anything."

"The witnesses say it was two Moroccans in djellabas. Those two might have pulled off a clumsy kidnapping of one boy, but I don't believe that they did any of the other abductions."

"I see," Melville said with a smirk. "Your preconceived notions may not allow you to see the truth."

"Yeah, I happened to say the same thing to a certain police captain."

"I heard about the discovery of bodies near where Sabine de Graaf was found. A terrible tragedy." He held up his whiskey glass. "Can I buy you a drink?"

"No, thanks. I'm going with my preconceived notions and do a little canvassing of the medina. I'm stubborn that way."

"Then allow me to accompany you. You'll need a translator, and I know the haunts of the medina better than you."

"Sure, I could use the help. German doesn't help me in this neck of the woods."

Melville downed his drink, put on his panama hat, collected his cane, and struggled to his feet. He wobbled a little. "Perhaps I've stayed too long."

"Witnesses last saw the men leading the boy past the Marine Gate. Are you able to make it that far without falling down?"

Melville pointed rather badly with his cane. "Lead on."

They entered the medina on Rue Siaghins, turning right almost immediately, then taking a circuitous route parallel to the outer medina wall. Mason managed to come across two locals who verified that they were on the right track. Their route took them north, passing the U.S. legation. They finally came to the Marine Gate, one of the seven gates in the medina's outer walls. The gate led to the marina, hence the name. Tourists from the ferries and occasional cruise vessel, or sailors on shore leave, passed through the gate at regular intervals.

Mason said, "If these guys were trying to get away with minimal witnesses, this gate is a bad choice."

"That's assuming they intended to use this gate, or leave the medina at all."

Mason nodded. "This is the last spot they were seen, which

means they either kept going or are holed up in one of these buildings." He looked around at the tangle of streets and tightly packed buildings. "If I were with this police force, I'd organize a house-to-house search. You know the medina better than I do. Put yourself in their shoes. Where would you go if you wanted to slip away?"

Melville rubbed his hands together. "I've always wanted to do this, be like a detective in one of those novels." He thought a moment. "Assuming these men had a whit of intelligence, and they wanted to get out of the medina, I would take the streets skirting the northern wall until reaching the Kasbah. It's much quieter there. Outside the main gate of the Kasbah, the Marshan Gate, there's an area for cars."

Mason motioned toward the street heading north along the wall. "After you."

26

M elville's devil-may-care attitude had returned, and he smiled as he strode with big sweeps of his cane. He was right that this area of the medina was much quieter. They encountered mostly children playing in the narrow streets, feral cats, an old man struggling under a formless bundle. Melville switched comfortably between French and Spanish when they questioned the few residents out in the streets. A boy and an old woman had noticed the two Moroccans with the Nazarene boy, and both pointed in the direction of the Kasbah. The descriptions of the men and the boy matched those given to the police, and both confirmed that the boy had a strange, blank stare.

While Melville enjoyed his role of police inspector, Mason kept a vigilant watch. He estimated he had another day before the arrival of the professional assassins. And that wasn't counting the current danger of Jennings's men or hired guns. Every blind curve or dark corner could conceal a possible killer.

Mason and Melville eventually made it to the smallest of the inner gates in the Kasbah fortifications. On either side of the opening, there were two policemen questioning a pair of teenage

Moroccan boys. When Mason got close, he saw that Tazim was one of them.

Tazim saw Mason and Melville approach and stepped away to meet them. He looked sullen, without his characteristic smile.

Mason said, "Have you traced the abductors to the Kasbah?"

"No, we were posted here to watch and question. And what are you two gentlemen doing here?"

"Just taking an evening stroll," Melville said.

Tazim ignored Melville. He said to Mason, "Capitaine Rousselot is very angry at you for withholding information about the murdered Moroccan girl. I am not to talk to you." He managed a slight smile. "But, as you can see, the captain is not here. I am guessing that you suspect the abductors are in the Kasbah. I would like to help."

"And disobey another of Captain Rousselot's orders by leaving your post?"

"I can say that I am following a possible lead."

Mason turned to Melville. "We could use another pair of eyes. And one who speaks Arabic."

Melville looked displeased being relegated to third place. "If you think it necessary."

Tazim spoke to his partner, another Moroccan policeman, and then the three passed through the gate and entered a large rectangular plaza of the Kasbah. On their right, another gate led out to the cliffs overlooking the sea and a number of houses or other buildings built outside the towering walls. To the left was the old sultan's palace, its gardens, and the Kasbah mosque.

Tazim said, "It does not seem logical that the two men would take the boy through here. Straight ahead is the old jail, which was once the sultan's dungeon. We still use this jail for certain prisoners, so there are a few policemen here at all times."

"But beyond the palace, the streets are very quiet," Melville said.

"Perhaps they went out that right-hand gate, the Bab Bhar," Tazim said.

"The cliffs and houses make it difficult going," countered Melville, "especially with the burden of a drugged boy."

"The Marshan Gate, then," Tazim said. "Cars can be parked very near the gate for a rapid escape."

"That's what we were thinking," Mason said.

Melville pointed with his cane to two opposite streets. "There are only two streets leading to the other half of the Kasbah, one by the south wall and one by the north. I propose we take the street along the south wall, as it's quieter. There's a street, Rue Touila, which joins the north and south streets in the middle. Once there, we can decide how to divide up our search of the western half of the Kasbah."

Mason agreed, and they began to skirt the southern wall. The old sultan's palace created a long, solid wall on their right. The Kasbah was roughly rectangular, with the west end sprouting two stunted wings. And it was the western end where a labyrinth of narrow streets served densely packed residential buildings. The area was quiet except for a radio and scattered conversations coming from inside the houses.

Mason tensed when he saw two Moroccan men in djellabas walking toward them. A single streetlight shone behind them, putting them in silhouette. Slowly, Mason put his hand in his pocket and readied his pistol.

As they came closer, Mason saw one was bald and wore a gray beard. The other looked to be in his fifties, with a broad black mustache. They both greeted Mason and Tazim in Arabic. Mason removed his hand from his pocket and told Tazim to ask them if they'd seen the two Moroccan abductors.

A few minutes of conversation later, the two men gave Mason a slight bow and walked away. Tazim said, "The old man is an imam of the Kasbah mosque. The other man is the assistant to the Mendoub. They saw nothing, but talked to some residents who were concerned about the stories of two Moroccans taking a Nazarene boy. The residents fear what the Nazarenes will do if it is true. This could make things very tense."

Mason nodded. "I have a feeling that's exactly what some Nazarenes want."

They continued to walk toward the meeting place.

"I, too, wonder if this is not a ruse," Tazim said. "A *ruse de guerre*."

"The problem is proving it," Melville said.

"Unless we find the real abductors."

They turned on Rue Touila. The buildings on the narrow street hemmed them in. A few moments later, they stopped at the halfway point defined by a perpendicular street that formed a small square. Halfway to the intersection, a Moroccan man came running up to them. He spoke to Tazim in Arabic.

Tazim spun to Mason. "This man says that he heard noises like fighting and a boy scream out once, then nothing."

The Moroccan man said something else and motioned for them to follow him. At a fast pace, they all went up to a door that stood partially open to a dark interior. The man pointed at the door, and he said something else to Tazim.

Melville tried to peer into the dark interior. "I believe I'd rather remain where I am."

Mason saw the fright in Melville's face. "Are you going to be all right out here?"

Melville nodded, and Mason and Tazim entered the pitch-black room. There was an odor of burned matches in the still air. Mason fished out his lighter and lit it. He found a wall light switch, and tried it with the sleeve of his jacket, but the electrical service seemed to be disconnected. There was a candelabrum on a table near the door. Being careful not to touch the holder, he removed one of the candles and lit it. With the candle held high, he and Tazim moved deeper into the room.

The boy's bare feet became visible at the far end. As they got closer, the candlelight fell onto the boy's body. He was naked, lying on his back, his legs akimbo. Mason knelt by the boy, whose blue eyes were now glazed with death. Mason checked for a pulse anyway.

"No pulse. His skin is warm. Maybe an hour ago." He pointed to the boy's neck. "See those impression marks? Looks like manual strangulation. Those abrasions are probably fingernail marks—the boy's while he tried to break the assailant's grasp. The murderer killed the boy face-to-face."

Behind him, Tazim uttered a short prayer.

Mason looked at Tazim. "You'd better go report this, right away."

"The poor boy," Tazim said as he continued to stare at the body.

"Tazim, go."

"Oh, this is going to be very bad." And with that, he left.

Mason met Melville outside and noticed he was alone. "Where's the man who heard the commotion?"

"It was all very strange. He waited a few moments, then just ran off without a by-your-leave."

Mason looked in the direction Melville had indicated. The whole thing felt odd. The man heard noises of a scuffle that had occurred at least an hour ago. Then he happened upon Mason and his companions after doing or saying nothing for an hour.

"Stay here," Mason said, and went back inside.

He searched the living room as best he could by candlelight. Most of the furniture had been covered, and the only sign of a struggle was near where the boy lay—the sofa covering had been partially pulled off and was draped across the boy's left arm. Even the dust on the bookshelves remained undisturbed.

The police out on patrols began to arrive in twos and threes. Mason briefed them and stepped outside to wait with Melville. Verger and his partner showed up fifteen minutes later. Verger glared at Mason, then said something in French to two of the uniformed cops. He went inside, and the two cops moved over to stand on either side of Mason and Melville.

"It appears we're under guard," Melville said.

"I'd do the same."

"You don't suppose we're now suspects?"

Verger emerged from the apartment and came up to them. "How did you find the body?" he asked in English.

"I knew you could speak English," Mason said.

"Answer the question."

"A Moroccan came up to us, saying he'd heard noises of a struggle coming from that apartment," Melville said.

Verger eyed Melville like he didn't buy it any more than Mason. "And what were you two doing in the Kasbah?"

"We were out enjoying the night air," Mason said.

"With one of our police officers?"

"Is that against the law?" Melville asked.

"It is against the law to violate a crime scene."

"Then how would Mr. Collins ever have discovered the boy?" Melville said.

"You alert the police about a reported disturbance," Verger said, and turned to Mason. "I wonder, as a former policeman, how you would have reacted to such interference, Monsieur Collins."

"I would have lectured them about why that's not a good thing to do, then thanked them for their assistance."

"Then thank you for your assistance, but I demand that you not interfere with police matters again. The next time, I will have you arrested. And for your information, Capitaine Rousselot no longer has any involvement with this case. Commandant Lambert has decided to personally supervise this investigation."

"The commandant who killed the investigation into the Moroccan children's disappearances?"

"We will find those two men. It is only a matter of time. Whatever purpose you served as a private investigator is now at an end. You may both leave, but please be available if we have more questions. Good night, gentlemen." With that, Verger went back inside.

"I require several drinks after this episode," Melville said.

"Not for me. Not tonight."

"Don't brood about this, Mason. This may well be the break in the case you've been hoping for, but you're too stubborn to see it."

"I like brooding. Nothing gets my investigative juices flowing like a good brood. Good night, Mr. Melville."

S ara sat on the sofa with a sketch pad, drawing the craggy face of a Moroccan man in charcoal. She didn't look up when Mason entered. Mason poured two fingers of whiskey and dropped into an armchair with a tired sigh.

"Busy day?" Sara said.

"Something like that."

"I heard about the horrible discovery today. I will never forgive the police for not doing more."

Mason took a long swig. "Even if they had, I don't think they would have solved anything."

Sara had yet to look at him. She sketched with an intensity in her eyes that Mason figured was only part artistic concentration. She looked unnerved by everything that had happened, and more than likely scared. With the assassins due at any time, and Jennings feeling cornered, things were bound to take a hazardous turn.

"I also heard about the boy," Sara said.

"Bad news travels fast."

"You don't think for a minute that two Moroccan men are responsible for all the abductions."

"Not for a minute," Mason said, and took a sip of the whiskey.

"If they catch those two, they deserve what they get for murdering an innocent boy, but they'll be paraded around like trophies for the Nazarenes to feel better about the white race."

"There's no proof the two Moroccans killed the boy."

Sara looked up from her sketch pad. "You think someone else strangled him?"

"I think those two goons were paid to abduct the boy, and they were too stupid or greedy to consider the consequences."

"Then the police will find them murdered somewhere like the boy, like the children."

Mason shook his head. "The real bad guy needs *live* scapegoats. Otherwise, there'll be too many unanswered questions. It'll be all tied up in a neat package: The two Moroccans will have no idea who really hired them—probably another Moroccan. And everyone's going to jump to the conclusion it was Moroccans all the time."

"Are you getting any closer to identifying the real killer?"

Mason told her about his interview with de Graaf, his membership in the fascist organization, and the sexual rites with child prostitutes. He told her about the child prostitute who died after one of the organization's rape sessions. "Everything points to one of the fanatical members going off the deep end, but nobody's talking. De Graaf refused to give me any names." He then told her about de Graaf's suicidal visit to Jennings.

"Do you think Jennings is at the center of it? That he's the evil Nazarene paying Moroccans to do terrible things, like the Berber parents said?"

"If he is, he's done a hell of a job covering his tracks."

Mason downed his drink, rubbed his eyes, and dropped his head onto the back of the chair. Sara came over and sat on the arm of the chair.

"Why don't you go lie down? I'll join you."

"Tempting, but I've got to think this thing through."

"You're not thinking at all. What do you hope to accomplish in the next few hours? You ought to try acting like a human being instead of a machine for a change."

Sara grabbed his hand and pulled him to his feet. She led him to the bedroom, and Mason let her begin to strip him and caress him until the tragedies, the haunting visions, the pain, began to fade.

He was almost in a frenzy as he tore away her clothes and pushed her onto the bed. Sara had to calm him several times to keep him from climaxing too soon, and her soft touch and warm voice finally soothed him. They found a rhythm and climaxed together.

After they had broken their embrace, Mason lay for a long time in the dark. Despite his exhaustion, he had a difficult time falling asleep. When sleep finally came, he dreamed of the corpse of the Moroccan girl lying on the unforgiving earth and him kneeling next to her. The girl's empty eye sockets suddenly had eyes. They stared at him with a look of fright, and they pleaded for him to help her, but all he could do was stand and back away, muttering a pathetic apology.

MASON WOKE UP THE NEXT MORNING TO THE SMELL OF COFFEE. He opened his eyes and saw Sara sitting in a chair next to the bed, drawing something on her sketch pad.

"Ah, you moved," Sara said. "I was almost finished." She laid the pad on her lap. "I've never sketched someone while they're having a bad dream."

She turned the pad so Mason could see her work. It showed Mason's three-day beard and sunburned face, sunken eyes with his lids clamped shut, and his jaw muscles bulging from clenching his teeth. All in all, looking like a man ten years older than his age.

"I look like a bum, who's just stepped on a hot coal and likes it too much."

"You look like that when you orgasm."

"Thanks. Nice image. You want me to show you what you look like?" Mason started to exaggerate his face, but Sara kicked him with her bare foot and ran out of the room.

Mason put on a button-down shirt and boxer shorts and went into the living room. Sara sat on the sofa and worked to finish her sketch.

"There's coffee in the kitchen," she said.

Mason poured a cup and returned to the living room. He leaned over Sara and kissed her. She kissed him back and Mason lingered there for a moment before straightening and heading for the bedroom.

"I know you can't stay in one place for too long," Sara said.

Mason stopped and turned to her. She continued to concentrate on her sketch, though the intention behind the question seemed clear. He tried to summon an explanation or apology, but instead said, "Not in Tangier, anyway."

Sara glanced at him, gave him a nod, and then went back to her sketch. Mason went into the bedroom, where he had begun to tape to the wall all the case notes, article clippings, and photographs he'd gotten from Tazim or acquired on his own.

Someone knocked on the front door. Mason stopped what he was doing and stepped quietly into the living room. Sara and he exchanged glances. A second knock came, harder this time.

"You'd better answer that before they kick in the door," Sara said.

Mason went to the credenza, where he'd left his pistol. He

checked the chamber, held the gun at his thigh, and went to the door.

Tazim was standing on the other side, wearing a suit and tie instead of his uniform. "I'm sorry to disturb you."

Before Mason let Tazim in, he looked back to Sara and watched her zip into the bedroom. This was more for Tazim's sensibilities than Sara's modesty.

Tazim caught a glimpse of her and swallowed hard. "Sorry."

Mason let Tazim enter, then glanced out on the street before closing the door.

"How did you know where to find me?"

"I heard from a friend of mine that you were at the big party the other night and left with that ..." Tazim swallowed hard again. "That woman. I only had to make a few inquiries about her possible location. This is not the first place that I tried."

"Are you sure no one followed you?"

Tazim nodded. "I am sure."

When Tazim spied Mason's pistol, Mason said, "Jennings's associates will have assassins in Tangier by now." Mason then noticed Tazim's attire. "Wait a minute, why are you out of uniform? You on the late shift?"

Tazim glanced at the floor. "I am suspended. Commandant Lambert and Inspecteur Verger are unhappy that I left my post to help you and Mr. Melville."

"Bastards."

Sara came out of the bedroom fully dressed. Mason introduced them and said Sara was a friend. Tazim seemed embarrassed to even look at her.

"Sara's the one who told me about the missing Moroccan children."

This further embarrassed Tazim, who suddenly took interest in the floor tiles.

"What's up? You didn't pound on the door just to tell me you were suspended."

"Oh, yes. The police have captured the two Moroccans."

"Alive?" Sara said.

When Tazim nodded, Mason said, "That's faster than I expected."

"An anonymous caller telephoned this morning and told them where the two men were hiding. They are in custody at police headquarters."

"An anonymous tip? How convenient. All wrapped up, nice and neat."

"Part of the ruse?" Tazim said.

"No doubt about it."

"I think other Tanjawis believe as we do, because a large crowd has gathered outside police headquarters to protest. The commandant is scheduled to meet the press outside headquarters to announce their successful arrests."

"Do you think that was part of the plan?" Sara asked Mason.

Mason shook his head. "I don't know. But this is something I've got to see."

"Is it not too dangerous?" Tazim said. "Why risk being in a big crowd without good reason?"

"I want to see who's there on the sidelines—besides a bunch of angry Tanjawis—admiring their handiwork. And who's not."

M ason had Sara pull the car into a space on the street three buildings before police headquarters. He had dispensed with the djellaba disguise, opting for sunglasses and a wide-brimmed panama hat. He, Sara, and Tazim sat in the car and watched the group of fifty-plus Moroccans in a horseshoe-shaped line across the street in front of police headquarters. Four policemen kept the line from advancing any farther, while one Moroccan man led the group in chants in Arabic.

"Let me guess. They want justice and the white men aren't giving it to them," Mason said. When Sara nodded, he asked, "Who's their cheerleader?"

"He's the leader of the local Istiqlal Party. They are the party most vocal about independence. Some of the party members in French Morocco are suspected of bombings and violent acts. They've been tolerated in Tangier, for now, as the group has avoided making trouble here."

"Until now," Mason said, and pointed to a man taking notes and his partner photographing the crowd and the leader. "French intelligence, I'm betting."

Parked cars packed the headquarters lot, probably attending

dignitaries for the press conference. Standing out from the rest, Mason spotted a chauffeur rubbing the hood of a blue-and-black Rolls-Royce Phantom III limousine to a spotless shine.

Mason pointed it out. "Meunier's limo."

"He's here for the press conference, I expect," Sara said.

"That or he wants a closer look at who he thinks are his daughter's abductors."

Mason scanned the protesters' faces. Among them, he saw two of the Moroccan punks who had confronted him in the shantytown. They were shouting the loudest and pumping their fists in the air. Then, toward the back of the crowd, he spotted a group of older men and women, and one man in particular.

"Rachid," Mason said. "There, in the back, with the other parents."

As they watched, more Moroccans arrived, some carrying placards. A group of reporters waited for Commandant Lambert to come out to make his announcement. In the meantime, they took notes or photos of the demonstration. Then there were the Westerners gathered at the edges of the spectacle; some seemed curious, while others looked horrified or yelled back at the crowd.

Then, Mason spotted a black Renault sedan parked just beyond the Western gawkers and on the other side of the demonstrators and police headquarters. It faced Sara's car. Through the reflection on the windshield, Mason could just make out the silhouette of a broad-shouldered man sitting in the driver's seat. His arms were raised, and he held something to his eyes.

Mason pulled down the brim of his hat to cover his face, and he slid lower in the seat. "There's a guy in a black Renault, opposite us, with a pair of binoculars."

"Is he looking for you?" Sara asked.

"That's the only reason I can think of to use binoculars so close to the crowd," Mason said, and scanned the area again. Among the gawking Westerners near the police headquarters parking lot, he saw one of the assassins who had stalked him in Marseille. "Yeah. Definitely looking for me."

Mason then spied a man on a hotel roof, two buildings down on the other side of police headquarters. He, too, watched the crowd below with a pair of binoculars.

"We should leave," Tazim said, following Mason's gaze.

"No, not yet."

Sara tied a scarf to cover her head and opened the car door.

"Sara, what are you doing?" Mason said.

"I want to talk to the parents."

"It's too dangerous. Jennings could have given them your description."

"I'll be fine." And with that, Sara got out of the car and walked toward the crowd.

Mason kept his eyes on the assassin from Marseille. Sara started to chant and pumped her fist as she wove her way through the crowd. She met up with the parents and said something into Rachid's ear. At the same moment, a team of uniformed policemen came out of police headquarters, followed by Commandant Lambert. The commandant stepped up to a podium and microphone. The reporters forgot the protesters and rushed to the podium. The crowd burst into louder chants, spurred on by the emergence of the commandant. Lambert began his speech, but the chanting grew so loud that he stopped. He glared at the crowd before walking back to the entrance. The reporters followed. It seemed the announcement would be conducted inside. That inflamed the crowd even more.

Sara and a small group of the parents broke away from the crowd that now pressed into the four hapless cops trying to hold them back.

To Mason's alarm, the group was heading straight for the car. "This isn't good," Mason murmured.

"We should leave," Tazim said. "Now!"

"Not without Sara."

The group gathered around Mason's side of the car.

Mason rolled down the window. "Sara, why don't you bring the reporters over here while you're at it—"

Rachid thrust his hand into the car with a mixture of somberness and gratitude.

"Rachid wants to thank you for all you've done," Sara said.

Mason took the man's hand, and Rachid shook it vigorously. He said a few words in Arabic as tears rolled down his cheeks.

"You're welcome," Mason said, then looked at Sara. "Tell him I only found some bodies, not the killers."

"He realizes that. But you brought the issue to attention and forced the police to search for the men responsible."

Rachid said something else, emphasizing each word with a jerk of Mason's hand. Sara translated, but Mason knew the gist of what he was saying. He concentrated on the three assassins. His heart jumped into high gear when he saw the assassin standing among the Western gawkers looking their way.

"Shit." Mason slid farther down in his seat.

At that same moment Tazim opened his door and got out. He began to talk to the parents like long-lost friends. Rachid finally let go of Mason's hand and turned to Tazim.

The parents looked bewildered by Tazim's enthusiastic talking, but Mason knew what Tazim was doing. Very clever. Now that Tazim and Sara were by the car, it looked like a Tanjawi homecoming. It worked. The assassin lost interest and turned his attention back to the area around the protesters. Mason felt relief at the close call, but he hated hiding in the car. He hated the whole idea of cowering, and he tried to think of how he could end it. The more he eyed the assassins, the angrier he became.

After a few tense moments, the parents, still somewhat bewildered by Tazim's antics, moved back toward the demonstration. Sara and Tazim got back in the car.

Mason cracked open the door. "Wait ten minutes, then create a diversion."

"Now where are you going?" Sara said.

"I'm going to have a talk with one of those pricks." He looked at Sara. "Make the distraction good. Something that makes a lot of noise. Can you do that?"

Sara nodded with determination in her eyes. Mason adored her for that. He said to Tazim, "When Sara gets it started, take the car and park it on the other side, about thirty meters from that building." Mason pointed to the hotel where the shooter was perched on the rooftop.

Mason slipped out of the car, keeping his back to the crowd. He walked away from the commotion and turned left into a narrow alley. It took him only a few minutes to loop around behind police headquarters and reach the wall of the hotel's rear parking lot. Up and over the wall, he walked with quick strides across the lot and entered the hotel via a side entrance.

On the eighth floor of the rear staircase, he found the roof access. A few steps up and he stood inside the door leading to the roof. It was slightly open, and Mason stared at the sunlit patch of the wall so as not to be blinded by the sun. By the orientation of the access door to the front of the building, Mason estimated that the assassin's position was to the right. The tarred roof would help him move silently.

He checked his watch and waited.

Not a minute later, the crowd of demonstrators burst into an angry roar. Police blew their whistles in a desperate attempt to control the surging crowd. A riot had broken out. Sara had done well.

In one quick motion, Mason was out the door. He pressed his back against the elevated structure of the access stairs. To his right, the assassin was on his knees, leaning over the short roof wall and peering down on the street. His sniper rifle lay by his side, on top of its transport case.

The noise below echoed up the surrounding buildings, a din of yelling, screaming, and police whistles.

Mason took quick, sure strides across the rooftop. Just when he was within ten feet of the assassin, the man turned in alarm. He jumped to his feet and went for the pistol in his shoulder holster. Mason charged, and with his left hand, he trapped the man's gun hand to his chest.

The man was quick with his left cross, but Mason was ready for it. He brought his right arm under and inside the arc of the swing and trapped the man's free arm to his rib cage. At the same moment he yanked his arm in with all his strength, bending the man's elbow backward. Mason heard the crack of bone.

The man stiffened and cried out, even while he desperately fought to free his gun hand. The excruciating pain drained him of strength. He tried kicking Mason, then head-butting him. He wouldn't give up, despite his broken arm. He fought as if he was about to die.

Mason had to take him down quick, before he cried out for help to his companions. Mason kneed him in the stomach. The man doubled over and his mouth popped wide, trying to breathe with his paralyzed diaphragm.

Mason yanked the gun from the now helpless assassin and swung it, striking the man just behind the ear.

The man fell on his side and rolled into a ball, stunned and breathless.

Mason turned him on his back, held the gun to the man's temple, and got in the man's face. The assassin's diaphragm recovered and he sucked in air.

"Who hired you? Who put the contract out on my life?"

The man spit up blood and sputtered, "I don't know."

Mason pressed the gun harder into his temple. "Bullshit. Who hired you?"

"The guy in the Renault. Archie Cameron. But he's just the team leader. He hired me. That's all I know. I swear."

"How many teams are here to kill me?"

The man hesitated. Mason put his knee on the man's shattered elbow. The man groaned, then screamed when Mason put on more pressure.

"Three teams. Maybe seven shooters in all."

"Six now. I'm tempted to throw you off the roof, but I want you to tell the others that I don't like being a target. Tell them I'm going to hunt them all down. One by one."

The man began to fade into unconsciousness, but Mason jerked him awake. "You got that?"

The man lifted his head in anger. "You're dead, asshole. You got *that*?"

With all his strength, Mason struck the man's jaw. The blow was so hard, the man's head jerked back and slammed against the roof. He groaned once and was still. And his jaw now sat at an odd angle.

Mason got up and took a moment to peer over the roof wall. The other two assassins seemed unaware of what just happened to their companion. They were too fixed on the melee. The police had resorted to using their nightsticks against the protesters trying to fight their way across the street. The surge of the crowd was threatening to overwhelm the contingent of police.

Then Mason saw Meunier's limo, the driver attempting to pull out onto the street. The chauffeur blew his horn as he inched forward.

Mason ran for the stairway.

29

No one noticed a disheveled Mason walk through the hotel lobby and exit onto the street. He turned right, and despite the temptation to turn back to look for the assassins or at the rioting crowds, he kept his gaze straight ahead. Sara's car was right where he'd instructed Tazim to park it.

Mason got in the backseat. Tazim sat behind the wheel, but the front passenger's seat was empty. "Where's Sara?"

"She is still with the protesters."

Mason took a chance and looked out the rear window. There was too much chaos to see whether Sara was on her way or injured in the riot. The police had increased their number and were getting the upper hand, but it involved swinging their clubs indiscriminately.

"Meunier's limo just passed a moment ago," Tazim said.

"We need to follow him. We're going to lose him at this rate." Mason looked back again. "Come on, Sara. Come on."

Just then Sara emerged from the crowd. She pulled her scarf forward to cover her face. Amid all the chaos, she wove around protesters scrambling to escape the police batons. It seemed like a minor miracle that she finally made it past without being noticed

—or beaten down by a police baton. She reached the car and got in.

"Go, Tazim," Mason said.

Tazim hit the accelerator and drove off. Sara was out of breath and held her upper arm as if in pain.

"Are you okay?" Mason asked Sara.

"A policeman tried to hit me in the head, and I used my arm to protect myself. I'll be all right."

Tazim glared at her. "Your idea of a distraction could get people seriously injured."

"They were already very angry. All I had to say was that they shouldn't be forced to stay on the other side of the street. The parents broke the barricade first, but not one of them threatened violence. The police were waiting for an excuse to beat us." Sara was near tears, either from the painful arm or witnessing the violence—or both.

Mason put a hand on her shoulder and leaned forward to inspect her arm. Sara pulled up her sleeve to show Mason. Her arm was red and swelling, but the injury didn't look too bad.

Tazim raced up to an intersection of three roads branching off in different directions. "Which one?"

"There he is," Mason said. "Three blocks ahead."

Meunier's limo took a right toward the marina and the beach. Tazim rushed through the intersection. Traffic slowed them down; the flow of cars was being diverted because of the demonstration. Tazim finally made it to the street Meunier's chauffeur had used, and the street sloped down toward the marina. From their high vantage point, they could see Meunier's limo had parked in the marina parking lot.

Mason spotted Meunier, along with his chauffeur and another man, walking on one of the piers toward a large luxury cruiser docked at the end of the pier.

"Do you think he intends to leave Tangier?" Tazim said.

"If you get there fast enough, I'll ask him."

Tazim stomped on the accelerator and skillfully negotiated the sharp turns and busy traffic. A few moments later, he pulled the car into a parking space.

Mason told Tazim and Sara to stay in the car. He got out and walked swiftly for Meunier's luxury cruiser. As he approached the boat, a crewman dressed in all white stood by the gangway. He had a 9mm pistol tucked in his belt and stared at Mason.

Mason didn't know if the guy was working for Meunier or for Jennings. He did a mental check of his surroundings in case he was under shoot-to-kill orders. Unfortunately, there was little cover. Only diving into the water would provide a means of escape, which gave Mason an involuntary shiver.

Mason stopped some yards from the man.

"That's far enough," the crewman said in a British accent. "Mr. Meunier doesn't want to be disturbed."

A few of the boat's crew had stopped what they were doing to watch what might happen next.

Mason looked up at the deck and saw Meunier standing near the pilothouse. He stared at Mason for a long moment.

Finally Meunier said, "Monsieur Adams. Let this man come aboard."

The crewman stepped aside, and Mason boarded the boat. Meunier met Mason at the gangplank. He was dressed in black— not sailing clothes—and looked as grim as ever.

"What's with the guard?" Mason asked in German.

"This vessel has been vandalized several times."

"Uh-huh," Mason said. "Are you planning on sailing off into the sunset?"

"Follow me, please."

The crew resumed their duties, though Mason didn't know what those duties would be if they weren't going anywhere. He followed Meunier down the companionway to a plush salon. They continued past the salon bar and into an office of mahogany and brass. The small space was just big enough to accommodate two leather chairs, a small desk, and a padded bench seat. Meunier shut the door and opted for the bench. "Please, sit."

Mason scanned the room. "I guess if you're going to leave town, this is as nice a way as any." He sat in one of the chairs opposite Meunier.

"To answer your question, Herr Collins, I'm not planning to leave Tangier. Not while my daughter—" Meunier stopped, and for the first time, Mason saw a crack in Meunier's stern mask. "If you are correct, Valerie only has a few days left."

"You don't believe the police arrested the right men?"

"No, I do not."

"And how did you come to that conclusion?"

"It is obvious. Those two uneducated Moroccans could not have abducted three white children under everybody's noses and remained undetected."

"And you told the police that?"

"Yes, I told Commandant Lambert, but he refused to listen. He wants to close the case by charging these foolish men."

"Did you come to this conclusion before or after you saw the two Moroccans the police had arrested?"

Meunier paused, as if trying to discern Mason's line of questioning. "Does it make a difference? My reason for doubt would be the same."

"Maybe those two aren't so uneducated after all. Maybe they're criminal masterminds and just got careless, or their streak of luck just ran out—"

"Hardly likely. We are talking about primitives."

"Or maybe you have some firsthand knowledge about the real perpetrator, and after seeing those two men, you knew they weren't behind the other abductions."

Meunier remained rigid and expressionless, though his silence betrayed him.

Mason said, "You didn't have to let me on board. You have two armed guards to keep people off. I think there's something you want to get off your chest."

"I am a desperate father. I want my daughter back and safe in her mother's arms. The police are making fools of themselves. Therefore, you are the only one I can turn to."

"Then the first thing you have to do is tell me what you know. You've refused to say anything because it means risking exposure of who you are and what you've done. You've got two, maybe three days, Herr Meunier, to get Valerie back."

"I imagine this is the same speech you gave Herr de Graaf."

"You two seem to have a lot in common."

Meunier said nothing.

"The only difference is that Sabine is dead, and Valerie has a chance to live. Do you want to live the rest of your life knowing you could have done more for Valerie?"

"You are not my priest!"

Mason raised his voice to match Meunier's. "Then I'll talk to you as a cop. You're covering something up that might help your daughter, and the guilt is tearing you up inside. No, I'm not your priest, Herr Meunier. I'm not here to sit in judgment or forgive you. I'm not your mother. I'm not going to comfort you and tell you it's going to be all right. In a few days' time, your daughter, after weeks of anguish and rape, will be strangled and dumped like a rotting piece of meat."

"That's enough!" Meunier said.

A moment of quiet fell on the cabin. A motorboat passed by, and water thumped against the hull of the cruiser.

"How about I help you along?" Mason said. "De Graaf told me what went on at your brotherhood get-togethers. You bring in a Moroccan prostitute—the younger and more innocent, the better —drug her, and rape her."

Meunier flinched at the word *rape*, but said nothing to refute the narrative.

Mason continued. "Then one day, one of your victims died right after you and seven other members had their way with the girl."

"Please stop," Meunier said. He rubbed his forehead with a shaking hand.

Mason said, "The girl died because you thought raping a young girl gave you some kind of Aryan power. Then after you all were done with her, she died in the dressing room. And instead of going to the police, you dump the poor girl's body out in the brush. You let her rot. What are you going to say when someone comes across your daughter's shriveled corpse and you did nothing to save her?"

"The girl didn't die in a room," Meunier said, and his face distorted in mental anguish. "She expired right in front of us." His throat worked overtime trying to swallow. His mouth must have been as dry as the land where the dead children had been dumped.

"Did someone strangle her?"

Meunier lifted his head to Mason, his eyes flooded with tears. "No."

"Then how did she die?"

"I don't know." Meunier shuddered and fought to take a deep breath. "Her face was blue."

Meunier's tears flowed at the memory of it.

"Who was there with you?"

"It is unnecessary to divulge their names, as none of them is the killer."

"I need the other seven members' names."

"That is out of the question. Please don't ask that of me."

"How can you live with the idea that one of the members has

taken your daughter? How can you let a trivial oath of secrecy get in the way? More than likely, the same man who murdered that girl has your daughter. He's already strangled Sabine de Graaf. And what's happening to your daughter right now? Three weeks in captivity. Three weeks of rape and torture. I can't imagine what state she's in. Wondering why no one has come to rescue her. When is her daddy—"

Meunier groaned and writhed, like reacting to an agonizing pain deep in his gut. He dropped to his knees, clasped his hands, clamped his eyes shut, and began to mumble a prayer.

Mason leaned in close to Meunier's ear. "Prayers aren't going to help your daughter, Herr Meunier. God knows what you've done. Why would he listen to you now?"

Meunier ignored Mason.

"Talk to me, Herr Meunier. I'm right here. I'm all you've got, right now."

A woman's voice behind Mason said in German, "Did you consider the possibility that God sent you to help us?"

Mason turned to see Mrs. Meunier at the open door. Meunier stopped mumbling his prayer but remained as he was. Mason stood and faced Mrs. Meunier. She took a few steps into the room, her hands clasped in front. She wore an impassive expression, though there were tears in her eyes.

"I wouldn't presume to know what God wants, Mrs. Meunier. We don't get along very well."

Mrs. Meunier took solemn steps to her husband and stood over him with a look of pity a mother gives to an errant son. She watched him a moment as her husband resumed quiet prayers. She looked at Mason. "My husband is a weak-willed man. Brilliant in business, but he has lustful urges he cannot control, and this Aryan brotherhood was just an excuse to exercise those lusts."

"So, you're aware of his extracurricular activities?"

"Did you think me a bad wife and mother to forgive him his lust for young girls?"

"Let's leave my opinions out of this. You won't like what you hear."

"Forgiveness is one of the greatest Christian virtues."

"My interest is in finding your daughter before it's too late. Can you help me with that?"

"I think my husband should speak for himself," Mrs. Meunier said, and looked at her husband. "Henri, you will tell Herr Collins all that you know."

Meunier fell silent. His body relaxed, and he let out a long sigh. As Mrs. Meunier looked down at her husband, her nostrils flared, and her lip curled as if she looked upon something vile and disgusting. "Henri!"

Her reprimanding voice seemed to calm Meunier. As if unwinding from a tight coil, Meunier placed his hand on the bench and rose from his knees. Without looking at his wife or Mason, he pivoted on his heels and sat.

"Who are the other seven members, Herr Meunier?" Mason asked.

"I don't believe any one of them would go so far as to abduct three members' daughters."

"I don't care what you believe. Tell me. If one of the members didn't murder the girl, then it could be a member who is so racked with guilt that he unknowingly confessed to the killer. The point is, one of the members is the key to finding the man who abducted and is raping your daughter."

Meunier looked at his wife, then back to the ground. "Besides myself, Sir Wilfred Brisbane and Herr de Graaf, there is Anthony Jennings, Christiaan Lambert, Baron von Litchten, Francesco Morino, and Josef Magnusson. But Morino and Magnusson left the country shortly after the incident."

Somehow, Mason wasn't surprised to hear Lambert's name. It

explained a lot. The other two names Mason knew from the fascist club's master list: Morino an Italian judge, and Magnusson a Swedish diplomat.

"Of the other five members who remained, who do you think is most likely to be the abductor?"

Meunier looked at Mason with a puzzled expression. "I honestly don't think any of them would do such a thing. The worst I could say is that Anthony Jennings has been very persistent in forming investment partnerships with us. Although I suspect it's mostly to get at our money. He was particularly aggressive with de Graaf, which is why I think Herr de Graaf suspected Jennings was the abductor."

"What about Lambert?"

Meunier shook his head. "You are welcome to ask me each member's name, but my answer would be the same. And if I guess incorrectly, innocent men's lives could be ruined."

Mason bristled at Meunier's use of "innocent," but he pushed that down. "How did you acquire the prostitutes?"

"Norwood, Sir Wilfred's butler, went to several establishments and received a list along with photographs. The group would then select each candidate."

Mason was about to ask another question when Mrs. Meunier said, "I would like you to see something."

Meunier twisted on the bench to face his wife. "Camille, you must not show him that."

She returned a defiant look, and Meunier seemed to shrink. Mrs. Meunier turned to the desk and removed a piece of paper. "We received this the morning before you came to our house." She handed it to Mason.

Mason read the message written in English and in block letters:

KEEP QUIET OR YOUR DAUGHTER DIES LIKE THE MOROCCAN GIRL YOU KILLED

"Did you kill the girl?" Mason asked Meunier.

"Absolutely not."

Mrs. Meunier said, "'You' in English is vague, but I believe it refers to the collective 'you.' The entire group."

"Perhaps," Mason said. "And keep quiet about what? Aside from the girl's death, what else could it be referring to?"

"I don't know," Meunier said. "All of us were present." He pointed to the note. "But that is why we've been afraid to talk to you. The abductor still has our daughter. There's too much risk involved if the abductor finds out that I gave you the members' names. You must realize that, so please keep what has been said to yourself."

"Do you know if de Graaf got a similar warning?"

Meunier said, "If he refused to give you the names, then I would imagine he did."

Mrs. Meunier said, "I believe the note implies that our daughter's abduction was not perpetrated by someone in my husband's brotherhood. And if it is not one of the members, then it is as you said: one of the members felt so much guilt that he unknowingly told the killer."

Mason nodded. "But why Sabine, Valerie, and Cynthia? There has to be a reason. Which makes me think there's more you haven't told me."

Meunier's whole body began to tremble. "Stop! Both of you. Speculating will not get our daughter back. Talking and questions will not save her. I have told you everything. I have laid my sins bare, and I can't take it anymore." He clamped his eyes closed and raised his fists. "Oh, God, how vile and cruel we all were. How perverted we became. Sick. We exploited young girls and one died because of it. Valerie may die because of it."

Meunier sucked in a breath and opened his eyes, though he looked at nothing.

Mrs. Meunier said a few more soothing words, then turned to Mason. "It is time for you to leave, Herr Collins. My husband will answer no more of your questions."

Mason nodded. He knew he wouldn't get any more out of Meunier right now—if there was anything more to get. Besides, if he stayed in their presence much longer, he knew he'd lose control and beat Meunier to a pulp.

30

M ason found Sara and Tazim standing on opposite sides of the car, looking like two pouty children. "Lovers' quarrel?"

Tazim's eyes popped wide with alarm, obviously misunder-standing Mason's taunting remark. "I am married, sir. I am on this side of the car for my own safety."

"That's because he was behaving like every Muslim man I know," Sara said. "Self-righteous and judgmental. I feel sorry for his wife. Don't ever force us to be alone again."

"And I don't want to be seen alone with this woman."

"Both of you, get in the car," Mason said.

After exchanging scowls, Mason and Sara got in the front, and Tazim sat in the back.

"Start driving," Mason said to Sara. "It's hot in here."

"No kidding. After all the hot air that man expelled—"

Mason held up his index finger to stop her. To his surprise, it worked. As Sara drove out of the marina parking lot, Mason filled them in on the interview with Meunier: that the Moroccan girl didn't die in an isolated room, but right in front of the men; that Meunier had received a strange note in English, that Mason believed was written by someone outside the brotherhood; and the bombshell for Tazim, that Commandant Lambert was a member.

Tazim cursed Lambert's name. "That is why we've gotten nowhere. That is why he stopped the investigation into the Moroccan children's disappearances."

"Don't say anything to anyone about Lambert," Mason said firmly. "If he hears he's on the list, he might run for cover. Leave him to me. I promise that once I'm done, you can have him."

Mason turned to Sara. "I need for you to talk to the parents again. They talked about the stories of Moroccans working for the evil Nazarenes. I'm betting the two arrested Moroccans work for whoever took the white girls. Now that we know their identities, I want you to see if the parents might be able to name some of their associates. Who they've been seen with, their families. I'll take rumors or wild guesses. Anything they've got."

Sara nodded as she steered the car for downtown. "If the parents haven't been arrested during the riot."

"If that's the case, then talk to their friends. Friends of friends."

"And what are you and Mr. Righteous going to do?"

"There's Lambert and Brisbane, though I doubt I'm going to get anything out of either of them. Tazim, while I do that, I want you to try to find out anything more about the henna artists. If they're still not in the Grand Socco, then try to track down their families." He said to Sara, "Drop us off at the Grand Socco. I'll walk to the police headquarters while I figure out how to go at Lambert without getting thrown in jail."

"You walking around is too dangerous."

"I'll be fine. We'll meet back at the apartment this evening."

Sara stopped as close as she could to the Grand Socco. Traffic had stopped and people were pouring out onto the streets. "Whatever's going on, it doesn't look good," she said.

"Watch for anyone following you," Mason said to Sara.

"Don't forget you might be a target." He put on his panama hat and sunglasses. He started to get out, but Sara pulled him back in and kissed him hard on the mouth, then gave a taunting look at Tazim.

Mason got out with the other man, and they watched Sara drive away.

"Not a word, Tazim," Mason said.

Tazim held up his hands to indicate he would stay out of it.

The usual chaos and crowds had tripled in intensity, as a throng of Moroccan protesters had gathered in the plaza. They formed a dense circle around the outer ring. A man shouted slogans with the protesters shouting their response, shaking hand-painted signs nailed to posts or thrusting their fists in the air. The ten or so police looked on with tense expressions.

"This crowd is bigger and meaner than the group this morning," Mason said.

"The people are angry about a great many injustices," Tazim said. "The children's deaths and the police violence this morning only made things worse. If it is like protests in the past, they will gather here and then march through the medina. There are too many for the police to control, but as long as the demonstration is peaceful, it is better that they should let them protest."

Mason and Tazim split up. Tazim headed for the inner circle of the plaza. Mason headed for Rue du Statut and the police station. He had to take a circuitous route through the plaza to avoid the protesters. As he wound his way, he felt several tugs at the bottom of his suit coat. He turned around to see a boy of around ten looking up at him. He recognized the boy as the one who sat with the potter next to the henna artists.

"Yes, sir?" Mason said. "What can I do for you?"

To Mason's surprise, the boy responded in English with a British accent. "I am very worried for Auntie Jamila and Fatima."

Mason leaned over with his hands on his knees. "Is Jamila your aunt?"

"No. She is Fatima's aunt, but I call her that, too. Can you help them?"

"I'm trying, but I have to find them first. Do you know where they live?"

The boy shook his head. "In the medina, but I do not know where. You can ask Auntie Jamila's brother. His name is Barir."

"How do you know Barir?"

Tazim must have noticed the boy talking to Mason, because he trotted up to them.

The boy looked at Tazim. "You are a policeman. My father told me never talk to policemen."

"This is Tazim," Mason said. "He's my friend. You can talk to him. He's not a policeman today."

The boy studied Tazim for a moment, then said, "Barir comes by to talk to Auntie Jamila. He is not very nice to Fatima. I don't like him, because he is mean to her."

"Do you know where Barir lives?"

The boy scrunched his face in confusion. "He lives with Auntie Jamila."

"Ah," Mason said. "Of course. Can you describe him for me?"

The boy thought for a moment. "He is very big."

"You mean tall?"

"Tall and fat. He has a big mustache and ugly teeth. People say he is not a good man, but nobody will tell me why."

"Does he wear glasses, or a hat, or does he have scars?"

The boy pointed at Tazim. "He dresses like that man, but he wears a tarboosh."

Mason looked at Tazim for clarification, and Tazim said, "You know it as a fez hat."

Mason nodded and turned back to the boy. "What's your name?"

"Mohammed."

"Nice to meet you, Mohammed. You speak very good English."

"I learn at English school. My father wants me to go to England one day."

Mason was about to ask him another question when the boy's father rushed up and turned Mohammed around by his shoulders. He spoke firmly to him in Arabic, and said something to Tazim. Then to Mason, "No speak to my son." He seemed frightened and desperate to break up the conversation.

"I'm sorry, sir, but the boy is worried about Jamila and Fatima. We may be able to help."

Tazim translated, and then the man and Tazim exchanged several sentences. The father turned away and guided his son back to his booth. The boy looked back at Mason, smiled, and waved. Mason returned the wave.

Tazim said, "The father said the brother's name is Barir Assaraf. He works as a construction laborer, but the father has heard he has a reputation as a crook. He has heard Barir lives near the Kasbah in the medina. That is all he knows."

"His eyes said something different," Mason said. He moved for the potter's booth, but as he did so, the father and boy returned to them.

The father talked to Tazim for a few moments, and then ruffled the boy's hair. Tazim translated that the boy convinced the father to help. They all were concerned about the henna women, but the boy especially, because he was in love with Fatima.

Tazim said, "They have heard what you have done for the Tanjawi parents, so he feels he can trust you."

The potter gestured toward the Catherine Gate, and Tazim said, "He will show us where the brother, Barir, lives."

Mason and Tazim followed the potter and his son. He led them into the medina and past the Petit Socco. They took a relatively straight street, Calle Comercio, or Business Street, where it seemed the main enterprise was houses of prostitution clustered in long rows on both sides—the Select, the Monte Carlo, Le Chat Noir—where women, girls and even boys hung out in the doorways to entice the passersby. One Spanish-managed brothel displayed photographs of young Moroccan boys with come-hither looks to draw in customers. The Moroccan girl who'd been strangled was probably just another runaway, and the brothel would have chalked up her disappearance as the cost of doing business.

Mason kept a vigilant eye as they went farther. The medina was a perfect place for an ambush, and they passed men in hooded djellabas that provided perfect cover. After several turns, their path led uphill, toward the Kasbah. The final street, not much bigger than a sidewalk, ended in a small triangular plaza. Fifty yards beyond the plaza, they came to a tangle of streets, many dead-ending and dark.

The potter stopped and pointed toward a short, dead-end street. He spoke to Tazim while holding the boy tight to his body.

"He says he will go no farther," Tazim said. "He and the boy can't be seen. It's too dangerous. He said Barir, Jamila, Fatima, and several other family members live in a riad at the end of that street. It has a green door, with a blue-and-green tiled arch above the door."

Mason thanked the potter and his son, and watched as they disappeared around the corner. The street ran north to south, so even though it was narrow, the late-afternoon sun had found the opening and pierced the otherwise sunless street in vivid light. Two boys kicked a soccer ball that was gray with dirt and bulged at the many patches, making the ball roll like the severed head Mason had once seen after an artillery shell had decapitated a soldier. A dog with protruding ribs ran a zigzag pattern up the street, then down again, as if crazed by hunger.

Mason and Tazim stopped at the door, thick with layers of green paint applied over decades. An old man in a withered brown djellaba and a white kufi occupied a bench next to the door.

Mason knocked on the door, prompting the man to look up with glazed, sightless eyes. He said nothing as Mason knocked again. The door finally opened a crack, and a stubby, middle-aged woman, her face creased by time and hardship, glared at them.

Tazim greeted her with *as-salaam alaikum* and introduced them. Mason felt like a third wheel, useless as he stood and observed Tazim and the woman exchange words. It turned heated, and the woman tried to slam the door shut, but Tazim stuck his foot between the door and doorjamb to block it. That made the woman scream louder and bang the door against Tazim's foot. Tazim gave up and removed his foot. The door slammed in their faces.

"That didn't go well," Mason said.

"She is protecting her husband. She insists that Barir is not here—"

"Yeah, yeah, and she doesn't know where we could find him."

"You are English?" the old man on the bench said.

"American."

"Ah, in that case I can help you. Samira has less of a heart than her husband. I heard you offering to help discover where Jamila and Fatima have gone."

"Do you know where we can find Barir?"

The old man gave them a toothless grin. "Yes, but I will not tell you. That I cannot do if I want to continue to sit here in peace during my last days in the world. But—" He paused and held up his index finger. "I could let him know you only want to talk to him. As unpleasant as the man is, he loves his sister and niece. He would do much to help them." The old man leaned sideways toward them and lowered his voice. "Though I fear the women are beyond help."

"And why do you say that?" Mason asked.

"I have lived seventy-two years and traveled to many places. Seen many things. I know."

"Sir, we still need to talk to Barir. It's also about the abducted children. We don't think Barir has anything to do with the abductions and murders, but we think he may know someone who does."

"So, you are *that* American."

"Mason Collins, sir."

"No one has called me 'sir' in a very long time. I was a bosun on merchant vessels, some under the British flag, others American. I much preferred the Americans." He paused a moment, as if remembering. "I will convince him to see you."

"As soon as possible."

"Will the Golden Lantern at six o'clock in the Petit Socco be convenient? I cannot guarantee he will be there. Barir has a dark soul, but a soft heart. I think he will come."

B arir was late, if he was going to show up at all. Mason looked at his watch: 6:25 p.m. He sat at an outside table at the Golden Lantern. He had chosen a table against the building wall, with his seat facing the busy Petit Socco. Tazim had taken a table at another bar two down from Mason's. They didn't want to spook Barir by having a plainclothes cop with him, even if Tazim was Moroccan.

Mason and Tazim had arrived thirty minutes ahead of the appointed time to scope out the restaurant and be there if Barir had decided to show up early. Mason was taking another chance remaining in such a well-traveled plaza. The longer he waited, the greater the risk. There were a number of peak hours in the Petit Socco, and six thirty p.m. was when half the prospective customers arrived for dinner or drinks. The other half would be there at nine p.m. or after, following the Spanish tradition of dining late.

The sun was still above the horizon, but hidden in the confined space. The dome of the sky went from orange to azure, and it bathed the chaos of the plaza in a muted light. The restaurants' and bars' neon signs flashed the full spectrum of colors into the deepening shadows.

Mason nursed the same cup of coffee he'd ordered almost an hour ago, and the waiter eyed him with impatience for camping out and not spending more money. He took another sip, and at that moment a shadow fell across his table. Mason looked up to see Melville grinning at him.

"Mind if I join you?" Melville said as he sat.

"Under normal circumstances, I'd be happy for you to join me, but this isn't a good time."

"Meeting someone?"

"Something like that."

"Ah, a mysterious visitor. On the case, are we?"

Melville signaled for the waiter. "Two whiskeys, please. And not that Irish swill. Single malt if you have it."

"Actually, I'm waiting for someone who might get spooked if he sees you here."

"Someone with vital information, I hope."

"The brother of the two henna ladies from the Grand Socco. He might have a lead on some Moroccans working for the abductors."

"I thought the police already had their men."

The waiter came back with the whiskeys, and Melville held up his in a toast.

Mason left his on the table. "I tried to be nice; now I need you to get the hell out of here before the brother comes."

Melville continued to hold up his drink. "It's been several hours since my last drink, and I intend to have this." Melville smiled. "Chin, chin." And he downed his drink, then slapped the glass onto the table. "Actually, I'm here to watch the spectacle. There's a mass of protesters heading for the Petit Socco, and it's quite amusing to watch the uninitiated Westerners run for their lives."

Melville took off his straw trilby hat and commenced to fan himself. "I think this evening is hotter than it was at noon." He looked at Mason out of the corner of his eye and saw Mason's scowl. "Oh, very well. I'll go under the condition that you join me for dinner. Dean's Bar serves delicious American hamburgers. A taste of home, what?"

"Yeah, sure. Give me a couple of hours."

"Splendid," Melville said, and stood. "Eight thirty will do nicely. Sorry if I inadvertently scared off your quarry. I've been known to show up at inopportune times. Forgive me."

"Go, Melville. Now."

Melville tipped his hat and toddled off.

A man next to Mason's table suddenly yelled something in Spanish at his companion and shot to his feet. He'd obviously been drinking heavily, because when he stood, he stumbled backward into Mason. Mason caught the flailing man and set him upright, but not before the man's arms shook Mason's table and sloshed out half of his drink. Mason hefted the man away from the table and shoved him in the opposite direction. The man mumbled an apology and, with Mason's help, staggered away.

Mason settled back in his chair and downed what remained of the whiskey. That's when he noticed a Moroccan staring at him from the center of the plaza. The man scanned the plaza as the crowds moved around him, and then his stone-cold gaze returned to Mason. His cold eyes reminded Mason of many men he'd encountered, those who had seen a lifetime of hardship and violence.

Seemingly satisfied, Barir finally approached Mason's table and sat. "You do not ever again come to my house. If you do, I will kill you. You bring danger to my door."

"From what I've heard, you're used to danger."

"Never to my home. My family."

"You tell me what I need to know, and you'll never see me again."

The man gave Mason one sharp nod.

"I believe your sister Jamila, and maybe Fatima, are missing because they were working for some bottom-feeding Nazarenes. The ones responsible for kidnapping and murdering all those Moroccan children and Nazarene girls."

Barir shot to his feet. "You will not insult my sister and Fatima."

"Sit down and listen to what I have to say. Any information you can give me might help discover who these Nazarenes are. It might help find out what happened to Jamila and Fatima."

Barir sat but continued to glare at Mason.

"I'm not a cop," Mason said. "My only concern is finding the Nazarenes. The old man by your door said you might have some information for me, so don't waste my time or yours."

"The old man is my father. Jamila is his daughter and Fatima his granddaughter, but he cares nothing about them. He sits by that fucking door with no concern for his family."

"Yeah, we'll get to your childhood problems after you tell me about your sister's and Fatima's involvement."

Barir stared at Mason a moment. "A Tanjawi offered Jamila money if she substituted her henna with one he gave her. He would tell her which customer to use it. Jamila did not know what was in this henna. I told her to say yes. He would give her a lot of money. I told her to not ask questions and do as she is told."

"Do you know who this man is?"

"Jamila would not tell me, but she was afraid of this man."

The heat in the plaza seemed to intensify, and perspiration broke out on Mason's forehead. He should have known better than to have a whiskey on an empty stomach.

"Do you know either of the Moroccans arrested for kidnapping the Nazarene boy?"

Barir let out a long sigh, as if the question caused him to feel a great fatigue. "Yes, I know Issam. We worked together on a few jobs. Mostly smuggling. He is not honorable man. Only what money can buy him."

Mason's face felt numb, and he found it hard to focus his eyes. Then he heard a hissing in his ears almost drowning out the hammering pulse of his heart. Alarm took hold in his chest.

He'd been drugged.

He fought off the symptoms. He had to concentrate, get as much information as he could from Barir, and then get out quickly before the drug took him over completely. He said, "Did you know that Issam was working for the Nazarenes who abducted and killed the Moroccan children? The same ones who probably paid your sister and niece to unknowingly drug innocent mothers and their children?"

"They took money to use the henna. What happened to those children is not their responsibility."

"It's too bad they listened to you. Who knows what's happened to them?"

Mason wiped the perspiration from his face and had to take deep breaths to control his heart rate. He could swear there were other people sitting at the table, and he blinked to make them go away.

"What is wrong with you?" Barir said. "You like every Nazarene I know, a drunkard. This is serious, and you are drinking alcohol."

Mason had trouble concentrating. The hissing in his ears became voices, like a hundred people whispering at the same time.

"I'm feeling sick, is all," Mason said, waving it off. "Some kind of bug." He rubbed his forehead to help his concentration. "I'm trying to find any other associates of Issam and his buddy. I need names. Locations. Give me a name, Barir. These bastards snatched up your sister and niece."

Mason pounded the table as much to master his debilitating symptoms as it was to jar Barir into talking.

"I know one," Barir said. "Jibran. I do not know his family name. He lives off Rue de l'Abattoir, behind the old cannery, in a small area of workers' houses. I do not know if he is involved, but I think he is."

Mason fought back the urge to vomit. "I need a location."

Barir opened his mouth to speak, when a loud roar of voices echoed in the plaza. Mason looked in the direction of the sound. He remembered the mass of protesters were due to arrive, but he wondered whether he was hearing actual voices or the ones buzzing in his head.

Barir looked puzzled, then angry. "I just told you. Behind the old cannery. It's near the railroad tracks."

Mason couldn't feel his legs. He moved his hand to wipe more perspiration and the movement was a blur.

He looked around in panic, Barir's angry words unheard. He had to get out of there fast. He stood, knocking over his chair in the process. He used the wall for support as his head swirled.

Then, across the plaza, he saw the assassin from that morning, the one who had been sitting in the car. Barir stood and yelled in Arabic, then fled. Mason watched him go. He tried to yell after him, but his mouth couldn't form the words. Another assassin, the one who had stood facing the crowd of protesters, appeared in the street Barir had used to flee.

Mason tried to move, but he stumbled into the neighboring table. Suddenly hands grabbed him. Mason fought them off; he then realized Tazim was holding him upright. All Mason could say was, "Drugged me." He pointed. "Assassins." There were three men now, and they were heading straight for them. He was unsure if it was a hallucination, but Jennings stood at the far end of the plaza.

Mason looked around wildly, and just then a huge mob of demonstrating Moroccans entered the plaza. They chanted and banged drums.

Mason had to yell over the din. "Tazim. The demonstration. Run!"

Tazim took Mason under his shoulder, and they ran headlong at the angry mob. The ground seemed to heave and recede with every stride. The sounds were deafening. He looked back and saw the assassins pursuing them.

Mason and Tazim crashed into the mob. The demonstrators yelled at him. Fists flew. Mason took blow after blow. Tazim tried to shield him, as he pleaded for them to stop. Mason clung to Tazim as he forced his legs to pump and thrash at the ground. His feet became tangled, and he nearly fell. Tazim grabbed at him and yelled something in his ear.

Tazim's head exploded. Mason was splattered with hot blood and brains. Tazim collapsed in a heap, bringing Mason down with him. He fell on Tazim's chest, his face close to Tazim's lifeless eyes.

The crowd erupted in a frenzy. One of their own had been shot down. They charged forward, the stampede of feet stomping and kicking Mason.

Mason felt nothing. It all seemed like a dream, a nightmare.

The next moment, the sea of feet parted around him, and a man's face filled Mason's vision. Rachid was saying something to him with great urgency in his eyes. Then Mason felt himself being lifted to his feet.

Like Tazim had done earlier, Rachid put his shoulder under Mason's armpit and propelled him forward. Time slowed to a crawl as they waded through the onrushing crowd. Angry faces seemed to float past him. The wave of bodies became a blur.

Then, like some kind of trick photography, he saw a little girl standing stark against the blur. Hana, the Polish girl he could not save during the war. She stood still, hugging a doll to her chest and staring at him. She was angry with him, he knew, even though her face expressed no emotion. She got neither closer nor farther away as Rachid pulled him down the street. And then blood spilled from a hole in her head and covered her face and soaked her long blond hair.

The street became filled with victims he had not been able to save. Some bore their bloody wounds, and some appeared as they were in life. They stood all around him and watched as he passed. Mason uttered apologies and pleaded for their forgiveness.

Then darkness fell around him. Hands touched him. He was laid on cool, damp ground. His insides burned, though he shivered. He had no sense of time or place. Only the touch of hands and kind faces that floated in and out of his vision. Sadness overwhelmed him. Then out of the shadows, he saw his grandmother. It felt as if she were really there, smiling and assuring. She stroked his hair like when he was a child and had woken from a nightmare.

Then he remembered nothing.

M ason opened his eyes. He lay on a simple platform bed, drenched in sweat. He was in a small room lit by two dim lamps. He lifted his head, but a searing headache made him drop his head again. His ribs felt bruised, as did his arms and legs and jaw. And his chest throbbed around his heart, like he'd vomited up every emotion.

Movement in his peripheral vision startled him, and he gripped the bed. A middle-aged woman, a Moroccan with kind eyes, came up to him.

"Who are you? Where am I?"

The woman shook her head and said something in Spanish. She held out a bowl of soup. Mason sat up despite the grinding pain. His headache flared, then subsided. She said something else and brought the bowl close, urging him to take it.

The smell of the soup triggered his hunger. He took it with both hands and drank the hot soup, ignoring her offer of a spoon. When he had finished, he said, "*Shukran*," and gave the bowl back to the woman.

Rachid came into the room and stepped up to the bed. Mason rose to his feet. His head swirled, and the dozen bruised places on his body throbbed, but he straightened and held out his hand to Rachid. They shook hands as Mason thanked him.

Rachid said something in Arabic and gestured toward the bed. Mason shook his head and took a tentative step forward. "Tazim?" he asked Rachid.

Rachid's expression turned to pity and he shook his head. Mason's legs turned weak, and he sat on the bed. Another person, another friend, he couldn't save. A rising anger burned away the sadness, and he shot to his feet. He gathered his clothes and put them on, ignoring Rachid's and the woman's pleadings. He thanked them again and found his way to the street.

It took him several minutes to orient himself. He was still in the medina, on a narrow street near the Marine Gate. The streets were empty and silent after the riot. Mason encountered a couple of two-man police patrols. None of them bothered to question him, only warning about a few small groups of Moroccan troublemakers who still roamed the medina. Mason was able to get directions from one of them on how to find Rue de l'Abattoir and the old cannery.

Mason remained vigilant as he exited the medina through the Marine Gate. The assassins would know they had missed their target, and a failed attempt could stir them into more radical action.

The directions took Mason down past the train station and along Avenida España. As he descended the wide street to the beach, he ran through all the events in the Petit Socco in his mind. Someone had slipped the drug in the whiskey. But who? The restaurant's bartender or the waiter? There was Melville, but he couldn't see when Melville had had the time or opportunity to put a drug in his drink, let alone a reason why. Then he remembered the man who'd stumbled next to his table. The man had fallen over Mason and put his hands on Mason's table to steady himself. The impact had even sloshed out some of his drink. And that could be why Mason didn't go into a complete trance; some of the drug had spilled out along with the whiskey. Mason tried to remember the man's face. He'd never seen him before, but that meant nothing. It could be he was paid to slip in the drug, as the assassins and maybe Jennings were there, lying in wait until the drug had taken effect.

Mason crossed the beach to the railroad tracks and followed them until he was opposite the disused cannery. He walked through a wide patch of scrubland and crossed behind the factory. It seemed a long time ago now, but this area made him recall the music and bonfires when he was on the beach that first night in Tangier. Even now, music floated on the humid air and distant bonfires glowed orange.

Mason found a clump of small houses on an impromptu jumble of dirt roads, the houses planted haphazardly among the scrub and stunted trees. It was past two a.m., but people were out, neighbors socializing around bonfires, kids playing in the open spaces. Mason walked up to a group of men talking around a fire in a rusty oil barrel. They looked at him as an unwelcome intruder, but one of them understood enough English to point out Jibran's house. Mason walked over to the house. The interior was dark, and no one answered the door after several knocks. There was a twenty-year-old, well-maintained Peugeot sitting in front of the house. It was one of the few cars Mason had seen in this neighborhood of poor fishermen and underpaid workers. Obviously, the guy had another source of income.

Some of the men around the fire watched Mason with suspicion, but that didn't worry him. He went around the rear of the house, which had two windows and a back door. The back lot was nothing but scrub and dirt, with no houses behind. Mason used his elbow to smash out the back door's window. Reaching inside, he unlocked the door and entered.

There was one bedroom, a tiny kitchen, and a living room.

The furnishings were all in good condition and of high-end quality—another sign that Jibran was making a bundle of money compared with the paltry wages Moroccans were paid. Even a new polished-oak radio cabinet stood in one corner. He searched through the closets and cabinets in the kitchen. He found nothing helpful, except a flashlight. He pocketed that and went back outside.

Out front again, Mason lit the flashlight and examined a strip of dirt beside the Peugeot that looked churned up from a much heavier vehicle. He squatted next to the Peugeot and scanned the area with the flashlight. The worn impressions were clear: tire tracks from a truck of some kind, and the tread marks—recent by the look of the ridge impressions—showed what seemed to be the exact same wear pattern as those left near Sabine's body. Mason fished out his notepad and found the sketches of the tire track pattern. Sure enough, they were the same, including the missing chunk of tire tread. Jibran worked for the abductors, and more than likely was involved in dumping the bodies.

Just as Mason stood, he saw one of the men sitting around the barrel fire jump up and trot for a motorcycle. The man started the motor and drove off.

Mason returned to the group of men, and through a drawn-out session of hand gestures and a few English words, he learned that Jibran had loaded his family in another car and driven off several hours before. No one would admit to knowing why one of their companions had taken off in such haste.

"Who knows Jibran? What does he do to earn enough money to have two cars?"

Except for the crackling fire, there was silence.

"I bet half of you understand English," Mason said. "The tire tracks in Jibran's yard match the ones we found where the children's bodies were dumped. This man works for the Nazarene who killed Moroccan children. I need to know how to find him.

Anything you can tell me about him. You can't just sit there and let the man get away with it."

Mason eyed each one of them in turn, though none dared to meet his gaze. He growled, turned on his heels, and walked away. No more than fifty feet away from the group, he heard footsteps behind him. He whirled around, expecting a fight, but one of the men from the group stopped and held up his hands.

The man said in English, "I mean you no harm."

"What's your name?"

"Fayyad. I work as the head gardener for Mr. Renfield. What you said, I did not know Jibran did such things."

"What can you tell me about him?"

Fayyad shrugged his shoulders. "Not very much. But you said to tell you anything. Omar can be a violent man, so I was afraid to speak."

"Is Omar the one who left on the motorcycle?"

Fayyad nodded. "I am at Mr. Renfield's mansion every day but Saturday. And I have seen Jibran's car pass many times on the Mountain Road."

"How many times?"

"Almost every day. Some days several times. He passes the mansion going away from the city. Then, sometimes soon after, sometimes many hours later, he goes back to the city. I do not think he works at one of the villas, so I wonder, why does Jibran drive on this road every day? There are only villas for rich people, then nothing."

"When he goes and returns quickly, how much time passes?"

"Perhaps fifteen minutes or a little more."

"Is there someone with him in the car?"

"Sometimes another Tanjawi, but I don't know him."

"Did he look like one of the Moroccans the police arrested?"

"I do not know these men, but I hope they suffer eternal hell."

"That'd be my guess. Where is Mr. Renfield's mansion?"

"It is called Las Palmas. It has a white iron gate with the name on it, and many rosebushes across the fence. There are not so many palm trees, so I do not understand why the mansion is called this."

"Anything else you can tell me about Jibran?"

Fayyad shrugged. "I live two houses from him, and often see him leaving his house late in the night."

"Thank you for coming to me, Fayyad. I need to ask one more favor. I'm going to steal Jibran's Peugeot, and I want you and the others to look the other way."

BANGS AND CLANGS AND URGENT FOOTSTEPS ROUSED CYNTHIA from her sleep. Cell doors were unlocked. The others moaned or cried out. Harsh voices urged them to move, and there was panic in those commands. The cell door next to hers was unlocked, and the man yelled, urging the other girl to move. The girl screamed; even the debilitating drug couldn't subdue the girl's terror.

Cynthia had only seconds. She'd known this day would come. Though some of the drugs were still in her system, she had managed to cut back on the drugs they were giving her over the last few days. She prayed she was lucid enough to carry out her plan. Her life depended on it.

She grabbed the foul bucket and scrambled across the cell floor. She pressed her back against the cell wall. She shook involuntarily. They would be coming for her any second. She had only one chance at this, and if she failed, they would take her away, never to be seen again. She pressed herself tightly against the wall, as if the rock would give way like magic. Then she remembered her vow.

Cynthia's door flew open, and the big woman in the mask stood at the threshold and yelled for her to come. Cynthia clung tightly to the bucket and tensed every muscle in her body. Even though the trauma, the lack of food, and the fitful sleep full of dreams had left her spent, she summoned all her courage and found a haven of calm in the tempest of her thoughts. *Don't panic,* she told herself.

The big woman charged for her. Cynthia screamed with fear and rage.

3 3

I t was close to four a.m. when the Peugeot Mason had stolen puttered up the New Mountain Road. He used his watch to keep track of the seconds after passing Renfield's Las Palmas mansion. Fayyad, the gardener, had said that Jibran's quick round trips took fifteen minutes or a little more. Figuring in the time it took for Jibran to park the car and perform a simple task meant the one-way drive up the road from Las Palmas would take five to six minutes. Of course that depended on Jibran's rate of speed, but Mason could calculate within a reasonable distance and cover all the mansions within that area. At thirty miles per hour, six minutes equaled a distance of three miles.

A hell of a long shot. But it was all he had to go on.

He'd dealt in long shots before, but taking this old Peugeot as it rattled up the incline of the New Mountain Road seemed like a doozy.

The gardener had said that he'd seen Jibran drive back and forth on this road, occasionally several times in one day. He was sure that Jibran worked for the Nazarene stealing children, so unless the man came up here for innocuous purposes, it could be that he ran errands for the killer. His trips were too frequent to be running bodies to a burial ground, so why, then? And here's where the long shot came in: he could be making runs to the place where the children were being held.

Mason had already passed Renfield's Las Palmas mansion, and now he was abreast of Brisbane's villa. There was a light on in what Mason figured was Brisbane's study, and Mason wondered if he was losing sleep over the worry that his daughter had a week left to live, or for his own reputation and livelihood.

Next came Jennings's villa, where all the windows were dark. Jennings was probably sleeping like a baby, comfortable in the satisfaction of another day's evil work.

At just under the five-minute mark after passing Las Palmas, he slowed to a stop and scanned mansions. He figured it was best to undershoot than over, so he would start there.

At this point the mansions were newer, bigger, and more lavish. Where he'd stopped, there were three mansions still under construction and a good hundred yards apart—two next to each other, and one across the street. The lots had been cleared for construction purposes, but many trees had been spared, including a thick line of growth separating the properties. Construction equipment and building supplies sat in various spots on the lots, and deep ruts and patterns of dirt on the road showed there had been a lot of heavy vehicles coming and going.

Issam, one of the Moroccans arrested for kidnapping the boy, was supposedly a construction worker, at least when he wasn't kidnapping children. So it was just as likely that his buddy Jibran worked construction as well, and his presence here could be explained by his going to and from work. Still, the isolated locations made one of them a good candidate for a place to hide the children.

The dented car door groaned loudly as Mason got out of the car. That set off several dogs somewhere at a neighboring mansion. The first mansion he searched was nothing but a foundation and the framed-out first floor. It took only a few minutes to search the place, including the unfinished basement. The second, though halfway to completion, yielded nothing. Mason was about to exit the second mansion when he heard a motorcycle.

He pulled back inside the doorless entry and into the shadows. The motorcycle came slowly down the road from the west. It was too dark to see the rider, but he wore loose-fitting clothes. The man kept looking left, then right, as the motorcycle idled and he used the slope to pull the motorcycle along. He was searching for something, or someone. He came to a stop in front of the mansion in which Mason was hiding and turned off the motor. He turned his head as if listening. It was too dark to see the man's face but he wore a djellaba. He definitely wasn't a resident in this swanky part of town. A gardener or servant? Maybe. But that would still be unusual at four a.m.

Mason felt certain the man was searching for someone, as he had no other reason to be on that road. He debated what to do. If he ran after the guy, the rider would be off in a flash.

The rider started up the motorcycle again and continued downhill, toward town. It took a few minutes for him to disappear and the sound of his motorcycle to fade. Mason ran out of the unfinished structure and up to his car. He got in and started up the engine. Now it was time to decide: follow the man, maybe catch him and interrogate him, or take a chance to go up the hill to see where he came from.

He put the car in gear and headed uphill.

At approximately seven minutes past Las Palmas, Mason reached the end of the line, where the mansions gave way to scrubland and the road dipped down toward the Atlantic coastline.

He stopped the car and studied the last mansion. It sat on the right side of the road, with the back of the property ending at the cliff and the sea below. After leaving the construction sites, he had approached the few remaining occupied mansions, waking the staff or the residents with his persistent knocking. But other than infuriating whoever answered the door, he had discovered nothing.

He now faced a mansion with a high brick wall that obscured the lower half of the structure. The wall arched in the middle, accommodating a thick wooden, reinforced gate. Mason slid over the car seats and got out on the passenger's side to avoid the creaking driver's door. He walked up to the gate. It was slightly open, and the heavy chain and padlock hung loose from a steel ring.

Mason pulled out his pistol and the flashlight he'd taken from Jibran's house, and then slipped through the gap. He stopped and studied the house. Constructed of brick, the house featured an odd mix of mock battlements, towers, and high chimneys, as if the architect couldn't decide between Tudor and a formidable castle. There were no lights anywhere, no cars in the driveway or porte cochere. The lawn grass stood high from many months of neglect. Weeds had taken over the gravel driveway, though many of those weeds had been crushed recently from vehicles. The windows lacked curtains, giving the impression that the house was empty.

The ornately carved front door was closed but unlocked. Mason entered without making a sound. All the furniture in the great rooms was covered with white cotton cloth, as if the owner had prepared the house for a long absence. But for all the trappings of a house shut down, the odors of cooking oil and burned candles lingered in the air.

As Mason searched the back rooms and the bedrooms, he discovered signs that the place had been quickly abandoned: a pot of soup left on the stove, clothing and linens left where they fell, and beds unmade.

When he entered the final and biggest bedroom, he felt sure he'd found the hideout. A boat-sized, four-poster bed sat at one end and seemed small in the immense room. Swaths of red-and-gold fabric hung from the high ceiling. Red-and-gold velvet covered the floor-to-ceiling window, and candles sat everywhere. But the real clincher was the Egyptian and Roman statues and busts lining the walls and arranged around the bed as if the bed were some kind of altar.

He searched through the rest of the rooms with growing excitement. Maybe in the culprits' hasty departure, they'd left the captives to rot in their cells. The cells had to be in the basement. But when he searched for the access to the basement, he found only closets or back stairs for the servants. His search turned frantic. He looked for signs that the door had been recently sealed or hidden behind furniture. Nothing.

Mason exited the rear of the house by the double doors of an immense dining hall. He found himself on a large back terrace, which led to a broad lawn. That, in turn, was divided by paths leading to a formal rose garden showing the same neglect as the front, and then a swimming pool containing nothing but muck and fallen leaves. Just beyond the garden was a long, rectangular outbuilding, originally a carriage house and stable. A pebbled driveway ran up to the front doors, indicating it had been converted into a parking garage.

He decided to search the outbuilding first. He avoided the pebble driveway and crossed the lawn. There were six windowless garage doors, but all of them were locked. He pounded on one of the doors to see if someone might cry out for help. Nothing. The building had only two small windows, one at each end. Mason stepped around to the far side to try peering in the window.

He froze. Leaning against the garden-side wall of the outbuilding was the same motorcycle he'd seen near Jibran's house. The same motorcycle the Moroccan Omar had used to race away from the group.

In the split second it took for Mason to process this, a man leapt out from the bushes and charged for Mason.

34

A man in a hooded djellaba was on Mason in an instant. Before Mason could turn and raise his pistol, the man swung a long lead pipe, striking Mason in the back. The impact forced the air from his lungs, and an electric shock of pain radiated out from his spine.

The man lunged with a knife in his left hand. Mason dodged it, but stumbled. The man swung the pipe again, hitting Mason in the arm and stomach. Mason lost his grip on the gun, and it fell into the deep weeds. He dodged another swipe of the knife, but the pipe caught him, clipping his jaw.

Mason fell against the outbuilding's wall and rolled, dodging swings of the pipe and lunges with the knife. He continued to roll away, using the wall for stability. He pushed off the wall at the last second and took three quick strides in an attempt to outflank the man.

The assailant yelled and charged, his knife out like a lance. Mason caught the man's lunging arm. He spun, kicked the man's feet out from under him, and flipped him on his back. The pipe fell from the attacker's hand and clattered along the pebbled driveway. Mason jammed his foot on his chest and wrenched the knife from his hand.

At the same moment, Mason heard a cry of panic behind him. He looked in the direction of the sound and saw a naked woman emerge from a clump of trees near the back of the property. That second of distraction gave his assailant an opening. He rolled out from under Mason's foot, pulling Mason off-balance. He then shot to his feet and fled toward the front of the house. Mason's first instinct was to go after the man, but he looked back at the woman. She ran now, in total panic, wailing as she fled. She was heading for the line of trees and the sea cliffs. In her terror, she might run right off the cliffs to her death.

Mason took off after her. The woman reached the line of trees and disappeared. Mason poured on the speed and plunged into the woods. In seconds, he reached the end. What he saw made him dig in his heels and come to a fast stop. The woman stood at the edge of the cliff, her toes instinctively curling around the smooth rock. She peered down at the beach, sixty feet below. She leaned forward, waist bent, as if struggling with the choice of jumping or being snatched by her pursuer.

Mason held out his hands, as if reaching for her, though he stood twenty feet behind her. "I'm a detective. I'm here to help you. You're safe now."

The woman continued to stare at the rocky shore below.

"I'm not here to harm you. I chased off the man who was after you."

He took a chance and stepped forward. "My name is Mason Collins. I'm a police detective. I won't hurt you. Now, step back before you fall. It's over now. You're safe."

Mason was within five feet of the woman when she teetered farther out, just balanced on the ledge.

"Stop, or I'll jump. I'm not going back there."

"What's your name?" Mason asked.

She didn't answer.

"Do you know Sir Wilfred Brisbane? He hired me to find you and the other abducted girls."

The woman sucked in her breath in surprise, and her knees buckled. Mason lunged and grabbed her from behind before she fell. The woman cried as she collapsed in his arms. Mason guided her back from the precipice and sat her on the ground next to him. He pulled off his coat and draped it over her shoulders. He shifted around to look into her eyes. She was covered in dirt, and one side of her face was bruised and swollen, but he recognized her immediately.

"Cynthia Brisbane?"

The woman—girl, really—looked at Mason. She shuddered, then wept, and laid her head against Mason's chest. There were scratches on her arms, and the bottoms of her feet bled in several places.

"Are you hurt bad anywhere?"

Cynthia shook her head, then tried to cover herself with the coat.

"Are there others like you, still being held?"

Cynthia wiped tears from her eyes, then said, "They are all gone."

"This is the house where you were being held?"

Cynthia nodded. "In the basement."

"Do you know if there are other men looking for you?"

Cynthia choked back her tears. "There are two. One left to search for me on his motorcycle, and the man who attacked you stayed to search the grounds."

"They could be coming back any minute. Let's get you out of here. Can you stand?"

Cynthia nodded and let Mason help her to her feet. As he guided Cynthia toward the house, she began to shiver.

"You could go into shock. I'll get you some blankets from the house."

Cynthia stiffened and pulled against his grasp. "I won't go back in there. Ever. You can't make me." There was terror in her voice.

"All right. I won't, but you've got to get warm. We'll get you to the car and turn on the heater."

Mason put his hat on her head. "Sorry, that's the best I can do to cover you up."

Cynthia pointed to a pile of firewood next to the garage. "My gown is over there. I took it off when I ran away. They would see my white gown in the moonlight."

"That was very clever of you," Mason said, and ran for the gown and brought it back. "It's damp, but I can't take you back to your parents dressed in just my coat and hat." He turned away so she could put on the gown in private.

"I don't want to go back there," Cynthia said as she pulled on the gown.

Mason was surprised to hear that, but he didn't want to argue and risk her fragile trust in him. "We'll talk about it in the car."

Mason draped his jacket over her shoulders. "Your feet are torn up. I could carry you, if you like."

Cynthia almost recoiled at the suggestion, but she caught herself and glanced at Mason. She shook her head and let Mason guide her toward the front of the house. All the while, he watched for one or both of the men searching for her. Once they were in the car, Mason started the engine and turned on the heater full blast. He made a U-turn and headed down the hill.

"Take me any place but my parents' house," Cynthia said as she stared out the windshield.

"I'm not going to ask why, but you've got to know that your parents are out of their minds with worry—"

"My crazy mother, maybe."

"Your father hired me to find you."

"I'm sure that was a great sacrifice on his part."

Mason looked at her, surprised how quickly she seemed to be recovering from such a traumatic experience—at least enough to show such anger at her father.

Cynthia returned the look. "I'm eighteen. I can choose where I want to go."

"Your parents can take care of you. You need medical attention and a safe place to recover. I can't think of a better place than with your parents."

"Are you insisting I go there because you want your reward?"

Mason glanced at her again, and this time she had anger in her eyes. She had recovered on the surface, but Mason knew some of this anger was just part of the reaction to her trauma. She would carry those wounds the rest of her life. Maybe anger was better than sinking into despair.

"I need to call the police right away, and your parents' house is the closest place for me to do that. Plus, you need a doctor. You'll have to talk to the police and let the doctor take care of your injuries, and then you can choose any place you'd like to go."

"Good. I choose your place."

"Oh, no, that's not going to happen."

Cynthia fell silent and turned her attention back to the road.

"Cynthia, it might be difficult, but I have to ask you a few questions."

She took a moment to respond. "Go ahead."

"Can you name any of your captors? Or anyone who might have harmed you?"

"Do you mean, who beat and raped me?"

"If this is too difficult, I understand. But if you can identify some of your captors and abusers, then we might be able to rescue the others."

Cynthia continued to stare at the road. "I only saw the faces of the two Moroccan guards, but I don't know any names."

"Did you ever see Valerie Meunier? She's one of the abducted girls."

"I don't know. We were never allowed to talk, and we never were together. One day they dragged a girl away. I couldn't see her face clearly, but I'm sure she never came back again."

Mason saw tears rolling down her face, though she maintained her stony expression. Mason wouldn't push any further on that subject. "You've been an incredibly brave girl—woman. How did you manage to escape?"

Cynthia took a deep breath and exhaled slowly. "A few hours ago the guards came to drag us out of our cells. I knew something bad would happen. The guards are always cruel to us, but this time they seemed more frightened or panicked than angry. They put drugs in our food, but I had found a way to throw some of the food away so I could be more aware. It still seemed like a terrible nightmare, so I can't trust exactly what I saw and what the drugs made me experience."

After being drugged in the Petit Socco, Mason knew that feeling well.

Cynthia continued. "I knew the day would come when they would take me away and I would never come back, so I devised a plan. When the woman guard came in, I threw the contents of my waste bucket into her face." Cynthia formed a brief smile despite her trauma.

"Good for you."

"Some of the others fought back or screamed and crumpled to the floor. There weren't enough guards to control so many, and in the confusion I was able to run through the basement without anyone stopping me. I didn't know where I was, or where I was going, but I managed to find the door to the outside. I heard yelling behind me, and footsteps, but that just made me run faster. It's only then that I realized we had been kept in a house.

"There was a high brick wall surrounding the property—too high for me to climb over. I was trapped. I pulled off my gown and I buried myself in dead leaves and branches under some trees behind the garage. They must have thought I had climbed over the wall or something, because the man who stayed behind didn't look for me very diligently. I knew I wouldn't get very far without shoes or clothes, so I stayed where I was. I heard the others crying, and I could just see a white truck near the back door. Then I heard the truck doors being slammed shut. The last sound was the truck and a couple of cars driving away."

"Did you get a good enough look at the truck to describe it?"

"I could only see a portion of the side. It had '*légumes*' painted on the panel in green lettering. I guess a fruit and vegetable delivery van." She shuddered, despite the blast of the car's heater. "I will never forget the screams of the others as they were taken away."

Cynthia hung her head and wept softly, but as soon as Mason pulled up to the gate to Brisbane's villa, she turned off the tears. Mason honked the horn. At five in the morning, it took the guard several minutes to come up to the gate. Instead of opening the main gate, the guard exited through the small gate and stomped over to the car.

The guard leaned over to peer in Mason's window. "What in bloody hell—" His eyes widened in surprise. "Good God, Miss Cynthia!"

The guard rushed to open the main gate and called the house from the kiosk. Mason stopped the car next to the front porch steps, but Cynthia remained rigid in her seat. Mason had to get out, then cajole her from the car. She scowled as Mason escorted her up the portico steps.

"Remember what you promised me," Cynthia said. "After this ordeal, I can go wherever I choose, and I could stay with you."

Mason jerked his head to look at her. "I never said—"

"Cynthia!" Sir Wilfred said, and rushed out the door in his pajamas and bathrobe. He threw his arms around her and his eyes were full of tears. Cynthia's were dry, expressionless. She barely hugged him back.

Norwood and a maid came out and chatted and cooed at Cynthia as they accompanied her and Brisbane inside. Mason followed them into the foyer.

"My darling Cynthia!"

Mrs. Brisbane rushed down the stairs. Cynthia broke away from her father's arms and ran to her mother. That's when Cynthia's stoic expression melted. Her face twisted in anguish and relief, though she didn't cry. Mrs. Brisbane cried enough for both of them. She kissed Cynthia all over her face, while emitting a kind of joyous chuckle. Sir Wilfred watched mother and child a moment, then instructed the maid to draw Cynthia a bath and lay out a clean nightgown. He turned stolidly to Mason.

"I suppose you want your reward."

Mason spun to him, his body rigid with anger.

Brisbane's expression changed to conciliatory. "Where did you find her?"

"The last mansion at the end of the New Mountain Road."

"Did you catch the villains who abducted her?"

"Everyone was gone. They had left shortly before I got there. Your daughter was very brave. She escaped when they were herding all the captives out of their cells."

"So, you didn't rescue her as much as run into her."

Mason restrained himself from responding verbally or physically. "I need to call the police."

Brisbane said to Norwood, "Take Mr. Collins to the telephone in the library, then ring the doctor from my office line."

Norwood showed Mason to the library, where he pulled out a telephone from a cabinet built into one of the bookcases. Mason waited until Norwood was gone before picking up the receiver. Instead of calling the police station, he dialed Rousselot's home phone. It took a number of rings before Rousselot answered.

Mason said, "I found the place where the children were being held captive." He then filled Rousselot in on everything he'd found out, and how he'd tracked down the location. He explained how Cynthia escaped, but the other children had been taken away before he got there.

"Cynthia couldn't identify the other captives?" Rousselot said.

"Unfortunately, no. She only got a glimpse of one girl they dragged away, and Cynthia never saw the girl again. I'm assuming that was Sabine de Graaf."

He then gave the captain Cynthia's description of the truck that was used to evacuate the other children. He also told him about the threatening note that Meunier had received, and that Meunier named Jennings as a member of the fascist organization. He held off telling him that Commandant Lambert was a member of the fascist club, or how the Moroccan girl had died. He didn't want to say either over the phone.

"I'm relieved to hear that you are still alive. No one knew if you had been killed or kidnapped during that riot in the medina."

The memory of what had happened hit Mason in the gut. "Tazim was killed by a bullet meant for me."

"I was very sorry to hear about his death. He was a good man. We have put out alerts to look for the assassins, but there is very little to go on."

Mason gave Rousselot detailed descriptions of the three assassins. "Tell your men to be careful. Those guys are pros."

"I suppose you will be leaving Tangier, now that you have fulfilled the conditions of your contract with Brisbane."

"The rest of the children are still out there."

"I admire your convictions and courage, but as long as you are a target, other people might get in the line of fire. Take Brisbane's money and leave town."

"I'll see you around, Captain," Mason said, and hung up.

35

M ason returned to the foyer. Brisbane was alone, standing at the base of the stairs, looking up to the second floor. Mason shook his head in disgust: the man's daughter had just come back from the dead, and Brisbane looked like he'd heard news that stock markets had dipped a couple of percentage points.

In a flat tone, he instructed Mason to follow him up to his office. Once there, Brisbane closed the door, being careful not to make any sound, and stepped behind his desk.

"My stipulation for payment was that you find and rescue my daughter. It turns out any random passerby, any fool, could have done what you did. Just be at the right place at the right time. Therefore, I don't believe you merit the full payment—"

"I don't want your money."

"Of course you do. I'm prepared to offer you five thousand pounds in lieu of the twenty. And it's far more than a man who misrepresents his experience deserves. You're just like every laborer who expects maximum reward for a minimum of effort." He sat in his office chair and opened his checkbook. "I suggest you accept the money and leave town immediately."

"Are you afraid I'll expose your nasty secrets?"

Brisbane squirmed in his chair as he began to write out the check. "If you're referring to the conservative men's club, that's well-known and has no effect on my position as consul general."

"I bet the press doesn't know about the Brotherhood of the Temple of Hercules, where you and some of the other members practice extreme Aryan rituals. Reborn Nazis raping drugged child prostitutes. And what if they found out that a representative of the British government was involved in the death of a child prostitute during one of the ceremonies?"

Brisbane slammed the checkbook closed. "This is blackmail." He said it with anger, but it came out as fear.

"I told you I don't want your money."

"Then what *do* you want?"

"To stop giving me the runaround and answer my questions."

Brisbane rubbed his forehead as he thought. He took his time, but Mason knew he was weighing his options. "You must promise that whatever I say doesn't leave this room. That's the bargain."

"Right now my interest is trying to save Valerie Meunier and any other children held captive, and find the killer. I can promise not to go to the press or tell any British authority, but if what you tell me has anything directly to do with the murders or the abductions, then I have to share it with the police. That's the best I can offer."

Mason took Brisbane's silence as a sign that he would answer Mason's questions, though not necessarily with the truth.

Mason continued, "De Graaf and Meunier said you were at the ceremony when the child died. That all eight members were present, including you. Someone in your group is responsible for the abductions and murder. I want to know who did it, and why."

"I haven't the foggiest."

"Did you receive a threatening letter today or in the last couple of days?"

Brisbane froze, except for one hand fiddling with the coins in his pants pocket.

"If you don't answer, I *will* follow through on my threat," Mason said.

It took Brisbane a few seconds, but finally he turned to his wall safe, hidden behind a painting of a naval battle. He turned the dial, opened it, and pulled out a sheet of paper. He then handed it to Mason. On the sheet of paper and written in the same block letters was the message:

YOUR DAUGHTER WILL DIE LIKE THE GIRL YOU ASPHYXIATED.

"Of course, I have no idea what the author of this note is talking about," Brisbane said. "I thought it was some kind of hoax."

"Who do you think sent this?"

"I've racked my brain trying to think of who, but I can't ..."

"The man abducts your daughter, and in his message he accuses you of asphyxiating the girl. That's an unusual way to talk about a girl dying of natural causes. Was it part of the Aryan ritual to asphyxiate the children?"

Brisbane said nothing, though his hands shook as he tugged at his bathrobe and wiped perspiration from his forehead.

"Suit yourself," Mason said, and moved for the door.

"Wait," Brisbane said without turning to the room.

Mason stopped and looked at Brisbane.

He let out a sigh and slowly turned to face Mason. "Yes, part of the ritual was to perform erotic asphyxiation during intercourse to heighten the orgasm, thereby increasing the power of transcendence. We believe asphyxiating the subject also increases our power. Therefore, sometimes the ritual included both partners, sometimes only the subject."

"Asphyxiation by simulated strangulation."

"Yes."

"Then someone in the group got carried away and strangled her to death."

Brisbane pounded the desk. "That's not how it happened. It was all done with safety, with witnesses to see that it never went … too far."

"Except, one time, it *did* go too far."

Brisbane's whole body started to tremble. "Yes."

Brisbane nodded. "De Graaf, Meunier, then I had just completed the transcendence ceremony. We were reciting the sacred text in preparation for the next member's rites, when the girl's face became terribly distorted. Her breathing became erratic. She convulsed and died." His face twisted in torment, and he stared at something unseen at his feet. "She was just lying there. No one was touching her. She must have been ill, or had a weak heart. It was an accident."

Mason took a moment to control his anger. "You all vowed to secrecy, made up the story of her dying in that room, then took her out to the desert and dumped her body."

Brisbane looked away and slowly nodded.

"All of you have performed this type of ritual on many occasions? And this is the first time this had happened?"

Brisbane looked at Mason. "Yes. We've performed this ceremony once every new moon, for about a year now."

"And always the same eight members?"

"Don't ask me to name them—"

"Meunier already gave me the names."

Brisbane rubbed his forehead and looked like he might collapse at any moment.

"I want you to write it all down: the members' names, the ritual that led to the girl's death, and a list of all the brothels that supplied you with the girls."

"If I write this, promise me it will not leave your hands, and that everything said in this room is confidential."

"I can't promise that. I have to talk to the police or I'll wind up in jail for withholding evidence. I'll try to leave out the details, but they're going to want to talk to you and the rest of the members."

"But I'm telling you that the girl's death was an accident."

"You raped a drugged child—"

A barely audible creak of door hinges made Mason stop and both of them turn to the noise. Cynthia stood just outside the door. She wore a bathrobe, though her face was still dirty. Brisbane stood and took two steps backward, as he struggled to appear calm.

"Darling, you should take your bath before the doctor arrives."

Cynthia stepped into the room as she glared at her father. "I knew it. I knew you were a depraved pedophile."

"You don't know what you're saying," Brisbane said. "It's the shock of captivity."

Cynthia looked at Mason. "I want you to know that he never did anything inappropriate to me. But ever since I was a child, he took too much interest in my girlfriends. Touching them, kissing them on the cheek, putting them on his lap."

"Cynthia," Brisbane said, "you will stop this nonsense immediately."

She stepped closer to the desk and her father. "And when I was older, he flirted with my girlfriends, fawning over them, acting so nervous around them that I thought he would have an orgasm in his trousers."

"That is enough!" Brisbane yelled. He advanced on Cynthia, but stopped himself at the last moment.

"And he would fly into a jealous rage whenever I talked about boys. Heaven forbid I dare declare my love for a boy." She looked at Brisbane. "He couldn't stand the idea of another man touching me, fondling my breasts—"

Brisbane backhanded Cynthia with such force that she spun and tumbled to the floor.

Mason grabbed him by the lapels and slammed him into the bookcase behind the desk. "You touch her again, I'll cut off your hands."

Mason shoved Brisbane again and went to Cynthia. He bent and gently pulled her hand from her face to see how badly she was hurt. The whole right side of her face glowed crimson, and Brisbane's ring had cut her right cheek. She tried to hold back her tears and wrapped her arms around Mason.

Brisbane growled with rage. He shoved books and art objects off the bookshelves, and then stormed out of the room. Mason watched him leave, while suppressing his temptation to run after him and carry out his threat.

Cynthia said into Mason's shoulder, "Now do you see why I don't want to spend any time in this house?"

"You need care and time to recover, and the best place to do that is with your mother."

Cynthia pulled away from Mason and snickered. "My mother is incapable of taking care of herself."

The sound of a throat clearing came from the door. Mason and Cynthia looked to see Mrs. Brisbane at the door. She glanced sympathetically at her daughter, then gave Mason a resentful glare.

"The doctor is here, darling. You should clean yourself up before you see him." She finally noticed the cut and swelling on Cynthia's cheek. She winced, then stiffened to get control of herself. "Your father has left. Please, go take a bath. Quickly, now. The doctor can't wait forever."

Cynthia looked at Mason. "Will you be here when I'm finished?"

Mason shook his head. "I have to go back to that house. There might be clues. Maybe some way to find the others. And I'm sure Inspecteur Verger will want to speak with you later."

"Then come back to me when you're finished. Please."

"Maybe in the afternoon."

"Cynthia," Mrs. Brisbane said, "I'm sure Mr. Collins has many pressing matters."

Cynthia kept her gaze on Mason. "If you don't come back for me, I *will* find you."

"Cynthia, please," Mrs. Brisbane said. "You must have the doctor look at you."

Mason tilted his head, telling Cynthia to do what her mother asked. He stood, prompting her to do the same. She looked more defiant and determined than mentally shattered, and Mason admired her strength. But he knew the trauma, the nightmares, would come flooding in once the shock wore off.

Cynthia finally moved toward the door and exited after one last glance back at Mason.

"Millie has your bath ready," Mrs. Brisbane said. "I'll see you in a minute, dear."

Mrs. Brisbane waited until Cynthia was down the hall before stepping up to Mason. "Now that I have my daughter back, I want you to leave her alone. I am deeply grateful to you for finding her, but now she needs the care of her mother. She's confused after such an ordeal, and is looking to you as a father figure. You must see that she doesn't need you around to confuse her further."

"Yeah, I see that."

"Good. I've already tolerated one man's possession of her. I have no intention of tolerating another."

Mason nodded. "You won't have to worry about me." He started to leave.

Mrs. Brisbane said more to the room than Mason, "Thank you for bringing my daughter back to me. I sincerely mean that."

Mason nodded once more and left.

The he mansion at the end of the road had police sedans and an ambulance parked in its circular driveway. As Mason walked up to the house, he saw two-man teams of police pacing the lawn and gardens. There was a gaggle of reporters cordoned off by a uniformed officer. Flashbulbs went off as Mason passed them.

The sun was above the horizon, bronzing the roof and upper floors of the house. The morning light gave Mason a clearer view of the house, and in hindsight, this house seemed an obvious place to set up a torture palace. Hopefully, finding out who owned this place would provide a clue, though the killer had done a good job of covering his tracks up to now. Mason shouldn't have let his assumptions blind his judgment. He'd assumed the hiding place would be in a remote part of the city, and not in the poshest neighborhood of Tangier.

He walked up the portico steps and was met by a uniformed policeman, who said something to him in French.

"Inspecteur Verger," Mason said.

The policeman gestured for him to stay put. Which Mason ignored, stepping into the house. The policeman stood next to

Verger and barked something at Mason. Mason ignored him. Verger dismissed the policeman, who managed to flash Mason an angry glare before departing.

"You have saved me the trouble of looking for you," Verger said.

"Happy to accommodate. Find anything?"

"First I want to learn how you discovered this place and the young lady."

Mason gave him a brief rundown.

"And you only saved one girl? The daughter of the man who hired you."

Mason ignored the snide remark. He knew Verger was probing for a weak spot. "How many have you saved, Inspecteur?"

Verger bristled; his smug grin vanished. "I telephoned Sir Wilfred's residence, and I was told he had left in a great hurry. Is that not odd? Just when his daughter is rescued and returns home. And you discover leads in a few days that eluded us for weeks. Again, very odd."

"Embarrassing for you, maybe. But not odd."

Captain Rousselot's entrance interrupted whatever Verger intended to say in return.

"Gentlemen," Rousselot said.

"Capitaine Rousselot," Verger said with feigned surprise. "Is not Commandant Lambert supervising this case?"

"Yes, thank you, Inspecteur Verger, that reminds me to speak to him about how Mr. Collins has accomplished more in a few days than you have in several weeks."

Verger looked like he might pull out his revolver and use it on both of them. He pointed to Mason and said, "This man—"

"Inspecteur, I suggest you speak to Cynthia Brisbane while her memories are still fresh. Her information could be vital." When Verger hesitated, Rousselot said, "Now, Inspecteur."

Verger gritted his teeth and left.

"Verger will make a good inspector one day," Rousselot said. "He is smart but has little homicide experience."

"His pride is stepping all over his intelligence."

Rousselot watched Verger exit, as if considering something. He then turned back to Mason. "Shall we explore the chamber of horrors?"

They walked through the house, examining things as they went. In a corridor tucked away from the main hallway, two policemen were using axes to chop through a massive butler's pantry.

"The interior access to the basement," Rousselot said. "They found it only when they entered the basement by the exterior door. The pantry is hinged by some kind of formidable mechanism."

"I suppose that wasn't the owner's idea."

"No. This was installed recently. However, the real feat of engineering waits for us in the basement. I suppose you saw the bedroom upstairs."

Mason nodded. "My guess is one of the members decided to continue the sex rituals on his own. Who is the owner?"

"A British earl. Apparently, the family has had financial difficulty for some time, and he hasn't been here since before the war."

They exited the house through the dining hall, and while they crossed the patio, Mason filled him in on what Brisbane had told him: that the ceremony included asphyxiating the girls during sex, though he'd insisted the girl died between rapes; that Brisbane had also received a letter threatening his daughter because of the asphyxiation; and finally that Brisbane had provided a list of the members, the brothels, and the locations of the ceremonies.

"I assume you intend to hand over that list to me," Rousselot said.

Mason had debated whether to tell Rousselot, but in the end, he decided he could trust the captain. "One of the eight members performing the rituals is Commandant Lambert."

The revelation stopped Rousselot. He balled his fists and gritted his teeth. "That is why the *trou de cul* took over the case. That is why our investigation led us nowhere. He must be suppressing evidence and warning witnesses."

Rousselot regained his self-control and turned to Mason. "Brisbane's word might be enough to force him out of the police force and ruin his reputation, but this is Tangier, and the girl was a prostitute. Plus, Lambert is very well connected."

"I want you to hold off saying anything to anyone."

"I will not let him serve one more day on the force."

"If it gets out, the others will skip town. We keep him in our back pockets. He could be useful."

Rousselot glared at him, but he said nothing. Finally, he growled in frustration and walked toward the west side of the house. Mason caught up to him, and they came to a reinforced door once used by the servants and to bring in supplies. There were many footprints leading in and out around the entrance. They descended a set of thick wooden steps to what had once been a large open space, bounded by the original servants' quarters and a crude kitchen. The far half of the space had been walled recently to make a long, narrow hallway serving several spacious rooms.

Mason and Rousselot passed two junior inspectors and two uniformed policemen gathering evidence and taking photographs, and they entered the first room off the hallway. This newly fashioned room had a series of open shower stalls. Shelves and simple closets stood against the wall and rose to the ceiling. The shelves held towels and white cotton gowns—like the one Cynthia had worn when she escaped. The closets contained various silk robes, period costumes, and leather corsets.

Mason shook his head, spun around, and walked out of the room.

The next room was even more disturbing than the last. Within this cinder-block room hung manacles from the ceiling over a cement concave floor that sloped down to a drain. There was a man-sized metal tub, a high-capacity water hose, and various whips and reed switches arranged on a primitive table.

The macabre scene brought up Mason's own memories of being tortured, and he could easily imagine the terror the children felt when they were brought into this room. His stomach constricted, accompanied by a slow, boiling rage.

"Shit," was all he could say.

Rousselot grunted in agreement. They reentered the hallway, which ended at a heavy wooden door. It sat open, and beyond it, a set of steps led down to another more primitively constructed hallway.

As they descended the stairs, Mason said, "They cut right through the foundation wall and tunneled into the rock. I can't figure it: all this time, money, and manpower for the sole purpose of exploiting children."

They entered the long corridor of hewn rock and earth, supported by thick beams. There were twelve cells on each side. Each cell was roughly cut into the earth, and contained a wooden bench and a bucket for a toilet. It stank of raw sewage, and the stale dankness made the air a stifling miasma.

When they reached the end, Mason turned and looked back down the dark corridor. The cells, now empty and silent, had held frightened and helpless children. It ate at him that he'd been unable to rescue the other children from these horrors. He grabbed one of the open cell doors and slammed it shut.

Rousselot put a hand on his shoulder. "Let us get some fresh air."

Mason nodded, and they walked back toward the exit and welcome daylight.

The cool, fresh air greeted them when they exited the basement. They entered the house again, and Rousselot discussed the search with a junior detective and the sergeant in charge of the uniformed squad. Meanwhile, Mason checked the upstairs rooms once again. He found signs of at least three people who had stayed in the rooms as "resident staff." The clothes and various toiletries pointed to there being at least one woman. There were no personal effects that might help determine their identities. Ironically, he did find a crucifix pendant on the floor by the nightstand in the room used by the woman. And some toiletries in another bathroom suggested a man of Western European origin.

All in all, they had been very thorough in clearing out any incriminating evidence. Obviously, they had prepared to abandon the house at a moment's notice.

Mason descended the stairs, and as he was about to reach the ground floor, Rousselot rushed up to him.

"We may have found the truck."

M ason accompanied Rousselot to one of the police sedans waiting in the circular driveway.

"Some road workers called into headquarters that they saw an abandoned truck that matches Cynthia Brisbane's description," Rousselot said as he climbed into the car. "We happen to be the closest to the location."

Mason got in beside Rousselot, and his chest constricted when he saw a new man behind the wheel, the place Tazim had once occupied. Their sedan turned right out of the driveway and headed away from the city, down a road that followed the ridgeline.

"What's out this way?"

"The Cap Spartel lighthouse and the Grottoes of Hercules. This road follows the cliffs along the Strait of Gibraltar, and it eventually turns south and follows the Atlantic coastline."

"Either they were planning to get out of the International Zone or trying to head south, then circle back to Tangier."

They fell into silence. Mason was worried about what they might find. If the truck had been abandoned because of engine trouble, the abductors could have panicked and slaughtered the children. He saw that Rousselot felt the same way, as the captain leaned forward to peer out the windshield in quiet vigilance.

Twenty minutes later, the lead motorcycle cop waved his right hand for them to pull off the road. And just below a rise, they came upon the truck. The sign along the side of the truck's cargo box declared in green paint, SOLOMON'S FRUITS ET LÉGUMES.

"That's got to be it," Mason said.

The ten-ton truck sat off the road at an oblique angle, with its hood open. Mason, Rousselot, and the other policemen approached the vehicle. The sun was above the tree line, but the rise of the road kept the area in shadow. The tall, dried grass had been trampled and plowed down by a multitude of feet and tracks of one or two other vehicles.

The men moved up to it with caution, as the cargo box doors were still shut. While the rest remained a few yards away, Mason, Rousselot, and a sergeant stopped in front of the rear doors. Mason's heart pounded in fear of what they might find. All three hesitated a moment before the captain motioned for the rear doors to be opened. The sergeant pulled down the latch and swung open a door. It stopped with a bang. Mason and Rousselot stepped up to the lip of the box. It was empty.

Mason surveyed the grassy hills. The captain seemed to know what Mason was thinking. "They could have taken them away to another location. They had plenty of time."

Mason nodded, but he feared the worst. He took careful steps into the brush, away from the road. They were in an area of hillocks, where the high plateau sloped down to the land at sea level. If the abductors had decided that hauling the children would be too risky, they could have killed them here and dumped the bodies in any one of the deep furrows.

Rousselot ordered the policemen to fan out in a line, and they all began to move along the ridgeline. Mason prayed they would find nothing, though that didn't mean the children were out of danger. The abductors may have just postponed the killing, or they would abandon them somewhere to starve or die of thirst. Or sell them off to slave traders.

The line advanced about two hundred yards before they decided to abandon the search. Mason wanted to continue, but Rousselot convinced him the abductors wouldn't have enough time or manpower to kill a dozen or so young people, then haul the bodies any farther than the two hundred yards. Plus, they had yet to come across any signs that someone, let alone a group, had moved through the tall grass for a long time.

Mason pointed to the several other tire tracks. "Looks like they transferred them to other vehicles."

"We should continue down the road to see if we see the other vehicles," Rousselot said.

"They're long gone. If they didn't kill them here, then they've decided to either get rid of them or wait to kill them in some isolated place."

"Then you should rest," Rousselot said. "You look like shit."

Rousselot had pronounced the word like "sheet," making Mason chuckle in spite of his dark mood, the brief release of tension making him aware of how exhausted he was.

He glanced at his reflection in the car window and had to agree. He had to rest for the long hunt that was ahead of him.

MASON FROZE IN FRONT OF THE APARTMENT DOOR. A SLOW BURN of worry radiated through his exhaustion. He had wedged a small piece of paper between the door of the apartment and the door-jamb before Sara and he had left to watch the police press conference that morning. That piece of paper now lay on the ground.

He jammed the key in the lock and shoved open the door. He

called out Sara's name as he went from room to room. His worry
turned to dread.

Sara was gone.

It was 8:40 a.m., which made it eighteen hours since they had
split up after Mason's visit to Meunier's boat. She could have left
for whatever mission she had planned for that morning. She could
have finally followed through on her threat to leave him and
never come back. Mason hoped it was one or the other, though
that hope faded when he found her clothes and toiletries were
right where she'd left them.

Had the assassins or some of Jennings's henchmen discovered
the hideout, just as Tazim had the day before? And, not finding
Mason, decided to take Sara instead?

Mason's senses bumped into high gear at the possible danger.
He moved to the living room and stood still and silent. He heard
footsteps outside the door, distinct from the normal foot traffic.

A man's footsteps. Then a vague shadow crossed the window
curtains near the door.

Mason moved to the side of the door, with his back to the
wall. He readied his pistol and cursed himself for not changing
locations earlier.

The man outside rapped tentatively on the door. A moment of
silence was followed by a whisper.

"Mason?"

Mason let out his breath and opened the door. Carson stood at
the threshold and grimaced.

"You look positively dreadful," Carson said.

Mason pulled him inside and shut the door.

"You'd better sit down before you fall down," Carson said.

Mason ignored the suggestion. "I thought you'd left for a run
to Spain."

"I changed my mind. Well, that is—" He looked at his feet. "I
felt ashamed for running out on you and Sara. I got on the boat

and was halfway to Spain, when I decided—much to my surprise—that I should face my fears. Stand up to mine enemies in the face of great peril—"

"I get it. You don't need to start quoting Shakespeare."

Carson looked at him with something Mason hadn't seen in his eyes before: sincere conviction. "I want to help."

"Okay, good. The first thing is Sara. She's not here, and she may not have come back after she, Tazim, and I decided to split up yesterday afternoon."

Carson stepped around Mason and surveyed the room, as if Mason had just overlooked her. "Oh, dear." He turned to Mason. "We have to find her."

"She might have come back last night and just left this morning on an errand." Mason rubbed his forehead, trying to clear his thoughts. "I don't know."

"Why don't I look for her? I know all her favorite haunts. And you get some rest. You're not doing anyone much good in your present condition."

"I can't stay here." Mason stopped rubbing his forehead before it started bleeding. He tried to focus his conflicting thoughts. Thoughts that would normally sort themselves out with ease and clarity. "But I can't leave without letting Sara know."

His head started spinning, forcing him to sit. Twenty-four hours with no sleep and little to eat, devastation by the drugs, Tazim's death, and everything else that had happened—it was pushing him to his limits.

"Look," Carson said, "I have a place that I use when things get a little hairy. I'll take you there. You get some rest, and I'll look for Sara. We'll leave a note in case she's just out and about, and I'll check back here from time to time."

Mason agreed. Carson helped him gather his things, including the case notes and photos he'd taped up on the wall. They then left a note that only Sara would understand: *THE TIN MAN HAS SOUGHT SHELTER WITH THE LION.*

Carson drove Mason to an area west of downtown, near the Spanish hospital. He owned a town house located at the end of a row fronting the wide street called Rue de San Francisco. Carson hung around just long enough to get Mason settled before he left on his quest to find Sara.

Despite his exhaustion, Mason picked a small ground-floor room to tape up his notes, newspaper clippings, sketches, and photos, and the strings that connected them. Where he didn't have photos, he used pieces of paper with the names from the conservative men's club and formed a wide circle, with the members of the sex cult in a tighter circle, and finally photos of Jennings, Lambert, and the fake Baron von Litchten in the center.

Lots of notes and photos and threads. Lots of pieces, but no coherent picture.

Mason still felt the money trail would lead to Jennings, though he was certain there was a central piece missing. And the strings connecting the guilty reflected that, as they all converged on a big question mark.

M ason opened his eyes to darkness, except for a ring of light around the edges of his peripheral vision. It took a moment for rational thought to rise to the surface. He remembered now: he'd lain down on the sofa, still clothed, in the early hours of the morning. Or was that yesterday morning?

Finally, Mason got his arms to move, and he lifted his fedora from where it lay across his eyes and forehead. He blinked at the daylight. His back and legs protested as he swung his feet over the edge of the sofa and hoisted his body into a seated position.

"Jesus!" Mason said as he flinched.

Cynthia sat in a chair, still and staring, as if she were a mannequin. Mason rubbed his eyes, thinking it might be a leftover from a dream.

"Did you know you snore?" Cynthia finally said. "You haven't moved a muscle for hours, but your lips flutter when you exhale."

"What are you doing here?"

"You sound like a trolling motor on a skiff."

A more pressing question came to Mason with his rising

consciousness. "Wait a minute. How did you find out where I am?"

"I knew Carson's been assisting you. I simply had to ask him, and he brought me here."

"I told you not to come—" Mason shook his head to clear his brain. "Wherever I am."

"You ought to be more careful. If you want your location to be a secret, staying with Carson isn't your best option. He loves to gossip, you know."

"Cynthia—"

"You forbade me to stay with you, but you said nothing about coming for a visit."

Mason stood and pulled on his suit jacket. "Come on. I'm taking you home." His head spun, and he had to steady himself on the back of Cynthia's chair, his body reminding him that he had consumed only a bowl of soup in the last twenty-four hours.

"I have coffee on," Cynthia said. "And there's enough in Carson's kitchen to make eggs and fry some merguez sausages. You need to eat something before you fall down."

Mason sat back down on the sofa. "What time is it, anyway?"

"Six thirty. That's evening, six thirty."

Mason nodded. "Okay, some coffee and food, and then I take you back home."

Cynthia gave him a half smile and headed for the kitchen.

Mason mustered his strength and shuffled over to a polished mahogany dining table. He'd been too out of it to register anything in Carson's apartment besides the welcoming sofa. The living/dining room was of modest size, but crammed full of antiques, objets d'art, and expensive-looking oil paintings. His thoughts then turned to Sara. She was smart, self-reliant, and certainly unorthodox. Someone could have flown within range of her radar and succumbed to her sexual advances. But aiding and abetting him meant she was in harm's way. He felt pulled in two directions: find the remaining captives or hunt for Sara. He silently apologized to Sara; the children would have to come first.

Cynthia came back in with the coffeepot and a mug. She displayed a smile like Mona Lisa as she poured Mason a cup.

"Your mother must have sent out a search party by now."

Cynthia's smile faded. "When I left, she'd retreated to her sanctuary and her shisha."

"I'm sorry you don't have a better home life. I just want you to get well. You've been through a horrible experience, an experience that could break the strongest person you can imagine."

Cynthia's hand trembled as she poured herself a cup. Mason gently took the pot from her hand and poured the rest of the coffee. Cynthia spun on her heels and fled for the kitchen.

"I'll start the eggs," she said.

Mason was no psychologist. He had no idea how to handle this: whether he should let her do comforting, routine things, like feeding him and pretending life was normal, or make her go home. He went to the kitchen and stood in the doorway to watch her. She had put on an apron and was breaking eggs in a bowl. The sausages were already sizzling in another pan. Cynthia turned and smiled, though her facial muscles were too tense to make much of one. She turned back and began beating the eggs with a fork.

"I hope you like scrambled eggs," Cynthia said as she poured the beaten eggs into a frying pan. "That's the only way I know how to make them. But if you let me stay here, I can learn how to make all sorts of things. You'll see."

"Cynthia ..."

She had started gently stirring the eggs, but it turned to an assault with the spoon, and she banged the sides of the pan with a clang. Mason stepped into the room, but Cynthia whirled around.

"Would you please sit down and let me do this? Please don't ruin this for me."

Mason nodded and returned to the table. Five minutes later, Cynthia put a plate of eggs and sausages in front of him and sat just across from him. The smell of the food triggered his hunger, and he shoveled in the food.

"You're not eating?" Mason asked between mouthfuls.

Cynthia shook her head. Her presence was growing on him, and his impulse to be her protector was clouding his judgment. He ate quickly, so he could get her home before he changed his mind.

"I never cared for domestic stuff before," Cynthia said. "I'd always wanted to be a lawyer."

Mason avoided asking her what brought on her change of heart. "I'm sure you'll make a fine one."

A moment of silence fell between them. Then Cynthia said, "I wonder if I'll ever be able to be with a man. Now I hate them all. Except you. And maybe Carson."

"You'll meet a nice guy one day, someone you can trust."

"I trust you."

Mason put down his fork. "Cynthia, it's normal to have feelings for the person who rescued you. The same goes for the rescuer. And that's fine. But that's all it is. To think it's something else is a mistake." He got up from the table. "It's time to go."

"Can't I stay a little longer?"

Mason leaned on the table for emphasis, but kept his tone tender. "We found the truck last night. The one transporting the other abductees. It was empty, meaning those kids are out there somewhere. I have to keep looking for them and the people who abducted you. I can't leave you here. I could be out all night."

"Then don't you want to hear what happened to me? It might help."

Mason hesitated. "Are you really ready to talk about it? It could stir up some awful memories."

"I'm stronger than you think."

"No, I know how strong you are. I've seen that."

Cynthia waited silently with a resolute expression.

"All right," Mason said, and tipped his head toward the living room.

Cynthia got to her feet and moved over to the sofa. Mason waited for her to get settled in before he sat across from her in a wingback chair. The sun had aligned with the direction of the street, and the umber light pierced the red-and-gold curtains with a glancing blow. Cynthia looked nervous and clasped her hands as she stared at a point of gold on the curtain. Mason waited for her to start, but she seemed to be waiting for a question in order to begin.

Mason accommodated her. "What do you remember of your abduction?"

"Shopping with my mother. We stopped by the Moroccan lady who does henna tattoos. Then we had some iced tea at one of the cafés in the Grand Socco."

"What about after that?"

Cynthia seemed to struggle to put her memories into words. "When we were inside the medina, I thought I was becoming ill. My heart pounded, and my face was hot. Then I felt dizzy. I tried to tell my mother, but I couldn't talk. Things became blurry. The people in the streets, too, like in old photographs when someone moved at the moment of exposure, and only a vague form is left. But then there were other people who were so sharp, so clear. They stared at me and spoke a language I couldn't understand. One sat in the old fountain in a small square, and it beckoned me. I looked for my mother, but she had disappeared." Cynthia hesitated and took in shallow breaths. "I panicked …"

"Cynthia. Maybe you're not ready."

"I want to tell you. Especially you."

Mason nodded. Cynthia took a deep breath and continued, "I remember hands holding me and urging me forward. They were like spirits, too. Indistinct faces and disembodied hands."

"You never saw their faces clearly?"

Cynthia shook her head. "They just kept pulling me along. Nothing else is clear in my memory until I woke up in a dark room. A stone floor, stone walls. A cot. The only light came from a dim bulb outside the room. It came in through the cracks in the wooden door. I screamed for help and heard other voices, young people—I couldn't tell their ages, but boys and girls. Some yelled at me to shut up or they would come. Some just cried and said nothing. I didn't know who 'they' were, and I didn't really care. All I wanted was to get out of there."

By this point Cynthia's eyes were unfocused, as if watching unseen images. Tears formed in them, but her body was still.

"I saw the cells," Mason said. "You don't have to describe them."

Her eyes remained fixed on the curtains, now glowing ruby red. "They did come."

"Who came?"

"A woman and a man."

"Moroccan?"

"No. White. The woman was bigger than the man. They both wore Venetian carnival masks—horrible, grinning faces like something out of an Edgar Allan Poe horror story. I never saw their faces. The woman had muscles and light brown hair. The man looked older, with gray hair. He was thin, but very strong."

"What did they say?"

"They only spoke to each other in Italian."

"Are you sure it was Italian?"

"I speak some Italian, French, and Spanish. A little Arabic. It was Italian."

"What happened when they came for you?"

"They took me to another room, attached my hands to chains hanging from the ceiling, and sprayed me with a hose. Like a fire hose. Then they left me hanging there. It seemed like hours. I was so cold, and the pain in my arms and shoulders was agonizing."

"Do you know why they did this to you?"

"They said nothing, but one of the other prisoners whispered that I must not make a sound. Never. And to obey every command, or the punishment would get worse."

"Did you ever hear their names, or learn more about them?"

"They were careful. I did get the sense that they were a couple. Or like brother and sister. They were always together and behaved as if they were intimate, somehow."

"What else can you tell me about the people who imprisoned you, or the ones …" Mason hesitated.

"The ones who raped me?"

Mason said in a soft tone, "Yes."

"I was drugged most of the time. They drugged all of us, I'm sure. Sometimes it was just to keep us calm. They deprived us of food and drink for long periods. Each time the drug wore off, they seemed to know it, and they would bring soup or greasy cabbage and tea. And I always knew when something bad was about to happen, because they'd bring me much more food—meat stews and vegetables. That's how I finally determined that the food contained the drugs.

"I tried to stop eating, but they would punish me if the plate was not empty. There was nowhere to conceal the uneaten food, except in the bucket for, you know, going to the bathroom. And they routinely checked the bucket for food scraps."

Cynthia paused and took a couple of deep breaths. "I finally got the idea of eating a portion and disposing the rest in the bucket, and, well … holding off number two until I had discarded the extra food in the bucket." She stopped and fidgeted with her hands, as if embarrassed and distressed by the memory.

Mason cleared his throat and leaned forward. "You're a very brave young lady. Why don't we talk about the rest later?"

"No, I want to finish. I have to."

When Mason nodded, Cynthia continued. "I ate less and less when I saw that it was working. I had to eat some of the food, so I was still ingesting the drug. I avoided going under completely, but neither was I ever fully aware. Sort of in a twilight, like a wakeful sleep. Sometimes I wasn't sure what was real or the drug. I still had hallucinations—people who weren't really there, or I found intense fascination with things. I became quite friendly with a cockroach." She half smiled at the black humor. "I have vague images of being led in the corridor, of them bathing me or dressing me in a clean gown."

"Was it always the same man and woman who did this?"

"As far as I know, yes. There were two Moroccan guards—the ones who searched for me when I escaped—but they never touched me."

"Do you know of anyone else who might have held back on eating?"

"One time, I heard screaming from another cell. A girl. It woke me, and I peeked through the cracks in the door. The woman came with two others. The girl sounded lucid. She screamed at them in German or Dutch, I think. Moments later, I saw the woman and two Moroccan men dragging her away. She seemed out of her mind, and I began to wonder if I was in an insane asylum." Cynthia looked at Mason. "Maybe she lost her mind. Maybe she had withheld food like me. I don't know, but I never saw her again. I kept wondering when it would be my turn. To be dragged off and never seen again."

The glow of twilight seeped through the curtains. Mason and Cynthia sat in silence as the muezzin summoned the devout to prayer.

Cynthia said, "I used to think that call to prayer quite lovely, but now it makes me feel sad and lonely."

In the dim light, Mason could see only the softness of

Cynthia's face, devoid of definition, and her body in silhouette. He made no move to turn on a lamp, guessing Cynthia would be more comfortable in the shadows because of what he was about to ask her.

"Do you remember any details about the rapist?"

"They always increased the dose of the drugs on those nights when I was taken to be bathed and dressed in a gown. And even when I started holding back food, I still felt the drug more intensely. After being bathed and dressed in a gown, someone dressed me in a white robe and then led me out of the basement."

"Were you taken someplace outside the mansion?"

"As far as I know, I was never taken outside. There was a long corridor, then a wide, sweeping staircase. It might have been the drugs, the hallucinations, but then I remember a profusion of silk fabric everywhere hanging from the ceilings. A mass of candles and pillows. It seemed so beautiful, moving through fabric as billowy as clouds. Like a dream before the nightmare. Despite being absolutely terrified, the drug heightened my senses. I tried to concentrate on looking for a way to run away, but I couldn't trust what I saw from moment to moment. And I was afraid that if I tried, I would end up like that Dutch girl, dragged away and never seen again.

"Music played somewhere—harp or flute, like ancient music. Not Moroccan. It was all like a beautiful nightmare. There was always this massive bed and candles. Someone would come. A doctor, perhaps, to check for cleanliness or … infections. He would check my eyes and pulse, and ask questions."

"To see if you were really under the influence of the drugs?"

"I assume so."

"Did he touch you inappropriately?"

"A few times. After that, he would leave. Often, I would lose track of time. The surroundings, the music, would put me into sort of a trance. I would imagine I was a fairy-tale princess, or like

Scheherazade, in some exotic palace. Anything to make what was ugly a pleasant dream. My lover would come, my prince, to take me away. Then someone *would* come, wearing a robe and mask, and the dream always turned into a nightmare. I tried to keep the dream going—this was the love of my life seducing me. But the grunting, breath that stank of cigars, the gray hair, the wrinkles …" Her voice faded into silence.

Mason thought he might be the one to lose control just listening and imagining, and he found his hands gripped the arms of the chair so hard that he had distorted the padding underneath. "You never saw any of the men's faces?"

Cynthia shook her head. "I only have vague images of a tall man."

"Think hard, Cynthia. You only recall one man coming to the bed?"

Cynthia thought a moment as she wiped her tears with her sleeve. "I don't know for sure. At least, by the time I was able to withhold some of the drugs, I believe it was only one man."

"Did he ever say anything?"

Cynthia took a few moments to respond. "He recited something in Latin, like a prayer or poem, as if he were performing some kind of ritual. 'Aphrodite' and 'Ishtar' are the only words I could understand." Her body shuddered at the thought of this. She bent forward as if she had lost her strength to sit upright.

Mason's anger forced him to his feet. "Okay, that's enough. You shouldn't have to remember any more, and I can't listen to another word."

Cynthia remained in the limp posture, but she said, "I could recognize his voice. He said these things in my ear. I will never forget the sound of his voice. Never."

Mason felt so angry that his skin crawled. His hands clenched fists as he looked down on Cynthia.

Night had come, and they were in darkness. Mason turned on

the floor lamp, fearing the gloom would make Cynthia worse. He sat next to her on the sofa, and saw that her face was puffed and red, her eyes swollen and bloodshot.

Mason was so upset that he'd neglected one important question. "I have to ask you one more thing."

She nodded. "If you let me stay here."

"I have to go out, and I can't leave you alone."

"Carson should be back soon, and I'll just come back anyway."

Mason knew she was right. "Cynthia, the doctor who would come to examine you, was it always the same man?"

When she nodded, Mason asked, "Can you describe him at all?"

Cynthia lifted her head and looked at Mason, as if an idea had come to her. "Maybe if you can find him ..."

"What did he look like?"

"I don't know how much of this is distorted by the drugs, but his face reminded me of Humpty Dumpty."

She cracked a smile at the absurdity of it. Mason felt a surge of adrenaline and not just a little bit of rage.

Cynthia went on: "A Humpty Dumpty with thick glasses perched on his nose. Oblong head, very white skin, and completely bald except for a preposterous little tuft in the back of his skull. And he smelled of cheap cologne."

Mason took her hands. "You're a remarkable girl." He then rose, walked over to another chair, grabbed his suit coat.

"You're leaving?"

"Cynthia, I know who that doctor is. And I'm going after the bastard."

"Then I can stay?"

Mason put on his hat and knelt to look at her. "You have to promise me you'll stay out of sight. Don't go upstairs. Stay in the kitchen and use only the lights you'll really need. If someone tries to break in, use the back door and run. Don't get trapped upstairs."

Cynthia nodded. "I promise."

As Mason went for the front door, Cynthia said, "Give him a pop in the nose for me."

"A pop in the nose is going to be the least of his problems."

I t took Mason several minutes to talk himself down from
wanton homicide to simmering rage. The most important
thing was to get Dr. Amoretti to talk; that's what his detective
training had taught him. Push too hard right off the bat and the
doc would just shut down and run for cover. And that would
cause whatever self-control he had just mustered to vanish, and he
really would murder the man.

Mason approached the hospital entrance. Two cops were
bringing in a victim of a knife fight, prompting Mason to lower
his head and slip through the front doors. He went up to the third
floor, where Amoretti had his office and exam room. He knew
Amoretti was there, as he had called, pretending to be the
concerned parent of one of the doctor's patients. He tried to act
calm, but he knew some of his rage showed through. The few
people wandering around at nine in the evening gave him double
takes or moved quickly out of his way.

The woman at the nurses' station directed him to wait, saying
Dr. Amoretti was busy with a patient. Mason didn't want to raise
any alarms—not yet, anyway—so he politely asked where he
could find the bathroom. He knew where the bathroom was, and

that it was in the same hallway as Amoretti's office. His practiced calm must have improved once he'd arrived on the third floor, because the nurse dutifully directed him and went back to doing her work.

Halfway down the hall, Mason entered Dr. Amoretti's waiting room. There was one other patient waiting, and, fortunately, no nurse to block Mason or call for help. Mason took a deep breath and entered Amoretti's exam room as if everything were just peachy.

Dr. Amoretti was leaning over the exam table, with his stethoscope against the chest of a twelve-year-old boy. That tableau pushed Mason's rage up a notch, but he didn't care at that point. He was inside and had the exit blocked. The boy's mother was the first to notice Mason. She looked surprised but not shocked. Then Amoretti saw him. He straightened as if his spine were on a tight spring, and yanked the stethoscope out of his ears.

"Mr. Collins. You can't come in here while I'm examining a patient. Please leave and tell Nurse Barker you would like an appointment." The doc had tried to sound commanding, but his voice quivered.

"Ma'am, please take your boy and step outside. The doctor and I have some very important issues to discuss."

"Madame," Amoretti said, "you will stay here, please. This man is just leaving."

"Now, ma'am. Please."

Mason said it firmly without raising his voice, but it was enough to prompt the mother to collect her son and whisk him out of the office. Amoretti tried to use the mother and son's exit to make one of his own, but Mason cut him off.

"You will let me pass," Amoretti said with panic in his voice.

"I'm guessing you didn't get the message: One of the abductees you examined for the rape sessions escaped last night and is talking. To me."

Amoretti tried a defiant expression on for size, but the trembling betrayed him.

"No, apparently you didn't," Mason said. "But guess who's one of the people she's been talking about?"

Amoretti backed up slowly as his gaze flitted around the room, looking for a magical exit or a weapon to defend himself. Mason kept up with him, advancing as the doctor retreated.

"The girl described you perfectly. It left no doubt that you are the doctor who gave them a clean bill of health before they were raped or sodomized."

"That is a lie!" Amoretti said, and looked over Mason's shoulder at the door. "Nurse! Help!"

"We're all alone, Doc. No one is coming to your rescue. Now, I want you to tell me who hired you. Tell me who is behind the abductions, rape, and murder, and I might let you keep your face."

"Help!"

Amoretti kept backing up; then, when he hit one wall, he would change direction. He held his hands out to fend off an attack. Mason's patience was wearing thin.

"I promise that if you tell me everything you know, you can walk out of here. You could even try getting out of Tangier before the cops come after you. You'll be gone before anyone finds out."

"I don't know what you're talking about!" Then, "Help!"

Mason grabbed him by his lab coat and pulled him in close. "I'm losing my patience. You're a weasel who deserves to have his dick cut off. I'm sure I can find the right instrument here somewhere. And someone can patch you up before you bleed to death."

The door burst open, and two orderlies came rushing in, one after the other. Amoretti squealed and ran for the door.

The two orderlies should have stayed together, but one was too confident of his abilities, and the other hesitated. Mason used the first man's bulk to perform a judo move, spinning him ass over end, and the orderly landed hard against the wall and the exam table.

The other orderly took a swing at Mason, but Mason blocked his arm and, with two blows to the chin and one to the stomach, sent him to the floor.

Mason rushed out into the hallway. He just caught a glimpse of a door closing, one that led to a back staircase. He ran to it and swung open the door. He heard running footsteps echoing in the concrete staircase, accompanied by grunts of panic. In his terror, the doctor had used poor judgment and run up the stairs.

Mason took two steps at a time. On the landing halfway between the fourth and fifth floors, he caught up to Amoretti. He didn't have to grab and tackle the man; the doctor panicked and threw himself in the corner. He held up his hands to fend off the assault and made a high-pitched whine.

Mason put his hands on the wall on either side of Amoretti's face. "I want answers, or I start breaking your bones. Who's behind the abductions and murders?"

All the doctor could say was "Please!"

The doctor's cowardice, especially after he'd exploited so many tranquilized children, sent Mason over the edge. He punched Amoretti with a rigid open hand just below the sternum. The sharp blow to the knot of nerves briefly paralyzed the man's lungs. He tried to scream. His mouth popped wide, but nothing came out.

"Names, Doctor!"

Mason heard a multitude of running footsteps in the stairwell. The orderlies had enlisted reinforcements, which probably included the two policemen he'd seen bringing in the knife-fight victim. Mason was out of time. He jammed his right hand into the doctor's crotch and grabbed his testicles. He squeezed and the doctor wailed.

"I'm going to crush your balls if you don't tell me."

Mason let off on the pressure.

"I don't know who the abductors are. I swear. I only serviced the children at the mansion."

"Who hired you?"

Amoretti hesitated as he gasped for air. Mason wrapped his left hand around Amoretti's throat and squeezed the man's testicles even harder this time. Mason had to yell over Amoretti's screams. "Who is he? Who hired you? Tell me now or I'll squeeze them until they burst."

The pursuers were no more than two flights below them. Amoretti signaled that he wanted to talk, and Mason let off the pressure on the man's throat and testicles.

"It was that American woman. Marjorie Ravenna!"

Mason hid his surprise by getting in Amoretti's face. "Who were you examining the children for? Who raped them?"

The pursuers were almost upon them, and Mason squeezed the man's crotch harder.

"I can't. He'll ruin me."

Strong hands tried to pry Mason away from the doctor, but that just made Mason squeeze harder. Fists pounded him, but Mason resisted. He yelled in Amoretti's ear. "Tell me who was there to rape the children."

Just as Mason felt a needle jabbed into his neck, Amoretti screamed, "Jennings. It was Jennings!"

Mason released Amoretti and whirled around to face four orderlies and two policemen. He swung wildly at one of them before his legs buckled and he fell to his knees. His ears hissed, he lost all feeling, then he passed out.

M ason felt like a car had dragged him across a field of stones while he was simultaneously suffering from a three-alarm hangover. The light of a bare bulb seemed to burn through his eyes and pierce his brain. He was the sole occupant of the small cell, and his nearest jailed neighbors were at the other end of the corridor.

He stood with some effort, using the bars of the cell to steady himself. At the hospital, he'd been so focused on Amoretti that he'd ignored the blows from fists and truncheons, compliments of the four orderlies and two cops, hence the multiple points of pain.

He coughed sharply, clearing his lungs. The sound alerted a guard, who opened the main access door at the left end of the corridor. The guard peeked in, glanced at Mason, then closed the door again.

Mason called out toward the door, "Hey, bring me some water. And tell Captain Rousselot to get in here. It's urgent."

When no one responded, he shuffled back to the bench and sat. He yelled a couple more times for water and for Rousselot, but no one came. It occurred to him that maybe the guards were keeping their distance because they knew someone was coming to shank him. He sat up straight and kept a vigilant watch.

Fifteen minutes later, the corridor door opened again, and Rousselot entered with the guard. The guard placed a wooden stool near the cell door and left. Rousselot wore his dress uniform, which was a little tight in the gut, causing him to sit with a sigh.

"What time is it?" Mason asked.

"Eight thirty in the morning."

Mason tried to rub away his grogginess. "You didn't have to get all dolled up just for me."

"I assume you are referring to my uniform. Tazim's funeral is set for eleven this morning. Most of the police force will be out to honor him. Usually Muslims are required to bury the dead within twenty-four hours, but the autopsy delayed it until today. That has made the locals quite upset."

"Not to mention being shot by a Nazarene protecting another Nazarene."

Rousselot returned only a cold stare. "Now, what is so urgent that you wanted to talk to me?"

"Before I get into that, I need to ask you a favor. I want you to check up on Cynthia Brisbane. I left her alone at Carson's when I went to go see the good doctor."

"Carson rang me when you didn't come home last night. Cynthia's with him, over my objections. Mrs. Brisbane demands her return, but the girl is old enough to decide where she wants to stay."

"Carson is harmless."

"I don't think Mrs. Brisbane is worried about Monsieur Carson."

Mason rubbed a sore spot on his neck. "What the hell did they shoot me with? I can't remember a worse hangover."

Rousselot smiled. "You made one of the orderlies very angry

for giving him a beating. He gave you enough sedative to subdue three people."

A prison guard walked past, prompting two of the inmates down the hall to demand water.

"Where am I?" Mason asked. "It looks like a dungeon."

"That's precisely what it was, the dungeon of the former pasha's palace, in the Kasbah. We use this for drunks, drug addicts, and difficult cases. We thought it best to keep you isolated."

"If that was to keep those assassins away from me, it won't work for long."

"Perhaps you should have thought of that before assaulting Dr. Amoretti—"

"You've got to pick up a Marjorie Ravenna at the equestrian center. Now. In fact, I'd pick up the stable manager, too, as I think he's partnered with Ravenna."

"Would you like to explain?"

"Amoretti provided his medical services at the mansion to make sure the children were healthy and drugged enough to be raped. And Amoretti told me that Marjorie Ravenna hired him for the job."

Rousselot showed a tick of surprise. "And how do you know all of this?"

"Cynthia Brisbane described the doctor to a T. She also told me about a woman and man who ran the cells with an iron fist, and Ravenna and the stable manager loosely fit her descriptions."

Rousselot called for a guard and told him to pass on his orders to arrest Marjorie Ravenna as quickly as possible.

Mason said, "You've also got to put a guard on Amoretti before he tries to make a run for it."

"He's not going very far. You put him in the hospital. He'll live, but has some—how shall I say—damaged organs. He may be guilty of despicable things, but you should not have—"

"He gave up Jennings."

That stopped Rousselot.

"Amoretti admitted that he saw Jennings at the mansion at the time of his exams. That means he's also got to be behind the abductions."

"We can question Jennings, but Amoretti is refusing to speak to us."

"You've got to at least search Amoretti's house before any evidence disappears."

"Would you please stop telling me how to do my job," Rousselot said, then took a moment to calm down. "We will question Madam Ravenna, but I'm sure Amoretti will claim he gave you her and Jennings's names to save his testicles." Rousselot couldn't help a faint smile. "With Cynthia Brisbane's testimony, we can detain the doctor, but it will be difficult to convince the prosecuting judge to make a case based on a witness who was under the influence of a very powerful hallucinogen."

"Then it's up to you to get Ravenna or Amoretti to talk. Or is Commandant Lambert going to quash that, too?"

Rousselot looked stung but offered no rebuttal. "Why do you think I am here? Because I enjoy visiting with you in this place? I respect you, but I don't like you. Your anger makes you brutal."

"When it comes to scumbags, and trying to save children, I'm willing to go a lot further."

"I am here because you are the only one who can bring this to an end."

"I thought you didn't like my methods."

"I do not like guns either, but I use one when I have no other choice. The commandant is suppressing our investigation. The city officials want the case resolved. But only as long as it keeps their hands clean and reputations intact. I am also turning to you because I am being transferred back to Lyon. You will have no one in authority on your side."

"So, you're the sacrificial lamb."

"I am happy to go back to France and get out of this rotten city. My only regret is that I will not be here to help you. Though I am not sure what can be accomplished in such a short time, with or without my help. The two Moroccans are refusing to talk, and the commandant and the prosecuting judge are putting forward the case against them tomorrow. That will put an official end to the investigation. Unless you can discover conclusive evidence against Jennings, or any other of the individuals, your efforts will come to nothing."

"I can't do much in here."

"Someone has posted your bail."

"I haven't had a bail hearing yet."

"The right amount of money in the correct hands can do wonders in Tangier."

Rousselot hoisted himself off the stool. "You are free to go. Despite what I have just said, I feel I must advise you to leave Tangier before you face a judge and jury. You will end up in prison, and I'm sure you will not make it out alive. I fear for your life, Monsieur Collins. There are too many people in high places who want this to go away."

"There's still a bunch of children out there, somewhere."

"Tomorrow morning I will no longer be captain. I can do nothing."

Mason stepped up to the cell door. "Help me, Jean-Marie. Make up an excuse to stay on a couple more days and help me get Jennings. You can't walk away from this."

Rousselot stopped at the door and turned to Mason. "And, by the way, your friend Sara Patterson was found early this morning by an oil-storage facility south of the city."

Mason grabbed the bars. "Is she still alive?"

"She was beaten and left for dead. She suffered some internal damage and has a severe concussion. She's due for surgery, but the doctors are optimistic that she will recover."

"It's got to be those assassins or else Jennings's henchmen."

"Once Mademoiselle Patterson is well enough to talk, we'll find out who did this."

"What hospital?"

"Seeing her would be a very bad idea. But since I know you will ignore logic, I can tell you that she is at the same hospital where you attacked Dr. Amoretti." Rousselot approached the cell and glared at Mason. "But if you cause any more mayhem, I will personally see that you are locked up for a very long time. Goodbye, Monsieur Collins. And good luck."

MASON STEPPED OUT OF THE OLD PALACE AND HAD TO SQUINT against the bright sunlight. As when he had exited the prison in Marseille, he wasn't sure who would be waiting for him. Word could have gotten out about his temporary incarceration, and there were even more people interested in silencing him than before. And, like last time, Carson waited for him in the shade of the Kasbah wall with his ubiquitous umbrella.

Mason made a beeline for Carson, and they met in the middle of the rectangular plaza.

"You're costing me a great deal of money, Mr. Collins."

"Put it on my tab. Sara was beaten last night."

"Yes, I'm aware of that. And I expected you would demand that I take you to her, despite the obvious dangers." Carson gestured toward the heart of the Kasbah. "Shall we? I have a vehicle waiting at the Marshan Gate. And I have a plan."

"What kind of plan?"

"You'll see."

Mason monitored the surroundings as they strolled—a little too slowly for Mason's taste.

"If you're worried about the assassins, they're looking for you in the wrong place. Someone spread the word that you're being held at police headquarters."

"Rousselot."

"Yes, the captain has turned out to be a good egg, despite being a Frenchman."

"Thanks for watching out for Cynthia."

"I caught her trying to crawl out the kitchen window. I thought she was a juvenile burglar, and she thought I was there to take her away." Carson rubbed his chin. "Did you know she has a rather effective right uppercut?"

Mason chuckled, and he felt Carson's eyes on him a moment.

"Cynthia told me why you went after that Italian doctor."

"Yeah, and? If you think I had another reason to put Amoretti in the hospital other than getting the truth out of him, you're wrong."

"Yes, of course," Carson said with little conviction.

"Maybe I get a little overprotective of kids—and Cynthia is still a kid. But beating Amoretti was the only way that worm was going to give me what I needed. Amoretti gave up Jennings as the principal rapist."

"Jennings? She actually recalls Jennings raping her?"

Mason shook his head.

"My, my. Difficult to prove, and even more difficult to get to a man like that."

"And it looks like I'm working this alone. Rousselot's being sent back to France, Melville has disappeared—"

"Not to mention you lack any solid evidence."

They passed through the Marshan Gate. To Mason's surprise, instead of Carson's Jaguar, an ambulance waited for them. A man in an ambulance driver's uniform stood by the back doors. Carson pointed to the driver. "That's Marlowe. He's a real ambulance driver, but he also works for me from time to time."

Mason looked at Carson. "You sly dog, you."

"I couldn't very well have you traipsing in the front door of the hospital with those assassins waiting for you."

Mason and Carson got into the back of the ambulance, and the driver closed the doors. A moment later, the vehicle took off. Carson handed Mason a folded ambulance uniform, and he took one for himself.

As they put them on, Carson said, "An orderly will be waiting for us by the back stairs and lead us to the fourth-floor surgical ward. A surgical nurse is expecting us. I offered to pay them, but when they heard the reasons why you assaulted Dr. Amoretti, they offered to help for nothing."

IT SEEMED EVERYONE ON THE SURGICAL WARD KNEW WHO MASON and Carson were, despite their attempts at keeping a low profile. The doctors were scared of Mason, while most of the nurses appreciated what he had done. Carson gabbed with the nurse who had arranged for their stealthy arrival, leaving Mason to fidget with a bulky surgical instrument on a rolling stand, the purpose of which was a mystery to him. Using the return wall as cover, he kept an eye on the swinging doors of the ward entrance. He looked at the wall clock once again. An hour had passed since they had arrived. Apparently, complications with another patient had delayed Sara's surgery.

The double doors swung open, and Mason ducked his head back until the doors closed. An orderly pushed a rolling bed into the ward. The nurse who was talking to Carson directed the orderly to park the bed halfway down the hall. Mason and Carson walked up to the bed and stood on either side.

Sara's face was bruised and swollen. Her lips, one eyebrow, and her left cheek now had fresh stitches.

"You have one minute," the nurse said. "Then we have to get her to surgery."

Mason and Carson each took one of her hands. Sara opened her eyes. She grimaced at the pain, then smiled.

"Both of my men came," she managed to say through her swollen lips. "Don't tell me you two are going to be my surgeons. I'd like to make it out of here in one piece."

Mason couldn't think of what to say. "I'm sorry, Sara."

"No need for that. I'm a big girl."

"Who did this to you?"

"I'm afraid we weren't properly introduced. Three of them jumped me after they ran my car off the road." Sara smiled with satisfaction. "I imagine their intent was to abduct me, but I managed to scratch out one of those cunts' eyes. They decided to beat me to death instead. I have no idea what prevented them from finishing the job."

"Darling," Carson said, "the doctors say you're going to be fine."

"Ruptured spleen, three broken ribs." She wiggled her fingers. "At least I can still do my art, but I'm not going to seduce anyone with my good looks anytime soon."

"You're still beautiful," Carson said.

"Liar. But thanks."

Mason struggled with his words. How could he tell her that this might be their last meeting? He could only squeeze her hand and stroke her forehead.

Sara looked at him. "I'll be fine. At least I got one piece of information out of the ordeal: the parents at the *bidonville* said that man named Jibran is an associate of the two arrested Moroccans. That he's a really bad guy. They heard he's in Tétouan, though they don't know where." She held up her head. "Now get those rapist, murdering bastards." She dropped her head, and she struggled to keep her eyes open.

"Time, gentlemen," the nurse said, and she signaled for the orderly.

As Mason watched the orderly wheel Sara into the operating room, he vowed he would do just that.

41

The ambulance driver dropped Mason and Carson off near the Marshan Gate, and this time a uniformed driver waited for them by a Mercedes sedan with the *corps diplomatique* license plates.

"What happened to your Jaguar?" Mason asked.

"The diplomatic corps plates offer greater anonymity and privilege. Something of an advantage with half the city looking for you."

The driver held the door open for Mason and Carson, who climbed in the back. The driver got in and drove downhill, skirting the medina's southern wall toward the modern part of the city. Carson pulled down the window shades and closed the driver's partition.

"How do you propose to implicate Jennings?" Carson said.

"I have no damned idea. Cynthia's my only witness, but her memories are pretty shaky. Amoretti's refusing to talk. The other kids are still missing, and the commandant and prosecuting judge are about to pin the whole thing on two dopey Moroccans. And I'm running out of time."

BONES OF THE INNOCENT

"I'm sure Cynthia wants the bad men behind bars as much or more than you do. Find a way to jog her memory."

"I push too hard and she could break."

"I imagine she's not as fragile as you think. She certainly has a boxer's right arm."

"I'm not going to be responsible for her winding up in a straitjacket."

"Short of going to the press, it seems you've run out of options. But even the gossip rags wouldn't touch this."

The frustration of it all made Mason squirm in his seat. "I should just line them all up and have Cynthia point out anyone she recognizes. Shame them in front of their wives. Hell, the world."

Carson was silent as he thought. He pulled out his gold cigarette case, removed a cigarette, and lit it.

"You think any harder, and your ears will start bleeding."

Carson seemed content to take a puff off his cigarette and blow it out with an air of reverie. "There's the big gala this evening. That might be the place to do it."

"What big gala?"

"Don't you look at a calendar once in a while? Today is the Fourth of July. The American legation, along with every other American organization, are cosponsoring a big bash at the El Minzah hotel this evening. The one hundred and seventieth anniversary—whatever significance that has for you Yanks. The Brits are reluctantly attending, no doubt for the free food and booze. And the French are coming, because the Americans promised to celebrate Bastille Day. Fireworks, a U.S. Air Force band, a navy band ..." He paused for effect. "Plus, a big charity ball benefiting the Children's Health Clinic and Welfare Center. Everyone who's anyone will be in attendance—top government officials, top police brass, royalty, diplomats—not to mention all the players in this sordid affair. Including Mr. Jennings, who's picking up the tab for the entertainment.

"The problem is, the place will be wall-to-wall security, personal bodyguards, and, not doubt, Jennings's personal protection. I'm sure he's hoping you might be idiotic enough to show up there."

"I'm just the kind of idiot to try."

"I have two invitations to the ball."

"Then I'll go as your date."

"I wouldn't go that far, but I might be able to keep you out of too much trouble."

The car stopped, and the chauffeur announced over the intercom that they had arrived.

Carson sat up straight when a thought came to him. "Wouldn't it be a shock to all those perverts if you brought Cynthia along?"

"Out of the question," Mason said, and got out of the car.

Carson got out and rushed around to catch up to Mason. "Just think of it—"

"No."

"But this is just what you wished for. She could confront the men right there, in front of everybody. Not to mention the press, the police. It could be sensational!"

Mason put his hand on the front doorknob and turned to Carson, raising his index finger and lowering his voice. "No!"

Carson pressed his lips together as if restraining himself from continuing the argument.

Mason said through the door, "Cynthia, it's Mason and Carson." He went inside, but Cynthia wasn't there. He moved quickly to the kitchen. "Cynthia?"

"In here," Cynthia said from the back bedroom.

Mason stepped into the room, with Carson right behind him. Cynthia was staring at the photos and lines of connections Mason had taped to the wall—including the photograph of her father and that of the corpses left in the desert.

"I asked you not to come in here," Mason said.

Without turning her head, Cynthia said, "Are these the men you think might be involved with the abductions?"

He stepped up to her. "You don't need to look at this stuff."

Cynthia pointed to the photos of Sabine de Graaf and Valerie Meunier. "I recognize those two. They were in the riding club. They were abducted, too?"

Mason laid his hands on Cynthia's shoulders. "Come on, let's get out of here."

Carson spoke up. "Yes, those are the men who are suspects, and those two were abducted along with a number of other children."

Mason gave Carson a look of warning.

"That's Sabine," Cynthia said, pointing to the photo. "I never saw her, but I think she's the one they dragged out of the dungeon. Poor girl. They killed her, just as I suspected." She turned to Mason with moist but fiery eyes. "And they're going to do the same to the ones they took away in the truck. What they planned to do to me, when they were done with me."

Mason tried to guide Cynthia out of the room, but she resisted.

"Yes, Cynthia," Carson said, "you're right on all counts."

"You stay out of this," Mason said to Carson.

"She has a right to know. She's not made of porcelain."

Cynthia pulled away from Mason and returned to the wall. She studied the photos a moment, and then she pointed to Jennings's photo. "You have a number of lines pointing to this man. Is he at the center of it all?"

"That's what I believe, but I don't have any real proof."

Cynthia stepped closer to examine Jennings's face. She did the same with each man, except her father: Meunier, de Graaf,

Commandant Lambert, von Litchten, the Italian judge Morino, and the Swedish diplomat Magnusson. She then returned to Jennings's photograph.

"Do you recognize him?" Carson asked.

"I don't know. There's something in his eyes. I only saw eyes …"

She turned away from the wall and held herself as if she had suddenly felt a cold wind. "I think I'm done looking now," she said as she stared at something unseen.

Mason walked over, put an arm around her shoulder, and led her out of the room. Carson looked at him with arched eyebrows as they passed. They all gathered in the living room. Cynthia sat on the sofa, still clutching herself and staring at nothing.

"I'll make some tea," Carson said. "Things always look better with a spot of tea."

"That would be lovely, thank you," Cynthia said. When Carson walked away, she added, "At least, that's the lie my mother always tells me." She smiled at Mason, as if really noticing him for the first time that morning. "I was worried about you all last night. I assume you did more than just talk to the doctor."

"He's still in one piece."

"He should be castrated, along with the rest."

Mason decided not to tell her that, for Amoretti, he had more or less made her wish come true.

"I hate to see you so frustrated," Cynthia said. "What can I do to help catch these men? And don't say nothing. I'm not a child any longer."

"Try to remember every detail. The slightest description. The way someone walked. An accent. Something you overheard. It could be anyone, not just the men on that wall."

"I'm trying to remember more. Maybe if I could hear each of them speak, I could connect a voice to a face."

Carson came in, carrying a tray with tea service for three. He had obviously been listening in, as he said, "She should go to the charity ball this evening."

"That's not happening," Mason said.

"What charity ball?"

Carson sat and started pouring the tea. "I'm sure all the rogues pinned up on that board will be there."

"I told you, she's not going."

Carson held up his hands in surrender. "Sorry. Only trying to help, old boy."

"It's perfect," Cynthia said.

"You're not going."

"If it can help—"

"You just escaped from those men, and you want to risk winding up in their hands again? They'd do anything to shut you up. I wouldn't be able to protect you."

Cynthia turned angry. "I have a right to confront my rapists! I think I deserve that much."

"She has a point," Carson said.

Mason jabbed his finger at him. "That's enough out of you." He said to Cynthia, "In that crowd anyone could grab you, and no one would notice. I'll have my hands full as it is without having to worry about you."

"You're going? When those killers are looking for you?"

"I can take care of myself. You can't."

Cynthia launched off the sofa. "You are not my father. Who appointed you my protector, anyway?"

Mason pointed back at the room with the pictures on the wall. "Do you want to end up like the girls in the photos? That's exactly what they'll do. They could be planning to do that anyway. You're the only witness, and the only thing that's saved you so far is that they think you can't remember anything because of the drugs. If they even get a hint that you withheld a portion of the drugs and could identify them—"

"Now you're just terrifying her," Carson said.

Mason stopped and took a deep breath. He said to Cynthia, "You've got to stay put. You're not safe out on the streets. And going to that ball could get you killed."

Mason had done what he'd intended—terrified her, as Carson had said. Cynthia's head hung low, and she stared at the rug with her shoulders pulled into her chest and her arms folded tight in her lap.

Mason rose from the chair and fetched the djellaba he'd draped over a dining room chair.

"Where are you going?" Carson asked as Mason pulled on the djellaba over his street clothes.

"To Tazim's funeral."

"That's insane. Were you not just lecturing Cynthia on the stupidity of walking into the lion's den?"

"The man saved my life. The least I can do is pay my respects."

Carson stood. "Then I'm going with you."

"You need to stay here and watch over Cynthia. Make sure she doesn't do anything foolish."

"You've developed a bad habit of giving everyone orders," Carson said. He glowered at Mason, then said, "At least let my driver take you."

He started to leave to find his chauffeur, but stopped in front of Mason, looking at him in his djellaba. "I would advise keeping that hood up. You look about as Moroccan as the king of Sweden."

The funeral procession was already underway when Mason slipped into the crowds lining both sides of Boulevard Pasteur. The procession began at police headquarters; then after proceeding down Boulevard Pasteur and Rue du Statut, it was to go around the Grand Socco, and finally end up at the Muslim cemetery along Rue de San Francisco. Boulevard Pasteur and the Grand Socco had the largest crowds, offering Mason the best chance to blend in and not be seen. He had no idea how popular Tazim had been, at least measured by the number of people who had turned out for the procession. It made Mason feel the pain of Tazim's loss even more acutely.

A phalanx of police, both Westerners and Moroccans dressed in uniforms of blue or white with gold braids and kepis, marched past. Then followed high-ranking police officers on horseback, including Commandant Lambert playing the part of a comrade in mourning.

Policemen had been placed at wide intervals along the route —an unusual measure for a funeral, but there was a palpable tension on the street. Mason scrutinized the faces in the crowds to see if there were any assassins lurking. He spotted Rousselot and Inspecteur Verger across and down the street to his left. They, too, scanned the spectators for any signs of possible violence. Mason figured that only respect for the solemn procession could have dissuaded the crowd from outbursts of anger.

The Mendoub's royal guard passed by on horseback and camels. As the Moroccan representative of the pasha, the Mendoub had little real power in the International Zone, but he did have an impressive contingent of Moroccan guards dressed in white flowing robes and bearing long, curved swords. The Mendoub's open carriage came close behind. White was the color of mourning for Moroccan funerals, and the Mendoub was decked out in his finest white djellaba with gold trimmings, topped with a white loosely wrapped turban.

A knotted train of Moroccans on foot came next. A handful of them bore the weight of a litter supporting Tazim's wrapped body. As it passed by, Mason closed his eyes and muttered a good-bye and thank-you to the man who had saved his life.

An array of women came after, with a young and pretty woman leading the way. The young woman was more than likely Tazim's wife, and Mason felt a sting of guilt.

Through the procession, Mason saw two policemen across the street cutting through the crowd of onlookers. They moved toward Rousselot and Verger with urgency. And when they reached the captain, they talked excitedly and gestured toward some unseen location. With Commandant Lambert on horseback in the procession, it seemed that Rousselot had been left in command of the security forces—hence the cops' decision to take their emergency to the captain.

Mason moved through the crowd and stopped at the curb. If he pushed through the procession to cross the street, he would draw the ire of the crowd and risk drawing attention to himself. He kept his gaze on Rousselot. One of the two policemen leaned in and spoke into the Rousselot's ear. Rousselot's eyes widened. He spun on his heels and followed the two uniformed cops.

Mason couldn't wait until the procession passed. With his head down and his djellaba hood up, he dashed through the tail end of the mourning relatives and broke through the other side. Some of the spectators yelled at him, but Mason zipped past before the angry spectators could do more.

Mason raced up to Rousselot just as they were clear of the crowd. One of the policemen mistook him for an angry Tanjawi bent on revenge, and he grabbed Mason.

"Captain!" Mason yelled, and pulled off his hood.

Rousselot turned and motioned for the policeman to release him. Verger seemed more amused to see Mason in a djellaba than annoyed by his presence.

"Follow us," Rousselot said, then checked his surroundings as if to see who might be watching or listening.

Mason followed him and Verger to a waiting police sedan. Verger got in the front passenger's side, and Mason joined the captain in the backseat.

Rousselot said something to the driver, and then turned to Mason. "A Berber sheepherder reported seeing a group of children being taken into a house about fifty kilometers southeast of here."

"When was this?"

"Earlier this morning. The sheepherder was coming to Tangier to barter for goods. Unfortunately, he only reported it once he reached the city."

Just as the driver put the car in gear, Mason saw one of the assassins run out from the crowd. Mason's and the man's eyes met as the car drove away.

Verger said something to Rousselot in French, and Mason heard Commandant Lambert's name.

Mason said in English, "Commandant Lambert isn't going to

be in charge much longer, Verger. Maybe they'll put you in charge."

"I am only advising Capitaine Rousselot that he has much to lose by ignoring the commandant's orders," Verger said.

Mason turned to Rousselot. "Did your men pick up Marjorie Ravenna and the stable manager?"

Rousselot shook his head. "Apparently, they have fled. According to one of the stable hands, the house at the equestrian center is their residence, but they rarely stayed there. We searched the premises but found nothing except a pile of burned papers behind the house. We have men watching the train station and the marina."

Mason nodded. "I was afraid of that. My guess is they lived at the mansion with the abductees, and made their getaway the night Cynthia escaped. We find them, we find the kids." He then asked Rousselot, "What about searching Amoretti's place?"

"We found a lot of money hidden in drawers, along with obscene magazines and photos of naked children, but—"

"Yeah, this is Tangier. What about the sheepherder? Did he say anything else?"

Rousselot shook his head. "Since the location is in the Spanish zone in the Rif Mountains, we called the Spanish police out of Tétouan to investigate. They should be there in about twenty minutes. We'll be there in forty-five."

They rode in tense silence as the driver took the same south-southeast road out of town. Thirty-five minutes later, they reached the border between the International Zone and Spanish Morocco. At the checkpoint on the border, a Spanish policeman escorted them the rest of the way. They turned off the two-lane highway and took a dirt road that climbed into the foothills of the Rif Mountains. After what seemed an interminable amount of time, they came to an isolated mud-brick house in a depression between bare hillocks.

Mason strained to see through the windshield. When they topped the rise and descended the slope, he slumped in his seat in disappointment: no truck or any sign the police had rounded up the children or the abductors.

Two other Spanish police jeeps were there as they pulled up. Three Spanish policemen milled around as if they didn't know what to do. A plainclothes man, probably a Spanish detective, came out of the house when Mason, Rousselot, and Verger got out of their car. The wind was up, and the surrounding hills caused it to blow in circular patterns, making the dusty earth swirl in mini-tornadoes.

Rousselot and Verger greeted the Spanish detective by name. They seemed to know one another, though the Spanish detective's voice and mannerisms indicated he would only tolerate their presence. Rousselot introduced Mason, and the detective gave Mason a curt handshake.

While the three policemen exchanged information, Mason surveyed the grounds. There were several sets of tire tracks, though the Spanish police had driven their vehicles over the same area. Most of the earlier footprints had been obscured by the winds, leaving only the shoe prints left by the Spanish police.

Mason entered the empty house. The original occupants had obviously abandoned the place some time ago, as there was a thick layer of dust laid down on the floors. The dust had been recently disturbed by a multitude of people. Discarded food cans, crumpled paper bags, and the remnants of fruit lay everywhere.

Rousselot and Verger entered the house, with the Spanish detective giving them a rundown of what they'd found.

Rousselot joined Mason. "It appears they stopped here for a day and moved on. The Spanish detective said they've already searched the entire area around the house. No signs of disturbed soil."

A diplomatic way of saying they hadn't found any fresh

graves.

Verger came up to them. "Tétouan is not far from here. The city has a reputation for piracy and slave traders."

"I saw Sara at the hospital this morning, and she said Jibran is in Tétouan."

"Did she say where?" Verger asked. After Mason shook his head, he said, "I will tell the Spanish police to look for him while they hunt for the other children."

Mason nodded as he scanned the floor and other surfaces for clues. He needed to find something, anything, that could act as a clue, no matter how insignificant. Some glimmer of hope. He felt exhausted from the lack of sleep and food, but his growing frustration and anger threatened to sap what strength he had left.

Rousselot, Verger, and the Spanish detective began discussing something in a mix of French and Spanish. The voices became a drone as Mason concentrated on the surroundings. There was nothing left to do but slowly wander the room. He imagined the children, helpless and panicked. No drugs to keep them sedated and compliant. From the disturbance in the dust, Mason could tell they sat on the floor in twos and threes, against the walls or in the corners.

In the bathroom there was only one set of prints left by soft-soled shoes or sandals. The Spanish police's footprints had stopped at the door. That solitary set of prints appeared similar to those around the area where Sabine had been found. The prints indicated that the person had entered the room, stopped at the window to close the shutters, and then exited.

Mason followed the footprints back into the living room. Now that he could fix upon one set of prints, he noted they were all over the living room and dining room. Then he caught the prints entering the kitchen. And along with those, he could see several distinct drag marks, like something had been dragged into the kitchen.

"Rousselot," Mason said from the kitchen.

When Rousselot and the detectives joined him, Mason pointed at the drag marks. Being careful not to step on them, he followed the marks that ended in a corner of the room. A pile of trash, remnants of wooden furniture and a tattered rug—all the detritus of an abandoned house—had been piled in the corner.

Mason attacked the pile, pulling away the junk. Verger pitched in, and in a few moments, they had cleared the area. Hidden underneath were the square seams of a trapdoor. The rope pull had been freshly cut. Mason pulled out his knife, and with Verger's help they lifted the trapdoor. A few flies escaped, and the smell of death reached their noses.

"Flashlight!" Mason said.

One of the policemen rushed over on the Spanish detective's orders and handed Mason his flashlight. Mason flicked it on, and they all peered into the darkness. The beam of light fell upon three bodies, facedown, in the six-foot-deep hole—two adults and one teenage boy.

Mason jumped into what had once been a root cellar. The two detectives quickly followed. Mason checked the boy. He was white, with light brown hair, and around fourteen. Mason checked for a pulse, even though the boy had a gaping bullet wound in his skull. He turned to the first adult. He knew who the two adults were, but he turned over the woman's body anyway. It was Marjorie Ravenna. Like the boy, she had been shot in the back of the head. The stable manager lay beside her, killed the same way.

Mason growled with frustration and slammed his fist into a foundation beam.

~

MASON FINISHED OFF HIS PACK OF CIGARETTES AS HE PACED THE front yard of the house. He was dying to get back to town, where he planned to wreak havoc on anyone remotely connected to the abductions. Maybe he'd string them all up and leave them hanging for all to see. Do it and slip out of town.

Captain Rousselot and the detectives were still inside, probably arguing about jurisdiction. Arguing was easier than catching the murderers. The Spanish police had brought in a coroner from Tétouan. They all would take photographs, measure and sketch, examine the bodies, and then they would wring their hands and shake their heads and be done with it.

The only glimmer of hope was that Valerie Meunier might still be alive, though being spared meant the abductors planned to hand her over to slave traders.

The sun sat on the mountaintops and the Fourth of July festivities were well under way back in Tangier.

"Happy fucking Fourth of July," Mason said to the western horizon.

The white teenage boy in the cellar didn't appear on anyone's list of abducted children, but Rousselot said there were numerous missing-persons reports from the impoverished Spanish families. Unfortunately, like the poor Moroccans, the Spanish kids sometimes disappeared for similar reasons: some ran away, some shacked up with a rich benefactor, or the parents were forced to give them up.

Marjorie and the stable manager had obviously outlived their usefulness. The man at the top of the evil food chain was erasing the evidence, covering his tracks by killing off the hired help. With Amoretti refusing to talk, and the rest of the staff either dead or on the run, Mason was running out of options. Very soon there would be nothing left; all the witnesses and evidence would vanish into thin air. The mystery would remain, but everyone would get on with their lives, making money and exploiting the downtrodden.

One piece remained: Cynthia. She was the last threat to deal with, and Mason worried she was vulnerable as long as he was away. But how long could that last? He couldn't protect her forever.

The coroner's assistants brought out the first body, covered and on a stretcher. Rousselot came out right behind and joined Mason. His hand shook as he offered Mason a cigarette.

Mason declined. "I'm guessing we've answered the question how the girls were abducted without anyone noticing. Marjorie and the stable manager were the ones who actually took the girls when they were under the drugs. They'd gained the girls' trust at the equestrian center, so even if the drugs didn't put them under completely, those two could take them away without too much of a fuss."

"And being a couple and white wouldn't raise questions."

Mason nodded and looked to the horizon. "I need a few stiff drinks."

Rousselot lit his cigarette, took a long drag, looking as haunted as Mason felt. "I know a very good place. I shall buy you as many drinks as you like."

"Thanks, but I've got something to do this evening."

Rousselot studied Mason a moment. "I've come to know that look of yours. You are planning something that will get you into trouble."

"I don't know what you're talking about."

"Ah. I was correct. I leave tomorrow, but for the rest of the day and night, I am at your disposal. What is your plan?"

"I don't have one."

"But you will."

"Maybe. Maybe by the time we get back to Tangier. But whatever my plan is, it involves walking into an ambush."

"Isn't it you who told me I couldn't walk away from this?"

Mason nodded. "Then I've got another one for you: be careful what you ask for."

A police driver dropped Mason off at Carson's house. There was no light in the windows and no car in the driveway. Mason rushed to unlock the door and enter.

"Cynthia? Carson? It's me."

He turned on the floor lamp and called her name again. He searched every room, but Cynthia and Carson were gone. When he went into his bedroom, he saw a tuxedo hanging on the door. There was a note sticking out of the breast pocket. It was from Carson.

It should fit you perfectly. Remember, I sized you up in Marseille.

Mason then picked up the phone and called the Brisbanes. Norwood answered and said Cynthia had come home about two hours ago. She was in her room and had asked not to be disturbed. His voice was icy and his answers curt. He added that Mrs. Brisbane was in her private study and indisposed. And Sir Wilfred had left last evening and had yet to come home.

Mason hung up the phone and had a strong urge to wipe out his ear. He took a bath and shaved off the four-day beard. While going through the process, he ran through every possible scenario he could think of for that evening. Every move and countermove. It finally came down to one option—one very risky option.

Mason put on the tux. It did fit perfectly.

Forty-five minutes later, Mason exited the apartment to find Rousselot waiting for him in his personal Renault. Mason got in and Rousselot took off. He wore his formal dress uniform with a pack of medals pinned on his chest.

"You talked to Meunier?" Mason asked.

Rousselot nodded. "I tried to appear hopeful about his daughter, but it was of little consolation."

"Is he on board?"

"His wife had to convince him, but he finally agreed. That woman frightens me. Considering she just learned that her daughter might be gone forever, she was like a stone."

"She keeps it so bottled up inside, she'll explode one of these days."

Luxury and chauffeur-driven cars lined up along Rue du Statut to discharge their passengers at the Hotel El Minzah. Two policemen directed curious onlookers to the other side of the street and kept the extraneous traffic moving on the two-lane street. Mason spotted Carson standing outside the hotel entrance nervously smoking a cigarette. He also saw another man, arms crossed and leaning against the wall just down the street. The man studied everyone who exited the cars or entered the hotel on foot.

Rousselot looked in the direction of Mason's gaze. "One of the assassins?"

Mason shrugged. "He could be one of Jennings's men, or a bodyguard for one of the dignitaries or government officials. We'll find out soon enough."

Rousselot grunted as he pulled the car forward to the head of the line. The two men got out, and the valet drove the car away. The policemen snapped to attention when they saw Captain Rousselot, though they looked puzzled to see him there.

Carson stomped out his cigarette and joined them at the entrance. He said to Mason in a muted voice, "Rousselot rang me and said you'd need my help. What are we all doing here?"

"I'll tell you inside."

Carson and Rousselot entered the hotel. Just before Mason stepped through the entrance, he looked back at the watcher. The man had come off the wall and attempted to look nonchalant as he eyed them entering the hotel.

The unremarkable exterior belied the hotel's tasteful elegance inside: Colorful Moroccan patterns of tile adorned the columns; arches of carved wood, brass chandeliers, and woven rugs all carried the same motif of complex geometric designs. The lobby was composed of several partitioned spaces, giving it an intimate air. But Mason paid more attention to the people either leisurely strolling through the lobby or seated in strategically placed chairs. Couples and groups, dressed in their finest, talked among themselves or slowly made their way to the terrace or the ballroom.

There was another watcher dressed in tropical whites and a straw trilby. He, too, studied them from a corner chair.

While Rousselot talked with one of his sergeants, Carson pulled Mason aside. "I reserved the private dining room, as Rousselot instructed, but exactly what is your plan?"

"You're going to help Rousselot corral Lambert and bring him to the room you reserved. We're going to see if we can get him to turn. Then we'll corner von Litchten, and use the both of them to lure Jennings in here without his bodyguards."

"And if you get Jennings in here, then what? Are you going to beat a confession out of him?"

"If it comes to that."

"That's not much of a plan."

"It's all I've got."

Carson arched his eyebrow at Mason as they joined Rousselot. The three men exited the lobby, passed through the dining room, and entered a small private dining room overlooking the broad terrace and lawn. They stood at one of the tall windows and observed the party through the gaps in the wooden lattice. The sun had set, leaving the terrace in the blue shadows of dusk. Two dozen tables had been arranged in a horseshoe around the terrace, with a temporarily installed dance floor that extended out onto the lawn. On a stage at the far end, a swing band played a Cole Porter tune as couples danced under the glow of Chinese lanterns. Everything had been decked out in red, white, and blue, from banners and balloons to American flags and iconic posters.

"There's Jennings," Carson said, and pointed to one of the tables near the band stage.

Jennings chatted with another well-heeled couple, with his wife seated next to him and looking bored.

Rousselot used his chin to point to an area under one of the arches that bordered the terrace. "Our illustrious commandant."

Commandant Lambert stood with cocktail in hand and trying to woo a woman not much older than Cynthia. Mason then noticed Baron von Litchten standing with his wife not far from Lambert.

Mason asked Rousselot, "Do you know if our other surprise guest arrived yet?"

"Yes, according to the sergeant I talked to in the lobby, he's here and seems resolute. But the sergeant didn't know how long that will last."

"He only needs to last long enough to confront the commandant," Mason said. He then signaled for his two companions to make their move.

Carson balked and said, "What could I possibly say to lure the commandant of police away from that young lady and his cocktail?"

"You're a smuggler and a con man. You'll think of something."

Mason watched as Carson and Rousselot walked out onto the terrace. The sole policeman saluted Rousselot as he passed. Carson looked nervous as he nodded hello to a few of the guests. They finally reached Commandant Lambert. The commandant appeared to have already had too many cocktails. He grinned at Rousselot and introduced the young lady. He didn't even seem to notice, let alone recognize, Carson for the notorious smuggler that he was. As Rousselot talked, the commandant's grin transformed into a scowl. They exchanged heated words, and it looked like Lambert would refuse to accompany them, but a moment later he straightened, tugged at his uniform, and followed Rousselot and Carson across the terrace.

A few moments later there was a light knock at the private-room door. Mason turned his back to the door as it opened. Carson, Rousselot, and Commandant Lambert chatted in French, the commandant sounding indignant, and the other two speaking in assuring tones.

Rousselot said in English, "*Voilà*, Commandant, the gentleman with the urgent matter."

Mason waited to hear the door close before he turned around.

Commandant Lambert started out yelling something in French, but then he shook his head and sputtered in English, "What is the meaning of this?"

Carson slipped out of the room as Lambert continued, "I will not be deceived in this way." He turned for the door.

"I wouldn't advise leaving until you hear what we have to say," Mason said.

The commandant stopped.

Mason continued, "Unless you want us to do this in public."

Commandant Lambert turned to glare at Rousselot. "What kind of treachery is this?"

"I'm the one with the information," Mason said. "Information I dug up despite your efforts to torpedo the investigation. We know you're in a fascist cult called the Brotherhood of the Temple of Hercules. That you, along with seven others, raped drugged children while you asphyxiated them."

"I do not have to stay here and listen to this nonsense." The commandant turned to retreat out of the room, when the door opened before he could reach it. Carson came in, followed by Meunier. The commandant gasped and took two steps back. Meunier wore all black and stood tall and rigid, as if straining to hold back his grief.

Lambert yelled at Meunier in French. Whether it was a reprimand or a warning, the effect emboldened Meunier. His eyes flared and he pointed his finger at the commandant. He declared something in French.

Carson translated, "The commandant is the one of the core members. He participated in the rituals that eventually caused the death of a young girl. He came up with the idea of disposing of the girl's body, and he personally dropped the girl's body out into the maquis."

Lambert seemed frozen in place as he stared at Meunier.

"Commandant," Mason said, "being a member of a fascist organization will look bad enough, but add in manslaughter, desecration of a human corpse, and obstruction of justice, you're looking at a prison sentence."

"Prove that. Prove that I was involved in any of these accusations, besides the word of this obviously deranged man."

Meunier took two steps toward Commandant Lambert and said something in French. He clenched his fist as he spoke, and Mason got ready to jump in if Meunier attacked the commandant.

"We also have Sir Wilfred Brisbane's testimony," Rousselot said in English.

The commandant's body seemed to shrink, the fight gone out of him.

Mason looked at Rousselot, who nodded for Mason to continue. "Commandant, we brought you here, out of the public eye, to offer you a deal."

Lambert looked up at Mason.

Mason continued. "We believe Anthony Jennings is involved in the abductions of the three daughters, and the murder of Sabine de Graaf. You help us get Jennings in here to confront him with these charges and without his bodyguards present. In addition—"

Commandant Lambert yelled at Rousselot in French.

Carson translated. "Is part of this deal having me killed?"

"So, he admits Jennings is the main guy?" Mason asked.

Commandant Lambert said in English, "I did not say this."

Rousselot and Lambert fell into a heated argument. Carson started to translate, but Mason said, "Don't bother."

"Commandant Lambert," Mason yelled, interrupting. "In addition, you must resign from the police department, promote Captain Rousselot, and leave town. For this, your membership and crimes will be kept private, and Captain Rousselot will not press charges."

"Commandant," Rousselot said, obviously having a difficult time getting past his anger to mouth his words. His face had turned red and sneered as he spoke. "You can leave the police with an excellent record, collect your pension, and nothing will ever go in your record to ruin your legacy." He swallowed hard. "You have my word."

The commandant gave one quick nod. Rousselot fetched a document he had made up in case they had successfully persuaded him. He put it in front of the commandant.

As the commandant scratched out his name on the resignation letter, he said, *"Bon débarras de cette putain de ville."*

Carson leaned over to Mason. "He says he's quite happy to be leaving Tangier."

Mason and Rousselot then instructed Lambert to lure Baron von Litchten to the room. The commandant growled and complained, but he finally stood and walked out the door with Rousselot.

Meunier stood in the corner. He kept rubbing his hands as he stared at nothing.

"You should go back to your wife," Mason said to Meunier in German. "I'm sure she needs you."

"My wife never needed me," Meunier said. "For anything. And I want to stay and look into Jennings's eyes when you force him to confess."

Something told Mason that forcing Jennings to confess to anything was going to be harder than it sounded.

The maneuvers to ensnare Commandant Lambert were repeated with Baron von Litchten. The fake baron crumbled much quicker than Lambert. In fact, the man curled up in a ball and wept into his hands. It took some time to calm him long enough to explain what he needed to do in exchange for his freedom.

Finally, the baron agreed to the terms; then he, Carson, and Lambert left to lure Jennings into the room. The plan was for the two to urge Jennings to come with them for a private and urgent discussion. They were to allude to breaks in the police investigation that could endanger them all. Mason hoped that the subject would be too incriminating for Jennings to allow his bodyguards to accompany him.

Carson was to keep an eye on Lambert and von Litchten, and intervene if the two appeared to crumble under pressure. And, in case Jennings decided to make a run for it, Rousselot had positioned himself by the front entrance with the two police officers.

Mason stood at the latticed window and watched as Lambert and the baron walked up to Jennings. The two were so rattled that there was no need for them to pretend they were frightened by the fabricated turn of events; it showed on their faces and hasty steps.

Jennings's table of eight talked and drank, laughed and toasted. Mrs. Jennings acted her part but barely cracked a smile.

It was full night, and the big fireworks show would start soon. The band had broken into a medley of John Philip Sousa marches in anticipation of the explosive climax.

Lambert and von Litchten reached Jennings's table. Lambert leaned into Jennings and said something. Jennings said something to his companions and rose. While the three conferred, a lovely young woman in a pink taffeta gown walked slowly up to the table, stopping a few feet behind Jennings. The three men were in such a vigorous discussion that they failed to notice the young lady. But Mason did.

It was Cynthia Brisbane.

Mason froze for a moment. He yelled at the window as he watched in disbelief. Cynthia stiffened as she listened to the men. She put a shaking hand to her mouth. Those five seconds seemed like an hour to Mason, but Cynthia finally moved off and headed toward the stage.

Mason bolted out of the room, dodging waiters and diners in the main restaurant salon, then through the lobby and out the door. He stopped at the elevated patio and watched as Cynthia mounted the band stage and grabbed the microphone from the male singer.

The band stopped. Jennings, Lambert, and von Litchten stopped. Everyone stopped. A buzz started as people talked hurriedly with their neighbors. Many knew who Cynthia was and what she'd been through.

Cynthia said into the microphone with a trembling voice, "Hello, everyone. My name is Cynthia Brisbane. I'm sorry to interrupt the festivities, but I have an announcement to make."

Mason glanced over at Jennings, who looked riveted to the

spot. What alarmed Mason was that the man had his hand just inside his tuxedo coat.

Cynthia continued. "Many of you know I was kidnapped, held in a cage for two weeks, and raped several times."

The onlookers gasped.

Cynthia looked at Mrs. Jennings. "I wasn't sure until I heard your husband's voice just now. He recited a poem in Latin while he raped me." Mrs. Jennings sucked in her breath and covered her mouth with her hand. Cynthia then pointed at Jennings. "Anthony Jennings held me captive and raped me repeatedly while I was incapacitated with drugs."

Jennings pulled out his pistol and shot at Cynthia. Mason jumped onto the terrace. People yelled and screamed. They fled in panic, and Mason had to fight his way through them.

The fireworks show began over the bay. Booms echoed across the beach and up into the hotel grounds. Flashes of colored light illuminated the terrace and the people running for their lives.

Mason had lost sight of Jennings. From somewhere beyond the tangle of guests, another gunshot rang out. A blockhouse of a man grabbed Mason, thinking he was a threat to whichever dignitary he was charged to protect. In three quick moves, Mason had him on the ground. He ran toward the sound of the gunshot.

He cleared the crowd at the edge of the terrace and saw Jennings running toward the back gate. The man was pulling his wife along, with two of his bodyguards taking up the rear. Mason stopped and looked toward the stage. Carson was on the stage cradling Cynthia. Mason took two steps toward them, but Carson waved him off, yelling that Cynthia was unharmed.

Mason ran toward the back of the property. He passed one policeman on the ground. The cop held his chest as blood seeped through his fingers, but Mason continued. In their panic, other guests ran for the back gate and streamed out onto the small side street.

Mason flew through the gate, only to see Jennings's car speed up the hill, heading for the main street. He raced up the side street with his gun drawn. The driver in Jennings's car had to swerve to avoid guests running away from the hotel. Just as Mason made it to the main street, Jennings's car made a left, rounded the Place de France, and turned onto Rue de Fez, heading south at a fast clip.

Mason ran up to the valet stand in front of the hotel. The valet had just brought a Mercedes up to the curb for the owner. Mason jumped into the open door, threw it in gear, and slammed on the accelerator.

The Mercedes's tires squealed as he sped off in pursuit. He passed the Place de France and took off down the same road. The city's buildings were a blur as he sped along. Jennings's Rolls-Royce limousine took the fork to the right. The Mercedes began to quickly overtake the heavy limo. He could see the silhouettes of the two bodyguards in front, with Jennings and his wife in the rear. The couple seemed to be fighting by the way their hands flailed in each other's direction.

Moments later, the city opened out to the sparse suburbs.

Mason glanced in the rearview mirror hoping to see a police car or two coming to his aid. He could use the help going up against two armed bodyguards and a desperate Jennings.

Mason returned his gaze to the limo. At that moment, the limo's back window lit up with three explosive flashes. Gunshots.

T he limo jacked to the left, then skidded. The tires smoked and the limo's forward momentum forced the back up as it came to a halt. Mason slammed on his brakes and stopped twenty-five feet away. He jumped out, pulled out his pistol, and used the open door as a shield. The bodyguard in the driver's seat was slumped against the door and not moving.

The next instant, Mrs. Jennings launched out of the backseat of the limo, took two steps back, and aimed a pistol at the interior. She fired four times. The bodyguard in the passenger's seat jumped out with his gun raised, but Mason fired twice, hitting him in the head and neck. The man fell dead to the pavement.

Mrs. Jennings pivoted to look at the man. She then turned her gaze back to the interior of the car. The pistol was at her side as she stared wide-eyed at what she'd done.

"Mrs. Jennings, put the gun down. It's all over."

When she didn't respond, Mason came around the open Mercedes door and took a step forward. Mrs. Jennings turned, raised her hand, and pointed the gun at Mason. "You caused this," she yelled with shock and rage. "You and that whore."

Mason laid his pistol on the hood of the sedan and held out his hands. "Mrs. Jennings, don't make this any worse."

Mason knew the Colt .380 held seven bullets. He'd seen three gun flashes inside the car, but was that three shots from her gun or did the one of the bodyguards get a shot off? At least four had gone into Jennings, but he didn't know how many she'd put into the driver. One or two? Empty or one bullet left? One was enough.

Mrs. Jennings started to cry now that the shock was wearing off. Her gun hand shook and her aim dipped. Mason took another step forward, but he was still a good twenty feet from her. She saw him move and raised the pistol. Her whole body shook. Her eyes popped wide.

Mrs. Jennings put the gun to her own temple.

"No, stop!" Mason yelled.

Mrs. Jennings clamped her eyes shut and pulled the trigger. The gun was empty.

She dropped the pistol and collapsed to the pavement. Mason walked past Mrs. Jennings and stepped up to the open limo door. Jennings had received four shots, one in the face. He was dead.

Mason checked the bodyguard in the driver's seat. He was alive, with one gunshot wound to his upper back. The man said nothing as he struggled with the paralyzing pain. Mason picked up the gun the driver had dropped. He removed the clip and ejected the bullet in the chamber before throwing it into the field. He checked the man's wound. It had gone through his back and exited above his left breast. He struggled to breathe as blood seeped from the hole in his chest. Mason took the man's hand and pressed it tight against the wound.

Mrs. Jennings recovered a little of her composure and looked at Mason. "My husband was a good man ... before. I tolerated his dalliances, but he became a monster. An evil thing. He was manipulated into this. He has—had a weakness, but he'd never exploited children before."

Mason decided not to say that she simply had refused to see it, or he was good at hiding it. He walked around the other side of the car and pulled off the dead bodyguard's coat.

Mrs. Jennings watched Mason as he returned to the wounded driver. He decided to let her talk, though he found it bizarre that she tried to justify her husband's sins after putting four bullets into him.

She leaned forward while pressing her point. "He was corrupted by temptation and manipulation."

Mason folded the coat and put it against the driver's wound, then took the man's hand and pressed it to his chest. "Keep pressure on it," he said to the man. He then stood and faced Mrs. Jennings. "Men don't acquire a taste for it. No one tempted him. No one manipulated him into abducting the Moroccan children and the three Western girls."

"He didn't abduct anyone. He told me everything in the car."

"What other reason would he try to kill Cynthia Brisbane and shoot a policeman?"

She pointed to the dead bodyguard lying near the passenger's door. "Ernie was the one who shot the cop."

"Why should I—why should you—believe him after everything he's done?"

"Why would he lie about that if he admitted to participating in those awful ceremonies? Why would he lie if he admitted he raped Cynthia Brisbane and some of the other children?"

Mason knew she had more to tell, so he waited for her to continue.

"A man came to him with a proposition. That person knew that Anthony was looking for a way to take over de Graaf's, Meunier's, and Brisbane's investments and property. He despised those three, calling them cowards. That they were more obsessed with their wealth and reputations than their daughters."

"And your husband claimed that the man who came to him abducted the children?"

"Yes. And he ran the cells where the children were kept. That man knew my husband's weaknesses, his desires, and that he had plenty of money to fund the scheme against the three fathers."

Mason hid his doubt and surprise. Was there someone else behind the whole sick scheme? Someone else was pulling the strings, including Jennings's?

He said, "You want me to believe that he confessed all this in the car? That he suddenly had a change of heart? I'm having a hard time swallowing this story."

Mrs. Jennings used the side of the car to help her stand. She stared at the pavement while wiping tears from her eyes. "He told me about the man and his scheme this evening, before the ball. I'm not defending him. I was shocked and appalled. It sickened me, and I wanted to run away, but I knew he'd hunt me down."

"So you shot him?"

Mrs. Jennings looked at Mason in a strange state of serenity. "I didn't just kill him to save myself. I killed him because he admitted to poisoning a girl during one of their cult ceremonies just to entrap the three fathers for monetary gain." Her expression turned to disgust. "He said he enjoyed it. And that he was going to enjoy doing that to me once we were out of the city." More tears welled in her eyes, and she yelled, "The monster deserved to die."

Sirens sounded in the distance. Someone in this sparse neighborhood had probably called the police.

"Did he tell you who this man was?" Mason asked.

Mrs. Jennings shook her head. "Only that the man prided himself in manipulating everyone. He bragged about bending people to his will. By knowing what someone needs, and becoming that person. To play with their minds and emotions. That's when I knew he was telling me the truth. The man had played my husband to a T."

Mason walked away, out of the glare of the headlights. As the sirens grew louder, he tried to think of who that master manipulator could be. Who, of everyone he knew or had contact with, had played him so masterfully?

He strode over to the driver and leaned in on him. "Where were you taking Jennings?"

The driver looked to be in shock, and blood bubbled from his mouth with each breath. Mason shook him to consciousness and repeated the question.

"Tétouan," the driver said.

"Where in Tétouan?"

"Off Rue de Fez. The tanners' quarter. A white house with blue shutters."

Mason headed for the Mercedes, but two police squad cars came to a screeching halt. He was hit by headlights, and through the glare, he heard car doors open and a now-familiar warning.

"Les mains en l'air!"

M ason was finishing up his statement with one of the policemen who'd arrived first on the scene. The cop spoke halting English, so it involved a lot of hand gestures. And that would have gone smoother if it weren't for the handcuffs binding Mason's wrists.

Mrs. Jennings sat in the back of one of the two squad cars. An ambulance driver and his assistant were tending to the limo driver. The first cops on the scene had come close to panic when they saw so many shooting victims. They had handcuffed Mason and called for immediate backup.

The interviewing cop seemed satisfied with Mason's statement, or he'd grown tired of the game of charades. He walked away as another squad car and an ambulance came rolling up. Rousselot, Verger, and Verger's junior partner got out of the squad car.

Rousselot rushed up to Mason and ordered his cuffs to be removed.

"Don't go anywhere," Rousselot said. "I will be back shortly." He then went off with the first responders and Verger to look over the scene.

Carson's Jaguar pulled up at that same moment, and Carson got out. Mason could see the silhouette of someone in the passenger's seat, but that person remained in the car. He recognized the curled hair and the collar of the dress—it was Cynthia.

Carson walked up to him, though he stared at the bodies now covered in bloodstained sheets. "I assume since you're standing that you're all right." He then looked back to where Mason was looking. "I told Cynthia to stay in the car. She doesn't need to see this bloody mess."

"How is she?" Mason asked.

They both glanced over at Cynthia, and Carson said, "Considering she was nearly shot, she's doing pretty good. She's an extraordinary young lady. I hope she can eventually put all this behind her."

"Her screwed-up family isn't going to help."

"You know, it's not your job to take care of her."

"Never said it was. I'm getting out of this insane asylum, the sooner the better. Just got one more loose end to tie up."

Rousselot came up to them. Mason filled them in on what Mrs. Jennings had said: Jennings wasn't behind the abductions, but he had raped the children and had poisoned a Moroccan girl during one of the fascist ceremonies to entrap the three fathers. He left off the part about the mysterious man orchestrating the whole thing. He wanted to take care of that particular loose end personally. "I hope you're going to go easy on Mrs. Jennings," he said to Rousselot.

"We'll write it up as self-defense, but I still have to take her in and charge her. I would have preferred to arrest and convict Jennings."

"The city bigwigs will be jumping for joy. Everything tied up in a nice, neat bow. They're going to love the way you solved the case."

"There is still what to do with you. Technically, I should bring you in for questioning for shooting that bodyguard."

"Those assassins would just find a way to get to me."

"That's why you are going to make a daring escape and disappear. Tonight."

Mason nodded. "What about Verger and the uniforms?"

"Verger is fine with it. You actually made a friend out of an enemy."

"That could ruin my reputation."

"I can handle the rest of them, but it has to be tonight."

"I, for one, am leaving tonight for Spain," Carson said.

Rousselot gave Carson a stern look.

"It's all perfectly legal this time," Carson said. "As far as Tangier is concerned, that is. The Spanish authorities might look at it differently." He turned to Mason. "You're welcome to come along. That is, if you manage to tie up your loose end."

"What is this?" Rousselot said.

"Nothing," Mason said, and to Carson, "Count me in."

"You know the boat. Before dawn."

"I want to say good-bye to Cynthia," Mason said to him, "but don't let on that I'm leaving for good."

"Of course not."

Mason took Carson by the arm. "In fact, let's talk about it while I walk to the car."

Once they had stepped away from Rousselot, Mason said, "I have another favor to ask."

"Lambert was close to shutting my operation down and throwing me in jail, so I believe I owe you great deal more than that."

"Good, because I want you to take your boat and wait for me in Tétouan."

"Tétouan? What have you got up your sleeve?"

"It has to do with that loose end."

Carson thought a moment. "There's a small dock for fishing boats, near the breakwater. I'll wait for you there."

"If I don't make it by three a.m., then feel free to leave without me."

"I would offer my assistance, but since it may involve bloodshed, I'll stay with the boat."

Carson stopped a discreet distance from the Jaguar, and Mason walked up to the car. Cynthia stepped out and hugged him.

"Thank you for everything," she said.

"That was a crazy thing to do," Mason said, and returned the hug. He then held her out at arm's length. "But walking up on that stage and announcing to the world what Jennings did was one of the bravest things I've ever seen."

Cynthia smiled. "I can't tell you how much—"

"You can tell me tomorrow," Mason said.

"I'll see you, then? Bright and early?"

Mason had to take a moment to answer. "Yes. Bright and early. Now, you should go home and get some rest."

"Perhaps I helped tame one or two of your demons."

"Yes, maybe you did."

"You'll sleep through the night once in a while without making that silly puttering noise."

"I might sleep a little better, but I have a feeling that noise isn't going anywhere."

Cynthia forced a smile, with tears in her eyes, revealing her complicity in the lie. "Well, don't come too early. I might sleep in a little."

Mason nodded. That was all he was capable of doing. Cynthia looked in his eyes for another moment before turning and climbing into the car.

Carson walked up to Mason. "I'll take her home now. I'll be at the breakwater at two a.m., and I'll wait as long as it takes." He got behind the wheel.

Cynthia stared at Mason and waved at him as the car pulled away. He watched it fade into the night.

She might have tamed one of his demons, at that.

Mason turned and joined Rousselot, who studied him with piercing eyes.

"I hope you are not planning to cause more trouble before you leave."

"Nope, not at all."

Rousselot showed that he didn't believe him. "And you will not require our assistance?"

"I want to do this on my own."

Mason held out his hand to Rousselot. "Thanks for everything. You're a pain in the ass, but a good cop."

Rousselot shook his hand. "Thanks to you, I'm stuck in this wretched place." He looked at the Mercedes, then returned his gaze to Mason. "I suppose you want to keep that car for a little while longer."

Mason held up the keys. "I just need to borrow it for a few more hours." He turned and walked toward the Mercedes.

Rousselot called after him, "Do not damage it."

"No, not the car."

M ason had the house in sight: white walls, blue shutters, and a blue-arched doorway. It sat one house away from Tétouan's medina wall and across from a gate that led out to the vast cemetery. The driver had said the house was in the tannery quarter, and the stench from the pigeon feces and cow urine used at the tanneries proved that to be true.

A single lamp mounted on another house threw a dim light onto the man standing on one side of the white house's door—enough light for Mason to recognize him: the man who had attacked him at the mansion the night he'd rescued Cynthia: Jibran. The man smoked a cigarette and kept glancing both ways, as if standing guard. That meant the person Mason had come for was inside.

It was 1:40 a.m., and the narrow street was quiet. That eliminated another concern, witnesses. He still had to get past Jibran, making as little noise as possible. He left the shadows and crept closer, using the recessed doorways as cover. Mason wore a djellaba, with the hood pulled up, and soft sandals. He had gone by Carson's apartment to gather his things and change out of his tuxedo and into street clothes, and as the djellaba provided no pockets, he had to carry his pistol and knife with his hands pulled up into the loose-fitting sleeves.

At thirty feet, he ran out of recessed doorways to use as cover. He transferred his long-bladed knife to his right hand. Minutes ticked by, yet Mason still waited. Finally, three Moroccans emerged from the cemetery and passed through the arched gate. They stopped a few feet inside the gate and talked as if in an argument. Jibran eyed them with suspicion—the opportunity Mason had waited to exploit.

The men's loud voices masked the sound of Mason's sandals. It was only at the last second that Jibran heard the zip of Mason's djellaba and turned. Too late. With one swipe of his knife, Mason cut deeply into Jibran's throat. He gurgled a final breath and collapsed onto the paving stones.

Mason picked the lock and entered the town house apartment. He gently closed the door and stepped into a small foyer. With his pistol now in his right hand, he took cautious steps into the living room.

Melville came out of a back bedroom with a suitcase. He stopped and smiled like his prodigal son had come home. "Mason. I was quite concerned about you. A rather reckless venture this evening, but I'm gratified you came out of it in one piece." He put the suitcase down next to the sofa and next to a second one.

Mason surged forward with his gun up. He put the barrel against Melville's forehead. "Give me one reason why I don't blow your head off."

Still smiling, Melville said, "Ah, you've come for me, then. I can think of several reasons why I would prefer my head remain intact, but I'm sure none would persuade you to spare my life. Except for one: your sense of justice. You won't shoot an unarmed man in cold blood."

With the gun still pointed at Melville's head, Mason patted

him down and found a Beretta .32-caliber pistol in Melville's suit jacket. He checked the safety and tucked it into his pants pocket underneath the djellaba.

"Abducting, raping, and murdering those children ought to be enough of a reason."

"For the record, I didn't rape the three white girls—"

Mason pushed the pistol so hard that it forced Melville's head back. "I'd advise you to stop, or I *will* pull the trigger."

Melville dipped his head as far as the gun barrel would allow, signaling compliance.

"Where are the other children you took from the mansion?"

"They're gone, I'm afraid."

"Gone where?"

"They were sold to slave traders yesterday. Where they are now, only the traders know, but certainly not in Tétouan."

Mason growled and grabbed Melville's head with his free hand. His finger gripped the trigger. Melville, still with the smile, closed his eyes as if daring Mason to shoot. Mason let off pressure as he shook in rage. He let go of Melville's head and took a step back.

Melville opened his eyes and seemed pleased with himself. "How did you find me? A fine bit of police work."

Mason took a few deep breaths, compensating his anger with the knowledge that Melville would soon get what he deserved. "Jennings's driver gave up the address. Jennings's idea was to come here, before his wife shot him to death."

"Jennings was a fool. He had more wealth than intellect. If there was ever a man who thought with his bollocks, it was he." Melville nodded toward his liquor cabinet. "A spot of whiskey?"

"I'll pour," Mason said, and moved to the cabinet. "I wouldn't want you to slip something in my drink this time."

"Ah, yes, you figured that out."

Mason poured two scotches and offered him one. Melville

held up his glass in a toast, but Mason ignored the gesture and downed his in one gulp.

"I underestimated you," Melville said.

"I get that a lot. Must be my face." He poured another scotch. "You had me going for most of the time."

"What gave me away?"

"Lots of little things didn't add up. Knowing more than you should. Steering me down dead ends. Showing up when I was getting warm and pumping me for information, all in the interest of being the town snoop. You scaring off those henna artists. Showing up at that café in the Petit Socco, and Jennings knowing exactly where I was. I had my suspicions, especially after getting drugged, but I didn't want to believe them. I liked you too much."

"Reminded you of your grandfather."

Mason nodded as he took a sip. "On my mother's side. My paternal grandfather was a real Nazi." He pointed at Melville's cane propped up in a corner. "You never needed that cane, did you? Another bit of theater, what?" Mason said, imitating Melville's British accent.

Melville simply shrugged.

"You suddenly missing in action was another tip-off. You can't be in two places at once. But even that didn't fully convince me until Mrs. Jennings said her husband had been manipulated by a master Svengali."

"Mrs. Jennings gives me too much credit. Jennings was easy. I simply played the devil on his shoulder. He and I adhered to the same Aryan tenets. And, as it turns out, we shared similar tastes. But that's where it ended. He used sexual magic as an excuse to pursue his lusts. I, on the other hand, believe in the transcendent power."

"Your proof of white superiority involves rape and murder."

"There is a natural hierarchy of the races, so who am I to disagree?" Melville continued his smile, but it had turned sour.

"That being said, these latest abductions were more philosophical. I believe that the only way to restore the old-world order is through revolution, and revolution begins with chaos. It is the only way forward. I abducted the Moroccan children and left their bodies to be found easily, so as to stir up the locals. I knew the police would do little, causing the locals to rise up in anger. However, while that did cause tensions, it wasn't enough."

"So you went after white children."

"I'd been working on Jennings for some time when he told me about the fascist cult, using children in their ceremonies."

"Mrs. Jennings said he confessed to poisoning a girl during one of the ceremonies."

Melville nodded. "That was my idea. Jennings wanted Meunier's, de Graaf's, and Brisbane's holdings, and I wanted to use the daughters' abductions to blame them on the Moroccans. Jennings provided the funds for my little scheme. We both would win." His genuine smile returned. "I made two miscalculations. You and Cynthia Brisbane. The cleverness and bravery of a pampered socialite, and the tenacity of an ex-cop."

"You thought you could play with me like some vaudeville hypnotist. Like you played Jennings."

"One must have his diversions," Melville said, and nodded toward his suitcases. "One of those suitcases is full of money: the remainder of Jennings's generous funding. You could help yourself if it would persuade you to let me go."

"There are some people waiting outside who wouldn't let you get very far."

"Of course. You brought the police."

"They let me talk to you first."

"To get me to confess?"

"To find out where the other children are."

"I'm sorry I wasn't able to accommodate you on that score."

"How about the henna-tattoo artists?"

"They had to be eliminated," Melville said. "I blame you for that one. If you hadn't suspected their involvement, I wouldn't have been forced to make them disappear." He held out his glass. "May I have another?"

"Why not? You're going to need it for what's going to come."

Mason poured the drink and handed it to him. Melville downed his drink and sighed with satisfaction, as if that gulp of scotch might be his last for a very long time. "Shall we get this over with?"

Mason took a step for the door, but Melville stopped him when he said, "Oh, I almost forgot. I planned for this contingency: you, somehow discovering the truth, coming for me. I alerted those assassins that you might show up tonight. Our little chat should have given them enough time to get here and find positions to cut off your escape. The police might serve as impediment, but only a little."

Melville made a move for the door, but it was Mason's turn to stop him. He held up his hand and said, "Wait here."

"They want to arrest me in here?"

"Something like that."

Mason went to the door and opened it. "Okay," he said to the street, and stepped aside.

Six Moroccans entered. They carried clubs and knives.

Melville's eyes popped wide. "What's this?" he asked. And then with rising panic in his voice: "Who are these men, and where are the police?"

Mason pointed to the men. "This is Rachid and four other fathers of the children you abducted, and the big fella is Barir. He's Jamila's brother." Mason said to Barir, "This man just admitted to having Jamila and Fatima murdered."

Barir looked fearsome enough before, but now he looked like he would spoil all the fun for the others and rip Melville limb from limb.

"Good-bye, Melville," Mason said, pulled the djellaba's hood over his head, and moved for the door.

"Mason, wait! I know where some of the children are."

Mason stopped and turned. He maintained his glare, though a spark of hope surged through him.

Melville raised his shaking hands as if to hold off an assault. "I lied about them being delivered to slave traders. I can show you where they are, but you have to promise me these men will not harm me."

Mason marched up to Melville and grabbed the lapels of his suit coat. "You don't use children as bargaining chips. Where are they?"

"You can turn me over to the police, but not to these men. Give me your word, and I'll tell you."

Melville's arrogance was gone, and for the first time he looked like a frail and defenseless old man. Or was this another ruse? As far as Mason could tell, Melville wasn't playing games this time. "All right, you have my word."

Barir charged up to Mason with balled fists. "You cannot give him to the Nazarene police. He had Jamila and Fatima murdered. I will have my revenge."

Mason answered Barir's glare with one of his own. "Not at the cost of the children's lives."

Barir growled in frustration and turned away.

Mason returned his gaze to Melville. "Where are they?"

Melville glanced over his left shoulder. "Behind that armoire is a door to the basement. You'll find them down there."

Rachid and Barir rushed over to the armoire and shoved it aside. Just as Melville had said, behind it stood a thick wooden door. Barir opened it, revealing steps that led downward.

"You're leading the way," Mason said to Melville. He then half dragged Melville to the door. Melville pulled a cord just inside the doorway, illuminating a bare bulb hanging a few steps down. It threw light onto the ancient stone walls and wooden steps leading down into the darkness.

Mason held Melville's collar and urged him forward. With Melville in the lead, they descended stairs that took them deep below street level. The air smelled of damp earth and mold. At the bottom of the stairs, Melville pulled another cord. A light came on, and just beyond the circle of illumination, six children were huddled on the bare earth in a corner. They shielded their eyes against the light. Their coarse cotton gowns were ragged and filthy.

Rachid and the other Moroccans rushed to the children, though Barir remained next to Mason.

Mason let out a long sigh of relief, as if he'd been holding his breath for far too long and a thousand-pound weight had been lifted off his chest. He shoved Melville toward Barir. "Hold him."

Mason strode up to the Moroccans and children. The parents searched the faces for their daughters or sons. There were three Moroccan girls, a Moroccan boy, and what appeared to be a Western boy. Then, behind all the rest, Valerie Meunier was still curled up in a ball. She stared at nothing, with her cheek pressed against the stone.

Rachid shouted with joy at finding his daughter. Two of the other men were hugging another boy and girl. The other fathers, despite their disappointment at not discovering their own children, cared for the others. Mason stepped over to Rachid, who embraced him. Valerie cowered from the Moroccan men, so Mason stepped over and squatted next to her.

"Valerie. You're safe now. These men will take you back to your mother and father."

Valerie perked up at the sound of Mason's voice. She seemed to understand some of what Mason said, as she uncurled and slowly turned to Mason. She cried out and hugged Mason. He lifted her in his arms and walked over to Barir.

"Tell Rachid to take the children upstairs."

A flash of a smile crossed Barir's face; then his expression turned to grim resolve. He had understood the underlying message behind Mason's words. Barir nodded and spoke to Rachid. Rachid corralled the children and urged them up the stairs. The other men stood by and watched.

"What are you doing?" Melville said to Mason. "Why are we still down here and not going to the police?"

Mason took two steps up the stairs with Valerie still in his arms. He turned to Melville. "I changed my mind," he said, and walked up the stairs.

"Mason! You can't do this!" Melville yelled.

Melville continued to plead with him as Mason mounted the stairs. He screamed for mercy. Mason reached the ground floor and used his foot to shove the heavy door shut.

The sound of clubs striking flesh and Melville's screams were muffled by the heavy door. None of the children looked frightened or upset at the sounds. Either they were too numb to care, or they'd heard too many screams during their captivity to be affected by them now.

Mason and Rachid moved the children to a corner and away from the basement door. Mason squatted so Valerie could stand. She seemed reluctant to let go of him, but finally she did.

Mason asked her, "Do you understand English?"

"A little," Valerie said. She pointed to one of the Moroccan girls. "She does, too."

"Good," Mason said, and said to the two girls, "There still may be some dangerous men outside. You'll be safe, but you all need to stay together. When we go out that door, stay against the buildings, and let the men protect you. I promise we'll get you all home. Now, tell the others, and we'll be going very soon."

As Valerie and the Moroccan girl translated Mason's words to the others, Mason stood and moved to the front door. He flattened himself against the wall near the door and opened it slightly. He listened as he peered through the crack. All was silent.

If the assassins were, indeed, waiting for him, Mason hoped wearing the djellaba with the hood up would at least give him a fighting chance to get away. Especially in a group of men all dressed the same way.

When approaching Melville's hideout, he had memorized the contours and characteristics of the surrounding streets and buildings. He now pictured the layout in his mind. He knew there would be a shooter on the rooftops across the street with a view of the doorway. To the right, the rooftop shooter would have an obstructed view, so the man would be on a rooftop to the left and maybe twenty feet down. The street to Mason's left ran straight for about one hundred feet before intersecting a cross street. To his right, at about eighty feet, was the entrance to the cemetery. There would be two waiting at each intersection, probably in djellabas. That accounted for five, minus the one he had put out of action the day of the demonstration. Though there could be more waiting in the shadows of the tight streets.

There was nowhere to go to but straight at them.

4 8

The noise from the basement quieted, and a few moments later the basement door opened. Barir and the other four Moroccans entered the living room. They were all breathing heavily from the effort. They remained silent, and all had grim faces. They shared no triumph from the task.

Everyone knew what to do. With his pistol in one hand and his Ka-Bar knife in the other, Mason pulled his hands up into the sleeves. They all gathered at the front door. Mason stepped out first, keeping in the shadows of the doorframe. Everyone filed out as a group, with the children in the middle of the group and skirting the building walls.

They moved swiftly as a pack toward the arched gate leading to the cemetery. The sniper, having a disadvantageous line of sight in this direction, would have to reposition. Mason counted on that, as well as the confusion about the presence of children and who was the actual target.

Mason heard footsteps on roof tiles, then the shooter jumping over the wall dividing one building from another. The assassins waiting at the intersection behind them would be moving forward by now.

Mason and his companions approached the gate. Mason counted down the distance, and at eight feet he whispered, "Now!"

The group broke into a run. They raced around the corner of the intersection. Two men in djellabas stood five feet from the corner with their backs against the wall, lying in wait.

Rachid and another man rushed the children forward. At the same time Mason and four of his companions grabbed both men and beat them with their clubs. The would-be assassins cried out in pain. A shot rang out, deafening in the silent streets.

They had to hurry. The other two ground shooters would be there in seconds. And if the sniper could find a good position, he would fire down into the group.

Lights came on in the surrounding buildings, and people shouted from windows and rooftop patios. Mason hoped the aroused neighbors would discourage the other assassins from continuing the pursuit.

Behind them, a door opened, and two more Moroccans rushed out to help take the children inside to safety. Mason and his four companions dragged the two stunned and bloodied men into the house, while Rachid and his partner shouted to their neighbors to call the police.

Mason chose the closest assassin and sat on the stunned man's chest. He trapped the man's arms with his knees. With the blade of his Ka-Bar knife across the man's throat, he slapped the man to consciousness. The man went rigid with fear.

Mason motioned for Rachid to move the children into a bedroom. Rachid and the two local Moroccans ushered the children into another room.

"Who sent you?"

Barir and one of the other fathers knelt on either side of the man's head. The sight of two enraged Moroccans with knives rattled the man. He cried out in panic.

357

Mason clamped his hand over the man's mouth. "If you don't tell me, we're going to start carving your face, then your groin. You might live through this, but only if you talk *now*."

The man jerked his head in a desperate nod. Mason lifted his hand off the man's mouth.

"I don't know who he is."

Mason shoved his hand onto the man's mouth. "Start with the ears," he said.

Barir and his companion put their knives against the man's ears. The man's wails were muffled against Mason's hand.

Mason signaled for them to hold, and he lifted his hand. "Talk. Last chance. I can work on your buddy once we're done with you."

"I swear I don't know. I only know his code name. Valerius. We've never seen him. Someone else hired us."

"Who?"

The man hesitated. He shook and panted with fear, as he looked from Rachid to the other father. "Rodger Spencer."

"Where is Valerius?"

The man hesitated again. With one swipe of his blade, Barir sliced off the top of the man's ear. The man screamed.

"Tell me where Valerius is, or they keep going!"

"I don't know! I swear. But the guy who hired me would know. Roger Spencer. He's in Lucerne. Switzerland. That's all I know. Please!"

Mason launched himself off the man's chest and stood. Barir and the Moroccan father delivered several blows to the man's face.

"That's enough," Mason said. "Tie them up, and we'll dump them in an alley."

"We should hurry," Barir said. "The police will be here soon."

Mason nodded. He didn't want the police to get involved.

There would be too many questions, which would lead the police to Melville's mangled corpse.

They acted quickly to tie up the men. With the bound men in tow, they joined the others waiting in the bedroom. The two local Moroccans led them out a back entrance and through a complex maze of alleys.

Finally, they came to where they had left the two vehicles: Mason's borrowed Mercedes and a limousine Barir had stolen for the occasion.

As everyone got into the vehicles, Mason said to Barir, "We have one more quick stop to make."

MASON STOPPED THE MERCEDES NEAR THE SMALL FISHING PIER. Barir's stolen limousine pulled up alongside. Mason looked at two Moroccans with two of the children in the backseat. He then looked at Valerie sitting next to him in the front. Valerie was in shock and said nothing. But Mason didn't need her to say a word. She and the other children would be safe now.

Mason got out of the car. The motors of Carson's boat were idling in a throaty rumble, as Barir and Rachid accompanied Mason down the pier.

Carson ran up to the stern with one of his crew and helped Mason aboard.

Mason turned to Rachid and Barir and shook their hands. "*Shukran.*"

The two men thanked Mason, and Rachid said something in Arabic.

Barir translated, "He says thank you, and it was a good night for justice."

Rachid kept saying his thanks, when Carson said, "Sorry gentlemen, but we have to be going."

Carson and the crewman cast off the lines, and Carson signaled the helmsman. The motors roared and the boat pulled away. Mason remained at the stern and waved a last good-bye.

It had, indeed, been a good night for justice.

But as the Moroccan coastline faded in the distance, Mason knew there would be no end to assassins pursuing him. He would have no peace until he cut off the head of the snake. He had no idea how to accomplish that, and had no idea who Valerius was, or where, but too many people had died. Too many lives had been ruined.

He had no choice but to return to the place he'd risked his life to escape.

The viper's den lay somewhere in worn-torn Europe.

GET A FREE MASON COLLINS NOVELLA

Get a free copy of a Mason Collins introductory novella, *In Malicious Hands,* when you sign up to join my Reader's Group. This novella is not available anywhere else.

You'll receive occasional newsletters from me with details on new releases, special offers, and other news relating to the Mason Collins series.

Just go to https://johnaconnell.com/subscribe/ to get your copy!

Did you enjoy this book? You can make a big difference in my career!

Reviews are the most powerful tools in my arsenal when it comes to getting attention for my books. Much as I'd like to, I don't have the financial muscle of a New York publisher. I can't take out full page ads in magazines or go on global book tours.

Maybe someday...

But there is something more powerful and effective than that, and it's something that those publishers would love to get their hands on:

A committed and generous group of readers.

Honest reviews of my books help bring them to the attention of other readers.

If you enjoyed this book, I would be very grateful if you could take five minutes to leave a review on the book's Amazon page.

Thank you very much!

ABOUT THE AUTHOR

John A. Connell is a 2016 Barry Award nominee and the author of the Mason Collins series. John has worked as a cameraman on films such as *Jurassic* Park and *Thelma and Louis* and on TV shows including *NYPD Blue* and *The Practice*. Atlanta-born, John spends his time between the U.S. and France.

You can visit John online at: http://johnaconnell.com

 facebook.com/johnconnellauthor1

 twitter.com/johnaconnell

BOOKS BY JOHN A. CONNELL

Madness in the Ruins

It is the winter of 1945, seven months after the Nazi defeat, and Munich is in ruins. A killer is stalking the devastated city—one who has knowledge of human anatomy, enacts mysterious rituals with his prey, and seems to pick victims at random.

It falls upon U.S. Army investigator Mason Collins—former Chicago police detective, U.S. soldier, and prisoner-of-war—to hunt down the brutal killer. In a city where chaos reigns, Mason must rely on his wits and instincts. And before Mason knows it, the murderer has made him a target. Now it's a high-stakes duel, and to win it Mason must bring into deadly play all that he values—even his life.

"...this is going to be a must-read series for me." *~ Lee Child, #1 New York Times bestselling author of the Jack Reacher novels*

∾

Haven of Vipers

Mason Collins risks everything to hunt down a gang of ruthless murderers in a case that will take him from a Hollywood-style nightclub and a speeding train, to the icy slopes of the Bavarian Alps. As both witnesses and evidence begin disappearing, it becomes obvious that someone on high is pulling strings to stifle the investigation—and that Mason must feel his way in the darkness if he is going to find out who in town has the most to gain—and the most to lose...

Haven of Vipers is the second in the Mason Collins crime-thriller series that Steve Berry, bestselling author of *The Patriot Threat* and *The Templar Legacy*, said: **"Excitement melds with adventure as the tangled** *threads gradually unwind, revealing treachery coming from all directions. The whole thing is reminiscent of early-Robert Ludlum, and makes you clamor for more."*

∼

Bones of the Innocent

Mason Collins grapples with a web of lies, secrets, and murder as he races against time to save the lives of abducted teenagers in a case as twisted as the streets of Tangier's medina. Then, as he digs deeper, he realizes everyone has a hidden agenda, including those who harbor a terrible secret. And just as Mason begins to unravel the mystery, the assassins have picked up his trail. Now, Mason must put his life on the line to find the girls and discover who's behind the heinous crimes before it's too late. If he lives that long…

∼

The Hunting of Men (coming fall of 2019)

When a shadowy organization fails to assassinate Mason Collins, they go after his colleagues, his friends, and the love of his life. Mason knows the only way to stop the killings is to cut off the head of the snake. Armed with only the leader's code name, Valerius, Mason will trek across Franco's Spain to war-torn Vienna to kill the man responsible. But targeting the most powerful crime boss in Vienna promises to be an impossible task, and Valerius has something special in store for Mason.

AUTHOR NOTES AND
ACKNOWLEDGMENTS

As hard as it is to believe, Tangier, Morocco was a crazy place from the 1930s to the mid-1950s. Several noted journalists of that time declared Tangier the "wickedest city in the world." With the exception of murder in broad daylight, just about anything went. In fact, some have stated that Tangier was the inspiration for the movie Casablanca. Whether that is true or not, I don't know. But after reading the following books on those years in Tangier, I tend to believe it. And that was just the tip of the iceberg! In fact, I had a hard time deciding what insanity to include.

The descriptions of the places, street names, and general circumstances of Tangier are as accurate as I could make them. The characters in the story are, of course, figments of my imagination.

Here's a list of the main sources I used when doing my research:

- 1) *The Dream at the End of the World: Paul Bowles and the Literary Renegades* by Michelle Green, Harper Collins, 1991

- 2) *Tangier; A Different Way*, by Lawdom Viadon, The Scarecrow Press, Inc., 1977
- 3) *Paul Bowles; Magic and Morocco*, by Allen Hibbard, Cadmus Editions, 2004
- 4) *Portrait of Tangier,* by Rom Landau, Robert Hale Limited, 1952
- 5) *Tangier: City of the Dream*, by Iain Finlayson, Harper Collins, 1992

~

As always, I am indebted to editor extraordinaire Ed Stackler for his intelligence, generosity, and insights. And to my family for all their kindness and support.

I've said it before, but I'll say it again: I would not have the joy and privilege to write these acknowledgements if it weren't for my wife, Janine. It is she who rekindled the writer in me. She supported me without question, pushed me, inspired me, and tolerated my silences and absent-mindedness as I "wrote" in my head. She slogged through many drafts, always offering encouragement and criticism whenever I needed them most. A most extraordinary woman.

CPSIA information can be obtained
at www.ICGtesting.com
Printed in the USA
LVHW111431010719
622873LV00001B/372/P